AND SO IT BEGINS...

Ludwig stared out the window, watching as the noonday sun chased away the shadows in the city streets below. Years ago, in an ill-conceived plan to escape his father's influence, he'd fled north, seeking to start a new life. Now, here he was, a decade later, the newly crowned king of the very kingdom he'd abandoned!

Nobody could've predicted the chain of events that would bring him here. After King Morgan assumed the Throne, the ruler ceased listening to reason and began purging nobles. With the aid of nearly half of the realm's barons, Ludwig waged a military campaign that ended with the death of his predecessor. Although he'd never been one to seek power for its own sake, Ludwig assumed the role of king, hoping he could repair the damage caused by the civil war.

"Having regrets?"

He turned to see his wife, Charlotte, moving towards him, a smile playing over her lips. She was in high spirits today, which he was thankful for. Neither knew when the lethargy would overwhelm her, requiring her to withdraw to the seclusion of their room.

He matched her welcoming smile. "How different things might've turned out if I'd remained in Hadenfeld instead of travelling north."

"But then you wouldn't have met Sig and Cyn." She paused, looking into his eyes. "Something is bothering you. Not me, I hope?"

Ludwig smiled. "No. Never."

"Then what is it?"

"When I returned to Hadenfeld all those years ago, I wanted only to settle down and live my life in peace. Now, here I am, the ruler of a realm ravaged by two civil wars in a span of only five years."

"That's not your fault. Had King Morgan been wise enough to listen to your advice, we wouldn't have had to remove him from the Throne."

"But I killed him."

"I hate to correct you," replied Charlotte, "but your archers were the ones who finished him off."

ALSO BY PAUL J BENNETT

<u>HEIR TO THE CROWN SERIES</u>

SERVANT OF THE CROWN

SWORD OF THE CROWN

MERCERIAN TALES: STORIES OF THE PAST

HEART OF THE CROWN

SHADOW OF THE CROWN

MERCERIAN TALES: THE CALL OF MAGIC

FATE OF THE CROWN

BURDEN OF THE CROWN

MERCERIAN TALES: THE MAKING OF A MAN

DEFENDER OF THE CROWN

FURY OF THE CROWN

MERCERIAN TALES: HONOUR THY ANCESTORS

WAR OF THE CROWN

TRIUMPH OF THE CROWN

MERCERIAN TALES: INTO THE FORGE

GUARDIAN OF THE CROWN

ENEMY OF THE CROWN

MERCERIAN TALES: THE SPARK OF CHANGE

PERIL OF THE CROWN

SAVIOUR OF THE CROWN

VICTORY OF THE CROWN

Power Ascending Series

Tempered Steel: Prequel

Temple Knight | Warrior Knight

Temple Captain | Warrior Lord

Temple Commander | Warrior Prince

Temple General | Warrior King

The Frozen Flame Series

Awakening - Prequels

Ashes | Embers | Flames | Inferno

Maelstrom | Vortex | Torrent | Cataclysm

The Chronicles of Cyric

Into the Maelstrom: Prequel

Midwinter Murder

The Beast of Brunhausen

A Plague on Zeiderbruch

Duality of Magic Series - Coming 2026

Voices From the Past

WARRIOR KING

POWER ASCENDING: BOOK EIGHT

PAUL J BENNETT

DEDICATION

To my wife, Carol, who gave me wings to let my imagination fly.

N
THE LAND OF
GREAT NORTHE
THE NETHERWOOD
HALVARIAN EMPIRE
SEA OF STORMS
TH
WILDERNESS

EIDDENWERThE
SEA
WILDERNESS
PETTY KINGDOMS
THE WILDLANDS
SHIMMERING SEA
THE PIRATE COAST
THE GREAT SEA

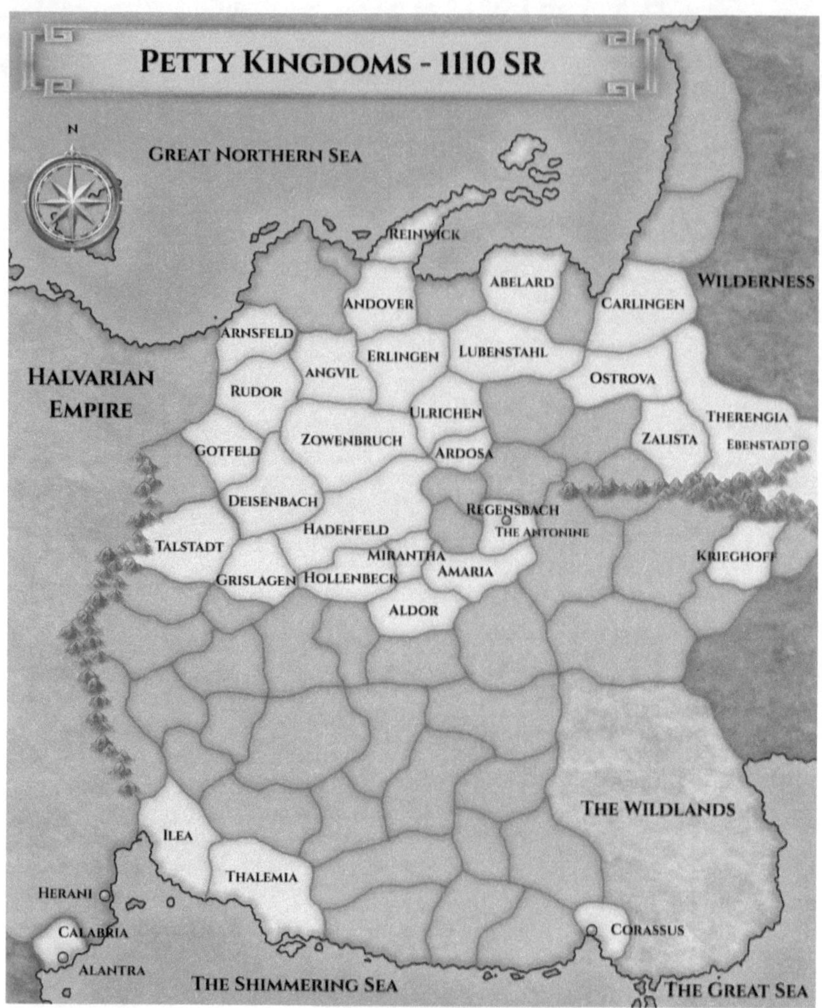

Map of the Petty Kingdoms

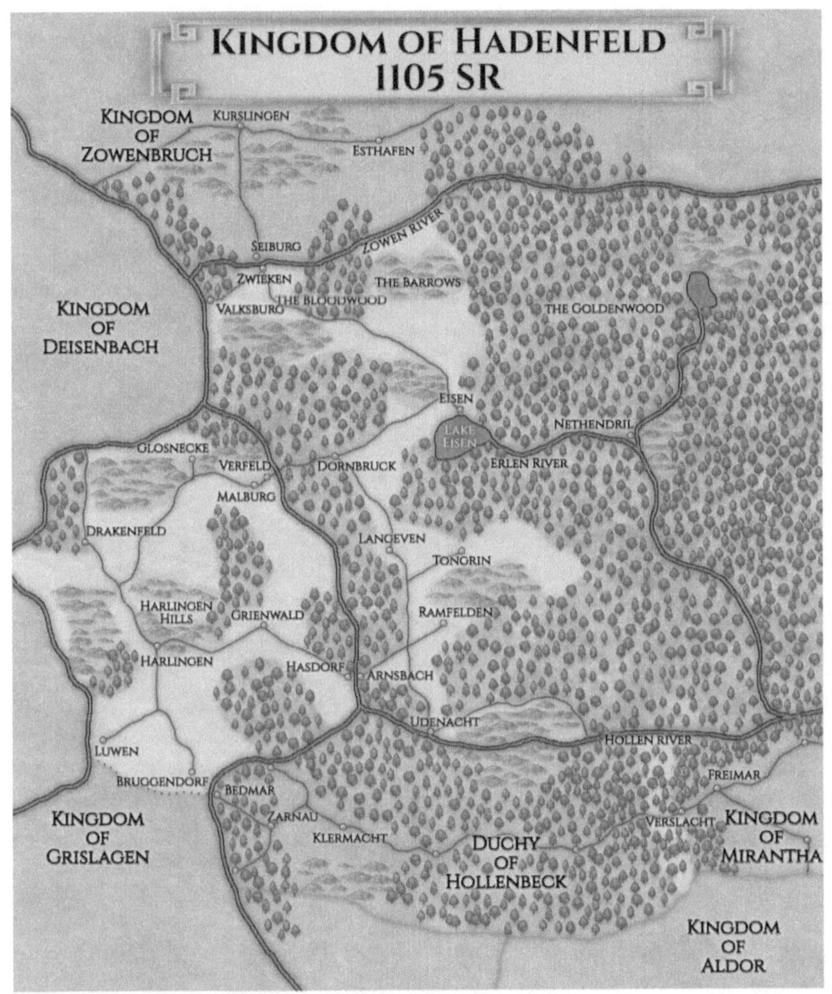

Kingdom of Hadenfeld

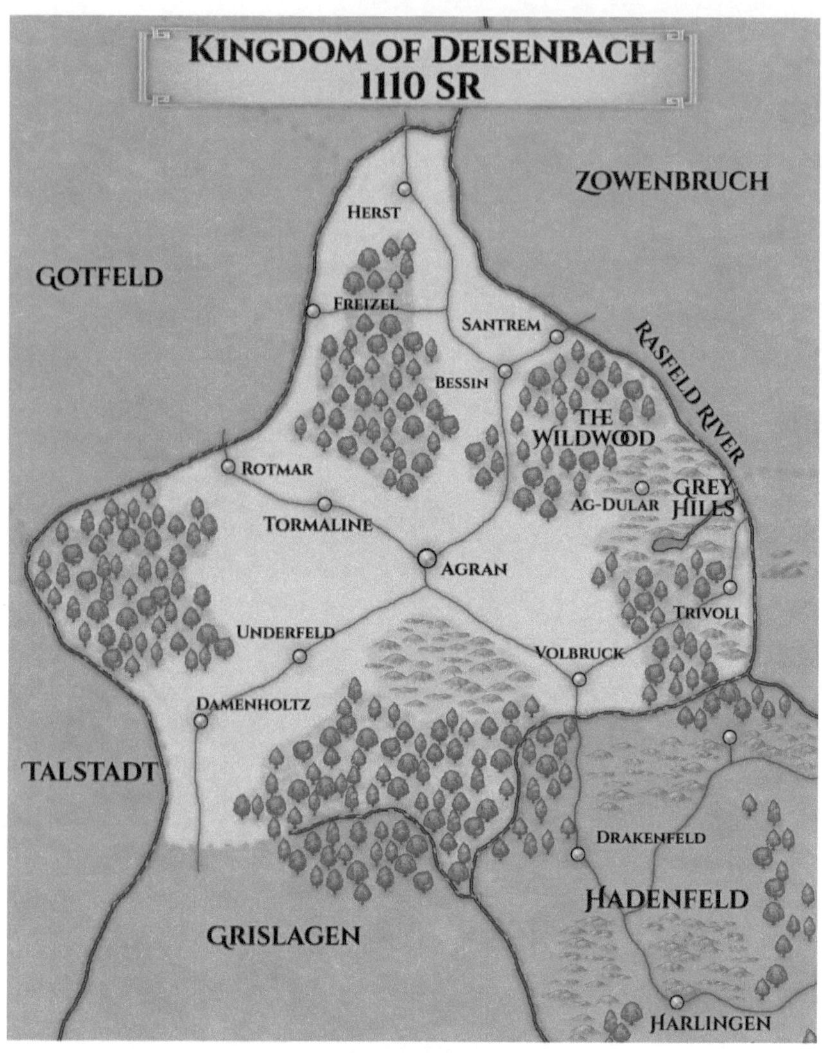

Kingdom of Deisenbach

1

THE CROWN

SPRING 1105 SR* (*SAINTS RECKONING)

With the spring buds bursting forth on the trees, and the days growing warmer, the nobles of Hadenfeld would soon descend upon the Royal Keep in the capital, eager to win favour with its new rulers.

Ludwig stared out the window, watching as the noonday sun chased away the shadows in the city streets below. Years ago, in an ill-conceived plan to escape his father's influence, he'd fled north, seeking to start a new life. Now, here he was, a decade later, the newly crowned king of the very kingdom he'd abandoned!

Nobody could've predicted the chain of events that would bring him here. After King Morgan assumed the Throne, the ruler ceased listening to reason and began purging nobles. With the aid of nearly half of the realm's barons, Ludwig waged a military campaign that ended with the death of his predecessor. Although he'd never been one to seek power for its own sake, Ludwig assumed the role of king, hoping he could repair the damage caused by the civil war.

"Having regrets?"

He turned to see his wife, Charlotte, moving towards him, a smile playing over her lips. She was in high spirits today, which he was thankful for. Neither knew when the lethargy would overwhelm her, requiring her to withdraw to the seclusion of their room.

He matched her welcoming smile. "How different things might've turned out if I'd remained in Hadenfeld instead of travelling north."

"But then you wouldn't have met Sig and Cyn." She paused, looking into his eyes. "Something is bothering you. Not me, I hope?"

Ludwig smiled. "No. Never."

"Then what is it?"

"When I returned to Hadenfeld all those years ago, I wanted only to settle down and live my life in peace. Now, here I am, the ruler of a realm ravaged by two civil wars in a span of only five years."

"That's not your fault. Had King Morgan been wise enough to listen to your advice, we wouldn't have had to remove him from the Throne."

"But I killed him."

"I hate to correct you," replied Charlotte, "but your archers were the ones who finished him off."

"Still, my assault on the capital led to his demise."

"You know as well as I that his survival would've only made things worse. His death spared you the need for a public trial."

"True," said Ludwig. "But by now, news of his demise will have spread across the Petty Kingdoms like wildfire, and the other rulers will view me as a pretender—an upstart who seized the Throne through force of arms."

"Most couldn't care less," replied Charlotte. "And, in any case, you had the support of the Church, which legitimizes your rule to many of them."

"It wasn't the Church, merely one order of Temple Knights."

"To a king, it's the same thing. Trust me, I heard it back in Reinwick enough times to know what I'm talking about."

Ludwig smiled. "You always know how to help me see sense."

"That's my magic."

He laughed. "You're not a mage."

"No, I'm not, but I'm aware of what's in your heart, and that's what makes us such a good match."

"Agreed."

She shifted her gaze to the streets below. "Have you finally decided what to do with the army?"

"I have, but I fear it won't be a popular choice."

"Do you mean to remove it from the barons' control?"

"I do," replied Ludwig. "The current method worked to our advantage during the war, but I can no longer permit each lord to command their own men. It's an open invitation for my enemies to oppose my rule."

"Then you must make efforts to bring our former adversaries once more into the warm and welcoming embrace of the Crown."

"Any suggestions about how we might do that?"

"The Duke of Reinwick would invite all his nobles to court on a regular basis. Reinwick isn't as large as Hadenfeld, but the principle is the same. When people gather together, they form bonds, which, in turn, leads to a greater sense of loyalty."

"I like the idea, but I must confess that's not my area of expertise."

"Then it's good I'm here to look after things. I'll ask Gita and Alexandra to help me organize everything."

"Then I shall leave it in your capable hands."

A soft knock came from the door, followed by Captain Gustavo's voice. "Majesty?"

"Yes?" replied Ludwig.

"My apologies, sire, but the Royal Council awaits your arrival."

"I shall be there directly."

"Yes, Majesty. I'll inform them at once."

Ludwig grinned. "It seems I'm now in trouble with the Royal Household for being late for a meeting I myself arranged."

Charlotte grinned. "Welcome to the life of a king."

Ludwig assumed the seat at the head of the table, flanked by Cyn and Sigwulf, with Lords Merrick and Emmett beside them. Rounding out the group was Father Vernan, representing the Church of the Saints.

"Good day, everyone," said Ludwig. "I hope you're all well?"

"That sounds a tad formal," noted Cyn, cracking a smile. "Are you certain you're feeling well?"

"I'm fine," replied Ludwig. "It's only that we have some serious business to attend to today."

"He means real work," offered Sigwulf, shifting uncomfortably in his seat.

"Problem, Sig?"

"It's these chairs. They're not made for the likes of me."

Ludwig turned to a servant standing nearby. "Let's see if we can find a chair with no arms, shall we?" He grinned at Sigwulf. "That's what you get for being so tall."

"Don't let me hold up the meeting."

Ludwig nodded. "I've called this assembly to discuss the army. Where do we stand regarding numbers?"

"We're down significantly since the war's end," replied Merrick. "We currently have twelve hundred men under arms, but it's draining our treasury. I'm afraid we'll need to make further cuts unless you have a way of increasing funds?"

"I wish I did," said Ludwig, "but Morgan drained the coffers dry. As it stands, we've barely enough for the day-to-day running of the realm."

"We could raise taxes," offered Emmett.

"I wouldn't advise that," replied Father Vernan. "There is already considerable resentment towards Ludwig's rule; that might be enough to push people into action."

"You think they'd rise up?"

"If our recent history taught us anything, it's that those unhappy with a monarch can force change at the point of the sword. I'm not saying I agree with it, but I keep a close eye on such things, and I assure you that I'm not exaggerating."

"No new taxes, then," said Ludwig. "I'm afraid we'll have to trim the fat a little more. If it helps, we can tell everyone it's meant to be a temporary measure."

"How temporary?" asked Merrick.

"The Royal Treasury needs refilling. I'm not suggesting it needs to be overflowing, but presently, there are no reserves. If we faced any sort of emergency requiring extra funds, we'd be unable to cope."

"And against this backdrop, you propose reorganizing the army?"

"We can't afford another civil war," replied Ludwig, "and the only way to prevent that is to place all soldiers under the direct control of the Crown or its designated generals."

"Generals?" said Merrick.

"Yes, that reminds me. Sig, Cyn—you're both promoted to the rank of general."

"Nice," replied Cyn. "Does that come with any extra coins?"

"Eventually, but I'm afraid for the moment, it's strictly a volunteer position."

She shrugged. "That's fine. I can make do. How about you, Siggy?"

The great northerner grinned. "General Sigwulf. I like the sound of that. Now, would that be Lord General Sigwulf or General Lord Sigwulf? I'm never sure where the titles fit in."

"It would actually be General Marhaven," said Ludwig. "We use last names in Hadenfeld, and your position as Baron of Verfeld is of secondary importance in terms of commanding the army."

"I can live with that."

Lord Merrick cleared his throat. "You appear to have some thoughts on the matter of the army, sire. If we are to make cuts, what troops do you want remaining?"

"I'd like at least half to be foot."

"And the rest?"

"Three hundred bow, the remainder horse. Is that possible?"

"Most certainly. I'll arrange for the armour and weapons of those dismissed to be stored in the Royal Armoury."

"Excellent. And ensure that each person we dismiss receives a letter documenting their service. Once our treasury is restored, we'll be looking to increase numbers, and they'll be the first people we contact."

"Anyone in particular you want to retain?"

"Plenty, but I'll leave that up to Cyn and Sig."

Ludwig surveyed the room, his gaze coming to rest on an ostentatious portrait taking up a good portion of the wall. His predecessor had expensive tastes, and the king needed to demonstrate to his subjects that he was willing to do his part. "I believe it's time we cleared out this keep of all these excesses, don't you?"

"Excesses?" replied Merrick. "Are you suggesting you wish to return to King Otto's more barren tastes?"

"Perhaps not quite as severe as his, but I'd like to avoid the more obvious displays of wealth."

"What would you have us do with all these paintings?"

"Sell them off. I'm certain there are plenty of wealthy people who'd love to get their hands on them. Having said that, we should be careful not to cause a panic, so let's keep our current financial situation to ourselves. I don't want anyone outside our circle here asking questions."

"We'll still have to address the reduction of our army," said Emmett. "How do you wish to explain that?"

"If anyone asks, we're concentrating on quality over quantity, and right now, we lack the facilities to house a large army."

"Good answer," said Father Vernan. "I see you've given this considerable thought."

"Not really. It only just occurred to me."

"Might I beg a question, sire?" said Emmett.

"Of course," replied Ludwig, "but only if you stop calling me sire. This is not court, and this assembly is one of mutual respect and friendship. Therefore, Ludwig will do fine. What's your question?"

"It concerns Eisen. It was formerly the capital of Neuhafen, but with reunification, there's no direct lord ruling over it. Are we to make it a barony or keep it operating as a Royal Holding?"

"For the short term, we shall leave it in the Crown's hands, but I'm open to suggestions about the best long-term solution. Creating a new barony is a valid consideration, but I'd prefer to hear some other ideas before I decide."

"You could designate it a free city," offered Cyn. "Like they did with Malburg?"

"Or give it to the army," added Sigwulf, "allowing us to maintain a garrison in case Zowenbruch decides to invade again?"

"Both excellent ideas," replied Ludwig, "but to make that decision, I'll need a lot more information. Cyn, see if you can dig out the original charter for Malburg, and we'll have Father Vernan consult with Temple Captain Hamelyn to determine what it would take to upgrade the facilities to house more men."

"Why the Temple Captain?" asked Emmett.

"With the numbers we're proposing, we'll need something along the lines of a commandery. I assume he has access to plans for those?"

"Most definitely," replied Vernan. "Though I must warn you; building a structure like that takes years."

"We have to start somewhere."

"Agreed. I shall seek out Temple Captain Hamelyn once we're finished here."

"Where are we in terms of loyalty?" asked Sigwulf. "I know the barons all pledged to serve you after the coronation, but who can we actually trust?"

"Most of the eastern provinces are good," replied Emmett, "but that's hardly surprising, considering they supported your efforts to win the Crown."

"Most of?" said Vernan. "I'm afraid you'll have to explain that one to me."

"When Ludwig called for aid, the barons of Arnsbach and Udenacht didn't respond. At the time, we thought it was their way of remaining neutral, but they've apparently developed close ties to Bruggendorf."

"That was to be expected," said Ludwig. "If you recall, they were implicated in Lord Jurgen's plot to start a war with Hollenbeck."

"Also true," added Emmett, "but we saw no indication of their men fighting against us." He swivelled to face Sigwulf. "You fought in the south. Did you run across any of their men?"

"We did at Arnsbach," replied the huge northerner, "but we never made it to Udenacht. Mind you, it's not as if the barons' men wore any distinguishing colours. For all we know, we may have been fighting men from any of the southern baronies, save for Luwen. Lord Meinhard would've been one of our staunchest defenders had he lived. I can't imagine his men fighting for Morgan, can you?"

"The trouble isn't only in the south," added Cyn. "Lord Darrian of Glosnecke is just as bad. I still say you should've thrown him into the dungeon after what he got up to."

"I won't lock up a man because he disagrees with me."

"A noble sentiment," said Father Vernan. "If only your detractors showed such sense."

"Presently, I have a considerable amount of support from the common folk, but that will change if things don't get better."

"What we need to do is boost the economy. If we drive up profits, thereby filling people's pockets, they'll forget about politics."

"You make a good point," said Ludwig. "What if we lowered the tax rates for businesses?"

"We can't," replied Merrick. "We need to fund the army."

"Ah, but if business picks up, more goods will be taxed, so we'd be trading a tax break for an increase in the number of items taxed. Stimulating trade is what we need, although admittedly, I'm no merchant."

"I suggest you consult Charlotte," said Emmett. "She has a good head for such things."

"An excellent idea. I believe that concludes our business of the day. Anyone want to bring something up while we're all together?"

"Yes," said Sigwulf. "I think it's time you assigned bodyguards to Frederick on a permanent basis. I know he's still young, but with questionable loyalty amongst some of your subjects, it seems like the prudent thing to do. I'd be happy to arrange it if you wish."

Ludwig had always been of the mind that his life, and by extension, the life of his family, would not change no matter his status, but now he was beginning to wonder if that was possible. As the king, he must accept that there'd always be those who viewed him as the enemy, regardless of his attempts to mend fences.

It saddened him to contemplate Frederick growing up in such surroundings, but there was no way to undo the past. "Very well," he said at last. "But please confer with Gustavo about who'd be most appropriate. He is, after all, the captain of the Royal Guard."

"Certainly," replied Sig. "I'll have a list of names for you by the end of the week."

"On another note," said Cyn, "there's the matter of the Elves of Nethendril. You agreed to come to their aid if they were attacked, but now that you're king, it needs to be formalized. I suggest inviting a delegation here, to Harlingen, to demonstrate your desire for a lasting peace." She grinned. "It might also serve to shock some of your more vocal critics when Elves show up in the streets."

Sigwulf chuckled. "And give them something else to gossip about in the parlours of the capital. I wish I'd thought of that."

"I'll compose a letter today," said Ludwig. "Cyn, can I rely on you to arrange a messenger to carry it to Nethendril?"

"My pleasure."

"Have the Temple Knights of Saint Mathew settled in?"

Father Vernan nodded. "Indeed. They've yet to build a commandery, but they found a couple of suitable buildings to provide them with sufficient shelter in the short term. While we're on the subject, might I make a suggestion?"

"By all means."

"The Temple Knights are well-respected by the people of Harlingen. Would you consider granting them permission to keep the peace on the city streets?"

"Why would he do that?" asked Sigwulf. "He has his own men to keep the peace."

"He does, but they are more likely to be viewed as enforcing the king's will rather than keeping the city safe. Seeing Temple Knights riding around would help allay fears that His Majesty is preparing to purge his enemies."

"And how would that work, precisely?" pressed Sig. "Are criminals now to be tried in an ecclesiastical court?"

"The intent would be to hand them over to the appropriate Royal Authorities for judgement. The Temple Knights would only arrest those who've broken the law."

"I like the idea," replied Ludwig, "but we'd have to work out the details before implementing it."

"I'm certain they'd be amenable to discussing the matter further."

"Good. Cyn, I'd like you to oversee that, if you don't mind."

"I'd be happy to," she replied.

"Excellent," said Father Vernan. "I shall arrange a meeting with Temple Captain Hamelyn."

"Would he need permission from his regional commander?"

"I doubt it. Temple Knights already patrol the streets of many cities in the Petty Kingdoms, so you'll find them most accommodating when it comes to rules and regulations. That is, after all, how they live their lives."

The door opened, revealing Charlotte, Gita, and Alexandra. "I hope I'm not interrupting anything important," said the queen, "but you're late for dinner, and the food is getting cold."

"My apologies," replied Ludwig, "but we had much to discuss."

"Is there a reason these matters cannot be discussed over the dinner table?"

"Not that I can see."

Sigwulf's belly rumbled.

Charlotte chuckled. "Then how about we get some food into Sig's belly before he passes out from lack of sustenance?"

"You heard her, my lords. We should not trifle with a northerner's hunger!" Ludwig stood, prompting the others to do likewise. "All things considered, I don't know why we didn't think of this before we began the meeting."

"Because you didn't have me here to suggest it," replied Charlotte. "Now, come along, all of you, before the servants tire of waiting and clear it all away."

2

STRUGGLES

SPRING 1105 SR

Ludwig was required to address a myriad of problems over the following weeks. He felt as if he was being bombarded with questions from sunup to sundown, everything from what food favoured his palate to who should be allowed entry to the Royal Keep without an invitation. He finally had enough and empowered the staff to make most decisions on his behalf.

Adding to his burden was the endless stream of individuals seeking the king's justice. Some were legitimate complaints, but many of the cases brought to his attention were one neighbour complaining about another, leading him to request a meeting with Lord Merrick, which the Baron of Drakenfeld hadn't been expecting.

"You wanted to see me, sire?" Merrick shifted as he waited for the king's response.

"I did. Don't worry. You're not in trouble, and please, it's Ludwig, remember? This is not a formal meeting." The king hesitated. "No. I suppose it is a formal meeting, but let's keep it friendly, shall we?"

The baron breathed a sigh of relief. "What do you want to talk to me about?"

"I'm inundated with demands for justice. I understand that's part of a king's duty to his subjects, but most complaints are trivial in nature, and I have far more important issues to tackle. To that end, I want to appoint you as my chancellor. As such, you'd be responsible for overseeing the laws of the land and a host of legal matters, save for those requiring intervention on my part."

"And what, for clarity, would warrant your attention?"

"I shall leave that up to your judgement," replied Ludwig. "Now, I wouldn't expect you to fill the position out of the goodness of your heart. There'd be a substantial financial stipend once our treasury is replenished. Would you be interested?"

"To be Lord High Chancellor? I'd be honoured. When would I start?"

"Immediately. You'll likely require a few days to acquaint yourself with procedures and responsibilities before you begin holding court, but I'll leave the scheduling up to you."

"I should begin by reading through our laws," said Merrick.

"That might prove a tad difficult. Previous kings have issued edicts and made laws, but to my knowledge, there's no single collection of laws, merely a profusion of individual documents."

"Then, with your permission, I'll undertake a revision of our legal system, creating a single book containing all our laws, which we'll then have scribes copy to distribute across the realm."

Ludwig smiled. "An excellent idea, although perhaps two books might be more suitable: a book of common laws and one for high crimes?"

"I assume high crimes would be those requiring a decision from the Crown?"

"Yes." Ludwig mulled it over. "On second thought, I don't like the idea of a single individual holding the power of life and death over someone accused of a high crime."

"But you are a just man," replied Merrick.

"And I will strive to continue to be so, but if we are to reform our laws, it must be for the benefit of the future, not only the present. We both saw what happened when King Morgan took matters into his own hands. I'll not allow that to happen again."

"Then I shall strive to carry out your will."

"Thank you."

Merrick grinned. "What do you intend to do now that you've put all this on my shoulders?"

"Don't worry. I've plenty to keep me busy."

"Are we still meeting this afternoon?"

"Yes. And remember to bring Gita. I value her insights."

Merrick rose, ready to leave, but then turned back to the table. "Isn't the ball this evening?"

"Is it?" said Ludwig. "I'd completely forgotten. I suppose I should probably postpone the meeting, then."

"You could always hold it afterwards. We'll all be here, anyway."

"An excellent suggestion."

Merrick made an exaggerated bow. "Then I shall see you this evening, Majesty."

Ludwig chuckled. "That you will. And remember, don't drink to excess; I want clear heads tonight, Chancellor."

Carriages lined the street, even though most of the barons had estates within walking distance. They pulled up before the main doors of the keep, one at a time, allowing each noble to make a spectacular entrance.

Charlotte had arranged the ball for Saint Augustine's Day, and the guests wore their finest outfits decorated with the symbols of their chosen saints. While her dress incorporated scarlet, along with the three waves of Saint Agnes, Ludwig wore an outfit in the more modest brown favoured by the Mathewites. It might not have impressed the lords of Hadenfeld, but many of the other guests appreciated the effort.

And what a guest list it was! The senior members of the Church of Saint Mathew, Agnes, and Cunar, were in attendance, along with the senior officers of the Temple Knights of Saint Mathew.

Ludwig had invited the officers of his own army to attend, peppering the room with captains aplenty. Added to that were the more influential members of the merchant class, people who, by their actions, bore a direct impact on the prosperity of the kingdom.

"Glad to see you, Master Kerrigan," said Ludwig as he stood in the receiving line, smiling and firmly grasping yet another hand. "We shall all be enjoying your fine wine this evening."

The vintner broke into a broad smile. "It is my honour, Your Majesty." He bowed, then moved along, repeating the process to Charlotte. She uttered words of encouragement, and then the fellow entered the great doors to the keep.

A familiar face was next in line, causing Ludwig to raise an eyebrow. "Master Grossman? I didn't expect you here tonight. You're a long way from Malburg."

"I trust I am not unwelcome?"

"Of course not. It's good to see you. It just took me by surprise. Are you in the capital on business?"

"I am. Malburg's ruling council sent me to enquire if we are still expected to maintain a militia. The war has been over for some time, and the expense is draining our coffers."

"I'm sorry I didn't think of this sooner," replied Ludwig. "As you say, the war is over. You may stand down your men with the knowledge that you have earned the Crown's gratitude."

"You are most gracious, Majesty." Grossman nodded, then moved along to Charlotte, offering an extended leg as he bowed and swept off his hat. "Majesty," he said. "It is a delight to see you gracing us with your presence."

"Thank you, Master Grossman. I trust Malburg is thriving?"

"It is, though that's not to say we're not without our troubles, but with the cessation of hostilities, things are definitely improving." He offered one more bow, then made his way inside.

Cyn appeared out of nowhere. "That's everyone, boss," she said. "Time to make your grand entrance."

"Are you certain this is absolutely necessary?" asked Ludwig. "We've already greeted everyone, and they know we're present."

"You're the king and queen now, Majesty. Appearances need to be kept up, whether you like it or not."

Charlotte nodded. "I agreed to welcome everyone to the keep alongside you. Now, you must return the favour and make a grand entrance."

"Let's get on with it, then, shall we?" Ludwig nodded to Cyn, who passed through the doors to speak with the Royal Herald.

The herald rapped his staff on the floor, silencing those in attendance. "Their Majesties, King Ludwig and Queen Charlotte of Hadenfeld. Long may they reign."

The two of them entered a room filled with people bowing, save for the guards. Ludwig surveyed the attendees, then waved for everyone to stand up straight. "Thank you. Your devotion is much appreciated." He paused to consider his next words. "This evening, we gather in celebration of Saint Augustine, a man who dedicated his life to the preservation of Holy Relics. Now, I am no relic, at least not yet." He waited as laughter broke out. "The coming months will be hectic. Although the war is over and the Throne secure, now, more than ever, we must work together to rebuild the realm." He nodded towards Charlotte, but she remained silent. "Enjoy," added Ludwig, "and let the music begin."

The musicians commenced playing, filling the room with a pleasant tune as the guests mingled, their voices rising as they started conversing with one another.

"That wasn't so bad," said Ludwig. He held out his hand. "Shall we dance?"

Charlotte gently grasped it, and he guided her onto the dance floor.

The dancing continued as the evening wore on, and Ludwig found himself in a philosophical discussion with the local Archprior of Saint Mathew. Father Hywell had been appointed to the position shortly after Ludwig and

Charlotte's coronation when his predecessor was recalled to the Antonine, although no one knew why. Ludwig believed it was because the Holy Father supported him during the recent war, but he had no proof. The inner workings of the Church were a mystery to those outside its walls.

As for the conversation, it concerned whether the Saints were of a divine nature.

"How else," the archprior said, "would their words have such a lasting impact?"

"I choose to believe they were mortal," responded Ludwig. "Their words carry such weight because they were meant to teach us how to behave."

"Exactly my point! How does one become so wise if not for divine inspiration?"

"Their words only became divine after the Church was formed. A feat, I might remind you, that didn't happen till well after their deaths."

Hywell chuckled. "I see we're not going to agree on this, but it hardly matters. What's more important is living in the spirit of the Saints, not where they obtained their inspiration."

"I couldn't have said it better myself."

Father Vernan wandered over, drink in hand.

"Come to help the archprior win me over to his point of view?" asked Ludwig.

"I try to avoid arguments concerning theology," replied Vernan. "It never goes well."

"Are you saying you hold no opinions on the matter?"

"No. Merely that this is a situation I could not win, for in taking a stand, I either annoy my superior or my king."

The archprior let loose with a chuckle. "Your time in His Majesty's presence has taught you well." Father Hywell's gaze locked on someone across the room. "I hope you will excuse me, Majesty, but there is someone I must speak with."

"Of course," said Ludwig.

Father Vernan waited until his superior was out of earshot. "Thank the Saints I was able to get here in time. The archprior would've talked your ear off."

"He seems an amiable enough fellow."

"Oh, he is, but once he starts, it's almost impossible to get him to stop."

"Then I am in your debt. Speaking of which, isn't it about time you became a prior?"

"I've only been a Holy Father for ten years."

"It feels like longer."

"That's because it's been an event-filled decade. For the record, I was offered a promotion but turned it down to continue as your spiritual advisor."

"You should've said something."

"I like to think we've established a firm friendship over the years, one that allows you to speak to me about anything that concerns you. I shudder to think what a new confessor might bring to the discussion."

"Then I am indebted to you," replied Ludwig. "And thankful that you are still with me now that I'm king."

"Yes, about that," said Vernan. "You have some hard decisions to make in the near future."

"Are you referring to something specific or merely in general?"

The Holy Father nodded towards the centre of the room, where Lord Darrian Forst, the Baron of Glosnecke, was taking a turn on the dance floor and proving to be most adept at it. "You and he have a history. Will that be a problem going forward?"

"Not on my part, but he's proven difficult to work with in the past."

"Might I suggest you take pains to reconcile? He is, after all, one of your barons."

"You make an excellent point, but I'm not entirely certain what I could say that would change his mind. He still blames me for preventing him from marrying Alexandra."

"Perhaps you could offer him a Royal Position? Such an appointment would raise his standing amongst the members of the court."

"I shall consider it, but I fear he won't soon forget that I also arrested his brother."

"That was all pushed aside by King Morgan, and in any case, he was only a prisoner for a few months. Hardly the type of thing to keep the anger burning, especially now that you're the king. As you so eloquently put it earlier this evening, it's time to work together to rebuild the realm."

Ludwig nodded. "I shall extend the hand of friendship once more. Perhaps this time, he might deign to accept it. I will, however, need some time to consider which position to grant him."

Father Vernan bowed. "You are wise beyond your years, Majesty. Quite the difference from the uncouth youth I met back in Erlingen all those years ago."

"Uncouth? I don't remember that."

"We both know you thought yourself invincible back then. Hardly the humble worshipper of Saint Mathew I see before me today."

Ludwig chuckled. "I'll admit I was quite full of myself in those days. Thankfully, I've had a little seasoning since then."

"More than your fair share. You've done well for yourself, taking each challenge on headfirst and always striving to do what's right instead of taking the easy way out. Lesser men would've bowed to Morgan's tyranny, but by seizing the Throne, you brought an end to his madness. History will remember your rule as a step in the right direction."

"Any other advice you'd care to impart?"

"Not at the moment," replied Father Vernan.

Ludwig peered into the Holy Father's cup. "Then we should refresh your drink. It appears you've emptied it!"

The hour was late, and with the last of the guests now departed, only Ludwig's most trusted advisors remained, having taken his advice to drink very little to maintain their wits. In some ways, it felt like more of a family gathering, but Ludwig knew there were serious subjects to address.

"The evening was a great success," he began. "I should especially like to thank Charlotte and Alexandra for their efforts in making all the arrangements."

Everyone offered their cups in salute.

"You're most welcome," replied the queen, "but the hour is late, so we'd best get to the topic at hand before our eyes start drooping." This last remark brought a chuckle from all.

"As you are aware," said Ludwig, "I intend to maintain central control over the Army of Hadenfeld, but to do that, we must somehow convince the barons to give up command of their personal armies. My question to you is how we might best go about doing so."

"Many of my fellow barons would be eager to do so," said Lord Emmett. "Maintaining these forces has been draining our treasuries for years."

"True," added Alexandra, "yet we cannot reduce our garrison when others maintain theirs. If we are to enforce this new arrangement, we must proceed carefully to ensure compliance. The last thing we want is for half the barons to give up their warriors, leaving the rest to undertake another civil war."

"A good point," offered Father Vernan. "If I may be so bold, I think I have a suggestion that might work."

"Go on," urged Ludwig.

"At the moment, each baron is charged with raising a certain number of men. I propose you reduce this number, ensuring that all comply before announcing the next round of reductions. The barons will notice the effect on their coffers immediately, allowing them to spend the coins elsewhere."

"I agree," said Lord Merrick, "but how do we measure compliance?"

"That's easy," replied Cyn. "We send inspectors out to ensure the barons are behaving."

"Those inspectors being?"

"The army."

"I fear that may be detrimental to the cause," said Father Vernan. "We're trying to unite the realm, not bully it into submission. Any presence of Royal Troops could be taken as a flexing of military might."

"But someone has to do it!" insisted Cyn.

"Hang on," said Sigwulf. "What if the Temple Knights carried out the inspections? No one would ever accuse them of being partisan."

"They fought for Ludwig during the war," replied Cyn. "That's about as partisan as you can get."

"I disagree," said Father Vernan. "I think the Temple Knights still hold a lot of goodwill. The more important question is whether the barons would allow them access to their estates."

"Why wouldn't they?" said Merrick. "It's not as if they'd be demanding entry into their manor houses."

"True," said Sigwulf, "but some of their keeps could house a company of men."

"That's not likely to be a problem in the short term," said Father Vernan. "After all, we'd be asking them to reduce their garrisons, not eliminate them entirely. A quick trip into the local village would corroborate the number of men under arms. Shall I broach the subject with Temple Captain Hamelyn?"

"If you would be so kind," replied Ludwig. "I shall be happy to discuss the matter with him in person if he has any questions."

"I'll be sure to mention that."

Alexandra cleared her throat. "Have we some idea of when we are to start this reduction?"

"I'd suggest at once," said Sigwulf, "although we should start slowly, say reducing them by only one company."

"I agree," said Gita, "and perhaps an incentive, like lowering taxes for those doing so, might prove effective?"

"We'd need to be careful," said Lord Emmett. "We're still operating on a treasury that's been robbed blind these last few years."

"Speaking of the coffers," said Ludwig, "how would you like to be the Royal Treasurer, Gita? You have a good head for numbers."

"I'd be honoured."

3

TITLES

SPRING 1105 SR

Darrian Forst entered the room with his head held high, his stiff posture indicating that his dislike of his host had not wavered since their last meeting. Forst came to a halt before Ludwig, neither nodding nor bowing in greeting. "You wanted to see me, sire?"

"I did. Come and sit. There's something I want to talk to you about."

Lord Darrian took a seat but did not relax.

"We've had our differences in the past," Ludwig continued, "but now that I am king, my duty is to tend to the well-being of all my subjects, including you."

"What is it you would have me do?"

"Do? I'm not punishing you. Quite the reverse. I want to give you a Royal Appointment."

The baron's eyebrows shot up. "Long has there been animosity between our families. Why would you even consider such a thing?"

"As I already explained, I want all my subjects to prosper. If my barons thrive, all thoughts of disloyalty disappear."

"So you're attempting to buy my loyalty?"

Ludwig found his ire rising and fought to keep it at bay. Losing his temper would do nothing except further antagonize the man, which was the last thing he wanted. He took a breath, then tried another approach. "Tell me, Lord Darrian, what is it you desire most? And don't say to marry Alexandra—that's not an option."

"I still require a wife, someone of good breeding."

"Is that your only requirement?"

"Yes. Why? What are you proposing?"

"My own marriage was arranged; would you be amenable to such?"

"I would," replied the lord. "Who do you have in mind?"

"Lord Merten, the Baron of Langeven, has a daughter who is seeking a suitable marriage."

"Has she a name?"

"Indeed," said Ludwig. "Esmerelda Boesch."

Darrian leaned forward, placing his elbows on his knees, no longer so stiff and formal. "Tell me more."

"I first became aware of her situation two years ago when I was in Eisen. At the time, there were no suitable candidates nearby, so we sent her to the court at Kurslingen, in Zowenbruch, in the hopes she might find a husband there."

"Is there something wrong with her?"

"Not at all. Why do you ask?"

"An eligible woman of her stature would be snapped up quickly. Why, then, is she still unwed?"

"If I were to give it a name, it would be politics. There's always been a stigma attached to the eastern baronies, but I assure you such behaviour will no longer be tolerated."

Lord Darrian remained silent.

"Have you any other questions?" pressed Ludwig.

"Would it be possible to meet her?"

"I shall write to her this very day, but it will take time to reach Kurslingen, so don't expect a quick reply. Does that mean you're interested?"

"Most definitely." He met Ludwig's gaze. "You surprise me, sire. I wasn't expecting this at all." Darrian hesitated for but a moment. "You mentioned a position; what did you have in mind?"

"There are several available. What sort of things interest you?"

"I am an avid rider, Majesty."

"Would you consider becoming Master of the Royal Stables?"

"Might I ask what that entails?"

"Your responsibilities would involve overseeing a breeding program, as well as purchasing new mounts for our cavalry and the Royal Household."

"I'd be honoured," replied Lord Darrian.

"Good. Then it's settled."

"When would I begin my duties?"

"As soon as you like, although there's no rush if other things need your attention."

"I shall report for duty tomorrow if that pleases Your Majesty."

"I'll let everyone know."

The baron stood and bowed but did not leave. "Might I ask a favour, sire?"

"You may ask, but I cannot guarantee an answer you'd like; it depends entirely on what you're asking for."

"Something for my brother, Gowan?"

"What did you have in mind?"

Darrian shrugged. "A captaincy, perhaps? I know he's not always easy to get along with, but a position of authority would give him some stability in his life. As it is now, he's aimless, which only leads to trouble."

"I'll find him something, but if either of my generals gives a reason to dismiss him, I'll not hesitate to approve their request."

"I shall ensure he understands the ramifications."

"Will he object to commanding footmen?"

"I doubt it."

"Good," replied Ludwig. "I'll send word once I've chosen which company to assign him to."

A look of relief flooded across Lord Darrian's face. "Thank you, Majesty. You've given me hope where I previously saw only despair." He bowed deeply before backing out of the room. As he reached the door, Cyn opened it and quickly moved aside, allowing him space to exit. She looked at the king, her eyebrows raised. "Trouble?" she asked.

"Not at all," replied Ludwig. "Are you here to see me, or were you just passing by?"

"I'm definitely here to see you." She entered the room and then took a seat. "But first, dare I ask what's going on with Lord Darrian?"

"I made him the Master of the Royal Stables."

"What is it you're not telling me?"

"What makes you think I'm not telling you something?"

"We've known each other for years, boss. You think I can't tell when you're avoiding something?"

Ludwig chuckled. "You're far too good at reading me. It just so happens I've decided to make Gowan Forst a captain in one of our foot companies."

"Which one?"

"That's for you and Sig to decide. Having said that, I want you two to give him a chance to prove himself."

"And if he doesn't?"

"Then you'll have the authority to dismiss him, but I'm hoping that won't prove necessary."

"When does he start?"

"It'll likely be a few weeks yet. I imagine he's up in Glosnecke, and it'll take time for word to reach him, then he'll have to ride all the way here."

"We'll be ready."

"Just what I wanted to hear. Now, you said you came here about something?"

"I did," replied Cyn. "I have it on good authority that some barons are struggling with paying their dues to the Crown."

"Let me guess, Tongrin?"

"That's certainly one, yes, but there are others."

"And how did you come by this information?"

"Gita might've mentioned it while she was poring over the accounts. She wanted to bring it to your attention, but I said I'd do it."

"Might I ask why?"

"Because I have an idea how we could deal with the issue."

"I'm all ears," replied Ludwig.

"Several baronies are struggling financially, largely due to the cost of raising all those warriors during the war. I propose those who can prove hardship pay less to the Crown. Not a permanent arrangement, just long enough for them to get back on their feet. It won't cost you anything since they can't afford to pay the full amount anyway."

"How many barons are we talking about?"

"Two or three, but if word gets out, others may try to claim hardship to pay less as well."

"I'm guessing you have an answer to that?"

"I do," said Cyn. "I travel to each barony to inspect their accounts and make an assessment of their finances."

"I wasn't aware you were an expert on finances."

"I used to keep track of the funds for my father's mercenary company."

"It might be dangerous," replied Ludwig. "I don't know too many barons who'd like someone poking around in their ledgers."

"Nor do I, but we would make it a requirement for anyone who wants to pay the lower amount."

"What will Gita think?"

"I've already discussed the matter with her, and she thinks it's worthwhile."

"And how much less would they pay?"

"She recommended half the full amount."

Ludwig nodded. "Get it all down in writing, then I'll sign it. Once we've sent word to the barons, and allowed them time to respond, you can decide who needs to be visited. As to your participation, I'll approve it, provided you travel with a suitable escort. You are going about the business of the Crown, and I shouldn't like to deprive the army of one of its generals if something untoward happened."

Cyn stood. "Right, then, boss. I'd better get hopping. It sounds like I'm about to be busy."

Ludwig sat with his feet up, facing the fire. It was a chilly spring evening, made even more so by the cold stone floors running throughout the Royal Keep. Beside him, Charlotte was reading a book. Frederick had been put to bed, and the two were enjoying a rare peaceful moment.

"How was your day?" she asked.

"Busy, as always. I trust you're feeling better?" She'd taken to her bed in the morning due to one of her bouts.

"Yes, remarkably so." She set her book down on the side table. "There's something we need to discuss."

"That being?"

"Grienwald."

"Ah," said Ludwig. "A bit of a difficult situation there. It belonged to Morgan before he became king."

"It did, yet he didn't see fit to name an heir despite fathering several potential candidates. Adding to that is the fact that you deposed him, making any claim by his family illegitimate."

"I hadn't thought of that. I suppose we should appoint someone as the new baron. Any suggestions on whom that should be?"

"No one comes to mind," replied Charlotte, "but that doesn't mean we shouldn't start looking. Ideally, it should be someone whose loyalty isn't in question."

"And someone who's willing to start a family to carry on the title."

"Or already has a family, so we wouldn't need to worry about who inherits. I'll begin making some discreet enquiries." She looked down at her book, then back at Ludwig. "What do we do about Luwen?"

"It belongs to Alexandra now that her father's no longer with us."

"Yes, but she's already the Baroness of Dornbruck. We need someone to look after the barony."

"She had a younger brother, but he died years ago. Does she have a cousin, perhaps?"

"She does," replied Charlotte, "although if memory serves, he lives in Deisenbach. Shall I follow up on that?"

"I think that would be for the best."

The door opened to the Calabrian, Captain Gustavo. "My apologies, Majesty, but Talon Elonin is here to see you."

"This is a surprise," said Ludwig. "I wasn't aware we were expecting her."

"Shall I take her to the audience chamber?"

"No. Bring her directly here."

"Yes, Majesty." Gustavo bowed, then left to fetch their visitor.

"What do you think this is all about?" asked Charlotte. "You don't suppose someone has invaded the Elven lands, do you?"

"No. In all probability, she's here to ratify our agreement. I recently sent a letter suggesting a visit, but it likely passed her on the road." He rose, stretched, and then offered his hand to Charlotte. "Shall we greet her?"

"I was just getting comfortable."

"Liar," he chuckled. "You've been comfortable for some time; you're already halfway through your book."

Her eyes flicked to the tome sitting beside her. "So I am. But in my defence, I was basking in companionable silence."

The door opened once more. "Talon Elonin," announced Gustavo. The Elf swept silently into the room.

Ludwig had spent a considerable amount of time amongst the Elves but always found it difficult to adjust to their appearance. Their elongated faces made him feel as if someone had stretched a Human head upward, distorting the features. Added to that were their slightly pointed ears and silver-white hair, giving the talon a striking presence.

"Greetings, Talon Elonin," he said.

"And to you, noble king," replied the Elf. "I am pleased to see you in good health." She turned to Charlotte. "And to you, noble queen."

"I'm sorry we didn't reach out to you sooner," said Ludwig, "but ruling Hadenfeld has proven more challenging than either of us would ever have imagined."

"I understand, as does High Lord Sindra. It was this very suspicion that convinced her to delay sending an emissary to your capital."

"I assume you're here to formally sign our agreement?"

"Not at all," replied Elonin. "I lack the necessary authority to do so. I am here, instead, to arrange a visit by the High Lord herself."

"Sindra wants to come here?" said Charlotte. "I must say that surprises me."

"As it did me," agreed the Elf. "It has been more than a millennia since a High Lord of Nethendril visited a foreign court."

"We shall have to send an escort," said Ludwig. "I shouldn't want anyone to think we've been invaded."

"I must insist she be allowed to bring her own guard."

"I have no objection, although I need to know how many to expect so we can make arrangements for their stay."

"Twenty, not including the delegation itself."

"Which consists of?"

"Myself, the High Lord, Galrandir, and six servants."

"I shall arrange for accommodations. Do you have a specific date in mind?"

"I should think the first day of summer most appropriate. Amongst our people, it is seen as a portent of good fortune. I took the liberty of consulting with your people in Eisen and discovered we mark the turning of the seasons on the same day."

"I wonder why that is?"

"I can answer that," offered Charlotte. "It dates back to the early days of Human civilization. At least, that's what the scholars claim. I suspect it was a tradition our early ancestors adapted from the Elves they are thought to have traded with."

"That appears to be the most logical explanation," replied Elonin. "As to our route, I suggest we emerge near Eisen, then travel along the northern road through Malburg, which is the route I came here upon."

"It shall be as you wish. Anything else you'd like to address while you're here?"

"Yes. The repulsion of Zowenbruch last summer convinced the people of the Goldenwood that we needed a larger standing army. To that end, we have increased the number of warbands. To put it in terms you might be more familiar with, we have added two companies to our expeditionary force."

"Expeditionary force?" said Charlotte. "I'm afraid you've lost me on that one."

"It refers to the number of warriors we would commit should Hadenfeld require aid."

"That is most generous," said Ludwig, "but as far as I recall, there was no specific mention of how many warriors we'd send, although naturally, we'd help in any way we can."

"The High Lord believes this particular item needs to be included as part of any agreement between our people. She trusts you, Lord King, but we must account for the relatively short lifespans of you Humans. Without that stipulation, a future king might deign to send only a token force."

"A fair point, but at present, we're still recovering from a civil war and haven't many men to spare."

"We have every confidence that your realm will recover in time, and, as I said, we trust you to provide whatever aid you deem suitable should that prove necessary."

"Thank you. You've given me much to consider."

"With your permission," said Elonin, "I shall withdraw."

"By all means. Captain Gustavo will show you to one of our guest quarters."

The talon bowed, then allowed herself to be shown from the room.

Ludwig turned to Charlotte. "What did you make of that?" he asked.

"They're worried about something."

"They have every right to be. By allying with us, they've entered the politics of the Petty Kingdoms, a difficult thing to navigate."

"Perhaps they fear further attacks?" suggested Charlotte. "Could Zowenbruch be plotting something?"

"I doubt it. We gave them a good trouncing last year, and King Konrad gave his word to remain on his side of the border."

"True, but while you negotiated that settlement, it was under the authority of King Morgan. Now that he no longer sits on the throne, Konrad may not consider the agreement valid."

"Which means I'll need to send someone to Zowenbruch to smooth things over and ensure the peace still holds. Yet another task I wasn't expecting. Is our entire rule to be like this?"

"Very likely," replied Charlotte. "It is the burden of monarchs across the Continent to deal with the unexpected. Why should we be any different?"

"It'd be nice if all the Petty Kingdoms could mind their own business and stop all this incessant warmongering. Imagine how prosperous we'd all be if we didn't constantly fear an enemy crossing our borders."

"If you break down the politics of the Continent, it all boils down to jealousy. Rulers covet what their neighbours possess, or rather what they think they have. They can't stand the idea that others are better off than themselves."

"That's a very astute observation. I suppose the question is, how do we counter that threat? Do we visit other realms and complain about how difficult life is in Hadenfeld?"

"Human nature being what it is, I doubt that would work. Others would claim you were lying to dissuade them from invading."

"Then what's the use of employing diplomacy?"

"We ensure the peace by building personal connections," replied Charlotte. "Friends don't go to war with one another, but strangers do."

"So I should travel around making friends?"

"That about sums it up, yes."

"Well, it would give me a break from court."

"From our court," she replied, "but you'd be visiting the courts of all our neighbours, so I'm not so certain you would consider it a break."

"Any suggestions on where to start? Zowenbruch, perhaps?"

"I'd suggest Hollenbeck. Sig already has a connection to the duke there, and he lent us some help during the siege of Harlingen."

"Then that shall be my first visit once we're finished with the High Lord of Nethendril."

4

EMISSARY

SUMMER 1105 SR

Hadenfeld's Knights of the Sacred Shield trotted through the city gates, the summer sun glinting off their armour as they led the procession. Behind them came the Elves of Nethendril, in silver and green, a delegation of warriors mounted on white horses that pranced as they entered Harlingen.

Sigwulf viewed the entourage from atop the northern gatehouse, curious how the people of the capital would react to these foreign visitors.

"Impressive, aren't they?" said Cyn. "Do you think all their horses are white or only these?"

"They were all white at the Battle of Eisen. I suspect that's the breed."

"I like the look of them."

"I never took you for someone who loves horses."

"I ride one, don't I?"

"That you do," said Sig, "but I've noticed you don't appear comfortable in the saddle."

"I'll admit it's not my favourite mode of travel, but I still appreciate a fine animal. We should discover if we can arrange for some of those horses for breeding purposes."

"They're too small to bear the weight of our armour."

"There is such a thing as light cavalry."

"Perhaps," he replied, "but as far as I know, Hadenfeld has never employed any."

"Then maybe it's time we started? It's not practical to use heavily armoured men to scout."

"It's worth considering. We'll bring it up to Ludwig once we finally get around to enlarging the army."

"Agreed. Now, we'd best get to the Royal Keep before anybody notices we're not there."

Ludwig had planned for himself and Charlotte to greet the delegation as it arrived at the keep, but she'd been unable to rise this day. Instead, the Baron and Baroness of Drakenfeld took her place, more to calm Ludwig's nerves than through any other necessity.

"I can hear the crowds cheering," said Merrick.

"And well they should," replied Gita. "It's not every day a foreign ruler visits Harlingen. Come to think of it, I don't believe a non-Human ruler has ever set foot in the city before."

"There's a first for everything."

"Indeed," added Ludwig. "Let us hope this visit is a portent of better times ahead for both our peoples."

"Very diplomatic of you," said Merrick. "Did you come up with that, or was it Charlotte's take on things?"

Ludwig smiled despite his frayed nerves. "Hers, of course. She's far more diplomatic than I am."

"Says the man who convinced the eastern barons to take his side during a civil war. Not that there's anything civil about war."

"I recall you supporting me, and you're not from the east."

Gita laughed. "He's got you there!"

The cheering grew louder as the parade of warriors turned onto the main street some blocks away, but even from this distance, the knights' gleaming armour and their large warhorses proved an impressive sight.

"They look lovely," said Gita.

"Lovely?" replied Merrick. "Hardly the description a warrior would appreciate. They are, perhaps, the finest knights in all the Petty Kingdoms."

"Hardly that," said Ludwig. "To be honest, they're a pain in the royal arse."

"Why?"

"I know the answer to that," said Gita. "When the kingdom was sundered fifty years ago, the order fractured, with many of its members joining Neuhafen. Both sets of knights claim the right to the name, leading to two separate orders of chivalry with the same name."

"Yes," said Merrick, "but we're all one big happy kingdom now, aren't we?"

"We are," said Ludwig, "but we're dealing with knights who, until last year, fought on opposite sides. Then there's the matter of their current organization. Whose grand master gets to rule the order?"

"I thought their grand master died at Erhard's Folly?"

"He did, or rather the king's grand master did."

"But we didn't have any knights when we faced them."

"That's because Morgan disbanded those from the east. They didn't fight, but ever since I became king, they've begged me to reinstate their membership in the order."

"And will you?" asked Gita.

"Eventually, but I must first determine how to reintegrate them into the order. I'd hate for fighting to break out between knights."

The men in question approached, passing by the keep, their leader offering a salute with his sword. Ludwig nodded a quick acknowledgement, then focused on the Elves and their silver mail that reminded him so much of fish scales. The lead riders proceeded past him, slowing their pace and coming to a rest as High Lord Sindra's horse came even with the entrance to the keep.

Elonin, who rode beside her lord, dismounted first, handing her reins to one of her warriors. She then moved to steady Sindra's mount while the High Lord climbed out of the saddle.

"King Ludwig," said Sindra. "I bring you greetings from the people of the Goldenwood."

"Welcome," he replied. "I trust your trip was uneventful?"

"On the contrary, it was full of marvellous sights. You have a green and pleasant land full of farms and pastures—a vastly different appearance from our own lands."

"And your escort?"

"They largely kept to themselves, which, admittedly, is how we preferred it. I assure you, however, they were well-behaved."

Ludwig turned to his companions. "May I present Lord Merrick and Lady Gita Sternhassen, Baron and Baroness of Drakenfeld."

"It is always a pleasure to meet like-minded individuals."

"Like-minded?" said Gita. "What makes you say that?"

"By the very fact that King Ludwig introduced you. We have observed him at length in the east and judge him to be a man of principles." She turned to Elonin. "Is that the correct term?"

"It is," replied the talon.

"You must excuse me," said Sindra. "Your language is new to us."

"You speak it well," said Merrick.

"It is good to hear you say so, as it is a recent development. After we worked together to defeat Zowenbruch, I thought it useful to learn your language, if only to prevent misunderstandings. Am I correct in assuming the same language is used elsewhere in the Petty Kingdoms?"

"You are," said Ludwig.

"Perhaps we should go inside?" suggested Gita. "There is a feast laid out in your honour, High Lord."

"Yes, of course," replied Sindra. "I forgot how much you Humans like to bond over food."

The dinner was a formal affair with tables piled high with enticing delicacies. It wasn't that Ludwig wanted everyone to be stuffed, but he was uncertain what the Elves would eat, so he'd instructed the kitchen to prepare everything they could think of, resulting in much of the cooking having to be done elsewhere, where more ovens were available.

Part of him considered it an exceptional extravagance, but he consoled himself by arranging for the Mathewite mission to receive whatever was left over.

As Charlotte was still unable to attend, Merrick and Gita helped keep the conversation flowing, along with Emmett and Alexandra. Rounding out this group was Father Vernan, who seemed greatly interested in learning more about the Elves of Nethendril.

"There's something I don't understand," he was saying. "Is your realm called Nethendril or the Goldenwood? Or is it customary to call it both?"

Sindra looked at Elonin and nodded.

"Nethendril is one of our cities," replied the talon, "whereas the Goldenwood is both the name of the forest and our realm."

"And how far does your border extend?"

"Right to the edge of the woodlands or the rivers, in those places where it forms a natural barrier."

"I'm led to believe your lands are close to Eisen."

"We have yet to formalize where our territory ends and yours begins, but as neither of us has expressed a desire to claim that particular region, it makes little difference. Also, we do not claim the land as you Humans do. Rather, we seek guardianship over it in the name of Tauril."

"Ah, yes. The Goddess of the Woods, said to hold domain over all the trees and plants of Eiddenwerthe."

"Said?" replied Elonin. "It is a fact, not a speculation held up for scrutiny. Her domain includes all natural denizens of the forest."

"Are you suggesting there are unnatural denizens?"

"There are, indeed," said Sindra. "Aberrations and animated constructs, the results of delving into matters best left unexplored."

"Aberrations?" said Vernan. "I don't believe I'm familiar with that term."

"They are the result of willful tampering with nature. Although I am ashamed to admit it, some Elves have ventured into forbidden studies, creating mockeries of Tauril's creatures. One such example is using magic to merge two creatures together, resulting in horrific results. Scores of the creatures have been released into the Goldenwood over the centuries, and some may still survive."

"And constructs?"

"Constructs are a different matter: creatures with no mind of their own that must be controlled by a wielder of magic, be it Enchantments or some fouler study of the dark arts."

"Astounding! No wonder the woods are considered so dangerous."

"That reputation came about because our people executed those who crossed our border. It had nothing to do with the creatures living beneath the boughs of the Goldenwood."

"You're very open about all of this," said Father Vernan.

"It is no longer necessary to keep it a secret," replied the High Lord. "We rescinded the law that required the execution of interlopers, and the trade route to Nethendril is now kept safe by our glade wardens. Your people have nothing to fear so long as they use the approved method of travel."

"Which is the Erlen River," offered Ludwig. "Boats from Eisen carry goods all the way downstream to Nethendril, then return with Elven goods for sale in Hadenfeld. It is, I'm told, a profitable venture."

"Astounding," said the Holy Father. "Who would ever have thought we'd end up trading with the woodland folk?"

"Our trade, at present, is small," replied Sindra, "but I hope this may increase over time."

"What types of things have you for trade?"

"The better question to ask is, what goods do you seek?"

"I'm afraid you've got me there," said Vernan. "I'm a Holy Father, not a merchant." He turned to Ludwig. "You'd have a better idea, Majesty. What are your thoughts on the matter?"

"I've seen their carpenters' work, and I can attest to its quality. I should think the nobles of Hadenfeld would be eager to purchase furniture made by the Elves. They also have shadowbark."

"Shadowbark?" said Emmett. "That stuff's worth a fortune! I remember my uncle having a desk made of it, and it cost him more than two thousand crowns." The baron leaned forward towards Sindra. "How much do you have?"

"Enough that we pave our streets with it."

"Truly?"

"I can vouch for that," said Ludwig. "Their streets are covered by it, presumably to keep the mud at bay. It also has the added advantage of resisting the elements."

"By the Saints," said Merrick. "I can scarcely believe it. The most expensive wood in the entire Continent, and they use it to pave their roads! I tell you, Eiddenwerthe has gone completely mad."

"There is no madness in building something that lasts," replied Elonin. "Shadowbark is common to us; thus, we place no great value on using it other than its ability to resist the seasons. You Humans, however, worship it simply for the sake that it's rare."

"You're not wrong there," said Ludwig. "Wine, food, and, as we've already said, even wood, is considered of greater value when it's difficult to find, regardless of its actual properties. I daresay if gold were as rare as some of these things I've mentioned, you'd be able to purchase a keep for a single crown."

"Imagine that," said Emmett. "Everyone would own a palace."

"Not so," said Alexandra, "for less of it would be in circulation."

"Yes, of course. I should've realized."

"As interesting as this discussion is," said Sindra, "I believe our time might be better spent discussing the terms of our agreement."

"Where would you like to start?" asked Ludwig.

"We each agree to come to the aid of the other should enemy troops threaten our lands."

"Agreed."

"How long would this mutual defence treaty last?" asked Gita.

"I would suggest fifty years, or until either of us passes to the Afterlife. It could always be extended by our descendants if they deem it beneficial. I should point out, however, that it does not bind us to assist in any war outside the borders of the Goldenwood or Hadenfeld. We hold no interest in conquering others, only protecting our homes."

"I see no problem with that," said Ludwig. "We still need to work out some additional details, though."

"Such as?"

"How are we to notify each other in the event of an emergency, and how many warriors are we to commit to the cause, should one erupt?"

"Our entire army," replied the High Lord, "save for those required to protect our cities, would march to your aid, were it deemed necessary."

"And in return, we would do the same, although, at present, our army is undergoing a reorganization."

"Is there a current threat to your realm?"

"Not that I'm aware of," replied Ludwig.

"Then the current state of your army is of little consequence. We are making long-term plans here today, not taking immediate action."

Father Vernan stood. "With your permission, sire, I shall go and finish preparing the documents for tomorrow's signing. I'll be certain to include the changes discussed here."

"Thank you," said Ludwig, who then turned to face the Elven High Lord. "Do you wish a copy in your own language?"

"That will be unnecessary," she replied. "Your tongue is sufficient."

Two copies of the agreement waited on a table in the great hall the next morning. Ludwig and Charlotte signed them, followed by High Lord Sindra. To add further weight to the document, the Archprior of Saint Mathew scribed his name as a witness, along with several Church elders. Elonin added her name as the Elven witness, and then seals were attached at the bottom of each.

Once the wax cooled, the archprior announced the document completed and that Hadenfeld and the Goldenwood were now bound in a defensive alliance, each expected to come to the aid of the other should it prove necessary.

Ludwig thought to celebrate the occasion with a meal, but after the excesses of the day before, there was little appetite for more heavy food. Instead, wine was poured, and smaller plates of bread and cheese, an Elven favourite, were brought out.

"Finally," said Sigwulf. "I was beginning to think I'd pass out from hunger."

"Really?" replied Cyn. "You ate enough last night to last you three entire days."

"What can I say? All this training builds up an appetite."

Their discussion was interrupted by the arrival of Captain Gustavo, who made his way to Ludwig's side and whispered in his ear.

The king stood up. "Please excuse me. I must attend to something." He glanced around the table. "Enjoy yourselves. I shall rejoin you directly. Sig, Cyn, with me, if you would." The two warriors followed him to a nearby room where they had some privacy.

"This sounds serious," said Sigwulf.

"It is," replied Ludwig. "The Temple Knights just informed us that Lord Jurgen is refusing to reduce the number of warriors under his command."

"But it's a Royal Decree!" exclaimed Cyn. "Is the fellow simply mad, or is he planning something?"

"We can't overlook that he was a firm supporter of King Morgan, even going so far as attempting to plot a border incident on the king's behalf. Did you ever get a chance to review his accounts?"

"No. I only spoke with those having financial trouble, and he wasn't on the list."

"You can't let the fellow get away with this," said Sigwulf. "It sets a bad precedent."

"I agree," added Cyn. "If the barons think they can ignore the king's commands, we're doomed. What do you want us to do?"

Ludwig looked at Captain Gustavo. "Have we any idea the number of men he has under arms?"

"Yes, sire. Captain Hamelyn estimates it to be close to three hundred. He based that on what the baron sent to aid Morgan during the war, so he may have raised more."

"I doubt that," said Sigwulf. "Even if he had twice that number, he'd still be badly outnumbered by the Crown. Unless you think he's in collusion with other barons?"

"We can't dismiss the possibility," replied Ludwig, "but whether he is or not, we must do something."

"I could take the army and force him to disband his men?"

"I have a better idea," said Cyn, "or at least a more diplomatic one. Summon Lord Jurgen here, to Harlingen."

"And who is to deliver this summons?"

"I'll go," she offered.

"Very well," said Ludwig. "But I shan't send you alone."

"What have you got in mind?"

"I'd like you to mount a small expedition, say four hundred men. I'll let you decide on its composition."

"And if he asks why we came in force?"

"You insist you were conducting a training exercise when you received word of the summons."

"Clever," said Sigwulf. "A show of strength to indicate you mean business. If he is plotting rebellion, he'd be forced to make his move now rather than later."

"I'm hoping it won't come to that," said Ludwig, "but it's better to force his hand instead of giving him time to consolidate his forces."

"When do I leave?" asked Cyn.

"First thing tomorrow. In the meantime, you'd best pick out who you want to take; you've got a long march ahead of you."

"I'll see to their provisioning," offered Sigwulf. "It appears we'll be missing the rest of the festivities."

"I shall make your excuses," said Ludwig. "Remember, Cyn, you're a general now. Any attack on you or your men is considered a direct attack on the Crown."

5

TROUBLE BREWS

SUMMER 1105 SR

The trip to Bruggendorf was seventy miles, with the mostly open terrain making for swift progress. Cyn had elected to bring along two hundred foot, a hundred archers, and most importantly, all the Knights of the Sacred Shield. A reasonably large force, but she had to weigh the chances Lord Jurgen might fight rather than submit.

She'd chosen Captain Paran to act as her aide, knowing his loyalties lay with the king, for he'd been recruited in the Barony of Verfeld some years ago and had proven himself many times since in battle.

Bruggendorf was a wealthy barony with lush, green, open fields ideal for raising horses. With King Morgan, there'd been a push to increase the number of horsemen under arms, resulting in an increase in the size of Jurgen's herds. That, in turn, led to more coins flowing into his coffers, which worried Cyn, for Ludwig's own treasury was only just beginning to recover from the war, while the baron was under no such restrictions.

Cyn called a halt as the village of Bruggendorf came into sight. Paran rode over, looking uncomfortable in the saddle.

"Orders, General?" he asked.

"I think we should avoid making a show of our strength right away."

"Shall I ride up and deliver the king's message?"

Cyn nodded. "I'll order some of our archers to keep an eye on the estate. I'd hate for you to run into trouble. Do you want a couple of guards to accompany you?"

"I doubt that would be necessary. After all, I'm only a captain."

Cyn handed over the scroll case containing Ludwig's summons, then looked up at the sky, estimating the time. "I'll expect you back before noon." The captain nodded, then urged his horse down the road.

She found the waiting far more nerve-racking than the march down here. So many things could go wrong, and the last thing she wanted was to start another civil war.

She tried thinking of something else, but her present circumstances kept gnawing at her. In a desperate attempt to divert her thoughts, she decided to inspect the men under her command, even though nothing was wrong with them, for most of them had served Ludwig during the war. The knights were the only exception, but they appeared eager to prove their loyalty to their new king.

Cyn was chatting with the archers when she was called to the road, for Paran was galloping back to them, not precisely the best indication of success.

"Trouble?" she called out.

"You might say that. Lord Jurgen refused to receive me."

"Did he give a reason?"

"I was told that, as a mere captain, I possess no authority to issue a summons."

"Did he not see the Royal Seal?"

Paran shrugged. "The sergeant I spoke with certainly did, but he refused to acknowledge it."

"It appears I shall have to see to this myself. It's one thing to refuse the visit of a captain, quite another to ignore the presence of a king's general."

"It might help if you brought an escort," said Paran.

"Good point. Find Edwig and Rikal, then join me back here."

"You think three is enough?"

"Three captains is a suitable number to ensure I'm not arrested. Any more, and it could be taken as an aggressive move."

The Calabrian chuckled. "And arresting the baron isn't?"

Cyn smiled. "We're not arresting him, merely escorting him to the capital."

"Fair point." Paran noticed his two friends off in the distance. All of them had been recruited in Roshlag, one of Ludwig's villages, and after serving him during his bid to seize the Throne, they'd been promoted to captains. He waved his comrades over. "We're escorting the general, so keep your wits about you."

"Is there likely to be fighting?" asked Edwig.

Paran turned to Cyn. "Good question. Your thoughts, General?"

"I'm hoping not," she replied, "but I won't back down in the face of resistance."

"So fighting, then," said Paran. "Don't worry, General. We'll keep you safe."

"Thank you, gentlemen. I appreciate that."

"We're not gentlemen, we're commoners."

"So am I. What's your point?"

"Just that we shouldn't be called gentlemen?"

Cyn leaned on the pommel of her saddle. "Ah, but you're the king's warriors, which makes the title appropriate. Now, let's get going, shall we? I should like this settled and be well on our way by dinner-time."

While the village of Bruggendorf was like any other of the Petty Kingdoms, the baron's estate was another matter entirely. Rather than a fortified keep, Lord Jurgen's ancestors elected to build a sprawling manor house. And why wouldn't they? The neighbouring realms of Hollenbeck and Grislagen had never been considered a threat.

The manor overlooked a green and pleasant valley, where his horses roamed at will. Cyn's visit two years earlier resulted in her becoming a prisoner, along with Siggy and Ludwig. They'd escaped, but she doubted Lord Jurgen would forget the subsequent events. She only hoped he wouldn't hold it against her.

As they drew closer, additional men issued from the building, joining the two who stood guard at the entrance. The three captains all put their hands on their hilts, but Cyn remained calm, waiting for the inevitable challenge.

Finally, one of the armoured warriors stepped out in front of the others. "Identify yourselves."

"I am General Cynthia Hoffman, appointed by His Majesty, King Ludwig, to deliver unto Lord Jurgen Voltz, Baron of Bruggendorf, the king's wishes that the baron should present himself at court."

"And if he chooses not to?"

"Failure to comply with His Majesty's wishes will result in arrest and forfeiture of his lands." Cyn nodded behind her. "Up the road a little, four hundred men wait to enforce the king's request."

"And we have more than three hundred defending this manor."

"Perhaps," she replied, "but your men cannot be everywhere at once, and while you're protecting the manor, mine will round up every single horse out in those fields."

"You wouldn't dare!"

"Wouldn't I? Clearly, you don't know me, Captain, or you wouldn't even suggest such a thing. I was a mercenary long before I took command of the king's men, and as such, I'm familiar with the art of pillaging. Now, will you take the summons to Lord Jurgen, or do you wish me to unleash my men on the baron's lands?"

The fellow looked around nervously and with good reason. It wouldn't take much to surround the manor, leaving plenty of her men to plunder the herds.

"Remain where you are," the fellow finally announced, then turned, hurrying back into the manor house.

"Well," said Paran. "That was interesting. Do you think the baron will submit, or will we end up having to take him by force?"

"Submit," she replied. "Doing so still earns him a reprimand, but refusing is more likely to result in a charge of treason, which could cost him his life."

"Not to mention his fortune," said Paran. "That, perhaps more than anything else, is likely to sway his response."

The guard captain returned, his attitude much less haughty. "The baron will see you now," he announced, then motioned towards the open door.

"These men are to accompany me," said Cyn.

"As you wish."

She ignored the guards as she passed by, though her hand never strayed far from the mace hanging from her belt. Paran, Edwig, and Rikal followed behind her, eyeballing the guards every step they took.

"His Lordship is down this way," said the captain, leading them through the entrance hall and down a side corridor, halting at one of the many decorative doors. He then knocked. "They are here, my lord."

"Send them in," came the reply.

The captain opened the door, and the group entered to find Lord Jurgen sitting in an oversized chair, his feet up on a small cushion, a bandage covering one.

"Are you injured, my lord?" asked Cyn.

The baron wore a look of disapproval. "A flare-up of gout, nothing you need to worry about."

"The king has a gifted healer at court."

"Healer? Don't make me laugh. The finest healers in all of Hadenfeld know of no cure for me."

"Ah," said Cyn, "but Kandam is not any ordinary healer; he's a Life Mage."

"I am not familiar with the name."

"I don't see why you should be, all things considered, but I assure you, he's more than capable of caring for your condition."

"My condition has nothing to do with your visit here."

"No, it doesn't. The king has summoned you to court."

"To what end?" asked Lord Jurgen.

"I couldn't really say," replied Cyn.

"Couldn't? Or won't?"

She offered a forced smile. "Does it matter, Lord? Your king called on you to come to the capital. Will you refuse his summons?"

Jurgen cast his gaze about like a cornered dog. "You may inform His Majesty that I will comply with his request."

"Excellent. We shall leave first thing in the morning."

"We shall leave when I'm good and ready."

"I shall honour your pledge," said Cyn, "provided you are 'good and ready' first thing tomorrow."

"And if I'm not?"

"Then I begin rounding up your horses in the name of the Crown."

"You wouldn't dare!"

"You seem to be under the impression you have a choice in the matter. Now, will you join us tomorrow, or are we to put you in chains? The choice is yours."

Jurgen stared back, and to Cyn, it appeared as though his eyes were bulging. For a moment, she imagined them popping out, and she stifled a giggle in an attempt to remain serious.

"I… shall be ready to leave in the morning," he finally replied.

She offered a bow. "I look forward to travelling in your company, my lord."

Ludwig sat at his desk, composing a letter to Temple Commander Charlaine. He hadn't heard from her in some time and was beginning to worry that Halvaria had attempted another invasion. A shadow graced his doorway, causing him to look up to see Gustavo waiting there.

"Problem?" said Ludwig.

"The general has returned, sire, along with Lord Jurgen and a small escort."

"Is he in chains?"

"No."

"Good. That indicates he came of his own free will." Ludwig rose, then moved around the table to stand before his captain. "Don't look so glum. We've managed to avert another civil war."

Gustavo frowned. "Can he be trusted?"

"Let's find out, shall we?" Ludwig exited the room, making his way towards the great hall. "Come along, Captain. I'd like a second set of ears at this meeting."

They arrived to find Lord Jurgen pacing back and forth before the throne, his pronounced limp making it easy for Cyn and six warriors to keep a close eye on him. At Ludwig's entrance, she bowed while her men briefly stood to attention.

The baron halted, his eyes following his king's every step. Ludwig sat on the throne, leaning back before he returned the man's gaze. Jurgen had been a loyal follower of King Morgan, even participating in a plot to foment a war with Hollenbeck, but the drawn and haggard man standing before Ludwig was a shadow of his former self.

"Are you injured, Lord?" asked Ludwig.

"A flare-up of gout, sire. A common ailment in my family."

"Shall I fetch Kandam?" asked Cyn.

"By all means," replied Ludwig, "and something for Lord Jurgen to sit on while you're at it." She nodded towards one of her men, who then left the room.

The baron looked around nervously before finally settling his gaze once more on his king. "You summoned me, Your Majesty?"

"I did," replied Ludwig. "It has come to my attention you are openly defying my orders to reduce the number of warriors under your command."

"I need those men to protect my land."

"From whom?"

"We have enemies everywhere, sire. One can never be too careful."

"Your estate lies close to both Grislagen and Hollenbeck. Surely you're not suggesting one of those realms is threatening war?"

"I speak of bandits, Majesty. They're a plague on the kingdom."

"Were that the case, your men would've been out patrolling the roads, nor would you require so many. How many companies did he have?" This last question he directed towards Cyn.

"Seven companies, from what we observed."

"Three hundred and fifty men? That seems a little excessive to me, especially when we're not at war."

Jurgen, finding his spine, stood straighter. "Yet you sent hundreds to arrest me."

"Arrest?" said Ludwig. "All I did was send someone to summon you to court. Are you now suggesting those numbers were not needed to safeguard my general from bandits?"

"I... no, sire." The baron's head sank; indeed, his whole body sagged, a realization his fate now lay in the king's hands.

The door opened, letting in Cyn's warrior, along with Kandam. The healer's Kurathian heritage was even more pronounced, for with the completion of his training as a Life Mage, he'd adopted the flowing robes common to his ancestors.

The warrior placed a three-legged stool before his king, and then Ludwig motioned for Jurgen to sit on it. The baron complied, although he still looked nervous.

"You and I've had our differences," began Ludwig, "but I am no longer a baron. As king, my responsibility is to look after this realm and its inhabitants, regardless of my personal feelings on the matter. Were I to execute you or throw you in the dungeon, I would be no better than Morgan. I invited you here to discuss matters in a civilized manner."

Jurgen's pale face belied his fear. "That is most generous of you, sire."

"Under my rule, barons are no longer required to raise troops in time of war." He held up his hand to forestall any objection. "You'll be permitted to retain a small number of warriors to keep the king's peace in your domain, but that's a far cry from raising a private army."

Ludwig paused, watching the baron with keen interest. Was he accepting this argument or merely cowed by the threat of imprisonment? Part of him wanted to punish the man for his aid in supporting Morgan, but he must put such feelings aside for the good of the kingdom.

"You stand to make a lot under this arrangement."

Jurgen sat up a bit straighter. "Will you not tax us to pay for the army?"

"I will, but you'll find it less of a burden than maintaining your own soldiers. There's also the matter of your horses, which will soon be in demand."

"So you mean to increase the size of the army?"

"Eventually, but first, I must put the kingdom's finances in order."

Jurgen nodded. "Morgan was terrible with that, a trait I'm told he inherited from his father." His gaze flicked to Kandam. "What's he here for?"

"He is going to heal your gout."

"That will take weeks. I should know, I've dealt with it often enough."

"I don't think you understand his position here. He's not a physician who relies on herbs and poultices; he's a practitioner of magic. You yourself employed a Fire Mage. Now you can witness first-hand the healing effects of Life Magic." Ludwig nodded to Kandam, who moved closer, kneeling beside the baron.

"Will this hurt?" asked Lord Jurgen.

"Not at all," replied the Kurathian, "although you might feel a slight tingle while the spell does its work. Would you be so good as to remove your boot?"

Jurgen did as he was asked, and then Kandam lifted the foot, rolling down the sock to reveal its red and swollen state. Strange words emanated from the mage while his hands began glowing with a white light that seeped into the baron's foot, causing it to glow as if lit from within. The swelling slowly subsided, and then the colour returned to that of a normal, healthy foot.

"Remarkable!" said Jurgen. "I never would've thought such a thing possible."

"I must warn you, however," said Kandam. "Your affliction is removed, but the root cause of the gout must be eliminated, or it may return."

"What is that?"

"It's been suggested the consumption of strong drink might be a contributing factor, as well as diet."

"Surely you're not proposing I give up on eating?"

"No, though you might want to give more consideration to what you consume."

"What do you suggest?"

"Less meat, although I'm not an expert in such things."

"But you're a Life Mage!"

"Yes, I can use magic to cure those afflicted by injury or disease. However, I cannot prevent your gout from flaring up again any more than you could prevent me from falling from a ladder at some point in the future."

"Yet you suggest less drink and meat?"

"I'm led to understand those who limit how much they imbibe are less likely to suffer from your ailment, but there are no guarantees."

"You did say it ran in the family," said Ludwig, "but perhaps that's a result of having the same habits as your father?"

"I shall consider your advice," replied Jurgen. He moved his foot around, twisting his ankle and bending his toes. "Most remarkable."

"You may put your boot back on," said Kandam. "The treatment is complete."

"My thanks to you… How exactly do I address you?"

"That is an excellent question." The mage turned to his king.

"You've mastered Life Magic," said Ludwig. "I suppose Master Kandam would be the most appropriate."

"Indeed, Majesty."

"Then I thank you, Master Kandam," added Lord Jurgen. He pulled his boot on, then gave the king a wide smile. "You have proved far more gracious than I would've thought, Majesty. I throw myself at your mercy for my temerity in refusing your orders and accept whatever punishment you deem appropriate."

"You are free to go, my lord. There will be no punishment, provided there are no further refusals to follow the king's commands. Break your word, however, and I shall consider a charge of treason. I shouldn't have to remind you of the punishment for that."

The baron turned white as a sheet. "I assure you, Majesty, I will reduce my garrison as soon as I return to my estate."

"Good. Now, you are free to leave the Palace, but before you leave Harlingen, I want you to meet with my generals."

"Dare I ask to what end?"

"To discuss the matter of horses. The Royal Army will need to purchase some soon, and I'm led to believe you produce the finest breeders in the kingdom."

"You honour me, sire." Jurgen made a grand bow before his king.

"My men will see you out," said Cyn.

The Baron of Bruggendorf offered her a nod, then turned and left the room with the warriors, leaving only Ludwig, Cyn, and Kandam.

Cyn waited until the door closed before speaking. "That was very diplomatic of you, boss."

"You find that surprising?" replied Ludwig.

"I've seen your diplomatic side before. I just didn't think you'd be using it with Jurgen."

"He is a king now," offered Kandam. "As such, he must put personal grudges aside to do what is best for the realm."

6

THE SOUTH

SUMMER 1105 SR

Ludwig looked up from the papers scattered atop his desk. "Interesting. It appears I've received an invitation."

"That's not unusual for a king," replied Charlotte, who was sitting on a well-padded chair nearby, reading a book. "Who's it from?"

"Duke Ulfric of Hollenbeck."

"Hollenbeck? Isn't that the realm Morgan tried to lure into a war?"

"It is. He's invited me to his capital, Klermacht."

"Convenient since you were planning on visiting. Have you ever been there?"

"No, but as you know, Sig has. He warned the duke about Lord Jurgen's ruse."

"Yes, I remember now. If I recall, that was the reason His Grace helped him and Cyn get their men into Harlingen during the siege. You should accept his invitation and reassure him we have no designs on his territory."

"Would you be up to accompanying me?"

"Much as it would please me, I fear my ongoing health concerns would be more of a hindrance than help. I think it best I remain here in Harlingen to rule in your absence."

Ludwig smiled. "It pleases me to know the kingdom is in your hands. Now remember, you're the Queen of Hadenfeld; don't let anyone try to tell you otherwise."

"You worry too much," replied Charlotte. "And, anyway, I have plenty of people to look after me in your absence. Now, concerning your trip, you'll need to arrange a suitable escort. I also recommend you take Sig since he's on good terms with the duke."

"You enjoy planning things far more than I do."

"That's why we make such a good team. Now, who else do you think should accompany you?"

"Father Vernan might prove useful."

"And for your escort?"

"I'll let Sig take care of that particular detail." He glanced around his office. "I suppose I should consider how much of this I should bring with me."

"There's nothing here that requires your immediate attention, and if anything needs a Royal Presence in your absence, I'm more than capable of fulfilling that role." Her smile warmed his heart. "Treat this as an opportunity to get away from the pressures of being king for a few weeks."

"I like the sound of that. I shall leave the day after tomorrow."

Ludwig reckoned the distance to Hollenbeck was close to a hundred sixty miles, a trip that would take more than a week. He'd intended to travel by horse, but Father Vernan was not the most able rider, so they went by carriage instead.

Sig selected twelve riders for their escort, half of whom were Knights of the Sacred Shield, and the rest were mounted men who'd served Ludwig during the war.

They set a brisk pace, and within three days, they'd passed Bruggendorf and were waiting on their side of the river that formed the border with Hollenbeck. Ludwig stood on the bank, watching as two men poled the ferry across.

"This will take some doing," noted Sigwulf. "I doubt we'd get more than four horses across at a time."

"There's no hurry," replied Ludwig. "By my reckoning, we're ahead of schedule. Do you know if the duke is particular about courtly protocol?"

"Not that I saw. Then again, I was only there for a couple of days. Are we surprising him with your visit?"

"I sent a rider ahead before we left Harlingen, but that won't give him more than a couple of days' warning."

"I'm certain he'll do his best to impress you with his hospitality. After all, Hadenfeld has a much larger army than Hollenbeck, despite our recent reductions."

"Did you see any of his warriors?"

"I did," replied Sigwulf. "If you recall, he marched some of his men to the border to oppose a possible invasion. Of course, it never came to that, but those under his command appeared capable enough."

"Does he employ knights?"

"No, and very little cavalry, or so I was told. The terrain over there is heavily forested and not well-suited to the deployment of horsemen."

"I'll have to remember that if we ever find ourselves in a position to render aid."

"You mean to form an alliance with the duke?"

"I do," replied Ludwig, "but purely a defensive one. Don't worry. I'm not looking to expand the realm—that was Morgan's folly."

The ferry bumped against their side of the river. The two men who'd been poling tied off to posts on the bank, waving the group of horsemen forward. Ludwig ordered the knights to go across, and the first four walked their horses onto the boat, calming their mounts as the rickety vessel sank down in the water.

"It's their warhorses," said Sigwulf. "They're heavier than our other horses. Perhaps we should send them three at a time?"

"A good idea."

Sigwulf walked over to the knights to tell them to reduce their numbers for the crossing. He soon returned, shaking his head.

"Something wrong?" asked Ludwig.

"Is it me, or do those knights seem a little thick-headed?"

"In what way?"

"They insisted they should cross four at a time despite the water sloshing over the side of the ferry."

"Yet they are now proceeding as a trio."

"Only because I refused to put up with their nonsense. I suppose that's what we get when we have nobles for our cavalry." He stopped suddenly, turning to Ludwig. "Pardon me. I didn't mean to imply you were a problem."

Ludwig laughed. "That's what I like about you, Sig. You're never afraid to tell the truth. And just for the record, you're one of my nobles now, too, remember? After all, you're the Baron of Verfeld."

"Only until Frederick is of age."

"I think you misunderstood my intention. Frederick needs no barony; he's a prince. That land is all yours, Sig... Well, yours and Cyn's."

Sigwulf straightened. "I never realized. Surely there's someone else more worthy?"

"I know of no one else I'd entrust with Verfeld's care. You are a loyal servant, Sig, but more importantly, a good friend. Now tell me more about Duke Ulfric."

"You met him after we captured Harlingen."

"I did, but we scarcely spent any time together. Those days were an endless whirlwind of faces and names, all trying to ingratiate themselves with their new king. I want to know what type of man he is."

"He's very plain-spoken. In some ways, he's much like you, concerned for the welfare of his subjects. I think you two will get along well."

"That's promising."

"As it should be. After all, we're not at war."

They were peering through the dusk by the time they hitched the horses back to the carriage. Light from the village of Bedmar lay a stone's throw from the ferry, so they headed there in the dark, seeking something to eat.

The Gryphon's Rest was busy, but the proprietor managed to squeeze everyone in. Thus it was that Ludwig, Sigwulf, and Father Vernan found themselves at a table with three locals: a farmer, his wife, and her brother.

Giles, the farmer, appeared pleased with the company of the travellers, although Ludwig declined to inform anyone of his status.

"So, what brings you lot down to Bedmar?" the old fellow asked. "You're not one of those Miranthans come to spy on us, are you?"

"Mirantha lies to the east of Hollenbeck," replied Father Vernan, "and we came from the northwest."

"Aye, but that could be a ruse. Spies are said to be clever folk."

"They are," agreed his wife.

"Why would Mirantha send spies here?" asked Ludwig.

"We heard there's been trouble on the border recently. Mind you, that's a long way from here in Bedmar."

"What kind of trouble?" asked Father Vernan.

"Can't rightly say," replied Giles, "but it was serious enough that the duke readied his men to travel to the border."

"And how do you know this?"

"Our son serves in the duke's army. He wrote to us about it."

The Holy Father looked at Ludwig. "I wonder if that's why he invited you here?"

"Are you someone important, then?"

Vernan opened his mouth to reply, but Ludwig beat him to it. "I'm an acquaintance of the duke, travelling here at his invitation."

"I had no idea we were in the presence of such important folk," said Giles. "I suppose you'll be on your way to Klermacht by morning?"

"That we will. Any idea how long that'll take?"

"Several days, at least; it's sixty-odd miles to the capital."

"You've been a great help to us," said Ludwig. "Let me buy a round of drinks to express our gratitude."

"That's very kind of you, Lord."

Their first day and a half in Hollenbeck had them travelling through dense forest, the road little more than a trail, but once they reached Zarnau, the trees lessened, and the path became easier to traverse.

After setting out one morning, they came upon a fork in the road with a sign indicating the capital lay to the right. However, of greater interest to Ludwig were the seven horsemen waiting there, watching their approach.

Sigwulf rode ahead, exchanged words with them, then returned to the carriage. "We have an escort," he said. "Sir Roderick of Tollingsbruck, the same fellow who helped us get inside the walls of Harlingen during the war. He brings greetings from His Grace, the Duke, but prefers we press on to Klermacht."

"How far is it?"

"Twenty miles. We probably wouldn't get there till well after dark."

"Tell him we accept and look forward to meeting Lord Ulfric."

Sigwulf returned to the knight and spoke briefly, then their new escort turned around and headed off in the direction of the capital. They set a brisk pace, stopping only to rest and water the horses.

With nothing else to occupy his mind, Ludwig began to worry that a war was brewing here. That, in turn, led him to the idea that a Stormwind or Sartellian might be causing trouble.

Klermacht, once it came into view, lacked walls like Harlingen but proved to be much larger than he'd expected. The duke's castle sat upon a hill in the centre of town, dominating the flat land surrounding it. Ludwig's Royal Keep back home paled in comparison to this stronghold, and he found himself staring at it in fascination, even as they rode through the city.

"This is quite the place," noted Father Vernan. "I shall have to see if I can arrange a visit to the Cathedral of the Saints while I'm here. It's said to be a wonder of the Continent."

"Cathedral of the Saints? I don't believe I'm familiar with that."

"It's an immense building with prayer houses for all six Saints. Originally, they intended it to house the hierarchy of the Church, but then we grew so large we required more space, so the Antonine was selected instead."

"How long ago was this?" asked Ludwig.

"Centuries before the downfall of the Old Kingdom."

"But wouldn't that place it within the borders of Therengia?"

"Indeed, but they found many converts amongst the population, and the local governor didn't mind if it kept the people happy."

"Fascinating," said Ludwig. "I was under the impression the Old Kingdom suppressed the Church of the Saints."

"That's what they want you to believe," said Father Vernan.

"They, being?"

"The rulers of the Petty Kingdoms. Ever since the Old Kingdom was destroyed, there's been this fear that it would rise from the ashes and its people would exact their revenge."

"And now it appears they have," said Ludwig. "At least that's the rumour, although I've a hard time believing they'd come seeking retribution. I imagine they'd prefer to be left alone, but now I'm getting off topic. Are you suggesting the Church flourished under them?"

"I'm not certain I'd use that particular term, but the worship of the Saints did become more commonplace. In those days, the temples of the Old Gods were still common, and I've read that in some places, our own Holy Fathers worked hand in hand with them for the betterment of the community. It stands to reason, considering we preach acceptance, but not every member of the Church agrees with those teachings, particularly those higher up."

"I'm surprised to hear you say that," said Ludwig. "Don't tell me you're becoming disenchanted with your faith?"

"Not my faith, merely those who twist the words of the Saints to their own advantage." He hesitated. "I'm sorry. I didn't mean to speak of this, but it's become clear to me over the last few years that the Church of the Saints is becoming more fractious."

"Temple Commander Charlaine wrote about the Cunars' treachery. Could that be related?"

"Perhaps," replied Father Vernan, "but there's nothing you or I can do about it. It might be best if we concentrate instead on our visit here, to Hollenbeck?"

"I agree, but let me know if you hear anything further on the matter. As king, I need to keep informed about anything that may impact my subjects."

"I will, most assuredly."

They entered the castle's courtyard gate, where His Grace stood waiting, an imposing figure with a mane of red hair matching his bushy beard. He wasn't quite as tall as Sigwulf but was broader of chest than the northerner.

Ludwig waited until the carriage rolled to a halt, then stepped down onto the cobblestones.

"Your Majesty," said Duke Ulfric. "You honour us with your visit."

"It is I who am honoured," replied Ludwig. "I'm only sorry I couldn't have come sooner." He beckoned the Holy Father forward. "This is Father Vernan, and you know Lord Sigwulf; he's one of my generals now."

"A general, you say? How fortuitous. We may have need of his services."

"Are you at war, Your Grace?"

"No, not as yet, but there've been some demands of late. Come inside, and I'll inform you of the details." He led Ludwig and the Holy Father inside while Sigwulf and Sir Roderick saw to the escort.

"You must pardon the lack of festivities," the duke continued. "We only learned of your arrival two days ago. Not that we don't appreciate it, but there was little time to prepare for a king's visit."

"Think of me not as a king but as an equal. After all, we are both rulers of our respective lands. Now, let's dispense with all this formality, shall we? Tell me about this trouble you're having? I understand it's with Mirantha?"

"Yes. A border dispute. Lacking a river to our east, there is no clear demarcation of our respective borders."

"Have you had any border issues before?"

"Not for centuries, but recent developments have changed that."

"What's happened?"

"Not long ago, a bright light fell from the sky. This is all speculation, but it is reported to have landed in the disputed territory."

"And you think it may be ithilium?"

"Ithilium?"

"Sorry," said Ludwig. "I meant godstone, or perhaps sky metal might be more appropriate, considering Father Vernan's presence."

"Yes, which means that somewhere out there is a rare metal worth a king's ransom."

"In an area you both claim?"

"Precisely," replied Ulfric.

"Is there anything else there of import?"

"No. It's largely wilderness."

"An interesting development," said Ludwig. "I assume your counterpart sent some form of demand?"

"Yes. He warned us not to interfere with his expedition. Presumably, he's sending people there to search for the sky metal."

"I assume you plan a similar action?"

Lord Ulfric's mouth hung open, but to his credit, he recovered quickly. "How in the name of the Saints did you know that?"

"It's what I would've done."

Father Vernan interrupted. "Who rules in Mirantha?"

"Augustinian the Second, named, I'm told, after the Saint himself."

"Might I suggest I talk to him on your behalf? The Church is renowned for being neutral in such disputes."

"I have a better idea," offered Ludwig. "I shall travel there myself and arrange a meeting between the two of you. I'm certain we can come to a reasonable settlement if we sit down and discuss things face to face."

"Where would we meet?" asked Ulfric. "I doubt he'd be willing to come to Klermacht, and I'm certainly not going to risk entering his lands, not while he's making claims on my territory."

"Would you find it acceptable to meet in Hadenfeld if I can arrange it?"

"Yes, but I fear you'll have a difficult job convincing him. He's said to be an unreasonable fellow, subject to fits of rage on occasion."

"And where did you hear this?"

"From one of my advisors."

"This advisor wouldn't happen to have the name Sartellian by chance?"

"No," replied the duke. "Her name is Sirellia, Sirellia Stormwind."

"Ah, I understand now," said Ludwig. "I'm sorry, I should have warned you sooner. The Stormwinds have been involved in several troubling situations in the last few years."

"But they're renowned throughout the Petty Kingdoms."

"I have it on good authority they serve Halvaria."

At the mention of the empire's name, the duke went silent. Ludwig waited, allowing him to consider the ramifications.

"What is the source of this information?" asked Ulfric.

"I was told so by none other than a Temple Commander of Saint Agnes, who witnessed their treachery first-hand."

"It would not be wise to question the honesty of such an individual," added Father Vernan.

"No," said the duke. "I suppose it wouldn't." He shifted his gaze back to Ludwig. "If what you say is true, does that mean they plot to incite war?"

"Most likely," replied Ludwig, "but our knowledge gives us the advantage."

"How so?"

"I will travel to Mirantha and convince Augustinian to meet with you in Hadenfeld. I'll send word once I've arranged where this meeting is to take place."

"And in the meantime?"

"Do nothing to antagonize Mirantha, and if Sirellia Stormwind pushes you on the matter, delay her by any means necessary."

"And if Augustinian marches into my lands with his army?"

"It won't come to that, but should it prove necessary, I'll march the Army of Hadenfeld to help you repel the invasion."

7

THE CAPITAL

SUMMER 1105 SR

Charlotte watched Frederick and Kenley take turns hitting a training dummy with wooden swords.

Gita nodded towards the young prince. "Your son wants to be a warrior like his father."

"He's only five. I don't think he even understands what that means. It is nice, however, to see him enjoying himself. He and Kenley are inseparable despite the three years separating them."

"My son sees Frederick as a brother. I've tried to explain he's a prince now, but you know how children are."

"It's fine," said Charlotte. "And when they grow up, Kenley can remind Frederick that even a royal must behave."

Captain Gustavo opened the door and stepped in.

"Not trouble, I hope?" asked Charlotte.

"I couldn't actually say," the captain replied. "You have a visitor, Majesty, or rather, the court has a visitor. A Temple Commander of Saint Cunar."

"Is there any indication of what he wants?"

"He has not deigned to reveal his intentions, although he graciously requested an audience. He also surrendered his sword without being asked. I sensed he's dealt with royalty before."

Charlotte stood, meeting the gaze of Liesel, her personal caregiver, when she needed one. "Would you be so kind as to keep an eye on the children? I'm required in the throne room and wish Gita to accompany me."

The woman offered a bow. "Of course, Majesty. I'd be delighted."

"Gustavo, fetch this Cunar, but give us a few minutes before you bring him in."

"As you wish," replied the captain.

Charlotte headed towards the throne room, her friend walking beside her.

"A Temple Commander," said Gita. "What do you suppose he wants?"

"I can't imagine, but whatever it is, it won't be good."

"What makes you say that?"

"If you recall, Temple Commander Charlaine revealed the Cunars tried to intervene in the defence of Angvil."

"Yes, but we're nowhere near the empire. Perhaps they seek permission to build a new temple?"

"Then why send a Temple Knight? Wouldn't a prior or a Holy Father be more appropriate? And why a Temple Commander—that's a senior rank."

"I suppose we'll have to wait and see," replied Gita. "Should I fetch the general?"

"Yes. That would be for the best. And while you're at it, find your husband; I might need his counsel. Don't worry. I won't start without you."

Gita quickened her pace, turning down a side corridor.

"Let him in," said the queen. Gita and Merrick stood on her left, with Cyn on her right. Captain Gustavo and six guards entered the throne room, then the guards split to either side. Gustavo continued, halting ten paces into the room before offering a bow. "Temple Commander Amarand of the Temple Knights of Saint Cunar," he announced, then stepped aside and allowed the knight to proceed.

The Temple Commander cut a fine figure in his plate armour and dark grey surcoat, a sword emblazoned in gold thread on his tabard denoting his rank. Other than that, he could've passed for any other member of the order.

He advanced to the throne, then went down on one knee and offered a bow. "Your Majesty, I am honoured that you granted me an audience." He stood and made a show of surveying the room. "Your pardon, Majesty, but I was led to believe the king would be present as well."

Charlotte looked at Gustavo, her head tilted to the side, an eyebrow raised in question. The captain stood his ground. "I informed the Temple Commander he'd been granted an audience with the ruler of Hadenfeld, Majesty. My apologies if I neglected to indicate which one."

She looked back at her guest. "My husband and I are co-rulers, Temple Commander. It's not common amongst the Petty Kingdoms, but then again, my husband is no ordinary king." She paused, letting her words sink in. "Do I know you?"

"Not that I'm aware of," replied Amarand, "but I assure you, I was chosen for this duty because I am an exemplary member of my order."

"And a humble one at that, Temple Commander. What makes you such an example of excellence?"

The fellow stood up straighter as he puffed out his chest. "I have served the order for more than twenty years, Majesty, fighting with great distinction in the Church's name many times."

"Were you at the Battle of the Wilderness?"

Charlotte noted the clenching of his jaw, but he kept control of his emotions. That defeat had seen the death of hundreds of Temple Knights, resulting in a loss of face for the entire Cunar order.

"I regret I was not, Majesty, although I did serve in the previous campaign in the east. I was only a Temple Captain at that time."

"And what brings you to my court today?"

"I seek an audience with the King of Hadenfeld, Majesty."

"To what end?"

He offered a smile. "I come bearing glorious news. Harlingen has been selected to host a new commandery for the order."

"Have you come here to gloat?"

"My apologies, Majesty. I was under the impression you were familiar with requests of this nature. It is customary for the realm bestowed such an honour to offer a grant of land for the commandery to be built on."

Charlotte knew the custom, for she and Ludwig had done precisely that for the Temple Knights of Saint Mathew. However, this visitor believed her to be uneducated in such things, something which she intended to use to her advantage.

Amarand, perhaps taking her silence for confusion, pressed his case. "A commandery here will bring glory to the Saints."

"You mean to Saint Cunar," corrected Merrick.

"I am addressing the Crown, not a mere courtier. You should keep your comments to yourself."

"My apologies, Temple Commander. I meant no offence."

"Lord Merrick is the Baron of Drakenfeld," said Charlotte, "and a close friend of both the king and myself."

The Temple Commander bowed his head. "Please forgive me, Majesty. It is a long way from the Antonine, and the trip proved exhausting."

"Then perhaps you should seek a rest before coming before this court." She stood. "You may return in two days, once you've properly rested. Hopefully, you can then demonstrate the behaviour appropriate to one of your rank."

The commander opened his mouth to speak, but she interrupted him. "Captain Gustavo, you may escort the visitor from the keep."

"Yes, Majesty." The captain stood before the Temple Commander, with the men of the Royal Guard assuming positions on either side. Amarand made a curt bow, then turned and strode from the room.

Charlotte waited until the doors closed before collapsing back onto her throne.

Gita moved closer, taking the queen's shaking hands in her own. "It's all over now."

"Not over, merely delayed."

"But the worst of it is past. You've faced down the dragon; the next time he visits, he'll show you proper respect."

"What if I've only made things worse?"

"Have no fear on that account," said Merrick. "Ludwig would've likely done exactly as you did."

"I disagree," said Gita. "I believe the queen handled that far better than the king would've. You are a true diplomat, Charlotte. It's not an easy thing to stand up to someone like that."

Charlotte turned to Merrick. "As Chancellor of the Realm, you know the law better than anyone. Are Temple Commander Amarand's claims valid?"

"It is certainly customary to grant land to the Church on occasion, but I am aware of no law compelling you to do so. Then again, we have the precedent of granting land for the building of a commandery for the Temple Knights of Saint Mathew. He'll likely use that as leverage when he returns."

"Leverage? Are you suggesting he will try to bully his way into Harlingen?"

Merrick cleared his throat. "The Church of the Saints wields power at the highest levels across the length and breadth of the Petty Kingdoms. By extension, the Temple Knights are the protectors of that institution, and I think the Temple Commander will do whatever he feels necessary to accomplish his objectives."

"To what end? Am I to meekly submit to his demands? Is Hadenfeld no longer able to chart its own course?"

"I'm not suggesting anything of the sort, Majesty. I merely strive to inform you of possible consequences regardless of what you decide to do."

"Then let us discuss those consequences. Let's begin by supposing I gave in to his request."

Merrick took time to think before answering. "As you know, a commandery takes years to build, but I doubt that would stop the Cunars from sending a company to us while it was under construction."

"And we already know that means trouble," added Gita. "Thanks to Temple Commander Charlaine, we know they serve the empire's interests."

"Yes," replied Charlotte, "but what would that look like here in Hadenfeld? We're a long way from the Halvarian border."

"I suspect they fear Ludwig may take a more active role in the politics of the region. The presence of a full company of Cunars in Harlingen might be seen by some as enforcing the will of the Church."

"Which means what, precisely?"

"They," replied Gita, "along with their Holy Fathers, could call into question the legitimacy of your rule—Ludwig did take the Crown by force. Were they to spread those stories to the other Petty Kingdoms, it might make diplomatic overtures more difficult."

"There is also the military threat," offered Merrick. "The presence of so many potentially hostile Temple Knights in our capital would require us to maintain a larger garrison."

"I have no desire to see a Cunar commandery anywhere in Hadenfeld," said Charlotte, "but what are the possible ramifications should I refuse their request?"

"Legally, none, but a refusal could result in a reprisal from the Church."

"What exactly would that mean?"

"I'm no expert in Church law, but I imagine it would consist of some public rebuke, a slap in the face, so to speak. Of course, that depends largely on who's behind this request in the first place. If it's the Temple Knights of Cunar trying to extend their reach, there's little to worry about. If, however, the entire Antonine is behind it, that's more concerning."

Charlotte sighed. "I must give this considerable thought."

"We'll support you whatever you decide," offered Gita.

"Thank you both. I appreciate hearing that, although it doesn't make this decision any easier. I wish Ludwig were here to deal with it."

"You are the queen, and he trusts you to make a decision that serves the people of Hadenfeld. Do not doubt yourself, Majesty. You have it in you to deal with this issue."

"Then deal with it, I shall. Merrick, you've been amalgamating the laws of the land into some semblance of order, so I need you to search through them and ensure there is nothing stipulating the Crown must bend to the will of the Church."

"And if I do find something to that effect?"

"Then I shall exercise my powers as queen to change it."

"I shall begin at once."

"What can I do to help?" asked Gita.

"I'd like you to host an informal gathering of any noble's wives who are currently in Harlingen. The aim is to discover their thoughts on Church politics without making it too obvious. Do you think you can do that?"

"I assume you want answers before the Temple Commander returns?"

"I do, but if you need more time, we can send word delaying his second audience."

"Give me half a day to make some enquiries," said Gita. "I'll let you know this afternoon if we need to delay his return visit any further."

"Thank you."

Two days later found the four of them, back in the throne room, awaiting the arrival of Temple Commander Amarand.

"I must say you surprised me," said Charlotte. "I never would've expected people to accept an invitation on such short notice."

"I took the liberty of presenting it as a Royal Invitation," replied Gita. "Few would refuse an opportunity to be a guest of the queen."

"But I wasn't present."

"True, but they didn't know that when they received the invitation. And for the record, I never actually said you'd be there, merely that you invited them, which was true. It was your idea after all."

"You can be very devious on occasion, Gita, which is one of the things I like best about you. Now, you're certain about your findings?"

"The guests were adamant they were devoted worshippers of Saint Agnes or Saint Mathew, but I found none who concerned themselves with Saint Cunar at all. Not surprising, as it's an order devoted to war and battle. Some of their husbands were worshippers, but from what I could determine, none took any interest in Church politics."

"Ah, yes," said Merrick. "The apathy of the ruling class. Most are only concerned with what affects them personally, which works to our advantage in this situation."

"It does," replied Charlotte. "And, as you reported earlier, there is no law suggesting I must comply with the Cunar's request, so I am free to choose whatever I may."

"Which is?"

"I shall refuse them, but in the interest of the realm, I must hear him out. Now, let's get our best court faces on, shall we? The battle is about to commence." Charlotte nodded at the servant standing by the door. "You may inform Captain Gustavo we are ready to receive our guest."

They waited as Temple Commander Amarand entered, escorted, as before, by the Royal Guard. He knelt and bowed as he did on his first visit, then locked eyes with Charlotte.

"I bring you greetings, Majesty, and the blessings of the Saints."

She waved her hand, indicating he should stand. "You've come seeking land for the building of a commandery. What you haven't told me is why?"

The question seemed to take him aback. "There's not a ruler in all the Petty Kingdoms who would not welcome a Cunar commandery in their capital."

"We are not talking of other Petty Kingdoms; we are talking about Hadenfeld. My question to you is not why I would want a company of your knights in this realm, but rather why YOU want them here."

"With all due respect, Majesty, were the king here, he'd doubtless tell you about the esteem a warrior such as he would hold our order in. When can we expect His Majesty to entertain an audience?"

"He is not currently here in Harlingen."

"I am a patient man and more than willing to wait, regardless of the duration."

"You still haven't answered my question," pressed Charlotte. "Why do you want a commandery in Harlingen?"

"Hadenfeld holds a strategic place in the midst of the Petty Kingdoms. From here, our Temple Knights would be able to respond quickly to the threat of invasion."

"Invasion? Are you speaking about the Halvarians?"

"They are the greatest threat to us, Majesty."

"Then why did your entire order withdraw from those kingdoms bordering the empire?"

"That was a strategic decision based on sound military thinking."

"That thinking left the Kingdom of Arnsfeld to fend for itself."

Amarand took a deep breath, letting it out slowly. "My superiors made that decision. It is not my place to question them."

"What guarantee would you provide were your knights stationed here?"

"Guarantee?"

"Would your Temple Knights help defend this realm from invasion?"

"The Church of the Saints does not concern itself with secular matters."

"Yet," said Charlotte, "the Temple Knights of Saint Mathew help keep our streets safe."

"With all due respect, Majesty, the Mathewites are hardly equipped to march into battle in their archaic mail."

"But that's precisely what they did. They stood beside us when my husband claimed the Throne while your own order was nowhere to be seen."

"Their actions were contrary to Church doctrine, but I am not here to besmirch the reputation of a fellow order. If you want me to make assurances that my own order will patrol the streets, I must disappoint you. Cunars are trained for battle. Our training, and reputation, for that matter, are second to none."

"I seek not to denigrate your reputation, merely to clarify your purpose. Will you march to protect us if the Halvarian Empire invades the Petty Kingdoms?"

"If my superiors command that, then yes." He forced a smile. "I fear we've drifted from the purpose of my visit. Might I return to the benefits of having our order stationed here in Harlingen?"

"By all means," replied Charlotte.

"People, your subjects, feel secure knowing Temple Knights are nearby to keep them safe."

"I am well aware of this, which is why the Mathewites are building a commandery as we speak."

A flash of annoyance flickered across the Cunar's face. "Only the most influential realms are granted the opportunity to house a commandery dedicated to the Temple Knights of Saint Cunar. It is a singular honour."

"You contradict yourself, Temple Commander. Your commanderies are, as you say, present in the most influential realms. Thus, the presence of one in a kingdom's capital is hardly singular."

Amarand's face hardened. "I am here as a courtesy, Majesty. My superiors have already made the decision to construct a commandery in Harlingen. I am merely informing you of that decision. If you are unwilling to grant us the land on which to build, then we shall purchase it."

Charlotte stood, her temper rising. "You shall do no such thing. Let me make this perfectly clear, Commander. Without Royal Assent, construction of a commandery is explicitly forbidden, and any attempt to carry on against my wishes will result in the arrest of anyone assisting in its construction." She hardened her tone. "I will brook no further defiance to my rule or that of my husband, the king."

"So you do not approve our request?"

"I am not prepared to render my decision at this time. Return to wherever you're staying, Temple Commander. I will summon you when I have made my final decision."

"How long should I expect to wait?"

"As long as it takes. The alternative would be for you to return to your superiors and admit that you failed in your endeavours, but I doubt that would win you any accolades."

"I shall do as you suggest." Amarand offered a slight bow of his head, then turned and departed.

Gustavo's men fell in behind him.

"Keep an eye on him, Captain. He could spell trouble."

"Yes, Majesty."

8

MIRANTHA
SUMMER 1105 SR

The King of Mirantha, Augustinian the Second, regarded Ludwig with a solitary eye, the other sealed shut by a thick scar. His short stature and well-trimmed beard were in direct contrast to King Ulfric, whom Ludwig was here on behalf of. He now had to play the role of diplomat rather than warrior, forcing him to avoid any topic which might upset his host.

"Your Majesty," began Ludwig. "I bring you greetings from the Kingdom of Hadenfeld."

"I am pleased to meet you," replied Augustinian, a bevy of men standing nearby, presumably his advisors. "Although I'm at a loss as to why you're here. Our two kingdoms share a border, but the area north of the Hollen River is nothing but dense forest."

"I've received word that your realm is at odds with the Duchy of Hollenbeck, so I'm here to see if I can help your two kingdoms come to a peaceful solution."

"Then you must inform the Duke of Hollenbeck he is not to interfere with my lawful rule of the territory in question."

"May we speak about the border? I'm given to understand it has never been formally recognized, and am most curious to know why."

"Our two realms were founded after the Old Kingdom collapsed, and the area in question was considered unusable. The forest there is so thick that even hardened hunters avoid its depths. Were it not for a single trail, it'd be impossible to reach Hollenbeck from here."

"But, apparently," said Ludwig, "that's changed?"

"It has. No doubt you've heard the rumours. If sky metal fell into that region, it belongs to Mirantha."

"My understanding is that few smiths have the skill to work metal of that nature."

"That's true," replied Augustinian, "but we could sell it to others, thereby filling my kingdom's coffers."

"To what end?" Ludwig took in the room. "You surround yourself with luxury, Majesty, as is your right, but I see no pressing need for more coins."

"Traditionally, the Army of Mirantha is small, only a few hundred warriors, but recent events in the south demonstrate a need for an increase in numbers."

"I'm afraid I'm not familiar with that realm."

"It's called Aldor, and their new king is rumoured to be casting his gaze at his neighbours with an eye to expanding his borders. You must understand that the realms south of Hadenfeld have relatively small populations; our villages and towns are often miles apart, making it difficult to provide effective garrisons."

"I understand your desire to increase your army," said Ludwig. "I'm in the same situation myself, but the acquisition of sky metal will only provide temporary relief. Even a king's ransom runs out one day, and an army increased in such a manner still requires the funds to maintain it once those coins are spent."

"Perhaps, but it will keep my kingdom intact in the short term. As king, I must protect my subjects. Without that sky metal, I'd have to raise taxes, something that would take a toll on those I'm sworn to defend."

"I sympathize with your plight, but your fear of Aldor is pushing you into a confrontation with Hollenbeck."

"What else am I to do? Surrender our sovereignty?"

"There must be another option," replied Ludwig. "Your current course could easily lead to war."

"Not if Hollenbeck minds its own business."

"You take exception at the thought that they lay claim to that region, yet they've considered it their land for centuries, just as you have."

"If you've come here to lecture me," replied Augustinian, "you can leave."

"My pardon," said Ludwig. "I'm only trying to understand the situation. Your realms share a long and peaceful coexistence, do they not?"

"The area in question has always been disputed, but up until now, it's been considered inconsequential."

"There might be no sky metal in the region at all, and even if there is, it could prove impossible to find."

"That is a chance I'm willing to take."

"Even if it causes a war?"

"Let me ask you this," said Augustinian. "How far would you go to ensure the survival of your people? No, don't answer that. I know your history. You usurped the rule of a king! I'm not suggesting it wasn't warranted, but it does illustrate how we're all capable of extreme action when the occasion demands it."

Ludwig mulled over his fellow ruler's words. He'd disliked the excesses of Morgan's rule, which had eventually forced him to take up arms. Was this situation any different? He tried to imagine himself in Mirantha's position. They were a small realm, perhaps the smallest in all the Petty Kingdoms, yet they'd managed well enough for centuries. Who was he to suggest what they were doing was wrong? Was there another solution? Something that could appease both sides?

"My apologies," said Augustinian. "I did not mean to cause offence, but recent events have proved most draining."

"Might I ask how you first learned of the lights that fell from the sky?"

"One of my advisors reported it to me."

"Might I ask which one?"

A bald, clean-shaven man spoke up. "That would be me."

"And you are?"

The fellow offered a bow. "Eduardo Stormwind."

"Stormwind?"

Eduardo smiled. "The family is dedicated to helping rulers across the Petty Kingdoms, regardless of how extensive their lands are."

"What can you tell me about these lights?"

"They were seen by the people of Verslacht, one of our smaller villages that lies close to our western border. You likely passed it on your way here from Hollenbeck. That is where you travelled from?"

Everything fell into place. The Stormwinds had invested a considerable amount of their influence in destabilizing the Continent; he must be careful not to reveal his knowledge. "It is," he replied, "though we were in far too much of a rush to take note of which villages we passed."

"A pity. That area of the country can be quite pleasant, I'm told."

"Might I ask how long you've been here at court?"

"Two years," replied Augustinian, "and his advice has proven most valuable to me. Why, there are times I wonder how I'd manage were he not here to advise me."

"My apologies for any perceived slight, Majesty," said Ludwig, "but it's been a long day."

The king, most pleased with the apology, broke into a smile. "I shall provide you and your advisors with rooms. We can tackle this in more depth once you've had time to reflect on the situation."

Ludwig bowed, then left the room.

"Another Stormwind," said Sigwulf. "Not the best of news. I'm beginning to think there's no truth to this rumour of sky metal."

"I wouldn't be so quick to judge," said Father Vernan. "We heard the same rumours back in Hollenbeck."

"True," said Ludwig, "but then again, they had a Stormwind of their own."

"What do we do?" asked Sigwulf.

"That largely depends on the truth. Either lights were seen in the sky, and the Stormwinds are simply taking advantage of the opportunity, or they're lying about everything in hopes of starting a conflict."

"Which is more likely?"

"I'd say the latter," replied Vernan. "We know they like to stir up trouble."

"True," said Ludwig, "but these rumours would be relatively easy to disprove. All we'd have to do is send one of our people to Verslacht to ask the right questions."

"Shall I take care of that?" asked Sigwulf.

"Yes, but let's not make it too obvious. The last thing I need is word getting back to court that we're causing trouble."

"And in the meantime?"

"I need to gather information, so I won't be pressing King Augustinian on the matter."

"But you can't just ignore him," said Father Vernan. "He's the king of this land, for Saint's sake."

"I intend to get to know him a little better. Perhaps, by spending time in his company, I'll come to understand his true motives."

"I thought we knew his motives! He wants the sky metal!"

"I doubt it's that simple. He feels threatened, which is making him react defensively."

"You mean the threat from Aldor?"

"We have no guarantee it's real," said Ludwig. "It could be another ploy on the part of the Stormwinds.

"We only brought a few men with us," said Sigwulf. "I can't spare any to send south."

"Nor would I expect you to. If Aldor were massing at the border, Augustinian would be mustering his army, not trying to organize an expedition into an uncharted part of his kingdom."

"So you suspect this sky metal might be real?"

"I do," replied Ludwig, "and who better to arrange for its sale than someone who has contacts amongst many of the courts of the Petty Kingdoms. Who knows, maybe the Stormwinds want it for themselves."

"You make a good point," said Father Vernan. "Sky metal is commonly used to create magic weapons."

"Not only weapons," noted Sigwulf. "In theory, it can be used for anything magical."

"Such as?"

"Magic rings, wands, belts: you name something made of metal, and there's likely something magical that can be associated with it. That's what makes it so priceless."

"Yes," said Ludwig. "The term 'king's ransom' comes up a lot when discussing sky metal."

"If we confirm the lights in the sky were real, what's our next step?"

"I'd prefer to get the two rulers face to face."

"I doubt that would work," said Vernan. "They don't trust each other."

"True, but I intend to host them both in a neutral location, most likely Udenacht."

"That certainly has possibilities, although it would require King Augustinian to cross into Hollenbeck to get there."

"Not necessarily," said Sigwulf. "We could meet east of the disputed region and escort him the rest of the way on our side of the border, thus avoiding Hollenbeck altogether."

"A good idea," said the Holy Father, "if we can convince Augustinian of it."

"Then that's what I'll do," replied Ludwig. "But let's hold off on that till we've confirmed this whole sky metal theory. How long do you think that would take, Sig?"

"We're only a short distance from the border. Give our man two days to gather information, and he can be back by the end of the week."

"Until then, I shall content myself with playing the role of guest and avoiding the topic."

"I'll make some enquiries of my own," offered Father Vernan.

"What did you have in mind?"

"I thought I might speak with the local prior of my order and see what I can learn about this Eduardo Stormwind fellow."

"Why do you think the prior would be of assistance?"

The Holy Father smiled. "I doubt you noticed, but that Stormwind wore a ring bearing the axe of Saint Mathew. Now, I'm not suggesting he's a true worshipper, but I wouldn't be surprised to learn he's been going through the motions to ingratiate himself with the king. If that's true, he'd likely insist on praying before someone befitting his station as a Royal Mage."

"No offence, but you're the king's spiritual advisor," said Sigwulf, "and you're only a Holy Father. What makes you think a prior more suitable?"

"I can answer that," said Ludwig. "Father Vernan turned down a priorship to remain with me."

"But wouldn't a prior be a more suitable rank for such a position?"

"It would," said Vernan, "but then I'd have other duties needing my attention, duties that would require a great amount of my time."

"You must've been sorely tempted to accept."

"Surprisingly, I was not. When I refused the offer, it was more of a relief. I have nothing against priors, but when one moves up to a position like that, they are often required to spend more time on administrative matters rather than spiritual ones."

"You are a true devotee of Saint Mathew."

Five days later, they had the news they needed from Verslacht. There had indeed been lights in the sky, although there were varying accounts of exactly where it fell relative to the village. All agreed it landed to the west, but some pointed in a northwesterly direction, while others claimed it lay to the southwest. No one had ventured out looking for sky metal, as the woods were said to be teeming with all sorts of dangerous wildlife, but all accounts placed the landing in the disputed border zone.

"And you're absolutely certain of this?" asked Ludwig.

Kalen Hasrich shifted his feet. He'd been recruited in Roshlag after Ludwig returned to Verfeld to claim the title of baron and had been in service to him ever since. Although trained as an archer, he now rode as part of the king's bodyguard. "Aye. I spent a few coins to loosen tongues. I also rode out to some nearby farms."

"It could be a clever trick," offered Sigwulf. "I doubt the Stormwinds would balk at a small expense to achieve their objectives."

"I thought of that, sir," replied the archer, "but my gut tells me they're telling the truth."

"That's good enough for me," said Ludwig. "You've done well, Kalen." He handed over some coins. "Here, this should cover your expenses. You may return to your post."

"Thank you, Majesty." Kalen slipped out the door to join his fellow guardsman keeping watch in the hallway.

"What now?" asked Father Vernan.

"It's time we requested a private audience with King Augustinian."

"But if there truly is sky metal in that region, how do we persuade him not to go looking for it?"

"By offering him a better option."

The Miranthan ruler sat quietly, staring as his visitors entered, his elbows resting on the arms of his throne as he tapped his fingertips together.

"I'm curious as to why you requested a meeting without my advisors?"

"I think I have a solution to your problem."

"Which problem?"

"The sky metal," replied Ludwig. "More specifically, how you might go about searching for it without causing a war."

"A most intriguing idea, but why did you request a private audience?"

"You and I make decisions on behalf of those we rule. Other voices serve only to distract us from our sworn duty."

Augustinian raised his eyebrow. "You think my advisors do not work in the best interest of my kingdom?"

"I think those who value influence are keen to wield it, perhaps not always to the benefit of the realm."

"I may not agree with your assessment of my advisors, but I shall listen to your proposal without their presence. Please proceed."

"The disputed region is hundreds of square miles of dense forest. It could take years to locate the deposit, time which would be better spent dealing with the Kingdom of Aldor."

"I cannot ignore the presence of such a valuable commodity."

"I'm not suggesting you do, merely that it would serve your more immediate interests to locate it sooner rather than later."

"Make up your mind, Majesty," said Augustinian. "Either it takes a long time to find this sky metal, or it doesn't. Which is it?"

"Many hands make for a lighter burden."

"I'm familiar with the words of Saint Mathew, but I fail to see how they apply in this instance."

"Then let me clarify," said Ludwig. "We all know sky metal is valuable, while being extremely difficult to work with."

"True, but as I previously stated, my intention is to sell it, not smelt it."

"Yes, but first, it must be found in an area your own hunters avoid. And even if you did find it, you'd have to dig it out, another labour-intensive task. Once that's done, there's transporting it. To my understanding, sky metal is a dense material, requiring a wagon and a team of horses, not the easiest thing to navigate through the trees. I suppose what I'm trying to say is the entire endeavour would prove difficult and expensive, particularly in manpower."

"I accept that," replied Augustinian, "but I fail to see the point you're getting at."

"Which do you think would be a better option? Half the value of the treasure now, or waiting years to claim all of it? Let me remind you that Aldor is unlikely to wait."

"What are you proposing?"

"Instead of risking war with Hollenbeck, you invite them to participate in the hunt for the sky metal and split the findings equally."

"How can I trust them? They could find it themselves and claim it all."

"I don't have all the details as to how this might be arranged, but the first step would be agreeing to meet with His Grace, the duke."

"Is that his idea?"

"No," said Ludwig. "It's mine. It makes more sense to work together instead of against each other. You double the chances of discovery and avert creating an incident that could lead to war."

"But the area in question is claimed by both of us."

"All the more reason to work cooperatively."

Augustinian nodded. "I will agree to meet with the duke. I shall send word at once inviting him here to Freimar so we can make arrangements."

"Might I suggest a more neutral location, one that resides in neither Mirantha nor Hollenbeck?"

"And where would that be?"

"Udenacht, which lies across the border in Hadenfeld. I'd offer my own services as host and ensure each delegation is given a proper escort to keep them safe."

"I agree, providing Duke Ulfric is of a similar mind."

"Then I shall send one of my men to Klermacht to deliver the invitation," replied Ludwig. "Meanwhile, I'll travel to Udenacht to make arrangements, then send word once everything is in place."

"I do have one question," said Augustinian. "Mirantha's border with Hadenfeld is covered with the same dense forest as the disputed area."

"I'll make arrangements for boats to carry your party, Majesty."

"How much time will you need?"

"Several weeks, I should think, but I'll try to speed that along as best I can. You may rest assured that I consider this a matter of great import."

"I am grateful," said Augustinian, "although I am curious why you take such an interest in our affairs. Neither Mirantha nor Hollenbeck are considered powerful compared with other Petty Kingdoms."

"We are neighbouring realms," replied Ludwig, "and I would have peace on the southern borders of Hadenfeld. To that end, I shall do all in my power to keep war from disrupting the land."

"Yet your reputation is that of a warrior king."

"While it's true I took the Throne by force of arms, it was never my intention to seize power."

"Then why did you?"

"To prevent the chaos that would inevitably result from the rule of a mad king."

9

THE ARCHPRIOR
SUMMER 1105 SR

L ord Emmett raised his eyebrows. "He demanded what?"

"Land for a commandery," replied Alexandra.

"It is the custom," said Charlotte, "but I've never heard of an order making it a demand. Perhaps I'm overthinking this?"

"You're not," insisted Gita. "Merrick and I were there, and we both perceived it as a demand. The Temple Commander thought quite highly of himself, if you ask me."

"How long has he been waiting for your answer?" asked Merrick.

"Three weeks now," replied the queen, "but I fear if I stall much longer, he'll bring the pressure of the Church to bear."

"Then tell him you deny his request," said Alexandra. "We all know the Cunars can't be trusted."

"It's not that simple," said Merrick. "I agree the request should be denied, but we can't tell him why without revealing how we came by this information."

"This puts us in a most difficult position," said Alexandra. "Perhaps we should consult with Father Hywell. He is, after all, an archprior."

"Do we reveal to him what we've learned?" asked Charlotte. "That could, in turn, create problems for Temple Commander Charlaine."

"How so?"

"By telling us, wouldn't she have broken her oath to her superiors?"

"Perhaps, but Father Hywell is a Mathewite, not an Agnesite. Thus, he'd have no jurisdiction."

"What you say is true," offered Emmett, "but all the orders serve the

Church of the Saints. I don't claim to be an expert in such things, but he might be required to pass that information on to his superiors."

"I wish Father Vernan were here," said Charlotte. "He'd be able to tell us whether that's true or not." She looked around the table. "Who's in favour of consulting the archprior?"

"I think it's worth the risk," said Alexandra.

"As do I," added Emmett, "although it might be best if the topic were presented to him as theoretical rather than an actual problem?"

"An excellent idea," replied Charlotte. "How about you, Gita?"

"I'll agree, but with some reservations. The archprior didn't get to his position by being a fool. He has to know the Temple Commander is here in Harlingen, and I think he'll see through the ruse. It might be better to tell Father Hywell the truth from the beginning."

"I shall consider that. And you, Merrick?"

"I agree with Gita. We are stepping on dangerous ground here, and the last thing we want is to upset the entire Church."

"Yes, but would it?" asked Alexandra. "The Temple Knights of Saint Cunar are only one part of it."

"True," replied her husband, "but what we're proposing is in contradiction to the accepted way of handling such things. Were we any other Petty Kingdom, we'd likely grant their request for land."

"But we're not any other kingdom," said Charlotte. "We're Hadenfeld."

"I didn't mean to imply we shouldn't refuse their offer, merely that the Church may not look kindly upon our response. Your Majesty does not wish them to build a commandery here—that's not a matter of debate. What we're trying to do is to determine the best way to inform them of that decision, hopefully in a way that will reduce any feeling of being slighted."

"I wonder," said Alexandra, "could we come up with another reason to deny their request?"

"I'm open to suggestions," replied Charlotte.

"How about something financial?" Alexandra looked at Gita.

"I wouldn't advise that. If word gets out we're short of funds, it may be an invitation to take advantage of us, perhaps even lead to an invasion, and war is the last thing we need right now."

"Could we claim there is no land available within the walls of Harlingen?"

"No," said Charlotte. "Then they'd ask for some outside the city's walls. It's a common enough practice in other Petty Kingdoms."

Everyone fell silent, leaving the final decision to Charlotte. "I will inform the Temple Commander that we do not wish a commandery in

Hadenfeld, but before I do that, I'll speak with the archprior. Perhaps, once he knows the truth, he might suggest another way to proceed."

Father Hywell sat in a large armchair, sipping wine, while the Queen of Hadenfeld regarded him. He was a man of forty-odd years, blessed with the appearance of one at least ten years younger. He claimed that his faith gave him his youthful appearance, but Charlotte thought it more likely due to his strict diet.

"I trust all is well, Majesty?" said the archprior. "Admittedly, it's not every day I receive an invitation to the Royal Keep." He leaned forward, offering a chuckle. "I trust I am not to be put in irons?"

"I assure Your Grace that you're safe here."

"Then might I ask the purpose of this invitation?"

"I am seeking advice," she replied. "Doubtless by now, you're aware that a Temple Commander of Saint Cunar is in Harlingen."

"I think I see where this is going. You mean to deny him permission to build a commandery."

"How did you know?"

"The reason for his visit is not the best-kept secret, and the fact that it wasn't immediately approved speaks volumes." He held up his hand. "I'm not suggesting you be forced into doing anything you don't wish, Majesty, but I must admit to some curiosity about how you came to that decision. Assuming the rumours are true, of course."

"They are," replied Charlotte. "Are you familiar with events surrounding the invasion of Arnsfeld two years ago?"

"Somewhat, although I can't admit to being an expert in the matter. The land battle involved the Temple Knights of Saint Agnes and Mathew. Is that what concerns you?"

"Were you aware that those of Saint Cunar sought to interfere with the Agnesites marching to aid in the war?"

Father Hywell set down his glass. "I was not. Might I ask where you heard this?"

"I cannot reveal my sources other than to state they are beyond reproach."

"Are you suggesting the Church sanctioned their interference?"

"The Church, no, but in all probability, someone higher up within their order was involved."

"I must admit I find this news alarming. Given the circumstances, I understand your hesitancy in permitting them to build a commandery here." He sat silently, waiting. "What advice is it you seek from me?" he finally asked.

"As an archprior, you're much more familiar with the Church bureaucracy than my advisors. My concern isn't about how the Temple Knights will take rejection, but how the Church hierarchy will react."

"The Cunars are the senior order of Temple Knights, not to mention the largest. Your refusal to allow them into your realm will be taken as an insult."

"I expected that," said Charlotte, "but what would be the result of that?"

"That's difficult to say. It might consist of nothing or a simple rebuke, but whatever happens, you probably wouldn't hear of it for months, perhaps even a year or more. The bureaucracy of the Church is notoriously slow, even when dealing with important matters. It's hundreds of miles to the Antonine, and that's not accounting for the normal chain of command. Your refusal would be passed on to the Grand Master of the Order. At that point, assuming he wanted to pursue it further, he'd have to take it to the Patriarch of Saint Cunar, who'd then decide whether or not to raise the issue with the Council of Peers, and they're exceedingly busy. Just convincing them to consider discussing the matter would be a major undertaking."

"Are you familiar with the Cunar Grand Master?"

"I'm afraid not," replied Father Hywell, "but if you wish, I could deliver a letter to the Archprior of Saint Cunar? Admittedly, he's not a Temple Knight, but he does report to the same patriarch."

"Do you think that would do any good?"

"Not likely, unfortunately. My own experience with the Cunars is that they are, by and large, very… what's the word?"

"Haughty?"

"I was going to say arrogant, but your word serves just as well." The archprior stopped himself, realizing what he'd just said. "I'd prefer that not be repeated; it could prove a major embarrassment to me, particularly when I work so closely with the other archpriors."

"I promise I shall breathe no word of it." Charlotte took a sip of her wine as she contemplated her next move. It sounded as though the chances of the issue making its way back to the Council of Peers was remote, but for some reason, she couldn't shake off the feeling of impending doom. The Church of the Saints wielded significant influence over the general populace. Could they use that influence to cause unrest in Harlingen? The army was more than capable of suppressing such activity, but significant damage would be done, both to the Crown and to the loyalty of its subjects.

"I hope I have not caused offence," said the archprior. "That was certainly not my intent."

She forced a smile. "I am not offended, only worried about the future of Hadenfeld."

"Over this commandery business? It is but a minor thing."

"I fear it may be the drop that overflows the bucket."

"Why would you say that?" He must've sensed her hesitation, for he did not wait for her to answer the question. "I assure you this discussion will remain confidential."

"I fear the Temple Knights of Saint Cunar have taken measures to assist the Empire of Halvaria. Their actions in Arnsfeld prove they are no longer working in the best interests of the Petty Kingdoms."

"Perhaps, but Hadenfeld is a long way from the empire's borders."

"Do you know much of Hadenfeld's history, Your Grace?"

"Only the events of the last ten years. Why? Is there something I should be aware of?"

"Hadenfeld has traditionally been one of the major powers of the Petty Kingdoms. With such a sizable army at hand, it was feared by its neighbours, at least until Otto was crowned."

"Ah, yes," said Father Hywell. "The war that split the kingdom in two. That was an unfortunate state of affairs, yet Otto reunited the realm just before his death, largely due to your husband's actions, I'm told."

"Other factors were involved, including agents of the empire who wished to cause a massive loss of warriors on both sides."

"I can well understand the politics of backing a war, but both sides? Wars are waged to seize control of a region, not wear down the forces involved. Are you certain you know the true story?"

"I am confident of my husband's interpretation of events, and, knowing the details, I agree with his conclusion."

"I shall have to take your word for it, but how would that benefit the empire?"

"They intend to invade," said Charlotte.

"Every decade or so, they swallow up another Petty Kingdom; I'll not deny that, but they lost at Arnsfeld, and Hadenfeld is hundreds of miles from the border."

"The next time they attack, it won't be a single kingdom they target; it'll be the entire Continent."

"That's a bleak outlook," said the archprior. "I'm prepared to believe some Cunars worked against the betterment of the Petty Kingdoms in Arnsfeld, but that doesn't mean the entire order is corrupt."

"Then why did they withdraw all their Temple Knights from those realms bordering the empire?"

"Because that's the best strategy to defend against them."

"But it's not; don't you see? If realms are only swallowed up every decade, why mass the knights so far away, in the heart of the Continent? Wouldn't it be wiser to keep them in those very kingdoms that are most threatened?"

"You make a compelling argument."

"There's more," said Charlotte. "May I continue?"

"By all means."

"Are you aware of the events that led up to the invasion of Arnsfeld?"

"Only in a very general sense. Why? Do you possess information I don't?"

"It appears I do. It began with a crisis, one that arose when the Temple Knights of Saint Cunar withdrew from the Kingdom of Arnsfeld. Thankfully, those of Saint Agnes responded quickly, replacing the local garrison with Temple Knights of their own."

"That explains their part in the battle. I always wondered why so many were present, but that still doesn't explain your leap of logic. How does the empire's defeat in Arnsfeld suggest they'd aim their next invasion at the entire Continent?"

"Let me answer that by asking you a question. What has been the greatest deterrent to the empire expanding at a faster pace?"

"That's easy—the Holy Army. Any protracted war would bring all the fighting orders to bear. Now that I think of it, I suppose that's the justification for withdrawing the Cunars from the border regions in the first place."

"And what constitutes the Holy Army?" asked Charlotte.

"The fighting orders, the majority of which are the Cunars." He paused, then it was as if a fire were lit behind his eyes. "Saints alive, do you know what this means? I see now why you fear an invasion by the Halvarians. Without the Cunars, there is nothing to stop them."

"Not nothing. The Petty Kingdoms still have their armies, but the recent conflict here has weakened us. Should a continental war erupt, we'd be hard-pressed to send aid to our allies, let alone defend our own lands."

Father Hywell shook his head. "If what you say is true, it speaks to corruption in the highest levels of the fighting orders."

"Not all of them," said Charlotte. "Your own Temple Knights fought at the Battle of the Brinwald, as did the Sisters of Saint Agnes."

"Yes, of course. Sorry. I was getting carried away. You're correct, but it does indicate troubles in the Temple Knights of Saint Cunar, perhaps even the rest of their order. Oh dear, how can I trust their archprior now, knowing this?"

"It's important you don't let on what you've learned here today, Your Grace."

"Yes, yes. Of course. The question now, I suppose, is whom I can trust?"

"Temple Captain Hamelyn and the other Temple Knights of Saint Mathew all supported my husband's bid for the Throne despite the Church's orders regarding non-interference."

"Yes," said Father Hywell, "but that particular matter saw my predecessor recalled to the Antonine, which suggests those actions were not condoned by the Church. Could that mean my own superiors are in league with whoever's behind all this?"

"I'd hate to speculate at this point, but I suggest you take care when dealing with your superiors in future, just to be on the safe side."

"Wise words, Majesty." The archprior downed the last of his wine, then stood and offered a bow. "You've opened my eyes, Majesty. Though I don't take pleasure in what I've seen, it prepares me for what may come, and for that, I thank you. Now, I must beg leave to return to my priory; I've much to consider."

"May the Saints guide you," said Charlotte.

"And you," he replied.

"How did it go?" asked Gita.

Charlotte shrugged her shoulders. "I spent the bulk of my time explaining why the Cunars can't be trusted. They've done an excellent job of hiding their actions."

"And the archprior had heard nothing about any of this?"

"Other than believing the Cunars were arrogant, no, but I'm hopeful that I opened his eyes to what is happening."

"Had he any suggestions on how we might proceed?"

"He said refusing the Cunars would likely be taken as an insult, but doubts it would go very far. Our refusal here has to go through many others before the Council of Peers, and it's not as if the Temple Knights have a shortage of commanderies."

"Then why do they want one here?"

"They fear our army would tip the balance of power should war come."

"You mean when," said Gita. "Though it must be a few years away, at least."

"What makes you say that?"

"The fact that they want to build a commandery. That takes time."

"Yes," said Charlotte, "but they'd likely use temporary housing while it was under construction, so that's not necessarily true. If I agreed to their request, they'd have an entire company here by the end of summer, which is not something I'd like to see, nor, I suspect, would Ludwig."

"When will you inform Temple Commander Amarand?"

"I was hoping Ludwig would return in time to make the announcement, but it appears I'll have to do it myself."

"I could inform him you're indisposed?"

"I refuse to use my health as an excuse. It gives them a reason to question my decision."

"Then don't give a reason at all," said Gita. "As queen, you're a busy person. He can't be granted a Royal Audience if you don't have time to see him."

"No," replied Charlotte. "That would be shirking my duty as queen, but I'll delay him a little longer to determine the best manner to inform him of my decision. I may be able to avoid any ramifications if I can deny his request without revealing what we know."

"I suspect that ship has sailed. The Temple Commander has shown himself to be prickly, although perhaps demanding would be a better description."

"Entitled might be even better," offered Charlotte. "I wonder if any other kingdom has ever refused their request to build a commandery?"

"I doubt it," said Gita. "If it hadn't been for Temple Commander Charlaine, we'd be unaware of their treachery. Prior to receiving that news, we'd have considered it a great honour to have a company here in Harlingen. We already have Temple Knights of Saint Mathew; might that work to our advantage?"

"No. That just makes it more personal. After all, why deny the Cunars when we've already agreed to the Mathewites' presence?"

"I don't envy you your task," replied Gita.

10

UDENACHT

SUMMER 1105 SR

Ludwig stood in Mirantha, staring across the Hollen River into Hadenfeld.

Sigwulf came up beside him. "Are you certain you want to cross here? The woods over there look tough to travel through."

"They do, but we need to ascertain if the river is navigable, and we can't do that by continuing on this side; it's even worse."

"It'll be slow going."

"I suspect we'll soon have help," said Ludwig.

"Help?"

"Yes, unless I'm mistaken, it'll only take a few days for the Elves of the Goldenwood to discover we're here."

"With all due respect, Ludwig, we must be at least two hundred miles from Nethendril."

"True, but there are other cities within their realm."

"Are you suggesting their kingdom extends this far south?"

"It's certainly a possibility, but even if it doesn't, they keep a close watch on the entire forest, always on the lookout for intrusions. That's how they knew we were coming last year."

Sigwulf shook his head. "It still amazes me how much things can change in so short a time. Last year, we were exiles in Eisen, and now here you are, King of Hadenfeld, with the Elves as allies, no less."

Father Vernan joined them by the riverbank. "I'm led to understand there's a ford here somewhere, although I'm at a loss as to where."

"Easily solved," replied Sigwulf. "I'll send a couple of riders in either direction. It won't take long for them to locate it." The huge northerner turned his horse around and rode back to their escort, who were standing guard.

"He's very dedicated," mused the Holy Father.

"Yes," said Ludwig. "I'm lucky to have him by my side."

"I don't know that it's so much luck as strength of character, Majesty."

"What do you mean?"

"You are the true embodiment of the Saints: a king who is both humble and concerned for the well-being of those he rules over."

"Ah, but I was no king when I first met Sig, or you, for that matter."

"True, and I remember you being somewhat conceited then, but unlike others, you learned from your mistakes and turned your life around, making you the man you are today. Not everyone is willing to undertake such a personal journey."

"I'm grateful for the acknowledgement," said Ludwig, "but I've had no choice but to learn to adapt. When I first returned to Hadenfeld, it was an adjustment, and becoming prince was even more so. Now, as king, there are some days I can't help but feel overwhelmed."

"That is understandable, considering the huge weight on your shoulders. Running any kingdom is difficult, let alone one that has seen so much turmoil in recent years."

"Perhaps it would've been better had I stayed in the north."

"If you had, the kingdom would have fallen into war."

"I might remind you it did precisely that."

"Agreed," said Father Vernan, "but your presence at the Second Battle of Harlingen changed history. Had you not stopped King Diedrich, the war would have dragged on for years."

"And then I waged a war to seize the Throne."

"Only because you had to. History has forced you into making difficult decisions, Majesty, and you've always responded by taking the high road rather than the easiest. I must commend you for that."

"Then tell me this," said Ludwig. "Am I making the right decision, interfering in the affairs of Hollenbeck and Mirantha?"

"You are guided by your conscience, and that, I know, is heavily influenced by the teachings of Saint Mathew. It is only natural that you should doubt yourself from time to time, but in your heart of hearts, only you can decide if what you're doing is right."

"Meaning?"

"If I were you, I'd trust your instincts. They've never led you astray."

"Except when I ran away to Erlingen," said Ludwig.

"True, but if I recall, you only truly embraced the teachings of Mathew AFTER you joined those mercenaries."

"Yes, after I was given a book of his writings by Rosalyn Haas." He tapped his saddlebag. "I still have it."

Sigwulf called out from downstream, beckoning them.

"It appears we've discovered our ford," said Father Vernan.

"Then it's time we crossed, and let's hope the Elves put in an appearance."

Two days later, they were making little headway, having only traversed an estimated twenty miles. Father Vernan was particularly distraught, for he'd expected the trees to lessen as they travelled westward, but the opposite had happened, necessitating retracing their steps on many occasions to find a passable path.

After one such endeavour, they entered a small glade, where an Elf, mounted on a white horse, waited, wearing the customary silver scales common to the warriors of the Goldenwood.

"Greetings," he called out in the Human tongue. "I am Nindaril, Talon of the Silver Eagle Glade Warriors."

"I am Ludwig, King of Hadenfeld."

"I know full well who you are, Majesty. I have been sent to render assistance. You are a long way from home and appear in need of a guide."

"I'd greatly appreciate that. I am curious, however, when you become aware of our presence?"

"My people have been watching you ever since you crossed the ford. There are few such places along the river, so we keep a close watch over them. I would have extended the hand of friendship sooner, but it took time for news of your incursion to reach me." He moved closer, offering a bow of his head. "Honoured are we to see our ally beneath the canopy of the Goldenwood. Might I ask what brings you here?"

"We were paralleling the river to determine if it would be navigable for a boat from Udenacht."

"You wish to transport something?"

"Not something," replied Ludwig, "someone. I'm hoping to arrange a meeting between the rulers of Mirantha and Hollenbeck, the Human realms that lie south of the river."

"And where would this meeting be held?"

"In one of our towns, Udenacht. Do you know it?"

"I know of it, although I have never entered it. There is an old road of sorts that lies along the Goldenwood's southwestern border that leads to Udenacht. I can show you the way if you wish."

"Thank you. That would be most appreciated."

The Elf paused, gazing over at the water, then turned to Ludwig. "The river to the south of us would prove a most suitable method of travel for your guests, provided you only use shallow-draft vessels. And even then, there are still points at which the boats would have to be dragged over the shallower sections."

"I thank you for the advice," said Ludwig. "I must admit your command of our language is most impressive. Is that due to magic?"

"Only partially. I understand a smattering of what you call the common tongue, and my spell enhances it."

"If you don't mind me asking, how is it that you know our language to begin with?"

"I have nothing to hide," replied Nindaril, "but perhaps it would be better if we discuss this as we ride rather than standing in the sun all afternoon?"

"Yes, of course." Ludwig advanced as the Elf talon turned his horse around. The two were soon riding off, Sigwulf and Father Vernan following, along with the remaining Royal Guards.

"When word reached us that Sindra had become the new High Lord, we sent a delegate to Nethendril."

"So you're not from there?" asked Ludwig.

"No. My home is Elandril, which lies some distance north of our present position. We have been keeping a watchful eye on your lands for the last century, particularly Udenacht and Ramfelden, always observing from a respectful distance. In recent months, several of us have ventured farther afield, communicating with farmers in the area to learn more about you Humans. It is through that contact that I learned the rudiments of your language."

"Just how far does your reach extend?" asked Ludwig.

"Tradition holds that our border is the edge of the Goldenwood, but we seldom venture that far west except for those who monitor your villages. There was some discussion of sending warriors to assist you in your recent war to claim the Throne. However, we Elves are not prone to making quick decisions, particularly in Elandril, and by the time we agreed, word reached us from the High Lord that the war had concluded."

"Would you consider sending merchants to Ramfelden and Udenacht? I'm certain both our people would benefit from the trade."

"I am a mere talon and thus not empowered to make such decisions, but I will pass the idea along to my superiors." They continued on in silence, following a trail that only their guide was able to spot.

It wasn't until later in the day when they'd paused to water the horses, that the Elf spoke again.

"Who rules in Udenacht?" asked Nindaril

"A baron named Lord Nikolaus Wendt."

"Do I detect a note of concern at the mention of his name?"

"That's perceptive of you," said Ludwig. "He supported the late King Morgan during the war." He noted the Elf's look of confusion. "The king I usurped?"

The Elf nodded. "Now I understand. You do not know if he will agree to host the rulers on your behalf."

"Correct."

"You are the king, are you not? Could you not command him?"

"I most certainly could, but a man forced to host would not be welcoming to guests, and there is far too much at stake here."

Even with the aid of the Elves, they took the rest of the week to reach the road, although the term road was being generous, for it was little more than stumps between the forest and hills to the south. It had been over half a century since the land had been cleared in hopes of starting a new barony at its end, but that all came to a halt with the ascension of King Otto and the war that splintered the kingdom.

Ludwig expected they would part ways with their guide, but to his surprise, Nindaril insisted on accompanying them to Udenacht. Once they cleared the Goldenwood, they were able to pick up the pace, and by the end of the week, they spotted a keep towering over the village itself.

They rode straight for the keep, where Lord Nikolaus stood there, waiting for them.

"Majesty." The baron nodded slightly. "We are delighted to see you, although I must admit to some surprise. I trust all is well?" He took notice of the Elf and stared.

"Allow me to introduce Talon Nindaril," said Ludwig. "He guided us through the wilderness."

"I'm afraid I don't understand. Did you not come from Harlingen?"

"No. We were south, visiting Hollenbeck and Mirantha, which is what I wish to speak to you about."

"Where are my manners?" said Lord Nikolaus. "Let's go inside, shall we? My men will take care of your horses."

"You know General Marhaven, of course, and Father Vernan?"

"Yes. I remember them from your coronation. I don't remember an Elf being present, however. I assume Talon is from the Elven realm?"

"He is, but talon is his rank, not his name."

"You may address me as Talon if you prefer," added the Elf. "It matters little to me."

"Astounding!" Lord Nikolaus led them up the steps to the keep's entrance. "You mentioned the kingdoms to our south. Has there been some sort of trouble?"

"In a manner of speaking, yes," replied Ludwig. "I'm hoping we can resolve their issues before it comes to violence, which leads me to the reason why I'm here. I'd like you to host a meeting of their respective leaders."

"Have you any idea when this meeting would occur?"

"My invitation will reach Klermacht in a week, but the capital of Mirantha will take considerably longer. Assuming they both agree, they'd still need to send a return message. I would say it's at least a month away, although six weeks is more likely."

"And if either side refuses to attend?"

"I doubt they will," replied Ludwig. "I intend to suggest that if only one shows, I'll throw the full support of Hadenfeld behind their claim." He paused as a look of horror crossed the baron's face. "Don't worry. I'll put it more diplomatically. I'm not aiming to start a war here, but I won't sit back and permit a war to erupt on my border."

They entered the keep, which was similar in layout to that of Verfeld, and were soon sitting in the great hall.

"You appear to have plenty of room here, my lord. I trust hosting a summit will not prove too difficult. The Crown will reimburse you for the cost."

"You are most generous, Majesty, although I am curious why you picked Udenacht. We were, after all, on different sides during the recent conflict."

"It's due to your location. As far as being on different sides, the war is over. You pledged your allegiance to me after my coronation, and I take people at their word. We may have had our differences in the past, Lord Nikolaus, but I am king now and bear the responsibility of looking after all my subjects, not just those who were on my side during the campaign. It's high time we put our differences aside and worked for the betterment of the kingdom, don't you agree?"

A look of relief flashed across the baron's face. "I do, most certainly, Majesty."

"We Elves will assist where we may," offered Nindaril. "I propose that my Glade Warriors escort the King of Mirantha rather than send his entourage by boat. Naturally, you would inform him of our offer to ensure he did not take offence at our presence."

"That is a most generous offer," said Ludwig, "and one which I'm pleased to accept."

The baron shifted in his chair. "Might I ask the reason for this meeting of rulers, Majesty?"

"Are you familiar with the concept of sky metal?"

"Vaguely. They say it's worth a fortune. Why?"

"There are reports that some of it landed in an area claimed by both Hollenbeck and Mirantha. I fear its very presence could lead to a war."

"Should we not leave them to settle this amongst themselves?"

"I might remind you that Hollenbeck lies across the river from you. Do you want to risk the war spreading to your own lands?"

"Certainly not," replied Lord Nikolaus, "but if the rumours are true, there's likely little we can do to sway them from this course of action."

"I'm hoping to come up with a solution that appeals to both rulers."

"Might it not be best to resolve the border dispute first? If you get them both to agree whose land is whose, then the realm with the sky metal would logically lay claim to it."

"I doubt either will accept that," said Ludwig, "especially when we don't know the actual location where it landed. To make matters worse, the area is densely forested, meaning a lot of manpower would be required to conduct the search, potentially placing two armies in territory claimed by both realms. A search, I might add, that could take months if not years."

"Even a minor incident could quickly grow out of control," offered Father Vernan. "And any war on our border could potentially expand as other Petty Kingdoms get involved."

"I'm afraid I'm not following," said the baron. "To my knowledge, neither kingdom has any alliances."

"True," replied Ludwig, "but it's possible a neighbouring realm might take advantage of the situation and attack while Hollenbeck and Mirantha were embroiled in a conflict."

"Saints alive, I hadn't thought of that." Lord Nikolaus noticed the disapproval on Father Vernan's face. "I apologize for the outburst, Father, but it caught me by surprise."

"Understandable," the Holy Father replied, "but we must always remain aware that actions have consequences, even those over which it appears we have no control. I've accompanied His Majesty to the courts of both Hollenbeck and Mirantha, and I believe neither ruler wishes a war. If we get them together for a civil discussion on the matter, I'm certain they'll come to an agreement."

"Let's hope," said Lord Nikolaus, "but I don't think you've accounted for the sky metal's potential worth. Perhaps we should march there ourselves and lay claim to it?"

"That would be an act of war," said Ludwig.

"True, but the Army of Hadenfeld could easily defeat Hollenbeck and Mirantha combined."

"I have no quarrel with either, my lord, and neither should you. I will not march warriors into a neighbouring realm without invitation, and I highly doubt that's going to be offered."

The baron bowed. "My apologies if I offended you, Majesty. I meant no disrespect. It is your prerogative as king to decide if and when we go to war. Regarding the summit, I am pleased to serve in any capacity I can. Do you need men to carry your messages to the respective rulers?"

"I'll take word to the duke," offered Sigwulf. "We have a history."

"And I shall take it to the king," said Father Vernan, "although I'll need an escort to the border."

"I would be pleased to assist," said Nindaril. "Perhaps, along the way, you could explain to me how your Saints work?"

"I should be delighted!"

"That reminds me," said Ludwig, "we left the carriage in Freimar. Perhaps you could arrange to have it sent here to Udenacht."

"If only we could travel in it ourselves, but yes, I'll see to it."

"And what of you, Majesty?" asked the baron. "Will you return to Harlingen while we await a reply or remain here in Udenacht?"

"I shall remain here, at least until we receive word back from our neighbours. I trust that won't prove too much of an inconvenience?"

"Not at all, Majesty."

11

HARLINGEN

SUMMER 1105 SR

Charlotte watched as Temple Commander Amarand surveyed the crowd. She'd invited him back to visit, but failed to mention the court would be in full session. She had asked several influential merchants to attend, in addition to her advisors, the better to spread word of her decision. Keeping it secret had been a daunting task, for it all had to be arranged without the Cunar learning of it, but the surprised look on his face told him she'd succeeded.

Amarand advanced towards the throne, all eyes on him. If he felt intimidated, he gave no sign of it, and she began to wonder if it had been a mistake for her to bestow her decision in such a manner.

He halted a few feet from her and knelt, offering a deep bow. "Your Majesty, I come today to humble myself before the throne."

"Rise," replied Charlotte.

He stood, his back straight, his dark grey tunic standing in stark contrast to the colourful clothes filling the court. "I come seeking an answer," he declared, his voice carrying to the corners of the room. "Have you decided to grant my order land?"

"After careful consideration, the Crown of Hadenfeld will NOT provide land for the building of a commandery for the Temple Knights of Saint Cunar."

Amarand gave a slight bow of his head. "Then we shall use our own funds." He turned to leave.

"I am not done," declared Charlotte.

The Temple Commander swivelled back to stare at the queen, his face a stone mask, but she suspected that beneath the calm exterior brewed a wave of great anger.

"As Queen of Hadenfeld, not only am I denying your order permission to build a commandery in Harlingen, but also any other city, town, or village in the realm."

"You cannot do that, Majesty. You have a duty to the Church to assist in spreading the teachings of the Saints."

"Temple Knights are the fighting arm of the Church; the Holy Fathers are responsible for the tenants. Are you now trying to claim otherwise?"

"The duty of my order is to keep the Church safe. We can hardly do that without a presence here."

Charlotte regarded those witnessing the exchange. "Temple Captain Hamelyn, does your order not protect the Temples of Saint Mathew in Hadenfeld?"

"It does, Majesty, and in the absence of other knights, we also protect those of Saint Agnes and Saint Cunar."

"There, you see, Commander? The presence of your order is not required."

Amarand clenched his teeth. "These are turbulent times, Majesty. A company or two of Cunars in your realm would go a long way to convince your subjects to refrain from rising up yet again."

"Rising up?" said Hamelyn. "Are you suggesting, Commander, that there is unrest? If so, where is your proof? My Temple Knights have patrolled the streets of Harlingen since the fall of King Morgan, and we've seen no evidence of trouble."

"With all due respect, Brother, your knights are not best suited to such a task."

"And you are?" snapped Charlotte. She pressed her lips together, upset at her outburst. It would do no good to further antagonize the commander, but he made it difficult not to.

"We Cunars are experienced in battle, Majesty. Were the king here, he'd undoubtedly make it clear our presence would have a calming effect."

She leaned forward on the throne. "I know my husband better than you, Temple Commander, and I assure you, he will agree with my decision."

"Then we must wait until his return!"

"No, we won't. I am a queen, not a consort. As such, I hold the same power to command as he does. Your order will not build a commandery or station any Temple Knights within the borders of this realm. Do I make myself clear?"

Colour crept up from his neck, flushing his cheeks. "I will accept your decision, Majesty, although I do wonder what prompted it. As you have just demonstrated, the Temple Knights of Saint Mathew are allowed within your borders; why not my order?"

"I do not have to explain myself to you or justify my reasoning."

"Not to me, you don't," replied Amarand. He glanced around the room. "But what do you suppose your subjects think of this decision of yours?"

A murmur went through those gathered, and Charlotte's resolve wavered. It appeared her plan had failed, and now she was in danger of the Crown losing face.

"If you want to know how I came to my decision, I shall tell you." All eyes were on her, while her focus remained on the Temple Commander. "Your order can no longer be trusted."

A collective gasp filled the room, and then everyone began speaking at once. She raised her hand, calling for silence. "Prior to the invasion of Arnsfeld, your order abandoned that realm, then tried to prevent the Temple Knights of Saint Agnes from marching to the kingdom's aid. Had your brothers succeeded in their endeavours, Arnsfeld would now lie in the hands of the Halvarian Empire."

"That's a lie!" said Amarand. "We did no such thing."

"I know of witnesses to this traitorous behaviour."

"With all due respect, Majesty—"

"With all due respect? That is precisely what you are NOT showing, Commander. Now, will you accept my decision, or am I to be forced to order my guards to escort you from the premises?"

He offered her a curt nod, then wheeled stiffly around and marched out, his footsteps heavy. As soon as the doors closed behind him, everyone started talking again, filling the room with noise.

Charlotte sat back, letting them discuss the matter. She'd not intended to reveal the treachery of the Cunars, and by doing so, she'd put the kingdom in a precarious position. Would the Church ignore the accusation, or was Hadenfeld doomed to feel their wrath?

That evening, she sat in front of the fire, pondering the day. Alexandra was across from her, while Kenley and Frederick sat in a corner, listening to Captain Gustavo quietly read them a book.

"That was quite the day," said Alexandra. "All things considered, I thought you handled it well."

"I let my emotions get the best of me," replied Charlotte. "It would have gone so much better had I kept a level head."

"Nonsense. That man deserved a dressing down. He was arrogant!"

"Still," replied Charlotte, "a little diplomacy wouldn't have gone amiss."

"I doubt that would've made a difference. Someone like that doesn't take no for an answer, which left you no choice. He was trying to force you to cave in to pressure from the Church. On the good side, you gave a magnificent display of strength in the face of a real threat."

"Did I? Or did I sound petty?"

"I have no doubt the capital will soon be talking about the queen with the steel back."

Charlotte laughed. "Now you're making me out to be some sort of hero."

"You did face down a Temple Commander; that's no small feat."

"I did, didn't I?"

"You don't sound convinced."

"You and I both suspect the Cunars now serve the empire. If that proves true, then my refusal to permit them to establish a commandery in Hadenfeld will likely have dire consequences."

"Remind me of what the archprior's opinion was?" asked Alexandra.

"That it would take years for it to reach the Antonine."

"Good. That gives us plenty of time to prepare a response. For now, however, we can celebrate." Alexandra refilled their goblets. "Let's talk of other things."

"A good idea. What shall we discuss?"

A knock interrupted, and then a servant appeared. "Temple Captain Hamelyn is requesting an audience, Majesty."

"Send him in."

"Shall I take the children away?" offered Gustavo.

Charlotte looked over to where both Frederick and Kenley were fast asleep on the floor. "Best leave them be for now, I think, but could you stay in case I need you?"

"Should I fetch Lady Gita?"

"No. She's busy seeing to the kingdom's finances. Let's leave her for now."

"Yes, Majesty."

Charlotte waved at the servant to let in the Temple Captain.

"You have news?" she asked.

"Yes, Majesty," replied the captain. "I've come to report Temple Commander Amarand has left the city."

"That's good news, but hardly worthy of a personal visit. Is something else troubling you?"

"I may be overstepping my duties, Majesty, but I had some people keep an eye on him since his last visit to court."

"Are you suggesting your knights were spying on him?"

"Not our knights, no, but I reached out to people we've met through our work with the sick and poor."

"And?" pressed Charlotte.

"It may interest you to know the Temple Commander visited several locations before his departure." Hamelyn pulled out a scroll that had been tucked into his belt. "I took the liberty of writing down the addresses, along with who lives there."

Charlotte unrolled the scroll and perused its contents. "Some of these people are surprisingly influential."

"And wealthy," added the captain. "I have no idea what they talked about, but according to our sources, the visits were brief."

"How brief? Could he simply have been bidding them farewell?"

"Doubtful. In each case, he was invited in while servants took his horse away. If he were only saying farewell, why let them take his mount?"

"You make a good point," said Charlotte. She handed the list to Alexandra. "Do you know anything about any of these people?"

"I'm afraid not. Most of my socializing in Harlingen has been confined to court, but I do have a few connections in the merchants' quarter. Shall I reach out to them?"

"If you would, but don't make it too obvious. I shouldn't like it to get out that we're looking into them, else they might hear about it and cover up whatever it is they're up to."

"I'll have my people keep an eye on them," said the Temple Captain. "Is there anything else I can do for Your Majesty?"

"I assume those whom Amarand visited are well-established?"

"That is my understanding."

"Then it's more than likely others would know more about them. Perhaps you could make some discreet enquiries of your own?"

"I shall see what I can do," replied Hamelyn, "but I must warn you, we Temple Knights are not spies; rather, we are warriors of faith who took an oath to always speak the truth."

"In other words," said Charlotte, "everything we've discussed is known by the Archprior of Hadenfeld."

"I don't report to the archprior, Majesty. My direct superior is our regional commander in Deisenbach."

"Yet if the archprior questioned you, you'd reveal what you know."

"Providing he asks, yes."

Charlotte smiled. "How very diplomatic, Temple Captain. You weren't by chance a politician before you joined the order, were you?"

"No, though admittedly, I've always had a fascination with how people rule."

"And what has this taught you?"

"That Hadenfeld is most unique, Majesty. From what I've observed, very few rulers believe in serving the interests of their subjects. They're more concerned with the accumulation of wealth and power."

"Yes," replied Charlotte. "That would be my conclusion as well. Then again, Ludwig never desired the Throne. He was forced to take it to end the reign of a mad king."

"An unwilling king," said Hamelyn, "yet he strives to make Hadenfeld a better place."

"He takes his duty as monarch very seriously, as do I. If that marks us as unique, then so be it."

"We have you to thank for that," piped in Alexandra.

"Me?" replied the Temple Knight.

"Well, not you, personally. I meant the teachings of your Saint, although I suppose we should acknowledge the influence of Father Vernan while we're at it. Speaking of whom, shouldn't they be returning soon?"

"Not for a while yet," said Charlotte. "Ludwig sent word he'll be spending some time in Udenacht as the baron's guest."

"Not trouble, I hope?" asked Hamelyn.

"He's hosting a meeting between the Duke of Hollenbeck and the King of Mirantha. His letter didn't relay all the details, merely that a conflict was brewing between the two, and he was determined to see them agree to a peaceful conclusion. It will be a few more weeks before we can expect him back in the capital."

Cyn opened the door. "Majesty, might I have a moment of your time?"

"Of course. Come and join us. Is this a personal visit or official?"

"A little of both."

"Let me guess, Gowan Forst?"

The general blinked. "How did you know?"

"I can think of no other person who'd cause you such distress."

"Who says I'm distressed?"

"I can tell when you're upset," said Charlotte. "You tend to clench your jaw. Now, come and sit. Have some wine; it'll help you relax."

Alexandra filled a goblet and passed it over.

Cyn drank deeply. "Thank you. I needed that."

"Now," said the queen. "Let's get to the bottom of this, shall we?"

"If he hadn't been born a noble, he'd be the village idiot. The man has no concept of responsibility!"

"Can you offer specifics?"

"He's always late to report for duty," replied Cyn, "and takes every opportunity to hold his nobility over others."

"Are you suggesting he misbehaves?"

"That's putting it mildly, Majesty. More like he flaunts it. He thinks that because his brother is a baron, he can do as he pleases. I've tried talking to him about it, but it goes in one ear and out the other."

"So you're saying he doesn't respect your authority?"

"He's under the impression that only noblemen are capable of being generals."

"You have the full authority of the Crown," said Charlotte. "Were he any other captain, how would you handle this situation?"

"I'd probably clap him in irons or maybe put him in the stocks for a few days."

"Then that is what you must do."

"His brother won't like that."

"Then his father should've taught him that bad behaviour has consequences. Lord Gowan Forst is to be treated as any other captain under your command."

"If I may," said Hamelyn. "Might I suggest an alternative?"

"By all means. I'm open to suggestions," replied Cyn.

"I'd be pleased for him to spend time amongst us Temple Knights."

"Are you suggesting he join your order?"

"No, merely become our guest for a week or two. Call it an exchange, if you wish—a chance for him to experience the need for rigid discipline."

"And if he refuses?"

Charlotte chuckled. "Then he'll be dismissed from service under a cloud of dishonour. I think, given the choice, he'll take the good Temple Captain up on his offer. I assume he will receive no special treatment amongst your order?"

"He shall be treated as any other initiate of the Temple Knights."

"Meaning?" asked Cyn.

"We are a humble order, seeing to our needs in every way, which includes scrubbing floors, preparing food, and even washing our own clothes."

Cyn laughed. "I'd love to see Lord Gowan doing laundry."

"We are trying to reform the man," said the queen, "not publicly embarrass him."

"Yes, of course. Sorry."

"Good. Then you may inform him that he is being sent to the Temple

Knights of Saint Mathew for training. Before you do that, I'll have it written up as a Royal Command, but give him the choice to accept the assignment before you present it. There's no sense in forcing him into it if he's willing to go of his own accord."

"Thank you, Majesty."

"Don't thank me; thank Temple Captain Hamelyn. It was his idea. Who knows, perhaps it will prove such a success, we'll consider sending others for training as well?"

"They would be most welcome," replied the captain. "We so seldom get visits from outsiders."

"Before you leave," said Charlotte, "may I ask you a question?"

"Most certainly."

"What do you think will be the result of our refusal to honour Temple Commander Amarand's request to build a commandery?"

"Cunars are not known for backing down. He will no doubt complain most vociferously to his superiors, which means his complaint will be taken to one of the Temple Generals of the order."

"They have more than one?"

"Indeed, they have two. One commands the Holy Army, the other the Holy Fleet, although he is often referred to as 'Admiral' to avoid confusion."

"And this Temple General reports to the Grand Master of the Order, I assume?"

"He does. At that point, it becomes more difficult to predict the response. At the very least, I expect a Cunar Archprior to come here seeking to either sway your opinion or rebuke you publicly. His order believes in the supremacy of the Church."

"Supremacy?" said Alexandra. "I'm not certain I follow."

"Within the Church of the Saints, there are two divergent beliefs. The Mathewites and Agnesites believe the Church is a servant of the people, and thus, secular law is seen as overruling Church law. Others, including the Cunars, believe the laws of the Church take precedence over any realm's individual laws. This debate spans centuries, but up until now, the discussion was only academic."

"And now we've pushed it to the forefront," said Charlotte.

"That seems to be the case. The hierarchy of the Church, however, is notoriously slow, so even if concerns were raised in the Antonine, it would be many months or even years before anything came of it."

"Thank you, Temple Captain. You've been most informative."

"It is my pleasure to serve, Majesty. Now, if you'll excuse me, I have duties to attend to." With that, he left, closing the door quietly behind him.

"He's a good man," offered Captain Gustavo, "and gave us a clear answer when he could've avoided the subject altogether. I wonder how long before a Cunar archprior arrives requesting an audience?"

"We already have one of those in Harlingen," said Alexandra.

"We do," agreed Charlotte, "but he's been here awhile and won't say anything that would risk his position. I think when the time comes, we'll see someone from higher up coming to lecture us."

12

DIPLOMACY

AUTUMN 1105 SR

Six Elven riders led the procession heading towards the baron's keep. Behind them came four of King Augustinian's knights, followed, in turn, by the horse bearing His Majesty.

From his vantage point atop the keep, Ludwig watched with great interest. He'd been worried the presence of the Elves might complicate the situation. However, when His Majesty came to a halt and dismounted, he appeared in good spirits, even going so far as to acknowledge his Elven escort with a slight bow. Lord Nikolaus came down the keep's stairs to greet King Augustinian.

"Quite the sight," said Sigwulf. "I hope all this work is worth it. The last thing we want is a war on our border."

"Let's hope they both see reason," replied Ludwig. Lord Ulfric, the Duke of Hollenbeck, had arrived two days earlier and now waited in the great hall. "Speaking of which, we should join them. I'd hate for their first introduction to each other to go astray."

"You think that likely? They've both travelled quite the distance to get here."

"Yes, during which they likely both rehearsed their demands."

"Do we restrain them if things get physical?"

"I doubt it'll come to that," replied Ludwig. "I believe they'll realize the merits of working side by side instead of being at each other's throats."

"Who's going to be the toughest to handle?" asked Sig.

"Handle? I intend for them to come to a reasonable solution without any form of coercion, not force a solution down their throats."

"Still, they're two very different people."

"Actually," said Ludwig, "I've found them both to be quite level-headed."

They entered the great hall to find Lord Ulfric waiting in the centre of the room, a pair of his guards standing off to one side.

Lord Nikolaus entered by way of the main door, leading King Augustinian. The King of Mirantha's gaze met that of his counterpart and he offered a nod, which was returned.

"Shall we?" said Ludwig. As the host, he sat at the head of the table, with the Miranthan delegation on one side, while the Hollenbeck group sat on the other. Lord Nikolaus took his seat at the far end, and then a bevy of servants moved up to pour drinks.

"Thank you," said Ludwig. "I know both of you travelled a great distance to come here today, but I think, given the circumstances, we can reach an agreement that's satisfactory to both your realms." He paused as the servants pulled away, then continued. "Before we discuss more recent matters, this would be a good opportunity to discuss the disputed region. Might I enquire how that land came to be claimed by both of you?"

"It is something we inherited from our ancestors," offered Ulfric. "Under the reign of the Old Kingdom, Hollenbeck and Mirantha were both provinces. With its demise, we became independent states, but the area between us was, and still is, dense forest."

"But there must've been a border during the reign of Therengia?"

"There likely was, but with their defeat, we no longer had any access to their records."

"Yes," agreed Augustinian, "and there's been no need for an established border, as the disputed area was of little use to either of us."

"And the area is still of no consequence," said Ludwig. "The sky metal is the real prize here."

"True, and therein lies the problem. That metal is in Mirantha's lands."

"I beg to differ," replied Lord Ulfric. "That area belongs to Hollenbeck."

"If I may continue?" said Ludwig. "I propose you work together to locate this sky metal and then split it evenly."

Lord Ulfric slammed his fist on the table. "Why in the name of the Saints would we agree to that?"

"I can think of two good reasons. Since you'd both be working towards the same goal, it lessens the chance of confrontation. Secondly, it means you'll have twice as many people searching for it."

"How do I know that if King Augustinian finds it first, he'll not claim it all?"

"Arrangements can be made," replied Ludwig. "Each search party would include at least one person from the other realm amongst its numbers, or, if you prefer, I can offer some of my own men to monitor both sides."

"Why would you do that?" asked the King of Mirantha. "Are you now demanding a share of the wealth?"

"I lay claim to nothing save the peaceful coexistence of those realms bordering my own."

"May I make a suggestion?" said Sigwulf.

They all stared at the great northerner.

"By all means," replied Augustinian.

"All this talk of sky metal is grand, but have either of you given any thought as to what to do with it?"

"What do you mean?" asked Ulfric. "It's worth a fortune; everyone knows that."

"Agreed, but it does nothing by sitting in someone's treasury. To gain any benefit from it, you'd need a buyer, someone who could work the stuff."

"And you know such a person?"

Sigwulf smiled. "Not personally, but I'm pretty sure I know where one can be found."

"Then out with it, man," said Augustinian. "Where is this fellow?"

"Nethendril."

Ludwig smiled. "Good point, Sig. I wish I'd thought of that myself." He turned to the two rulers. "Nethendril is an Elven city within the Goldenwood."

"Is that where my escort came from?"

"That realm, yes, but from another city named Elandril."

"Saints alive," said Ulfric. "How many cities do these Elves have?"

"That's an excellent question," replied Ludwig. "I shall be certain to ask High Lord Sindra the next time I see her."

"Her? Shouldn't she be the High Lady, then?"

"That's not their custom and has no bearing on our discussion here today. Lord Sigwulf is correct. They likely have a smith or two who can work sky metal. Oh, and they call it ithilium."

"Ah, yes," said the duke. "I remember you mentioning that word back in Klermacht. Does that mean they'd be interested in buying it from us?"

"I can't guarantee it, but from what I understand, ithilium is used for the construction of magical items, and the Elves seem to have lots of those. I suppose that's what comes from having so many mages."

"Mages?" said Augustine. "Just how many mages have they?"

"Their High Lord is certainly one, and I've met three others in person, two talons and a healer."

"And you trust the Elves not to use their magic against us?"

"Let me put your mind at ease, Majesty. Hadenfeld has a mutual defence pact with the Goldenwood."

"You're allies?"

"Only if either of our kingdoms is under threat of attack." Ludwig went quiet. Was that the answer to this situation? "What if I offered both of you the same?"

"How would that work if Hollenbeck invaded us?" asked Augustinian.

"The simple answer is it wouldn't, but if any other kingdom threatened you, say Aldor, for example, then we'd send warriors to defend your lands."

"Would that include taking the war to the enemy's lands?"

"If they were the aggressors, yes, but I'm not about to support an ally who goes to war for no good reason."

"I find that eminently acceptable," said Ulfric.

"As do I," added Augustinian, "although speaking of my realm, I possess few troops to contribute to the defence of a kingdom the size of Hadenfeld."

"Could you manage two hundred men, Majesty?"

"I believe so, yes."

"And you, Your Grace?"

"Two hundred would be acceptable."

"Good," replied Ludwig. "Then I shall instruct Father Vernan to draw up the document authorizing it. Now, with the threat of invasion dealt with, and a potential buyer for the sky metal, can we begin working out a method by which this saintly treasure may be located?"

The rulers both nodded.

Ludwig continued. "Have we any maps of the area?"

"Not on my part," said Ulfric.

"Nor on mine," added Augustinian. "But there is a road that cuts through the forest... well, more of a trail."

"Yes, I remember," said Ludwig. "My party took it when we travelled from Klermacht to Freimar, but we need to search the area north of that. I propose a joint expedition consisting of groups of three horsemen each."

"How many groups?" asked Ulfric.

"At least ten," replied Ludwig, "possibly twenty if we can manage it. Any more, and we risk them getting in each other's way."

"They should map as they go, making note of any landmarks for future use."

"An excellent idea. And we could also..." Their discussion continued well into the night.

Most of the servants had long since retired when Father Vernan found Ludwig sitting by the fire. "Your declaration of mutual defence is written, or at least the first draft is. You'll want to review it with everyone to ensure it meets their satisfaction. Once that's done, we can make a copy for each ruler to take home."

"Thank you. Your hard work is much appreciated."

"My work? You arranged all this, Majesty. My part was that of a simple scribe. You've become quite the diplomat."

"I didn't expect it would go so smoothly. I must thank Sig for that."

"Why? What did he do?"

"He suggested the Elves might purchase the sky metal. It's not as if many other realms could do anything with it."

"I've heard that Dwarves are skilled at smithing it."

"True," said Ludwig, "and if the Elves of Nethendril prove unwilling or unable to buy the ithilium, I shall use my connections with the smiths guild to locate a Dwarven smith who's capable in that regard."

"You know a Dwarven smith?"

"No, but I've made the acquaintance of one of their couriers, Rurlan, although I don't see him very often."

His own words gave him pause. Rurlan was his sole link to Charlaine, the means by which they'd exchanged correspondence over the last few years. It had been some time since he'd heard from the Temple Commander. Was she still in Arnsfeld, or had she been reassigned? "How long do Temple Commanders remain in their position?"

"It varies considerably," replied Vernan. "The regional commander of the Temple Knights of Saint Mathew has been in Deisenbach for a dozen years at least. Are you thinking specifically of Temple Commander Charlaine?"

"I am. Why? Does that make a difference?"

"I would say so. She's been at the centre of trouble since she joined the order." The good father held up his hands. "I'm not suggesting she caused trouble, merely that she has proven adept at dealing with it. With skills like that, she'll be in demand and likely to be reassigned to wherever something is brewing. Mind you, I have absolutely no idea where that would necessarily take her."

"Who decides such things?"

"The Grand Mistress of the Order."

"Not an archprior?"

"Saints, no. Commanding the Temple Knights is at the sole discretion of the appropriate grand master."

"Is there a rank between the Grand Mistress and a Temple Commander?"

"Not in my order, nor any other, so far as I know, except for the Temple Knights of Saint Cunar."

"Why is that?" asked Ludwig.

"What need has an order for a general unless it marches to war?"

"So if the Antonine goes to war, the Cunars will lead the Holy Army?"

"Absolutely. The same goes for the Holy Fleet. An admiral of theirs fought at the Battle of Alantra."

"So there's such a thing as a Temple Admiral?"

"Not exactly," replied Father Vernan. "Admiral is a position rather than a rank. At Alantra, that position was held by Temple General Marius, but I couldn't tell you if he's still the admiral. Bear in mind, I'm not a military expert, particularly when it comes to the fighting orders, but I believe the grand master decides when to replace Temple Generals, which I assume only happens when they're planning a Holy Crusade since there's nothing for a general to do in times of peace."

"But wouldn't Temple Commanders report to them?"

"Only when on the march. Temple Commanders of the orders are, in effect, regional commanders, each in charge of several commanderies. It varies by region, but what they all have in common is that they report to the office of the grand master. Think of a Temple General as a field rank rather than an administrative one."

Ludwig grinned. "You claim to be no military expert, yet here you are, telling me the inner workings of the fighting orders. Are all the orders organized in the same way?"

"There are a few obvious differences. The Ragnarites, for example, use the same ranks but don't operate commanderies other than their training facility in the Antonine. Similarly, the Augustines are only present in half a dozen locations to guard Holy Relics, while the Ansgarites send individuals out to conduct their investigations."

"I don't know much about them."

"Nor would I expect you to since they only operate within the confines of the Church hierarchy."

"So only the Mathewites, Cunars, and Agnesites operate commanderies?"

"Yes, except in more remote locations requiring fewer Temple Knights. We refer to those as detachments, and although smaller than a full company, they still operate under the command of a Temple Captain and report to a regional commander."

"Are the regions the same for each order?"

"I'm not certain what you're asking," said Father Vernan.

"I know Captain Hamelyn reports to a regional commander in Deisenbach. Would that realm host the regional commanders of the other orders?"

"As far as I'm aware, no, although there are some exceptions where all three can be found in one realm."

"And who makes that decision? The grand master?"

"You know, I'm not entirely certain. Why? What is it you want to do?"

"It occurs to me that it might be advantageous to have a regional commander based in Harlingen. It would certainly make it easier for Captain Hamelyn to coordinate things with his superior."

"True, but for that to happen, the regional commander would have to relocate from Deisenbach, which could be viewed as a slight against their king."

"It was just a thought," said Ludwig. "It's getting late. We should both get some sleep; it's going to be a busy couple of days."

As they hammered out details, Ulfric and Augustinian grew closer, warming to the thoughts of being allies, and the possibility of finding the sky metal. By the time they were done, they'd agreed to full cooperation and sharing the results, along with securing a promise from Ludwig that he'd send men to act as a neutral third party. The biggest surprise of all came when Lord Nikolaus volunteered to carry out the task on behalf of Hadenfeld, freeing up Ludwig to return to Harlingen.

The cool weather was a sign that autumn was fast approaching. Ludwig rubbed his hands together as he saw his guests on their way and then prepared to depart himself.

Baron Wendt came to see him off. "You've done well, Majesty. I must congratulate you on your success."

"Thank you, although you were as much a part of it as I was, and your offer to oversee things is greatly appreciated. I shall not forget your service."

The baron bowed. "The honour is mine, Majesty. Please give my regards to the queen."

"I shall. Farewell, Lord Nikolaus. I hope you enjoy your time in the south." Ludwig mounted his horse, waiting as Father Vernan did the same. Neither spoke until Udenacht was far behind them.

"You've made a new ally," said the Holy Father.

"Technically, two," replied Ludwig.

"I was referring to the baron. It's most remarkable, particularly when you consider that not so long ago, he fought alongside King Morgan. You hold an admirable ability to forgive in the truest tradition of Saint Mathew. It marks you as a great ruler."

"All I did was secure our southern border."

"Oh, you did a fair bit more than that. You took two rulers prepared to go to war and made them allies and, dare I say it, even friends. A most remarkable transformation."

"Ulfric feared a war with Mirantha, and Augustinian was afraid of Aldor threatening his southern border. All I did was reassure them that Hadenfeld would come to their aid if necessary."

"And at the same time, you convinced them to come to our aid if needed. That, in itself, was a stroke of genius."

"I do not intend to go to war anytime soon."

"True," said Father Vernan, "but who knows what fate has lined up for us. The future is uncertain, Majesty, but you've given us a steady hand with which to steer the ship."

Ludwig chuckled. "You're getting philosophical in your old age."

"Old age? I'm not much older than you!"

Ludwig sat back as he realized, with a shock, just how long he'd known the Holy Father. They'd met in ninety-five when Vernan was only a Brother of Saint Mathew, and Ludwig, a baron's spoiled son. Now, here they were, ten years later, he a king and Father Vernan, his spiritual advisor.

"Do you believe in fate?" asked Ludwig.

"They say the Saints move in mysterious ways."

"But you know as well as I that the Saints were mortal men and women. We venerate their teachings, not them as gods."

"True, yet some mysterious force led to our paths crossing back in Erlingen and again in Hadenfeld."

"Did it, or was that mere coincidence?"

Father Vernan rubbed his hands together. "Ah, just what I like: an ideological discussion, exactly what's needed to pass the time!"

13

HOME

AUTUMN 1105 SR

Ludwig didn't wait for the carriage to come to a complete stop before he opened the door and hopped down onto the cobblestones. Young Frederick was running towards him as fast as his five-year-old legs could go. He caught his son, lifted him up, and planted a kiss on his cheek.

"Good morning, Papa. I missed you."

"I missed you, too. How have you been?"

"A man in grey visited Mama, and she sent him away."

"A man in grey, you say? Was he a knight?"

"He wore armour like yours," replied his son, "but not as nice."

"Where's Mama?"

Frederick's face fell. "She's not feeling well today. Auntie Alex is looking after us."

Father Vernan stepped from the carriage. "Good afternoon, Highness. My, you're so tall. Why, you must've grown a head taller since we left."

The boy beamed. "Where's Siggy?"

"Seeing to my escort," replied Ludwig. "Don't worry. He'll join us shortly. Come. Let's get inside, shall we? Those clouds look like they're bringing rain."

Cyn stood by the door. "Welcome back, boss. I trust everything went well down south?"

"It did. Even better than I expected. We have two new allies, and I averted a possible war."

"And," added Father Vernan, "His Majesty secured the loyalty of Lord Nikolaus."

"That couldn't have been easy," noted Cyn. "How did you manage that?"

"I didn't do anything," said Ludwig. "He volunteered to oversee a joint venture with Hollenbeck and Mirantha. It seems there's some sky metal lying somewhere between their two realms, and we convinced them to work together to retrieve it."

They stepped inside, and he continued. "What's this I hear about a visitor in grey?"

"A Cunar Temple Commander by the name of Amarand sought an audience to request land for a commandery."

"I can see where this is going. The queen refused him?"

"Yes."

"That's exactly what I would've done, but I sense there's more to this story?"

"There is, boss, but I think it best if Lady Gita filled you in on the details. She and Lord Merrick are inside. They're sitting in for Her Majesty today."

Sigwulf's voice boomed out from behind Ludwig. "Is that the young prince I see? Look at you. You'll soon be as tall as me!"

Frederick rushed over to the huge northerner, then halted, offering a bow. "Greetings, General."

"What about me?" said Cyn. "Don't I get a greeting?"

Sigwulf grinned. "We'll celebrate later, in private."

"You must excuse me, Majesty. I need to go and speak with Siggy—in private." She rushed out the door.

Ludwig laughed. "Come along, my son. There's work to be done, and the generals need their privacy."

The great hall was currently furnished with an immense table, around which sat several individuals Ludwig vaguely remembered seeing before. Merrick sat at the head of the table while Gita took notes, but both stood as the king entered.

"Majesty," said Gita. "Welcome back to Harlingen."

"Thank you, although I must admit to some surprise. What's going on here?"

"We are completing the work of rewriting the laws of the land, Majesty, or rather, collating them. These are Royal Magistrates, here to offer their expertise on the matter."

"Please continue," said Ludwig. "However, I'd like to borrow Lady Gita, if I may, so I can catch up on what's been happening in my absence."

"We've been at this for a while now," said Merrick. "Why don't we take a break, gentlemen? I'll have the servants bring in something to stave off the pangs of hunger, shall I?"

Nods from around the table answered his question.

"I think it best we talk in private," said Gita, nodding towards the magistrates.

"Come, then," said Ludwig. "We'll adjourn to the parlour." He knelt before his son. "Frederick, I need you to go and find Auntie Alexandra. Can you do that for me?"

"Yes, Papa."

"Good lad. Now off you go." He watched his son tear out of the room. "I'll catch Sig up later. Father Vernan, I'd like you present as well, if you don't mind."

"It would be my honour, Majesty."

Ludwig set down his cup. "By the Saints, I would've had the man arrested."

"The queen remained remarkably calm," said Gita, "and we discussed the possible ramifications before informing him that his order wasn't welcome. Unfortunately, he left feeling slighted."

"I can well imagine."

"The queen is concerned her actions may have caused some ill will."

"Nonsense. She handled it much better than I would have. She was good to be rid of the fellow."

"The concern," said Merrick, "is that the Church may take some sort of reprisal against us."

"The Church relies on the generosity of its worshippers. I doubt they'd risk losing the income of an entire kingdom, especially one our size. There may be a public rebuke, likely delivered from the pulpit, but that would soon pass, and we would return to our previous relationship with the Church. In any case, it's not the Church we refused, only one order of Temple Knights. If anything, it's the Cunars who should be rebuked for making demands."

"There's more," said Alexandra. "We learned that the Temple Commander visited several notable people in Harlingen prior to his departure."

"Members of the Church?" asked Ludwig.

"No, influential merchants, for the most part, which is what makes it all the more disturbing. We're keeping an eye on them, just to be safe."

"A wise move."

"Do you think the timing was intentional?" asked Merrick. "Could he have waited for you to leave so he could intimidate the queen?"

Alexandra laughed. "If that was his plan, he failed miserably."

"True, but there is a common misconception that a queen is weaker than a king."

"Come to think of it," said Gita, "he did act deliberately antagonistic."

"That suggests he arrived in Harlingen some time before his audience," said Ludwig, "so he would've had to know I'd left."

"Not necessarily," said Father Vernan. "I agree he was likely here in the capital for a while and that he thought he could intimidate the queen, but members of the Church are often patient people, willing to wait when necessary. I suggest he would've waited even longer had you not travelled south. It takes years to build a commandery; what does it matter if the request is delayed a few months?"

"Here's a thought," said Alexandra. "If our suspicions were true, wouldn't that suggest they know about the king's communications with Temple Commander Charlaine?"

"I'm not following," said Gita.

"If we knew nothing about the treachery of the Cunars, their request would've been granted without another thought. Yet this Temple Commander specifically waits until the king is absent and then tries to bully his way into court, making demands of the queen. That indicates he believed His Majesty would refuse his offer."

"This is all speculation at this point," said Ludwig, "but I shall certainly take that possibility into consideration, although I can't see how. The courier we use is a member of the smiths guild, and the letters are sealed with a phoenix ring."

"Could the courier have been turned?" asked Merrick.

"I think that's highly unlikely, but there is another method by which they could've learned about my distaste for the Cunars." He looked around the room as the servant who'd refilled their cups left. He nodded at the door. "The Royal Keep employs many servants. It wouldn't take much effort for them to listen in on our discussions."

Merrick looked around the room. "Are you suggesting there's a spy in our midst?"

"Yes, possibly several, in fact. When I became king, I granted amnesty to any who served Morgan, including members of the Royal Household. In light of what we've discussed, I think it's someone on the inside leaking information to outsiders. Furthermore, those merchants whom this Temple Commander spoke to are likely funding the effort."

"The question now," said Gita, "is what we do about it."

"Shall I begin by questioning each member of the staff?" asked Merrick.

"No," said Alexandra. "Do that, and word will quickly spread that we're on the hunt for spies. We'd be better to..." Her voice trailed off as the servant returned with a fresh bottle. They made small talk as glasses were topped up, and then the servant left.

"As I was saying," Alexandra continued, her voice now quieter, "we can use this knowledge to our advantage."

Merrick grinned. "You mean to spread false rumours?"

"It's worth considering."

"I like it," said Ludwig. "But from now on, we'll take care to guard our privacy when discussing important subjects."

"That's easy enough," said Gita. "We'll pick a room and only allow food and drink to be brought in when we begin."

"And if they listen at the door?" asked Alexandra.

"We'll post guards unless you're accusing Captain Gustavo of being the spy?"

"No, I trust him," said Ludwig. "I'll leave you lot to make all the appropriate arrangements. Now, if you don't mind, I'm going to look in on my wife."

Everyone stood.

"It feels like, ever since I became king, I've dealt with nothing but problems. I am, however, thankful for the advice and counsel from each and every one of you." With that, he left.

The next few weeks proved busy ones for Ludwig. Merrick completed his compilation of the laws of Hadenfeld, and now they required the king's approval. Not one to shirk his duty, Ludwig insisted on reading the completed tomes himself, not the easiest of tasks, considering the sheer number of laws.

As a baron, he'd naturally assumed that the land was governed at the whim of the nobles. He understood that theft, murder, and the like were illegal but had neglected to educate himself on the finer points of the law. Now that he was king, however, he truly appreciated how the wording of a particular law might be misconstrued if not given a precise definition.

When Charlotte was up to it, she helped. Her mastery of writing was most advantageous, and her influence was keenly felt, so much so that on those days when she was coping with another episode, he postponed the work rather than carry on without her input.

On a warm autumn day, Frederick was showing his father a handful of leaves that he'd collected, their brilliant colours a sure sign the season was well underway. Ludwig cherished his moments with his son, yet the responsibility of being king always seemed to cut his time short, and today promised to be no exception as Father Vernan rushed into the room, his breathing laboured, sweat rolling down the sides of his red face.

"Whatever is the matter?" asked Ludwig.

The Holy Father took a moment to try to catch his breath. "The Antonine," he gasped. "They've chosen a new Primus."

"Good for them."

"Perhaps, but not so much for us. I've learned he's a former Temple Knight of Saint Cunar."

"Not Amarand, I hope?"

"No. Someone named Wilmar: at least that's the name he took when he was appointed."

"He changed his name?"

"Is that so strange?" asked Father Vernan. "There are many a king in the Petty Kingdoms who adopted a new name after being crowned."

"I suppose there is, now that I think of it. Has this ever happened before? Choosing a member of a fighting order, I mean."

"Not that I'm aware of. However, custom dictates that upon becoming Primus, the individual gives up membership in their previous sect. However, Temple Knights take oaths of lifetime service, except for Saint Agnes, as they're permitted to leave at any time."

"I don't suppose we know the previous name of this new Primus?"

"I'm afraid not," said Father Vernan. "Although, it's rumoured he served as a Temple General, or was it Father General? I can't quite remember."

"What's the difference?" asked Ludwig.

"Father General is a position rather than a rank and is typically assigned when a portion of the Holy Army goes on campaign."

"Wouldn't that be the Temple General's duty?"

"If the entire Holy Army marched, most certainly, but historically, that seldom happens. There was the Battle of Alantra, which was commanded by Temple General Marius. I believe I mentioned him to you previously. In any case, that has no bearing on this piece of information."

"This doesn't sound like good news for Hadenfeld."

"I don't think it is," said Father Vernan. "It means there's a much greater chance of Temple Commander Amarand bringing our rebuke to the attention of the Council of Peers."

"And would they be inclined to support an action that sought to punish us?"

"I would say so. You must remember, the Primus is elected by the patriarchs of all six orders. Obviously, Primus Wilmar received enough votes to get elected, so it only stands to reason he has the council's support."

"Is his election a lifetime appointment?"

"No. The Primus serves for five years, although it's often the custom for them to continue on for more than one term, should the Council of Peers choose."

"Then perhaps this entire affair will fade into history?"

"I doubt it. Primus Wilmar is relatively young for a Primus, which bodes ill for any thoughts that he might serve only one term."

"Are you saying that age is the only reason a Primus wouldn't be re-elected?"

"Age or physical infirmity. A number died in office over the centuries, but they were all of advanced years."

"People die of disease or sickness all the time," said Ludwig.

"True, but being a former Temple Knight suggests he's still in fine health. It'd be folly to think he might suddenly sicken. I'm afraid we're stuck with him for the time being."

"You don't appear to hold much trust in the Church."

"I'm not enamoured of those high up in the hierarchy, if that's what you mean."

"Are you now doubting your faith?"

"My faith, no, merely my supervisors. Archprior Hywell is a decent fellow, but if you recall, his predecessor made quite the spectacle at Morgan's coronation."

"Yes, I remember. He was bedecked in gold and jewels."

"Not the most fitting attire for an order devoted to humility and modesty. Unfortunately, I've noticed an increase in such displays in the last few years, even amongst my fellow Holy Fathers. It is, I fear, an indication our faith is lessening as personal wealth and comfort increasingly become more prevalent."

"Even amongst the fighting orders?"

"You'd have to ask Temple Captain Hamelyn to be absolutely certain, but I suspect there's little danger of it, considering their strict discipline and adherence to their own rules of conduct."

"Do you think this attitude is limited to the Church, or is it growing amongst the people of the Petty Kingdoms?"

"That's an interesting question," replied Father Vernan. "Certainly, society as a whole has changed significantly since the Church's early days, but I think there've always been those who seek influence and fortune. Even your predecessor flaunted his wealth, though thankfully, you've taken a more modest approach to ruling."

"I could do more."

"You are still a king and, as such, must present an image of strength and power. There is also a fine line between being modest and presenting your-self as a pauper, one which you've navigated quite effectively." He paused a moment. "My apologies, Majesty. We've strayed significantly from the topic of conversation."

"As we often do," replied Ludwig, "but I appreciate the diversion. Now, getting back to this new Primus for a moment, what do you suggest we do?"

"There's little we can do. We both agree that the queen made the right decision in disallowing the building of a commandery. We must pray that Amarand's superiors choose to let the matter rest rather than make things worse. Do you think otherwise?"

"I do. Don't get me wrong, Charlotte made the right decision, but now we must live with the consequences. When was this new Primus named? It couldn't have been because of us, could it?"

"No. The election was held while Amarand was still in Harlingen; it simply took time for the news to reach us. Not long ago, Hadenfeld would've been one of the first realms to hear such news, but I fear our standing amongst the Petty Kingdoms has fallen significantly these last fifty years or so. That's not your fault; it's a problem you inherited when you were crowned king."

"I couldn't care less if Hadenfeld is considered important or not," said Ludwig, "provided my subjects can live in peace."

"Yet you'd march to war if the occasion demanded it."

"Of course! To do otherwise invites our neighbours to take advantage of us."

"Yes, but you've surrounded us with allies. Even Zowenbruch has agreed to keep the peace, thanks to your efforts as prince."

"There's still so much to be done, yet it feels as though we're heading in the right direction. I don't want to merely rule; I want to make things better for my subjects. Is that madness?"

"Not at all," replied Father Vernan. "The actions you've taken so far would make Saint Mathew himself proud were he here."

"Isn't pride a sin?"

"Only when taken to excess. As he once said, 'Take pride in your work even if others fail to see its value but beware the sin of conceit.'"

"I shall endeavour to keep that in mind, going forward."

"I know you will. Now, I've interrupted your time with your son, and for that, I apologize most profusely."

"Thank you for bringing this to me," replied Ludwig. "It's not the greatest of news, I grant you, but at least we're now aware and can prepare accordingly."

"And how do we prepare?"

"By offering prayers that we have enough time to rebuild the army."

14

ENVOY

AUTUMN 1105 - SPRING 1107 SR

Autumn's red leaves were covered by snow early that winter, and the blanket of cold lasted far longer than in past years. The warmth of the spring sun was welcomed by all, and the hustle and bustle of a town coming out of hibernation permeated the city. If trouble was brewing, no sign of it could be seen in Hadenfeld, and life went on, oblivious to what might be happening within the halls of the Antonine.

The scorching heat of summer came early, and with it, news that Mirantha and Hollenbeck had finally located the sky metal. Enquiries were sent off to the Elves of the Goldenwood, and then the matter fell from memory as more important issues demanded Ludwig's attention.

The Temple Knights of Saint Mathew's commandery officially opened that autumn, although much of the interior work was still to be completed. Ludwig and Charlotte toured the building, curious about its layout. Like all commanderies, the Temple Captain's office faced west, towards the Holy City of Herani, while the interior halls had fittings for doors to segregate the building should an enemy gain access to its halls. The doors would be heavily reinforced and capable of being locked, but had yet to be constructed.

The Archprior of Saint Mathew consecrated the building, and then, instead of a feast, everyone was encouraged to donate funds to the Mathewite mission, which helped the sick and poor of Harlingen.

The icy winds of winter came once more, and the kingdom, having prospered from record harvests, ensured that pantries and bellies alike were filled. The work of codifying the laws of Hadenfeld into two volumes had been completed the year before, but the scribes were still labouring to make copies.

By spring, the leader of every town and village across the realm held the law of the land in their hands, and it felt as though a golden age had begun. The kingdom had settled into a time of peace and prosperity.

The arrival of an envoy from the Church in the form of Archprior Ramone reminded everyone that the Antonine had not forgotten them. His carriage befitted that of a king, drawn by six white horses and escorted by twelve Temple Knights of Saint Mathew. He was taken straight to the Temple of Saint Mathew, while news of his arrival was sent to the king.

At first, Ludwig thought to wait outside the keep, greeting His Grace as he exited the carriage, but he rejected that idea, as it would have signified that the kingdom was subservient to the Church of the Saints. To his mind, religion and politics shouldn't mix; they should coexist, one looking after the spiritual needs of the people while the other looks after the physical. Thus, the king found himself waiting in the great hall along with Charlotte and Father Vernan.

"I don't understand," said the queen. "Is this new archprior to replace Father Hywell?"

"If he is, I've had no word of it," replied Father Vernan. "Temple Captain Hamelyn suggested he's come as a special envoy, though to what end, I couldn't tell you."

"Could this have something to do with the Cunars?" asked Ludwig.

"Perhaps, but if that were the case, why send an Archprior of Saint Mathew?"

"Isn't it obvious?" replied Charlotte. "They're aware of our devotion to him. Who better to convince us to reconsider our decision?"

"I suggest we keep an open mind," offered the Holy Father. "Perhaps he's come on a different matter altogether?"

"Do you think that likely?"

"No, but I can hope, can't I?"

From outside came the muted sounds of horses, and then Captain Gustavo entered, announcing the arrival of Archprior Ramone. Guards opened both doors, and a procession of Holy Fathers preceded the entrance of His Grace. Notably absent from the retinue was Archprior Hywell, although this may have been due to an attempt to avoid diverting attention away from his counterpart.

The Holy Fathers assumed positions on either side while an elderly man with receding snow-white hair stepped forward. Archprior Ramone sported the well-trimmed beard common to the Mathewites, but it had thinned, and despite his advanced years, he walked with purpose, pausing some ten paces from Ludwig and Charlotte.

"Majesties," he began, his voice at once both clear and thunderous. "I bring greetings from the Council of Peers and its leader, Primus Wilmar."

"We are honoured by your presence," replied Ludwig. "Though I'm curious about the reason for your visit."

The archprior slowly surveyed those present in the room. "This is, perhaps, something best discussed in private."

"Then let us adjourn to another room where we may talk more openly."

Ludwig rose, offering his arm to Charlotte.

"Our discussion is for the ears of kings," said the archprior.

"My wife and I are joint rulers of Hadenfeld, Your Grace. Thus, she will be present for this discussion."

"As you wish."

"I should also insist on the presence of my spiritual advisor, Father Vernan, in case I require clarification on Church doctrine."

"Understood. I shall rely on my aide, Father Ignacious, to perform a similar role for myself."

Ludwig's gaze settled on the captain of his guard. "Captain Gustavo, I leave it to you to see to our usual precautions."

The captain replied with a bow, "Yes, Majesty."

"This way, Your Grace." Ludwig led them through the hallways of the keep, walking slowly to allow Gustavo time to clear out the servants and post guards at doorways. "I trust your trip was pleasant?"

"Pleasant enough," replied the archprior, "although it was much longer than I'd anticipated. According to the maps we have of the Petty Kingdoms, your eastern border is not far from the Antonine, yet it was impassable, requiring us to travel all the way to the north, through Zowenbruch, to reach you. Do you plan to construct a road to the east?"

"Not at present. The terrain is far too inhospitable." Ludwig neglected to mention that the Elves claimed the area, deciding it was to his advantage to keep their existence secret. Word would eventually get out now that Mirantha was aware of their existence, but he hoped the news had not yet reached those in charge of the Church of the Saints.

They turned a corner to see Gustavo waiting with two guards stationed on either side of a door.

"Is everything ready?" Ludwig asked.

"Yes, sire. All is in order."

"Good man." Ludwig turned back to his guest. "I recruited the captain myself when I was a baron. He's proved a most resourceful individual."

A guard opened the door into what Charlotte liked to call the sunroom, as the afternoon sun illuminated the entire area through the large, west-facing window. On the east side, a bookshelf was stocked with some of her favourite books, but the centrepiece was the fireplace beside the window, warming all against spring's chill.

"Please sit, Your Grace," offered Charlotte. "You, too, Father."

The Antonine's envoys took their seats while Father Vernan moved to the side table to pour drinks. Ludwig then sat, Charlotte taking the chair to his right. They sipped their drinks, waiting for someone to break the silence.

The archprior cleared his throat. "As I'm certain you've been informed, Majesty, Temple Knights visited Harlingen, seeking to build a commandery."

"Yes," replied Ludwig, "and this permission was granted."

"It was?"

"Yes. Captain Hamelyn took possession of it late last year."

"Captain Hamelyn?"

"Yes," said Father Vernan. "Or rather, Temple Captain."

"Of Saint Cunar?"

"Saints, no—of Saint Mathew."

"The good father is correct," added Ludwig. "The queen and I both attended its dedication."

"That is not the commandery to which I was referring," replied the arch-prior. "You were, I believe, offered the honour of hosting a commandery of the Temple Knights of Saint Cunar."

"We were, but we declined the honour."

"May I ask why?"

"We have no need for them in Hadenfeld."

"But you allowed a Mathewite commandery."

"Their dedication to bettering the lives of the sick and poor is renowned throughout the Petty Kingdoms."

"The Cunars are the preeminent fighting order of the Church. Their mere presence acts as a deterrent to those who seek to make war upon your realm."

"With all due respect, Your Grace, their presence has done little to lessen the threat of war, largely due, no doubt, to the Antonine's official refusal to intervene in secular matters. Taking that into account, I see no reason why the presence of a company here would be of any benefit."

"I urge you to reconsider, Majesty. Your refusal to allow them to build here has come to the Council of Peers' attention. Many have taken it as an affront to the very Church they serve so diligently. This refusal, on your part, could lead to dire consequences."

Ludwig took a sip of his wine, trying to project an air of confidence. Sitting here, listening to a lecture wasn't easy, but to back down now would be akin to prostrating himself before the Church, something a king should never do. "You speak of consequences, Your Grace. To my mind, that sounds remarkably like a threat."

"I am not your enemy, Majesty. Merely a friendly face bringing distasteful news. Submit to the will of the Church, and all is forgiven."

"I would've expected an Archprior of Saint Mathew to be more under-standing, but I see I'm mistaken." Ludwig set down his drink. "Let me make this perfectly clear, Your Grace. Hadenfeld refuses to condone the presence of Temple Knights of Saint Cunar anywhere in Hadenfeld."

"Even to guard the Temple of Saint Cunar?"

"That task is performed admirably by those of Saint Mathew, as I'm certain you're already aware."

The senior Church official took a sip of his wine before voicing his response. "I don't understand your reasoning, Majesty. It's not as if it would cost you anything. Any other kingdom would be proud to have such knights nearby."

"Any other kingdom? How do you think Arnsfeld feels about that claim? The Cunars' abandonment of that realm led directly to a Halvarian inva-sion, and that's not including their attempts to prevent the Agnesites from taking up the duty in their absence."

"I'd be careful of your next words, Majesty. You are close to insulting the Church."

"I hold no quarrel with the Church," replied Ludwig, "only the Temple Knights of Saint Cunar."

"Yet you maligned the entire institution. Continue in this manner, and you will leave us no choice but to punish your kingdom."

Charlotte placed a hand on Ludwig's arm while keeping her gaze on the archprior. "Am I to understand that unless we allow this Cunar comman-dery, the Church of the Saints will punish us?"

"That is correct, madam."

"That's Majesty," corrected Ludwig, standing. "This meeting has come to an end. As to your threats, they hold no weight here. Build more comman-deries for Saint Mathew if you wish, or even Saint Agnes, but as I said earlier, we will not permit the presence of Temple Knights of Saint Cunar under any circumstances. If that results in us being censured, then so be it."

"I beg you to reconsider, Majesty. Do you fully understand the conse-quences of such a statement?"

"Yes. Do you?"

Archprior Ramone shook his head. "I'm sorry that we have reached such an impasse, but I thank you all the same for at least having the decency to hear me out. I shall return to the Antonine with your response, although I fear it will not be taken lightly."

"I understand."

"May the Saints watch over you both, Majesties."

"And you, Your Grace. Captain Gustavo?"

The door opened. "Yes, Majesty?"

"You may escort our guests from the premises."

"This way, Your Grace."

Their footsteps echoed down the hall as the door closed.

Ludwig sat back in his chair. "I can't say I'm surprised at how that went, all things considered."

"At least we managed to keep it civil," noted Charlotte, "but I fear it won't continue in that manner much longer. Doubtless, Archprior Ramone will return to the Antonine with all haste. The only question remaining is how long before they act."

"For once, geography is on our side," mused Father Vernan. "It'll take more than a month for him to reach the Council of Peers, and then they'll have to discuss the matter. I expect it will be several months before we hear back, but when we do, it'll be a hammer rather than a few words."

"Surely you're not suggesting they'd invade?"

"I was speaking metaphorically. They're far more likely to order us Holy Fathers to cease performing ceremonies as a method of punishment. That, in turn, creates ill will between the people of Hadenfeld and you, their rulers. It's a way of applying pressure without resorting to war. Of course, this is mere speculation on my part."

"I fear it may come to more than that," replied Ludwig. "The Cunars are a fighting order; they could choose to take to the field of battle."

"If that happens, we're doomed," said Charlotte. "They're the fiercest knights in all the Petty Kingdoms."

A hurried call went out to Ludwig's advisors. Lord Merrick, who was at his home in Drakenfeld, was the last to arrive two weeks after the summons. He joined Gita, who'd remained in the capital, along with Lord Emmett and Lady Alexandra, who'd arrived earlier.

Sigwulf and Cyn were there, along with Ludwig and Charlotte, but surprisingly, Lord Darrian Forst, the Baron of Glosnecke, had been included in the invitations.

Ludwig, having just relayed the details of the archprior's visit, looked around the table. "Thoughts?"

"We need to prepare for war, boss," replied Cyn. "I know what you're all thinking, and yes, I realize going up against the Cunars is a tall order, but what choice do we have? We can't let them march unopposed into Hadenfeld."

"I agree," added Sigwulf.

"What is the current state of the treasury?" asked Ludwig.

Gita consulted her notes. "There's enough in the coffers, providing we don't intend to keep the war going for months on end."

"How many months?"

"That depends on how large an army you want to support."

"Our current size is a thousand men under arms," offered Cyn, "which doesn't include the Temple Knights of Saint Mathew. We can also rely on Mirantha and Hollenbeck to send men, providing we give them enough advanced warning, and then there's the Elves."

"That sounds promising," said Charlotte. "How many men can we expect from our southern neighbours?"

"Two hundred each, although, now I think of it, we neglected to specify what warriors they'd send."

"And the Elves?"

"Five hundred," replied Cyn.

"Will that be enough to stop a Holy Army from rampaging through the kingdom?"

"I doubt it," said Ludwig, "and we need to consider that Mirantha and Hollenbeck might not send men if they know we're fighting Temple Knights. We must increase our numbers to compensate."

"I agree," said Cyn, "but it takes time to train them."

"I'd like to see at least two more companies of cavalry, along with another four of foot. Is that something we can do reasonably fast?" He asked this of Lord Darrian.

"The Royal Stables can supply enough horses, provided you approve the purchase of additional mounts from Jurgen. The cavalry will, however, require some training if we rely on new recruits."

"Is that a problem, Cyn?"

"Not at all. If you recall, when we reduced our army after the war, we provided those we dismissed with a letter documenting their service and promised they'd be the first we contacted when we increased our numbers. Admittedly, it's been two years, but I imagine enough would be willing to return."

"And the mounted troops?"

"That's easier than you might think," offered Merrick. "Now that the barons support fewer companies of their own, many of their warriors are looking for employment, including some cavalry. I imagine a few weeks under the tutelage of the Temple Knights would quickly whip them into shape."

"I shall approach Temple Captain Hamelyn about it," offered Sig.

"We're a little short of archers," said Cyn. "Unfortunately, they're harder to replace."

"Why is that?" asked Alexandra.

"Footmen can be trained in a relatively short time, but it takes years to master the art of the bow."

"That's interesting," remarked Charlotte. "Perhaps we should take steps to encourage more archers in future?"

"What do you have in mind?" asked Ludwig.

"The Crown should purchase bows and arrows and distribute them across the villages and towns of Hadenfeld. We then promote their use through sponsoring archery tournaments. I realize this doesn't meet our short-term goals, but it lays out a foundation upon which we can build in the coming years."

"There are always crossbows," offered Merrick.

"Crossbows have their advantages," replied Ludwig, "as they're relatively easy to use, but they're not as versatile as bows."

"How so?"

"They take much longer to reload. Also, being mechanical devices, they require care to maintain them."

"So do bows."

"True, but a person using a bow has learned how to care for their weapon over years of use. Those armed with crossbows are typically lacking in such experience. Crossbows are also more difficult to produce; I'm not aware of anyone in Hadenfeld who can make them."

"I'll look into it," offered Sigwulf, "if only for emergencies."

"A good idea. It wouldn't hurt to keep a company or two in reserve."

"Actually," said Cyn, "they'd be handy for manning the walls of Harlingen, thus freeing up bowmen to accompany the army."

"I like that," said Charlotte. "We can form a group of reserve archers for just such a purpose. In the north, we call them a militia, although I believe the Old Kingdom used to call them a fyrd."

"The fyrd included footmen," added Ludwig. "That would also benefit us. We'll authorize the raising of a reserve militia for the purpose of freeing up our regular army to march when the time comes."

"If the time comes," said Merrick.

"I pray you're proven right, but in the meantime, we'll prepare for the worst. Let's start recalling what warriors we can. I want them trained and ready by summer."

15

TROUBLE IN THE EAST
SUMMER 1107 SR

Charlotte tossed and turned, sweat pouring off her to soak the sheets while her unfocused eyes darted around at an alarming rate.

Kandam felt her forehead. "I cannot explain it, sire. I've done all I can to heal her, but still, she thrashes around."

Ludwig held her hand in his. "Is there nothing we can do to help her?"

"I've sent word to Nethendril in the hopes that Galrandir might be able to do something, but I fear it will take him weeks to receive the message and return."

"She's been bedridden for three days. Has she kept any food down?"

"We're feeding her broth, as her stomach tolerates little else. Shall I give her some seaflower to help her sleep?"

Ludwig nodded, too overcome with emotion to speak any further. Although his marriage to Charlotte had been arranged, he'd come to love her deeply. Now, the thought of losing her threatened to overwhelm him.

Kandam reached for a small wooden bowl that contained a pale-green powder. "This is a temporary solution, Majesty, and I can only use it a few more times before she becomes dependent on it."

A hand rested on Ludwig's shoulder. "Come," said Father Vernan. "Let Kandam look after her; you need to rest as much as she does. Gita will keep an eye on her."

The Holy Father led the distraught king from the room. Ludwig was in a daze, unable to think of anything except the possibility he might lose his wife. Vernan brought him to the dining hall where his advisors all sat, save for Gita.

"Have we any news?" asked Alexandra.

"I'm afraid not," replied Father Vernan. "Kandam is doing all he can, but there is little change."

"That is most worrisome. How did she become sick?"

"We're not certain. She'd taken to bed due to one of her episodes, not an unusual occurrence, but when Liesel went to check on her, she found the queen tossing and turning. The sweating began shortly thereafter. That was three days ago, and we've yet to see any change despite Kandam's ministrations."

"Could it be poison?" asked Ludwig.

Everyone turned to him, for he suddenly looked alert despite his obviously exhausted state.

"Poison?" said Father Vernan. "I'd think that highly improbable. More than likely, it's a disease."

"I disagree," said Alexandra. "If that were so, why are none of us affected?"

Kandam stepped into the room. "The queen is sleeping," he said, "but I'm still at a loss to explain this malady."

"The king suspects it may be poison."

"I hadn't considered that. My training at the hands of Galrandir primarily concentrated on healing the flesh, not the effects of poison."

"If it were a poison," said Ludwig, "how would it have been administered?"

"That's difficult to say. I'm not an expert by any means, but the most common method would be ingestion, yet she hasn't eaten much these last few days."

"Perhaps it was inhaled?" offered Father Vernan. "I've heard that ground seaflower can be administered in such a manner."

"It can, but it only induces sleep, not these strange symptoms the queen is experiencing. One thing's for certain: if it is a poison, it has a strong hold on her. From what I know, if a poison doesn't kill outright, its symptoms usually vanish over a couple of days at most. This continues unabated."

"Could her condition be due to the application of magic?"

Kandam bristled. "I am a Life Mage. I would never hurt the queen!"

"My dear fellow," continued Father Vernan, "I'm not suggesting it was you. Rather, I'm putting forward the idea that someone used magic to afflict the queen. Perhaps there's a Necromancer somewhere in Harlingen or a Hex Mage?"

"We must consider every possibility," said Ludwig. "If such an individual were in the city, could they affect Charlotte without us knowing?"

"I doubt it," said Kandam. "One of the basic rules of magic is that a caster must be able to see their target."

"Yes, but aren't there spells that allow mages to view things from a great distance?"

"Yes, for some schools of magic. They refer to it as scrying."

"Is there any way to detect if someone was being scryed upon?" asked Alexandra.

"I know of a universal spell that can detect the presence of magic, but one must cast it while the scrying is in progress. Unfortunately, while I'm aware of it, it's not in my repertoire."

"So we can't dismiss the possibility entirely?"

"No."

"That's a fine conjecture," noted Father Vernan, "but even if it were true, how would we find such an individual? We knock on everyone's door and ask if they have a Necromancer in the house?"

Alexandra suddenly sat up straight in her chair. "Perhaps we don't have to."

All eyes turned to her.

"The list," she said.

"What list?" asked Father Vernan.

"Majesty, if you recall, Temple Captain Hamelyn had a list of names."

"Yes. That's right," said Ludwig. "The people whom Temple Commander Amarand visited before he left Harlingen."

Captain Gustavo, who was standing near the door, stepped forward. "Shall I go and arrest them, sire?"

"No, but it's a good place to start. Send men to pay them a visit and see if we can't connect someone to the staff here at the Royal Keep."

"So we're not looking for Necromancers?"

"I doubt a Death Mage would look any different from a normal person. Let's assume, for now, at least, that poison is responsible, and if one of these people is behind it, they would've needed some way to administer it. The most logical conclusion would be by coercing someone inside the keep's walls."

"Coercing?"

"Yes," replied Ludwig. "Bribe, compromise, or even threaten in some manner."

"Could it be the same person who passed on information to Temple Commander Amarand?"

"It's quite possible, but how would we find the one responsible?"

"I could have my guards make some enquiries of our staff as well; perhaps someone saw something suspicious?"

"It's worth a try," said Ludwig. "Have your men begin their questioning. Let's hope they can get to the bottom of this mystery."

Gustavo left, calling for guards even as he went through the doorway.

"There's something else that's bothering me," said Alexandra. "Why now?"

"What do you mean?" asked Ludwig.

"Well, Charlotte is loved by everyone. The only person who might bear her a grudge is that Cunar Temple Commander, and he's been gone for nigh on two years. That's a long time to wait to exact revenge, wouldn't you say?"

"Perhaps the poisoning was an accident?" mused Father Vernan. "By that, I mean she wasn't the intended target? I'm certain there are still some who oppose your reign, Majesty."

Captain Paran appeared at the door, clutching a scroll. He moved with some haste to stand before the king. "This just arrived, sire, from Nethendril."

Ludwig examined the seal, which featured the image of the Goldenwood surmounted by a crown, the mark of the ruling house of the Elves. He read through the contents while everyone watched with bated breath. "The Goldenwood is calling for aid. They've spotted a force of horsemen coming from the east. High Lord Sindra bids us muster the army and march for Tongrin with all haste."

"Tongrin?" said Sigwulf. "I would've thought Eisen more likely."

"We know so little about the Goldenwood's borders, but we did learn about the existence of Elandril, even if we don't know its precise location. I suspect that city is threatened, and Tongrin allows us to get closer to the general area without entering the Goldenwood."

"Have we any idea of who's come to fight the Elves? I thought we were the only ones who knew of their existence?"

"We were," said Ludwig, "but Mirantha and Hollenbeck both learned about them, so word has probably spread to the surrounding realms. The tone of this letter, however, indicates the High Lord isn't afraid for her own sake. I get the impression she thinks this army is coming for Hadenfeld."

"We must march at once," said Merrick.

"I can't," said Ludwig. "I need to remain here with Charlotte."

"Don't worry, boss," said Cyn. "Siggy and I can march the army to Tongrin."

"How soon can you leave?"

"It'll take a day or two to gather supplies for the march, but we'll send some cavalry on ahead."

"Are you certain that's wise?" said Father Vernan. "We have no idea what this army consists of. What if the Cunars are coming to take their revenge?" Everyone looked at him in disbelief. "Is that so far-fetched?" he asked.

"What lies to the east? I'll tell you what: the Antonine, where sits the Holy Army."

"Why march through the forest?" asked Lord Emmett. "Surely it makes more sense to come through Zowenbruch or even Mirantha?"

"Because coming at us through that great forest is the last thing we'd expect. We have a defensive pact with Mirantha and Hollenbeck, as well as an understanding with Zowenbruch. They'd have a hard time marching through those kingdoms without risking us hearing about it."

Ludwig beckoned to one of the guards. "I must write a reply; be so kind as to fetch me what I need."

"Yes, Majesty." The guard left, heading for Ludwig's office.

"I'll send a reply assuring High Lord Sindra that the army will march. Paran, I should like you to have a dispatch rider standing by to carry it."

"Yes, Majesty."

"Sig, Cyn, you two see to the mustering of the army. Gita, you go with them. They'll need funds from the treasury to speed things along."

"What can I do to help?" asked Father Vernan.

"Pray that we're able to stop this invasion."

Ludwig fretted as he sat on his horse, watching the Army of Hadenfeld march out of the city through the eastern gate, the shortest distance to Tongrin.

Since meeting with his advisors in the spring, the Royal Army had been increased to thirteen hundred souls, all of whom now marched to war, with Sigwulf leading them and Cyn as his second-in-command. Ludwig wanted to command the army himself, but Charlotte needed him, so he must trust his closest friends to do what was required.

"A formidable force."

The voice broke him from his musings, and he turned to see Temple Captain Hamelyn. "I'm surprised that you're here. I was led to believe your knights would remain in their commandery."

"And so they shall, and I'm not going either. It wouldn't be right for two orders of Temple Knights to face off against each other."

"We don't know for sure that it's a Holy Army."

"It's the only thing that makes sense." The Temple Captain shifted uncomfortably in the saddle. "There's something I should tell you."

"Go on."

"A dispatch rider arrived today from the Antonine."

"And?"

"There's no easy way to say this; the Council of Peers has branded you a heretic, or rather, Hadenfeld. I'm afraid it's only a matter of time before they declare a crusade."

"And when they do, will you fight alongside them?" asked Ludwig.

"I shall bear no arms against you, Majesty, nor will the men of my order."

"But you won't assist us; is that it?"

"That largely depends on what the archprior decides."

"The last I heard, you took your orders from a regional commander, not the archprior."

"That's true," said Hamelyn, "but our primary purpose is to guard the temples of the Saints. If Archprior Hywell decides to withdraw his people from Hadenfeld, I'd have no choice but to accompany them."

Ludwig sensed a dark cloud gathering over the kingdom, one that might well spell the end of Hadenfeld as he knew it. "Tell me what it means to be named heretical? Does that carry a death sentence? Are they going to slay everyone here or only the ruling class?"

"Theoretically, only those who refuse to acknowledge the Saints."

"You and I both know many commoners who worship the Saints in public but pray to the Old Gods in times of need. Are they to be sacrificed in the name of a Holy War?"

"I have no doubt that should a crusade be declared, many will die. Please don't make the mistake of believing I support the idea." The knight shook his head. "I don't. I'm merely trying to present you with the facts as I know them."

"I appreciate your honesty. I don't suppose you'd be willing to tell me how large this Holy Army of yours is?"

"I have no idea. The Cunars form the heart of any crusade, but they'll be supplemented by volunteers from across the Petty Kingdoms. Have you heard of the Battle of the Wilderness?"

"I have, although I know few details. Why?"

"At that battle, the crusade consisted of seven hundred Temple Knights, two hundred of which were on foot."

"On foot? That's strange, isn't it?"

"No," replied Hamelyn. "Unlike the other orders, those who join the Cunars are already knights. For the first year of their service, they serve on foot as a mark of their devotion to the cause."

"Seven hundred doesn't sound so bad."

"With all due respect, Majesty, I wasn't finished. They were assisted by an equal number of volunteers who came from across the Petty Kingdoms."

"Were they to field the same numbers in Hadenfeld, we'd find ourselves outnumbered."

"Your saving grace is the cities of Eisen and Harlingen, which are both walled and command strategic locations. You also have your Elven allies, giving you a slight numerical advantage, but that only holds true if the Cunars field similar numbers to the last crusade."

"Not the most encouraging of news."

"When I joined the order, I took an oath to always tell the truth."

"I appreciate that," said Ludwig. "Your order also helped me claim the Throne of Hadenfeld, so I'm thankful for that as well. I just wish the news were better."

"At least you now know that they're coming."

"True. When did they make this decision branding us heretics?"

"In the spring."

"If they're like us, it would take them a while to amass an army."

"Even more so," offered Hamelyn. "The normal practice when announcing a crusade is to spread the word to all the Petty Kingdoms, asking for volunteers. The Temple Knights of Saint Cunar are fine mounted warriors, but they still need archers and foot troops to carry out a campaign."

Ludwig considered the Temple Captain's words. They made perfect sense, for what army would march without foot, horse, and bow? It suddenly struck him that perhaps that was the weakness of any Holy Army. "Tell me what you know of the Battle of the Wilderness."

"The Holy Army marched to the east of Ebenstadt to pacify the region. They claimed the easterners were causing trouble in Ebenstadt. They called a crusade, and warriors from across the Petty Kingdoms gathered in Ebenstadt, under the command of the Duke of Erlingen."

"Lord Deiter? I fought alongside him back in ninety-five."

"Unfortunately, he died in the battle, while the Cunars fought to the last man, refusing to surrender. Those of the duke's forces who survived told us what we know about the battle, but I'm afraid it makes for a confusing account."

"You seem to know a bit about it."

"We Temple Knights try to learn from every battle, even a loss. Not that my order was involved, you understand. In fact, our grand master objected most strenuously to the idea of the crusade, which led to an entirely different matter."

"That being?" said Ludwig.

"Crusades can only be declared by the Council of Peers."

"Are you suggesting the crusade was unsanctioned?"

"So it would appear," replied Hamelyn. "Unfortunately, that has little bearing on Hadenfeld's current predicament."

"You've given me much to consider."

"I'm merely attempting to clarify what you're facing. Were it my choice, my men would stand beside you."

"Even against a fellow fighting order?"

"I've suspected for a while now that the Temple Knights of Saint Cunar have strayed from their original purpose. They are meant to lead the Holy Army in times of war, but of what use is that when all they do is wage crusades to punish unbelievers? They should stand shoulder to shoulder with the Petty Kingdoms and face the threat of the Halvarian Empire together." The Temple Captain took a cleansing breath. "Sorry, Majesty. I didn't mean to lose my composure."

"Understandable, given the circumstances," replied Ludwig. "Have you any theories when this change in policy originally came about?"

"The Church has always been careful to stay out of regional conflicts, and I understand why. War is so commonplace in the Petty Kingdoms that if the Antonine became involved, it could cause a lot of ill will."

"Yet the very presence of the Cunars has supposedly held the empire at bay for decades."

"That is the general belief. The threat of them marching to a kingdom's defence is, I think, the reason the empire expands by conquering one realm at a time."

"So that by the time the Cunars react, the war would be over?"

"Precisely, but their active interference in Arnsfeld is very troubling and indicates some within their order support Halvaria."

"And now," noted Ludwig, "due to the actions of one of their Temple Commanders, it appears we in Hadenfeld must fear the full power of their order."

"Not only the order, the entire Church. I might remind you that the Council of Peers approved the motion to declare you heretical." Hamelyn shook his head. "The Church has lost its way. The people of Hadenfeld are faithful in their devotion to the Saints; this manipulation of the council has another agenda, but for the life of me, I can't see what it is."

"I can," replied Ludwig. "They want to crush our army so it can't be used to repel the empire when it comes."

16

TEMPLE GENERAL

SUMMER 1107 SR

Ludwig paced, his mind in turmoil. Time dragged on, and still, Charlotte sweated, tossing and turning to no end. Kandam had tried everything, including consulting a local herbalist to enquire if there was a plant that might offer some relief, but nothing came of it.

Weeks passed, and while Charlotte could keep down broth, she'd grown thin and gaunt. He began to wonder if she'd survive the month.

Yelling came from outside the window, but he paid it no heed, his thoughts consumed by the imminent loss of his wife.

Footsteps approached, and then the door to the queen's chamber swung open, and Cyn, along with another woman dressed in white, entered.

"Who is this?" asked Ludwig.

"My name is Temple Captain Teresa," the woman replied. "Cynthia tells me the queen is ill. I've come to offer my services."

"I don't understand."

"She's a Sister of Mercy," offered Cyn. "A Life Mage."

"So is Kandam, and he's been unable to cure her."

"Your pardon, Majesty," said Teresa, "but from what I've been told, he lacks my experience." She looked down at Charlotte. "May I examine the patient?"

Ludwig nodded, and she moved closer, feeling Charlotte's forehead, then forcing the queen's eyelids open to peer into her eyes. "How long has she been like this?"

"Three weeks or so," replied Kandam. "She's taken broth for sustenance, but I've had to resort to powdered seaflower to allow her some measure of respite."

"We suspect it's the result of poison," added Ludwig, "but we've been unable to identify it."

"If it's truly poison," said Teresa, "I have a spell that would remedy her condition. Would you permit me to cast it?"

"Most certainly."

She closed her eyes, soft words issuing from her lips as the air surrounding her buzzed. A faint blue light glowed from her hands as the litany of magical incantations continued. The glowing increased in intensity, bathing the room in its soft light. Teresa abruptly fell silent and placed her hands on Charlotte's stomach, the colour draining from her into the queen, causing her to glow. It was a strange sight, for as her skin returned to its normal hue, the bones beneath still glowed, revealing Charlotte's skeleton. Once this, too, paled, the queen ceased all movement.

Ludwig caught his breath, fearing the worst. The Temple Captain reached for Charlotte's wrist, feeling for a pulse. "This is no ordinary poison. Has she been moved since she fell ill?"

"No. She's been here the entire time. Why?"

"There is a force at work here which defies logic."

Ludwig struggled to make sense of her words, finding it difficult to even think. "Can you cure her or not?" he snapped.

"Prepare another bed," said Teresa, "and ensure one of you watches the servants prepare it. Once you've moved her, seal this chamber. No one is to enter until I'm finished with it."

"Are you suggesting it's something to do with this room?"

"Is this her normal bed chamber?"

"Yes," replied Ludwig. "We share it."

"You haven't slept here since she fell ill, have you?"

"How did you know that?"

"I suspect that if you had, you would've fallen prey to this same sickness."

"Who sent you?"

"The Temple General of Saint Agnes."

"Temple General?"

"Yes, boss," said Cyn. "Charlaine."

Ludwig nodded at Gustavo. "Do as she says."

"At once, my lady," said the captain.

"Sister will do, or Temple Captain. Now, you'll need a couple of your men to move the queen, and be quick about it."

"I'll carry her," said Ludwig.

"With all due respect, Majesty, you're too weak. Have you even slept?"

"A little."

"Then the good captain here will have to suffice."

Gustavo moved up beside the bed and waited as a maid pulled back the sheets. He then lifted the queen as if she weighed nothing and carried her from the room.

Ludwig awoke to someone prodding him. He'd fallen asleep in the sunroom while waiting for news. The woman in white stood before him, her face filled with concern as he struggled to recall her name.

"The queen is recovering nicely," she said.

"You were able to cure her completely?"

"I was, although it will be a while before she's back to full health. You were lucky I arrived when I did; another day or two, and it might've been too late."

"I still don't understand what happened," said Ludwig. "Was she poisoned or not?"

"She was most definitely poisoned, although not by her food."

"Then how?"

"That, I've yet to determine, but I suspect the source is somewhere in that room." She stared at him for a moment. "You don't remember me, do you?"

"You must forgive me. I've been consumed by my wife's ill health."

"My name is Sister Teresa... Sorry, Temple Captain Teresa. I'm still getting used to that. I'm with the Five Hundred."

"Five hundred?"

"Ah, yes. I suppose there's an explanation due, but I'm not the one best equipped to do so. Charlaine can do that once she arrives."

"Charlaine is coming here?"

"Yes. Our forces met your army as we left the Goldenwood. General Hoffman informed me of the queen's malady, so she and I rode for Harlingen while your other general saw to the garrisoning of the troops."

"What troops? What's this all about? Sigwulf took the army east to deal with the Holy Army."

"Except it wasn't the Holy Army; it was us, five hundred Temple Knights of Saint Agnes."

"So we're not being invaded?"

"Not at present, although after all that's happened, I'm afraid that may be inevitable."

Cyn came through the door. "How you doing, boss? Feeling better now that you've had some sleep?"

"Yes, thank you. Although I'm still struggling to understand how five hundred Temple Knights suddenly ended up in eastern Hadenfeld. Where are they?"

"Siggy's taking them to Eisen for the time being."

"I remember someone telling me Charlaine was a Temple General?"

"Yes," replied Cyn. "That was me. She should be arriving here soon, along with her second-in-command. Siggy will remain in Eisen until he hears from you."

Ludwig stood, then stretched, using his hands to support his back. "My apologies. That chair is most uncomfortable."

"That's because it's made for sitting, not sleeping."

"Yes. Thank you, Cyn. I never would've guessed."

"That's what I'm here for, boss."

Ludwig turned to Teresa. "I owe you a great debt. However shall I reward you?"

"I'm rewarded by the knowledge that I was able to help a person in need. That's thanks enough."

"I seem to recall the term Sisters of Mercy being used. Is that a new order?"

"No, merely a new category of Temple Knights. I'm determined to teach some of my fellow sisters Life Magic, if I can find any who have the potential."

"May I ask where you learned your magic?"

"I was taught by Master Gwalinor, an Elven Life Mage of great learning."

"Yet you're a member of the Temple Knights of Saint Agnes."

"I was, and am again, but for many years, I was lost to the order."

"How so?"

"I was severely wounded at the Battle of Alantra, so Master Gwalinor brought me back to Eloria, the Island of the Sea Elves, to oversee my recovery. There, I learned the art of healing magic. Years later, I left to return to the Antonine."

"So you now serve the Church?"

"I serve the Order of Saint Agnes, but I'll let the Temple General explain that once she arrives."

Charlaine entered the great hall three days later, her plate armour covered by a scarlet surcoat bearing the three waves of Saint Agnes in gold thread, denoting her as a Temple Commander. However, a blue sash was slung over one shoulder, a mark of distinction that made her stand out from her companion, whose surcoat was adorned with silver-threaded waves.

Ludwig, sitting beside his nearly recovered wife, caught his breath as Captain Gustavo escorted the visitors into the room, his guards on either side, just as they'd been for Temple Commander Amarand. It was strange to see her here in Harlingen. He'd loved her once, still did in some measure, but the distance between them had served to temper those feelings. No longer did he harbour a passion for her; instead, he felt the warm glow of friendship, of their shared fight against the empire's influence.

Charlaine went down on one knee, same as the Cunar had, and for a moment, Ludwig worried that she was bringing another ultimatum from the Church. "Your Majesties," she began. "I come to you today to ask for sanctuary."

"From whom?" asked Charlotte.

"The Antonine."

"So you're not here at the behest of the Church?"

"No, Majesty. The Temple Knights of Saint Agnes were ordered disbanded by the Council of Peers. Instead of surrendering our weapons, we fled and came here to Hadenfeld, in the hopes of finding a place of safety."

"We are glad to see you," replied Ludwig, "and I welcome you and your sister knights to our realm, but if it's safety you seek, I'm afraid you've come to the wrong place."

The queen leaned over and whispered to her husband. "We have much to discuss with them. Should we not meet in more secure surroundings?"

Ludwig nodded, and the queen continued. "It pleases us to see you again," she said, rising from her throne and moving to stand directly in front of Charlaine. "I shall be ever thankful to you for the kindness you showed me back in Reinwick. Let us leave this room and talk of recent developments in more comfortable surroundings." She paused, looking at the woman beside Charlaine. "Would you do me the honour of introducing your companion?"

"This is Temple Captain Nicola, my aide. Since you appear to be free of your affliction, I assume you've already met with Temple Captain Teresa?"

"We have. Now, let's find you some refreshment. You must be parched after such a long ride." Charlotte nodded at Captain Gustavo, who went ahead with a few guards to prepare the room for visitors. "You must pardon our eagerness; much has happened of late, and we feared you were an invasion sent from the Antonine. Learning your order had travelled through the Goldenwood came as quite a shock."

"Did Teresa not tell you our story?"

"No, only her own. She thought it best you be the one to inform us of what you've been through."

Charlotte moved slowly, supporting herself on Charlaine's arm as they walked to the sunroom. Ludwig followed behind, alongside Temple Captain Nicola. They soon arrived to find Gustavo's men guarding the door.

"All set, boss," Cyn said through the open door, then motioned for them to step inside. A Royal Guardsman poured wine into goblets and passed them around as everyone took their seats.

"General Marhaven filled me in on recent events," began Charlaine, "but doubtless you're wondering what circumstances could've forced us to march here to Hadenfeld."

"The thought had crossed my mind," replied Ludwig.

"It's a complicated story, but I'll try to keep it as simple as possible. Shortly after I last wrote, Danica and I were ordered to the Antonine, where we heard rumours of a plan to amalgamate the fighting orders under the single command of the Cunars. That might have been acceptable to some of the other orders, but the Cunars' rules against women serving meant the disbandment of our own. Then, a new Primus was elected."

"Yes, we heard about that," said Charlotte. "A former Temple Commander of Saint Cunar."

"While in the Antonine, we learned that he was an agent of the Halvarian Empire. Unfortunately, it was too late to do anything about it. Shortly afterwards, we were ordered to lay down our weapons and submit to the Temple Knights of Saint Cunar. Needless to say, we refused."

"And now you're a Temple General?"

"That came about out of necessity. To ensure the order's survival, the grand mistress needed someone she could trust to lead them. You see, only the Matriarch of Saint Agnes can appoint or remove a grand mistress, but the rank of Temple General is a lifetime position."

Ludwig nodded. "She named you general to ensure no one could outrank you."

"Correct."

"Clever," said Cyn, "but couldn't the matriarch simply appoint a new grand mistress?"

"In theory, yes, but the Antonine had disbanded our order, so there'd be no need. The last grand mistress gave me specific instructions to do whatever was necessary to keep my fellow sister knights safe. When we learned that the Council of Peers had ruled against you, I realized you'd need allies, so I came here seeking refuge rather than risk another kingdom with closer ties to the Church. I know I'm asking a lot, but if it makes it any easier, you can turn me over to the Antonine, providing you allow my fellow sister knights to remain here in Hadenfeld."

"We will gladly grant you and your fellow knights refuge," said Ludwig, "but you may have to fight the Church to preserve your order. We are expecting a Holy Army to march on us at any time."

"Then, with your permission, we shall fight by your side."

"Temple Captain Teresa mentioned the Five Hundred. I assume that's how many knights you brought with you when you fled?"

"Yes, although we took some casualties along the way."

"Five hundred knights will require a significant amount of resources to maintain."

"I'll have them surrender their arms and leave the order if you'd prefer."

"We would not prefer," said Charlotte. "Five hundred trained Temple Knights is a force to be reckoned with and a valuable addition to the Army of Hadenfeld."

"True," added Ludwig, "but the cost involved is substantial."

"What about Eisen?" suggested Cyn. "You've never been able to make up your mind about what to do with it."

"It appears the Saints have provided," replied Ludwig. "I have an offer for you, Charlaine. I'll make your group the caretakers of Eisen. As such, you'll collect taxes to be used for the maintenance of your order and for the betterment of the city. In exchange, your knights will swear to defend Hadenfeld alongside the Royal Army."

"Do you mean to put us under its command?" asked Charlaine.

"No. You shall retain command of your own knights at all times, but I expect you to cooperate with the Army of Hadenfeld whenever possible."

"Then I accept your offer."

"I shall have Father Vernan draw up the agreement tomorrow."

"There is more," said Charlaine. "Once word gets out that we've found refuge in Hadenfeld, others may come, swelling our numbers. Am I to turn them away?"

"I assume, as Temple General, you will be in communication with those companies spread across the Petty Kingdoms?"

"Eventually. At least that is my intention."

"Then you may inform them that those who seek refuge will find it here in Hadenfeld. That's assuming a Holy Crusade doesn't wipe us off the Continent before they arrive."

"Thank you. You've done much to ease my mind."

"I suppose we must now decide the next steps."

"I have an idea," said Charlotte. "In essence, your order will be acting as a barony, or perhaps a free city would be a better comparison. You used to live in Malburg, if I'm not mistaken."

"That is correct," replied Charlaine.

"Then it's only proper you maintain a presence here at court. Say, a small detachment under one of your Temple Captains? We, in turn, will supply a Royal Advisor to Eisen to assist you in ruling over the city. Additionally, we'll continue to supply magistrates and other administrative personnel necessary to oversee the city. Your order, however, would be responsible for patrolling the streets and the surrounding area."

"You're also close to Nethendril," added Ludwig, "so we should arrange for an Elven advisor as well. I trust you have no issue dealing with Elves? You did, after all, fight alongside them at the Battle of the Brinwald."

"I have no objection," replied Charlaine.

"Good. Then it's settled." Ludwig fell silent for a moment. "I'm very sorry for the loss of your father. He was a good man."

"Though his loss was keenly felt, I know in my heart that he died fighting for what he believed in."

"Have you visited your mother?"

"No," replied Charlaine. "We came by way of Grienwald. I had hoped to visit Malburg on my return to Eisen."

"I should warn you, she blames me for your father's death. It might be to your advantage not to mention our arrangement regarding your order. Just so you know, I arranged for an annual stipend for her in recognition of your father's sacrifice."

"I appreciate that. My mother's always been a stubborn woman, but I'll endeavour to do what I can to comfort her. As far as my Temple Knights are concerned, I'll see them settled in Eisen and then return to Harlingen to determine how they may be employed alongside your own army should an invasion come."

Temple Captain Nicola cleared her throat. "While the Temple General returns to Eisen, I shall remain here to answer any questions you might have. It also allows me time to learn what's involved in running a city. I believe you have a Life Mage here? Someone by the name of Kandam?"

"Yes," said Charlotte.

"Then we'll have Temple Captain Teresa remain with me so she may teach him more spells of healing."

"That is most generous," replied Charlotte.

"Good," said Ludwig. "That reminds me. She still has to determine what poison was used to infect my wife."

"She hasn't done so already?" asked Charlaine.

"No, but then again, she was busy monitoring Charlotte's health. We sealed the room in question, and no one's been in there since. She seems to think some type of magic was used to cause the illness."

Charlaine smiled. "I shall leave that to Teresa's discretion. I'm certain once she begins looking for answers, she'll discover who's responsible."

17

THREATS

SUMMER 1107 SR

Teresa held up a small vial containing a bright green, glowing liquid.

"What is it?" asked Ludwig.

"The cause of your wife's illness. How familiar are you with the concept of magical energy?"

"It's what powers a mage's spells, isn't it? Are you suggesting that strange substance was drawn from a mage?"

"The common belief is that when a spellcaster uses their magic, they call upon a power that lies within them."

"Yes, I've heard that. It's said to be in the blood."

"An oversimplification, but essentially true, and just as blood carries magic through the body of a mage, so, too, do ley lines carry magic through the body of Eiddenwerthe."

"Ley lines?"

"There are rivers of power flowing beneath the surface, invisible to the naked eye. The Elves of Eloria refer to it as the Essence of Eiddenwerthe."

"Intriguing," replied Ludwig, "but if it's supposed to be invisible, why is it glowing green?"

"Sorry. I should've made myself clearer. The ley lines are only invisible because they run beneath the surface. If they were to erupt into the air, they would indeed glow green, though not, I suspect, as bright as this sample. This is more concentrated, as if someone distilled the essence into a purer form."

"And where was this vial found?"

"Beneath the mattress."

"It's that powerful?"

"Most certainly," said Teresa, "and insidious. In most cases, such an illness is said to be incurable, but in Her Majesty's case, it seems her previous condition worked in her favour, somehow preventing the infection from doing any permanent damage. My spell of neutralize toxins was able to remove its effects on the queen, but its proximity would've infected her again had we not moved her to a new room."

"That being the case, is it not dangerous for you to be handling it?"

"Gwalinor believes it requires long-term exposure to pose any real danger."

"He has experience with it?"

"Indeed. He even has a sample locked in a lead box back in his villa in Eloria. He showed it to me during my training."

"How did he come by it?" asked Ludwig.

Teresa smiled. "The Elves want you to believe they are a civilized race, but my time amongst them taught me they can be just as devious as Humans. It was recovered from an enemy agent who infiltrated the upper echelons of their ruling class."

"How does one distill such an essence?"

"That's an excellent question. Unfortunately, although I am familiar with its effects, I lack the knowledge of its creation. I would surmise, however, that it would take someone of exceptional potential to extract it from the ley lines."

"And by potential," said Ludwig, "you mean, a mage?"

"Yes."

"Would this mage need to be capable of a particular school of magic or simply well-trained?"

"The latter, I suspect. Why? Have you an inkling who might be responsible?"

"Only in a general sense. I trust Temple General Charlaine has seen fit to inform you of the treachery of the Stormwinds and Sartellians?"

"She has, and to answer your next question, one of those two families could easily have the capacity to extract something of this nature."

"Good to know," said Ludwig, "but we have none in Harlingen."

"That you're aware of," replied Teresa. "And the person who delivered this vial need not be the one who distilled it. It's even possible they weren't aware of its effects."

"Then why hide it under the mattress?"

"Humans are a superstitious lot. Perhaps someone took it as a charm? Something to ward off evil? Does the queen suffer from any recurring illness?"

"She alternates between extremes of melancholia and happiness. The Elf mage, Galrandir, tried curing her, but the effects of his treatment left her unable to enjoy life."

"I understand," said Teresa. "Magic can curb the extremes of the mind, but is incapable of distinguishing between sadness and joy."

"I suppose this means we must commission the construction of a lead-lined box?"

"That would be advisable. Burying it deep is another option, but then it might affect plants in the area, poisoning their roots. For now, I suggest we lock this vial in one of your cells in your dungeon, hiding it away from prying eyes."

"I shall see to it at once. Thank you, Temple Captain. You've been most helpful."

"The work is only just beginning, sire. There is still the matter of discovering who placed it beneath the mattress."

"I shall have Captain Gustavo question all the servants."

"I could, perhaps, be of assistance. My training under Gwalinor included spells that can ascertain if someone is lying. Were I to assist Captain Gustavo, we might get to the bottom of this sooner."

"I'd be pleased with any assistance you can render."

Cyn entered the sunroom, and Ludwig looked up from the book he was reading, as did Charlotte.

"Problem?" he asked.

Father Vernan, who was staring out the window, turned to join the conversation.

"We have a visitor," said Cyn. "Another emissary from the Church."

"Another archprior?"

"No. I suspect he's a lay brother, although I saw no signs of which Saint he represents. He insists on delivering his message in person."

"I assume you searched him for weapons?"

"Gustavo's men took care of that. Shall I bring him here, or would you prefer the throne room?"

"What do you think, Charlotte?"

"Here will be fine. If I'm going to be lectured by another member of the Church, I'd prefer to be comfortable."

"You heard the queen. Go and fetch the fellow."

"Yes, boss." Cyn left the room.

"I suppose it'll be more threats," said Charlotte. "They can't seem to take no for an answer."

"I suspect it's more than that. They're likely readying that Holy Army of theirs for the coming invasion… or should I call it a crusade?"

Charlotte shrugged her shoulders. "I daresay that depends entirely on who emerges victorious. It's an invasion to us, but if the Church wins, it will be written in history as a crusade to bring the true word of the Saints to the masses."

A few moments later, the door opened, and a young man wearing a brown cassock entered. "My name is Brother Erasmus," he said. "I've been sent to deliver a message from Primus Wilmar."

"Are you a worshipper of Saint Mathew?"

"No, Majesty. I am a Brother of Saint Ansgar."

"That's unusual," said Ludwig. "I thought your order wore blue?"

"Only on ceremonial occasions."

"Go ahead, then," urged Charlotte. "What is the message?"

The Ansgarite cleared his throat. "I am here to inform you that the fighting orders have all been dissolved, save for the Temple Knights of Saint Cunar."

"Isn't that a Church matter? Why would this be of particular concern to us?"

"The Antonine is sending messengers to all the Petty Kingdoms, not only Hadenfeld. I should also mention that harbouring any of the disbanded orders is considered a crime under Church law."

"Church law holds no sway over our realm."

"With all due respect, Majesty, harbouring such criminals would result in your entire kingdom being declared an enemy of the Church."

Ludwig laughed. "That is an empty threat. I know full well the Council of Peers has already declared us heretical. Even as we speak, they plot to march a Holy Army into our lands."

"We shall see how you feel when your subjects are clamouring for spiritual guidance." Erasmus's gaze fell on Father Vernan. "You are hereby ordered to return to the Antonine at once, Father, as are all Holy Fathers serving in Hadenfeld. No more services are to be conducted within the borders of this realm until the Primus determines the kingdom has paid its due penance."

"I follow the orders of my superior," replied Father Vernan, "not a mere messenger."

The visitor turned to face the king. "Your response is not unexpected, so I've been instructed to inform you that if you do not submit to the Church by the end of summer, Hadenfeld shall fall victim to a Holy Crusade."

Ludwig stood, fighting to control his temper. "Tell your masters that if they intend to invade, they are more than welcome to try. Be warned, however, that when they cross our borders, no mercy will be given."

The brother's thin smile did not reach his eyes. "Then I shall leave Your Majesties and withdraw from your realm."

Cyn escorted the visitor out.

"This doesn't bode well," mused Father Vernan.

"Could he be bluffing?" asked Charlotte. "Could they truly order all the Holy Fathers to leave?"

"That's a difficult question to answer. The Council of Peers can send out all the orders it wants, but the decision to obey ultimately falls squarely on the shoulders of the archpriors. They could recall an archprior, as they did with Hywell's predecessor, but that typically takes months."

"Why is that?"

"For one thing," replied the Holy Father, "the order has to come from the Patriarch of Saint Mathew, and then a replacement would have to be sent, necessitating more travel time."

"Yes, but couldn't they do that all at once?"

"I suppose, but there is a great amount of information that must be passed on from an archprior to his replacement. There's also the recent matter of the Temple Knights of Saint Agnes. I find it difficult to believe the Archprioress of Saint Agnes would abandon the sister knights."

"Are you suggesting she might refuse?" said Ludwig.

"We live in extraordinary times," replied Father Vernan. "Had you asked me only six months ago, I would've denied the possibility, but recent circumstances have seen fit to upset the normal rules of behaviour."

"And your own order?"

"I doubt Archprior Hywell will take the news well."

"You think he might disobey the edict?"

"That's difficult to predict. I cannot claim to know my superior well, and it's not his decision alone. He will need to consult the priors of Hadenfeld, for he cannot rule over the Church if he has no subordinates."

"But you must have some idea?"

"I know people need spiritual guidance," said Father Vernan. "What I don't know is whether or not my fellow Church leaders will make that a priority rather than follow the Antonine's orders. It's a complicated situation we find ourselves in."

"Would it be wise, do you think, for me to meet with the archprior?"

"It certainly couldn't hurt. Then again, it might be better for the queen to do so?"

"Me?" said Charlotte.

"Yes. You share a past. You met with him when Temple Commander Amarand visited two years ago."

"That hardly means I know the man."

"The life of a member of the clergy is one of constant service. As such, a visit to a Royal is apt to be something worthy of remembering, a high point of a career. They would view the offer of a second visit as a great honour."

"Then I shall make preparations immediately."

"And while you're doing that," said Ludwig, "I'll discuss strategy with Cyn and Sig now that he's returned to us."

"How much time do you reckon we have?" asked Sigwulf.

"The messenger indicated the invasion wouldn't come till the fall. His exact turn of phrase was that we had till the end of summer to give in to their demands."

"That, at least, gives us time to prepare."

"Agreed," said Cyn, "but what does that entail precisely? We know the enemy is coming, but not where they're coming from."

"A good point," said Ludwig, "and one which has been on my mind of late. We have no news at present of an army gathering near any of our borders, but I did receive a message from Erlingen that the Antonine is calling for volunteers to participate in a crusade. Unfortunately, my source neglected to mention where this army would gather."

"The two most likely prospects are Zowenbruch and Deisenbach," said Sigwulf. "We have people in Hollenbeck and Mirantha, and Grislagen has always kept close ties with Luwen, so I can't see them getting involved."

"Zowenbruch only has one invasion route, that of marching down the road to Eisen. Deisenbach, on the other hand, could potentially move on Drakenfeld, or even Glosnecke, making it much more difficult to anticipate their route of march."

"We need people at the borders," said Cyn. "Small groups that can fade away unnoticed and bring word should they spot anything suspicious."

"Agreed," added Ludwig, "but at the same time, we can't afford to mass the entire army in one place. To that end, I will divide it into two commands."

"I assume me and Siggy would command these divisions?"

"Naturally. We'll split it right down the middle, with equal numbers of foot, horse, and bow for each of you."

"And our allies?"

"The Elves will only march once an enemy crosses our border, so you two have the task of delaying the enemy while we wait for their assistance.

There's also the matter of the Temple Knights of Saint Agnes, but they'll have to remain in Eisen until we need them, else we'd have to assemble an extensive baggage train to keep them and their horses fed."

"Do we have anyone in the courts of Zowenbruch or Deisenbach?"

"Now that you mention it, yes," said Ludwig. "Lord Darrian is there."

"Lord Darrian is in Zowenbruch?"

"Yes. He travelled there to meet Esmerelda Boesch. I proposed an arranged marriage on his behalf, and she sounded interested, so he insisted on presenting the offer to her in person. Now that they're married, they've remained there to be our ears and eyes at King Konrad's court.

"Speaking of Lord Darrian," said Charlotte, "how's his brother doing?"

"He's a changed man," replied Cyn. "It's amazing the effect that a few weeks with the Temple Knights had on him. I daresay he's now one of our more accomplished captains, though if you tell him, I'll deny it."

"That's good to hear," said Ludwig. "I shall send Lord Darrian a letter. Perhaps he can make some enquiries on our behalf."

"Have we anyone in Deisenbach?"

"No, but you know who might? The Temple General. I'll write to her."

"Until then," said Sigwulf, "how do we proceed? Splitting the army is one thing, but where do we march? Eisen is now thick with Temple Knights, so it's not the best place to support an extra six hundred men."

"Take them to Dornbruck for now, but I'd prefer to deploy them farther north, halfway between Eisen and Zwieken."

Sigwulf nodded. "Dornbruck it shall be."

"What about me?" said Cyn. "Do I march to Drakenfeld or Glosnecke?"

"Drakenfeld is the more likely candidate, if only because of the road. If a Holy Army does come after us, I expect they'll be eager to capture the capital, and that's the most direct route."

"I'll let Lord Merrick know we'll be camping on his lands."

"We have some time yet; summer hasn't run its course, but by the first day of autumn, I want everyone in place. I'll also warn all the northern barons to secure their keeps, just in case."

"Do you believe the Church would siege them? That would take months, and they'd have to use siege engines."

"I doubt it. I suspect they'll go for the quickest victory instead of a prolonged conquest, which means the two main targets are Eisen and Harlingen."

"Harlingen is the capital," said Cyn. "Wouldn't that be their most logical target?"

"It's certainly a possibility, but if this Holy Army is serving the interests of Halvaria, capturing Eisen would be just as effective. They could invoke the memory of Neuhafen and split the kingdom in half."

"So we'd no longer be considered a threat to the empire?"

"Precisely. To prepare, you'll have to organize your respective baggage trains. To help expedite the process, I'll have Gita release additional funds. I shall send word once we receive confirmation of where they're massing, but until then, you'll need to be ready to fight on short notice."

"I assume you're going to remain here in Harlingen?"

"Only until we know which way they're coming. I'll notify both of you when I change my location."

"Any chance of a few Temple Knights of Saint Mathew lending us a hand?" asked Sigwulf.

"I wish I could say yes, but that appears unlikely unless the Archprior of Saint Mathew decides to defy his superiors. If anything changes, however, I shall be certain to mention it."

Ludwig paused to gather his thoughts. From a strategic perspective, he was in a difficult situation. His army, though experienced, was still rebuilding after a couple of lean years. Marching them to battle was bad enough, but putting them up against the toughest knights in all the Petty Kingdoms might be asking too much. Was he throwing their lives away in a vain attempt to prolong his rule? Would it be better to bend the knee to the Church and allow the Cunars to garrison knights here?

The very thought of doing so was repugnant. The Church was corrupt—he knew this with a certainty—and if he allowed them unfettered access to his realm, it spelled the end not only to Hadenfeld's future but likely that of the entire Continent. Without his army to assist them, his allies might be weakened to the point where the legions of Halvaria could crush them.

"I can't stress the import of these events," he continued. "I know this is a lot to put on your shoulders, but the very fate of the Petty Kingdoms may be decided by this coming campaign."

"We won't let you down, boss," said Cyn.

"Agreed," added Sig. "If those Holy Warriors cross into our lands, we'll send them to the Underworld!"

18

CONSULTATION

SUMMER 1107 SR

Charlotte waited as a palace guard poured the tea. It felt strange for a warrior to take the place of a servant, but if the archprior took issue, he didn't reveal it, nor, for that matter, did the Archprioress of Saint Agnes.

"I'm so glad you both accepted my invitation," said the queen. "Outside of official functions, it's rare we're together in the same room."

"Quite," replied Archprior Hywell. "Though I do wonder why Archprior Malakai is not present."

"He's chosen to obey the Antonine's orders," replied Archprioress Bernadine. "He's always been a stickler for protocol and is arranging his evacuation from the kingdom even as we speak." She shifted her gaze to their host. "I assume that's why you invited us here to the Royal Keep?"

"It is," replied Charlotte. "As you know, the Antonine has disbanded all the orders of Temple Knights save for those of Saint Cunar. I'm certain it won't be long before they want us to turn over the sister knights of Saint Agnes into the hands of the Church."

"No chance of that."

"Let us not make hasty decisions," said the archprior. "There is much to consider here."

"Consider?" said Bernadine. "Are you seriously suggesting I turn over faithful sister knights to an Antonine determined to put them behind bars? I shall never condone such an action."

"At the moment," said Charlotte, "I'm more interested in what your respective orders intend to do. Will you abandon the kingdom like your colleague, Archprior Malakai, or remain and continue giving spiritual guidance to the people of this realm?"

"It's interesting you should mention that," said Hywell. "We discussed that very subject this morning."

"And your conclusion?"

"We cannot make that decision without calling a conclave of our junior members. To that end, we've sent for all priors and prioresses to travel here to Harlingen, where we'll meet and discuss the matter."

"To discuss whether to remain or leave?"

"What my colleague is trying to say," said Bernadine, "is that we will abide by the majority decision. And to clarify, we invited all members of the clergy who conduct ceremonies, not only the priors."

"The orders went out this morning," added Hywell, "but it'll be some weeks before they arrive."

"And will they all be meeting together or separately by faith?"

"Separately, which may result in one or both of our orders remaining here in Hadenfeld, depending on the results."

"Or neither," offered Bernadine. "This is not a situation that has ever happened before, so I find it difficult to estimate which decision they'll favour."

"I understand," said Charlotte, "but I'm curious as to where your own preferences lie."

"I'm all for remaining, but that opens up a hornet's nest of problems."

"Such as?"

"It means a break from the Antonine and all that entails, and we'd have only Hadenfeld to support us. Now, I'm not saying the Church couldn't continue to function, but eventually, we need replacements, and that, in turn, requires training of Holy Members, something typically done elsewhere."

"It's not insurmountable," added Hywell, "but it means we'd no longer report to superiors elsewhere. In fact, we would become those very superiors, forcing us to take on additional responsibilities. There is also the ethical question of the temples themselves, which are the property of the Church of the Saints."

"That is not something you need to worry about," said Charlotte. "Were you to break with the Antonine, the Crown would seize those buildings and then gift them to you in perpetuity."

"Well, at least that's one thing off our plates."

"I'm curious about the disbandment of the Temple Knights. Why would the Church do that?"

"It was, I'm told, primarily a financial decision, but I have my reservations. I've written to our patriarch seeking clarification on that point, but the Antonine is a long way from Harlingen, and events are moving swiftly. I suggested to Temple Captain Hamelyn that he maintain his presence in Hadenfeld until he receives orders to the contrary."

"And if I may ask, how was that news received?"

"He was relieved, to say the least. He assured me he'd sent a courier to their regional commander in Deisenbach, but once again, we're waiting for a reply. I'll let Archprioress Bernadine answer for the Temple Knights of Saint Agnes."

"Their Temple General resides in Eisen," said the archprioress. "I should think that puts an end to any question about their intentions. I imagine she'll send riders to every Agnesite Commandery across the Petty Kingdoms."

"Speaking of which," said Charlotte, "what is your opinion of that? That is to say, what effect will the order's disbandment have across the Continent?"

"Once more, difficult to say. No doubt, some kingdoms will refuse the order to disband them. Take Arnsfeld, for example. The sister knights helped them defeat the Halvarian incursion. I can't imagine the king expelling them there, can you? And Reinwick is in a similar state. Come to think of it, most northern kingdoms would do the same."

"Why is that?"

"On account of the Temple Fleet that our sister knights command. I'm told sea trade has flourished under their control of the Great Northern Sea, and I don't imagine there's a ruler anywhere along the coast who'd see a return to the days of rampant piracy. The middle kingdoms, however, are a different story, as are the southern."

"Would you care to explain?"

"The Temple Knights of Saint Agnes don't typically maintain large contingents in most kingdoms, preferring instead to concentrate on their primary duty of guarding the places of worship. Having said that, a dozen sister knights are hardly going to be seen as a threat to the hosting realm, so their presence may be ignored."

"Interesting you should say that," added Hywell. "I've heard the order has expanded in recent years, thanks in no small part to the efforts of their new Temple General. Not that she's held that position for long, but her accomplishments thus far have resulted in an increase in women wishing to serve."

"It has certainly led to more enquiries about them," agreed Bernadine. "Of course, all that's on hold for the present. We can't very well send women off to be trained until we know which facilities are still in operation."

"I hadn't considered that," said Charlotte. "How many training facilities do they have?"

"Three. One each in Eidenburg, Corassus, and the last only recently moved to the Antonine, so we can safely assume that will no longer be available to them."

"I doubt Corassus would be either," said Hywell. "That's a Cunar stronghold, not to mention the home port of the Holy Fleet."

"In your opinion," asked Charlotte, "can they continue to exist without the Church's support?"

"Provided they can still recruit and train, I don't see why not. I suppose the same could be said about the Temple Knights of Saint Mathew. There will always be a need to keep our temples safe, and prior to these recent orders from the Council of Peers, they had no problem recruiting others to join the cause."

"And now?"

"I suspect some of the disbanded Temple Knights will join the Cunars, but a significant number would prefer to abandon their vows or choose to operate as individual chapters. Then again, the Mathewite regional commander in Deisenbach agreed to help put the king on the throne, so he'll likely be of a similar mind. I'm surprised he wasn't called to the Antonine for his audacity. Of course, officially, his position no longer exists, so they may have chosen to ignore him."

"Perhaps," said the archprioress, "but we are working on outdated information. Word travels slowly amongst the Petty Kingdoms, particularly when at the mercy of the Antonine's notoriously slow bureaucracy. For all we know, word is only just reaching him now of what happened with the fighting orders."

"Would he order his knights to participate in a crusade against Hadenfeld?" asked Charlotte.

"I doubt it, especially considering the assistance they lent you during the war. There's also a matter of history. Their Temple Knights have never participated in any of the countless crusades of the past, and I see no reason to expect them to do so now, even if commanded by the Primus himself."

"Thank you," said Charlotte. "You've been of immense help to me."

"These are difficult times," replied Archprior Hywell, "and one must tread carefully to ensure they take the proper path."

"And what, in your opinion, is the proper path?"

"I am not the ruler of Hadenfeld, thank the Saints."

"And if you were, would you bow to the Church to avoid conflict?"

"An interesting question. Conflict is to be avoided whenever possible, but where would we be if Saint Agnes had not stood up to Jaramel, the High Lord of Herani? The best choice is not always the easiest."

"How does one tell which choice to make?"

"By having faith," replied Hywell. "You are a remarkable woman, Your Majesty, and an even more remarkable queen. Let your faith be your guide."

"Even if it involves defying the Church of the Saints?"

"Let me ease your mind," said the archprioress. "It is the teachings of the Saints you should venerate, not the whims of mortal men. I may be marked as a heretic for saying so, but the Antonine no longer represents the true wishes of the Saints. Were that so, they would live in humble homes and conduct services on behalf of the common folk, not hide behind the massive walls living their lives in relative comfort and extravagance."

"Clearly, you're not enamoured of your superiors."

"The farther away we get from our worshippers, the less we understand what it means to be one of the faithful. To put it another way, as one grows in power or influence, they begin to prioritize their own interests to the exclusion of others. How can a person so out of touch with their worshippers make decisions concerning them?"

"Could the same not be said of kings?"

"Most definitely, and history provides us with plenty of stories of those who succumbed to this temptation. Even the Church has suffered on occasion, but in the past, such behaviour was punished; now it has become acceptable, perhaps even encouraged." Bernadine paused, shaking her head. "Don't mind me, Majesty; I'm just bitter. It's a result of the indifference of the Antonine. They're very supportive when it comes to collecting tithes or donations, but when we ask for something in return, all we receive is silence. It's enough to drive a person mad."

"I would agree," added Archprior Hywell. "What I don't understand is how we got to this point? Ten years ago, no one would've predicted this… situation."

"That doesn't mean this behaviour wasn't present at that time," said Charlotte, "merely that no one was looking for it."

"Wise words, Majesty. I think you may have hit upon the truth of the matter."

"Yes," agreed Bernadine. "A slow rot eating away at the Church unseen." She adjusted her cassock. "Is there anything else we can do for you, Majesty?"

"Not at present. Thank you for your time today."

"In that case, we'll take our leave of you. Please feel free to contact either one of us if you need to."

"Thank you. I will."

With that, they were escorted from the room.

Charlotte and Gita watched as Kenley sat in the saddle. The boy was nine now, almost ten, and had grown comfortable on ponies, but this was his first experience on a horse. The stable master stood nearby, ready to rush forward should the lad make a mistake, but he needn't have bothered, for the beast was a mild-mannered creature that responded well to the boy's commands.

"He's a natural horseman," offered the queen.

"Just like his father," replied Gita. Kenley made a circuit of the training area. "How did it go with the archpriors?"

"It was educational."

"And by that, you mean?"

"They have a lot of concerns, not the least of which is how their priors and Holy Fathers will act, given all that's occurred."

"In other words, they're sitting on the fence?"

"I think they'd both prefer to remain in Hadenfeld," said Charlotte, "but they can't do that without the Holy Fathers agreeing or Holy Mothers, in the case of the Agnesites. They've called a conclave of their respective orders to decide how to proceed."

"And how long is this to take?"

"Weeks to gather those needed, and then there's no telling how long to reach an agreement."

"And all this when our time is running out," said Gita. "Not the best of news."

"True, but not the worst either. They could've obeyed the orders of the Council of Peers and left Hadenfeld altogether."

"This Holy Crusade could be over by the time they come to a consensus. You don't think that's their intention, do you? To wait out the crisis and see who emerges victorious?"

"Neither one impresses me as the sort to avoid trouble; I think they'd prefer to face it head-on."

"This entire situation is so frustrating, and all because one man wanted to build a commandery in Harlingen."

"I doubt this was all Temple Commander Amarand's fault," said Charlotte. "Like most men of the fighting orders, I suspect he was following orders. Who knows, perhaps the Primus himself suggested this course of action?"

. . .

Temple General Charlaine stared out from the walls of Eisen Keep to the south, where the great lake fed the Erlen River. The sight of so much water reminded her of her time in Ilea.

"Peaceful, isn't it?"

She turned to see Sister Nicola, who'd been the grand mistress's aide and now helped oversee what remained of the order, a difficult task now that they were no longer in the Antonine.

"I was thinking about my first assignment," said Charlaine. "Of course, that was the Shimmering Sea, not a lake, and the weather was much warmer, but it's still a relaxing sight." She turned back to the water. "Have you heard from any of our other detachments?"

"Not yet, General, but our letters are likely still en route. I don't expect we'll hear much till autumn."

"True, but the weather is already turning cooler, which means it's coming early this year. Anything from the Elves?"

"Yes. The High Lord sent word she's assigned someone to act as an advisor."

"Anyone in particular?"

Nicola smiled. "Yes, Talon Fariel. The High Lord thought it best she send someone we're already familiar with."

"When is the talon due to arrive?"

"We're to expect her by the end of the week. I've taken the liberty of preparing quarters for her here in the Royal Keep." The Temple Captain hesitated. "Do we still call it the Royal Keep? It seems a strange name, considering it now belongs to us."

"Perhaps Temple Keep might be more appropriate, although logically, it's more of a castle than a keep."

"Do you remember Sister Rhea?"

"I remember Temple Captain Verushka commenting that she was full of initiative. Why do you ask?"

"It seems she comes from a long line of stonemasons."

"And?"

"She's of the opinion we could strengthen the outer castle walls."

"How?" asked Charlaine.

"By building small towers that allow archers to attack the flanks of attackers."

"We'd need archers for that."

"About that. When we first arrived in Eisen, I did a cursory inventory of the place."

"I'm guessing you found something," said Charlaine.

"Yes," replied Nicola. "A cache of crossbows, along with a significant number of bolts. It appears that, back in the day, the ruler of Neuhafen sought to raise a couple of crossbow companies to complement his archers."

"And yet they remained in stores. I would've thought he'd have taken them to Harlingen during the war."

"I can't explain why he didn't, but they appear to be in good shape. Sister Genevieve also found a ledger containing a record of their purchase, including the signature of King Ruger."

"Ah, that explains it," said Charlaine. "Ruger died before the invasion. His son, King Diedrich, led the attempt to conquer Hadenfeld."

"Why wouldn't he have used the crossbows?"

"From what Ludwig told me, he was an impulsive man, and likely didn't want to take the time needed to train with them. We, however, have plenty of time on our hands. How many did you say there were?"

"We haven't opened every crate," replied Nicola, "but according to the records, there were more than a hundred."

"It's uncharacteristic for you not to have the exact numbers," said Charlaine.

"The room where they're stored is jammed full. We're still doing a full inventory, but I thought you'd like to hear of our discovery."

"This is excellent news. Now, do we train our own sister knights to use them or hire people from Eisen to man the walls?"

"Have you a preference?"

"Danica trained all the sister knights of the Temple Fleet in the use of crossbows, which proved to be of great benefit. I'm not suggesting all our knights learn to use them, but it wouldn't hurt to find out who might prove proficient with them."

"I'll arrange for some targets to be set up in the courtyard so we can test everyone."

"Yes," said Charlaine. "While you're at it, send someone into town to make enquiries. If we intend to employ crossbows, we need to ensure we know how to look after them, and most likely, they were made in Eisen."

"They could've been imported."

"From where? No one else in Hadenfeld uses them, and Zuwenbruch was never on friendly terms with Neuhafen."

"You keep mentioning Neuhafen," said Nicola. "Is that the name for this area of Hadenfeld?"

"It was a breakaway kingdom. The eastern barons of Hadenfeld rebelled more than fifty years ago, declaring themselves the Kingdom of Neuhafen. The two realms were reunited after the Second Battle of Harlingen, back in 1104."

"Was that the first civil war, or the second?"

"Technically, the first was when they broke away."

"And the second?"

"That was when Ludwig seized power."

"But wasn't the kingdom reunited after fighting Neuhafen?"

"Yes, but there were two kingdoms in that conflict, so it's not seen as a civil war."

"All that fighting in so short a period," mused Nicola. "I'm beginning to think Hadenfeld wasn't our best choice."

"It was our only choice," replied Charlaine.

19

TEMPLE KNIGHTS
AUTUMN 1107 SR

"I fear this will not end well," said Charlotte. "Autumn is now upon us, and we've yet to hear from the archpriors concerning their decision."

"We must be patient," replied Ludwig.

"Have we any news from the borders with Deisenbach or Zowenbruch?"

"Not as yet. Cyn has her warriors in Drakenfeld, but reports nothing out of the usual."

"And Sig?"

"The northeast is quiet. He's sent people up to Zwieken and Valksburg, but none report the massing of troops on our border. Not that I find that surprising. To my mind, if you intend to assemble an army to invade your neighbour, you wouldn't do it within plain sight."

"So we're no better off than we were before."

"It appears not, but I have hopes that if there is indeed a Holy Army massing in Zowenbruch, we'll soon have proof of it."

"How so?"

"Lord Darrian has taken to riding around their countryside in search of Temple Knights of Saint Cunar. His missive indicated he'd yet to see any, but rumours are they're massing to the east, well out of sight of the border. If that's true, it means they plan to march on Eisen."

"You must warn Charlaine," said Charlotte.

"At this point, they're only rumours. We also can't rule out the possibility they might try a two-pronged attack, with a second army coming from Deisenbach, marching on us here in the capital."

"Still, you must inform her of the possibility."

"I shall send a messenger to both her and Sig, but until we have proof, I'll refrain from ordering our warriors to march."

"Is there nothing further we can do?"

"Esmerelda's been mingling with the nobility of Zowenbruch in the hopes one will reveal what King Konrad's up to."

"But he took an oath not to invade," said Charlotte.

"He did, but he's likely got the Church breathing down his neck. I can no longer count on his neutrality."

"But couldn't the same be said of Deisenbach?"

"King Justinian doesn't have a history of invading us."

"Perhaps, but if the Church called upon him to assist in the crusade, would he heed the call?"

"That's difficult to predict," said Ludwig. "I've never met the fellow, but I have heard he's more interested in wealth and entertainment than conquering."

"Entertainment?"

"Yes. He's said to enjoy jousting."

"That's common in the north, although I'm surprised a king would participate."

"Oh, he doesn't participate, merely spectates, but he's said to have his favourites. I'm led to believe that attempting to gain his favour is a popular pastime amongst the contestants. Is it like that in the north?"

"Not in Reinwick. Erlingen is the Petty Kingdom credited with making tournaments so popular. You competed yourself, did you not?"

"I did," replied Ludwig, "but only the once, and I ended up losing everything."

"But that's where you met Sig and Cyn, so it wasn't a total loss."

Ludwig smiled. "That's right, I did. Perhaps, when this crisis is over, we'll host a tournament here in Harlingen."

"What a wonderful idea."

"That's assuming we still exist."

"Don't be so glum," said Charlotte. "We will survive this."

"How can you be so certain?"

"Because I have faith in you. I've believed in you since we first met, and I've yet to be disappointed. You will find a way through this conflict, even if it means defeating the entire Holy Army."

A soft knock drew his attention. "Yes?"

"Temple Captain Hamelyn to see Your Majesties."

"By all means, send him in."

The door opened, allowing their visitor to enter.

"You bring news?" asked Ludwig.

"Indeed, Majesty, although I'm not quite certain where to begin."

"According to Temple General Charlaine, your order has been instructed to disband. Perhaps you should start there?"

"Yes. Unfortunately, that is true. I came here to tell you we have no intention of laying down our arms, or becoming Temple Knights of Saint Cunar. I understand this puts you in a difficult position, so if you want us to leave your realm, we shall abide by your wishes."

"Why would we want you to leave?"

"The Temple Knights of Saint Mathew are no longer sanctioned by the Church. Allowing us to continue to operate within Hadenfeld is a flagrant disregard of the Church's laws."

"The Antonine already branded us as unbelievers, my friend, and we've taken in close to five hundred Temple Knights of Saint Agnes. I doubt the presence of two companies of Mathewites could make the situation any worse."

"I'm curious where you stand," said Charlotte. "What of your superiors? Have they surrendered their positions of authority and joined the Cunars?"

"I cannot speak to the entire order, but I do know our regional commander in Deisenbach refused to dissolve the chapters under his command. Ultimately, that leaves the Temple Knights in Hadenfeld, Deisenbach, and Grislagen under the Temple Commander's control."

"And how many knights does that make?"

"I'm not entirely certain," said Hamelyn. "We have two companies here in Hadenfeld, but last I heard, there is only one each in Deisenbach and Grislagen. The rift in the Church, however, particularly amongst the orders, has seen some of our brothers give up their oaths of service."

"In other words," said Ludwig, "your numbers are decreasing."

"Quite the reverse, actually. Although some of our brethren chose not to fight the Antonine's edicts, other, more dedicated souls, are making the long trek to the region seeking to join us where we are accepted."

"And how are the Cunars taking this?"

"I think, to a large degree, they're ignoring us. To their mind, the Temple Knights of Saint Mathew offer little in terms of a threat."

"Yet your order fought in Arnsfeld, as well as Hadenfeld."

"True, sire, but only in limited numbers. Regardless, the Temple Commander implored me to make our case before the two of you to discover your thoughts on the matter."

"Your presence is always welcome," said Charlotte.

"Agreed," added Ludwig. "I recommend you keep your companies intact and remain here. If it's a matter of funds, we can arrange to undertake the expense of housing and feeding you."

"And what would we have to do in return?" asked Hamelyn.

"Help protect Hadenfeld."

"I assume that means placing my men under the command of the Crown, but I'm not altogether certain that would be appropriate. I would, however, like to propose an alternate arrangement."

"Go on."

"If you'd allow it, I'd place my companies under the command of Temple General Charlaine."

"She's from a different order," said Charlotte.

"True, but we've worked with our sister knights on many an occasion, and the Temple General is an experienced leader. Of all of us, she knows best how to employ Temple Knights in battle."

"I have no objection," said Ludwig.

"Nor do I," added Charlotte. "Your proposal makes perfectly good sense, but you'd need to organize this with the Temple General."

"Then I shall make arrangements to do so immediately."

"Has your regional commander in Deisenbach heard anything of a Holy Army massing in that realm?"

"His last instructions indicated nothing of that nature, and considering his stance on defying the Antonine's order to disband, he'd be on the lookout for any news like that."

"Before you go," said Ludwig. "Have you heard anything from Archprior Hywell?"

"I'm afraid not, Majesty. The conclave has been in full session for days on end, and my men have been specifically ordered not to enter the building while it's in session."

"And they say nothing when they leave each night?"

"That's just it; they don't leave at all. They've sequestered themselves in the Temple of Saint Mathew."

"But they must eat, surely?"

"Food is brought to the door, but the Holy Fathers carry it inside. Even then, little is spoken, save for matters concerning the meals."

"Out of curiosity," said Charlotte, "how does this new arrangement of yours sit with those of Saint Mathew?"

"I'm not sure I follow?" said Hamelyn.

"If I'm not mistaken, your order's grand master traditionally worked under the authority of the Patriarch of Saint Mathew. Now that you no longer have a grand master, who will your Temple Commander report to?"

"That, I'm told, is one of the many matters the conclave is considering. I'm afraid I have nothing else to report to you, Majesties, but should I hear of anything, I'd be pleased to pass it on to you."

"Thank you," said Ludwig. "That would be very much appreciated."

Two days later, Archprior Hywell sat in the sunroom with the king, making small talk while shifting around in his seat, unable to settle.

Ludwig decided to get to the subject at hand. "Has your conclave concluded, Your Grace?"

"It has," replied the archprior. "We discussed a great many things, particularly the matter of where we stand regarding the Antonine's edicts."

"And your conclusion?"

"The Church of the Saints has a long and storied history. For more than a thousand years, it's provided spiritual guidance to those in need, fulfilling a critical role in the very fabric of the Petty Kingdoms. In the past, we've always expected moderation from those in charge. We have a saying amongst our order, or at least we did: 'The bureaucracy of the Church moves slower than a snail.' In many ways, this was both a weakness and a strength, for it allowed radical changes to be resisted with every fibre of its being. Unfortunately, this appears to no longer be the case."

The archprior seemed to be struggling with what he'd come to say, but Ludwig remained silent, letting the fellow take his time.

"This is a most difficult decision, especially given that our finances are, by and large, controlled through the senior members of the Church. That is not to say we rely on them for the day-to-day operations of our temples, but any new construction or expenditure beyond that is only approved at the highest levels."

"Are you not an archprior?" said Ludwig. "The only person higher in position is the patriarch of your order, surely?"

"Although I oversee all aspects of our religion here in Hadenfeld, my power stops at the border. While only the patriarch outranks me, the Antonine is filled with archpriors, each taking care of a particular aspect of the order, including finances. If we break from the Church, those funds would cease to be accessible to us."

"But the donations you receive here would no longer be forwarded on to the Antonine."

"Yes," replied Hywell. "That point was brought up. We would suffer in the short term, but the general consensus is that our finances would be in a better state by this time next year. Until then, we'd have to weigh every expenditure carefully."

"So you've decided to split from the Church?"

"We have. The decision was a difficult one and not, by any means, unanimous, although we did, at last, reach a consensus. Once that was decided, there were a host of new problems to deal with, beginning with how this Hadenfeld Church of Saint Mathew should operate."

"And what did you come up with?"

"That the basic organization adopted by the Church of the Saints be maintained, although without a patriarch."

"My understanding was that only the fighting orders were affected by the Antonine's orders."

"Yes, but then we were ordered to cease administering religious services, a direct result, we were informed, of your refusal to permit a Cunar commandery in Hadenfeld. We felt the Council of Peers had overstepped its authority. Branding you a heretic for denying their request is a grave injustice, one which we cannot let stand. The result of all of this is that we will continue to conduct ceremonies in the name of our blessed Saint as we have for centuries."

"I'm pleased to hear it," said Ludwig, "although I must warn you that if the Holy Army succeeds in defeating us, it may well cost you your livelihood, possibly even your heads."

"That topic also came up at the conclave," said Archprior Hywell.

"And?"

"We'd be poor servants of Saint Mathew if we did not stand up for what we believe in. We've formed a new council to make decisions. I will be the chief arbiter, but the decisions shall be made by the priors and Holy Fathers of the realm."

"How do you plan to accomplish that? You can't have every Holy Father travel to Harlingen each time a decision needs to be made."

"True, but experience tells us very few decisions must be rushed in such a matter. In the meantime, votes can be tallied by gaining a consensus through correspondence."

"Voting by letters?" said Ludwig. "An ingenious solution, although I fear it makes debate more difficult."

"Some might say it makes things easier. The written word can be so much more expressive than a council hall, where emotions get the better of people. Putting ink to paper requires much more thought."

"You make a good point."

"Thank you. It will take time to set things in motion, but I feel it's the best option going forward." He paused briefly. "Having said that, I should stress we are committed to this endeavour, even if the Antonine should change its mind. We are now the Hadenfeld Church of Saint Mathew, and our links to the old Church of the Saints are irrevocably broken."

"Have you heard anything from the archprioress?"

"Their conclave is still in session, but I suspect they will arrive at a similar conclusion. They won't abandon the Temple Knights of Saint Agnes, and between you and me, they were given scant attention from the Antonine."

"Why is that?" asked Ludwig.

"When it came to the fighting orders, the Cunars always received the most attention. They were, after all, the pre-eminent fighting order of the Continent, or at least they were supposed to be."

"Yes, but the archprioress isn't a Temple Knight."

"While that's true, their order worked very closely with the sister knights. They also had the disadvantage of under-representation. You see, the Council of Peers consists of the patriarch of each Saint, or the matriarch in the Agnesite's case. The Antonine is, in essence, a court of sorts, with each member vying for a share of the resources. As the lone woman on the council, the Matriarch of Saint Agnes was already facing an uphill battle."

"I assume what they collected went into the Antonine's coffers?"

"Indeed," said Archprior Hywell, "and funds were seldom returned for the construction of new temples. If anything, they'll be much better off now. As an independent church, they will keep all the donations they receive."

"Do you think this decision by the Antonine will have far-reaching consequences beyond Hadenfeld?"

"Their decision concerning the fighting orders certainly will, but I'm afraid Hadenfeld is another matter entirely. I hate to admit it, but the Petty Kingdoms typically turn their backs when their neighbours are in trouble, and few would be willing to defy the Church under any circumstances. Even as we speak, Temple Knights are being instructed to leave realms across the Continent. Not all, mind you, especially those where the orders served in the best interest of those in charge."

"Have you any specific kingdoms in mind?"

"I can't imagine Arnsfeld kicking them out, can you? Not after they quite literally saved the kingdom, and Reinwick, I'm told, is in a similar state. However, both those kingdoms are some distance from the Antonine; I suspect those closer would be more inclined to follow the orders of the Primus."

"You say Primus," said Ludwig, "but isn't the Council of Peers responsible for such things?"

"In theory, yes, but Primus Wilmar appears to have solid control over the patriarchs. They say he was a Cunar Temple Knight, a most unusual situation."

"Father Vernan told me that's rare."

"Rare? Why, it's singular. Never before has a member of the fighting orders been chosen as a Primus." Hywell shook his head. "No, I must be more precise. There was one, a Mathewite to be exact, but he was invalided out of the Temple Knights due to an injury and became a Holy Father instead. He eventually became an archprior, which led to him being named Primus, but that was many years later."

"Was he an effective Primus?"

"Unfortunately, we never got a chance to find out. He died shortly after taking office, a victim of his advanced years. A pity, really, particularly considering his work with our missions across the Petty Kingdoms."

The archprior stared at the fireplace and sighed. "We live in difficult times, Majesty. This situation would try the patience of Saint Mathew himself were he here to witness it, but you are handling it with grace and humility. That marks you as a rare individual."

"I thank Your Grace for your kind words," said Ludwig, "but I had little choice in the matter. A king who subordinates himself to a higher authority puts himself at risk of becoming a vassal."

"That sounds like a quote, though I daresay it's not from the *Book of Saint Mathew*."

"It's attributed to *The Campaigns of Aeldred*. I haven't read it myself, but since becoming king, I've taken to reading anything about leadership I can find, and they all make reference to it. I must admit I find it strange that people who hate the Old Kingdom so much seem to savour the words of its founder."

"*The Campaigns of Aeldred*, you say? Were you aware that book is required reading for some of the fighting orders?"

"I was not," said Ludwig. "Does that mean Temple Captain Hamelyn might possess a copy?"

"I doubt it. That's usually reserved for Temple Commanders, but you should talk to Temple General Charlaine. She'd likely have one, provided, of course, she was able to bring it out of the Antonine with her."

"I shall be sure to ask next time I see her."

20

DEMANDS

AUTUMN 1107 SR

Ludwig was placing the saddle on his horse when he saw Charlotte enter the stables. "Come to see me off to Eisen? We already said our goodbyes."

"There's been a development. One that requires your immediate attention."

"I'm all ears."

"Temple Commander Amarand has returned under a flag of truce."

"To what end?"

"Perhaps we'd best go and find out?"

Ludwig removed the saddle, handing it off to a stable hand. "I shall delay my trip till we've dealt with this fellow."

They made their way towards the great hall. "Any idea what he's here for?" he asked.

"None whatsoever, but his coming in person indicates it's important. Cunars are not ones to go anywhere under a flag of truce."

"He wants something."

"Agreed, but what? Does he still expect us to bow to the Church when we've told him in no uncertain terms his demands are unacceptable?"

They entered the great hall, taking their seats on the twin thrones of Hadenfeld. A nearby guard waited, and with a nod from Ludwig, opened the door. Outside, stood Captain Gustavo and six men, the familiar form of Temple Commander Amarand in their midst.

They entered, but rather than the guards splitting off to either side, Gustavo kept them ringed around the Cunar.

"Majesties," said their visitor. "I bring you greetings in the name of the Primus."

"Indeed?" replied Ludwig. "I'm surprised to see you here, Temple Commander, especially considering the matter we discussed on your last visit."

"My apologies, sire, but I assure you the well wishes of the Primus are genuine."

"Why the sudden change?" asked Charlotte. "Since last we met, we've been declared heretics. Are you now saying Primus Wilmar had a change of heart?"

"He is a great believer in the power of redemption and sent me here to offer you a way to repair the rift that has torn us asunder."

"I see," said Charlotte.

"I don't," said Ludwig. "I would ask you to speak plainly, Temple Commander, so there is no misunderstanding. Why are you here?"

"The rift between Hadenfeld and the Antonine must be closed. To that end, I am here to extend an offer that can reinstate the good name of your realm."

"I refuse to subordinate myself to the will of the Church."

"Nor would you be expected to." Amarand took a deep breath. "I regret we came to heated words during my last visit, and my order accepts that you do not wish us to build a commandery in your lands."

"That's gracious of you to say; however, we both know you didn't come all this way to apologize. If you had, you wouldn't need a flag of truce."

"Majesty, we're both aware it's only a matter of time before Hadenfeld and the Church are at war. I'm offering you the chance to change all that."

"And what is it you would have us do?"

"If you would permit, I will get to that, but I must insist you hear me out fully before making your decision."

"You have my attention and that of my queen, but I shall not entertain foolishness or anything that might weaken our rule of this realm."

"You are too kind, Majesty. I'm not certain how much of this you know, so you'll pardon me if I start at the beginning. Last spring, the Council of Peers voted to amalgamate the fighting orders under the command of the Temple Knights of Saint Cunar, to avoid redundancy and to reduce the not-so-inconsiderable cost of maintaining six separate fighting orders. The other orders were instructed to surrender their arms until such time as they were inducted into the Temple Knights of Saint Cunar, at which point their weapons would be returned."

"Several refused to obey this order," he continued, "but the council was in a generous mood and allowed those knights to leave the service of the

Church. The Temple Knights of Saint Agnes, however, refused to a man... or rather, to a woman. They then attacked those sent to secure their arms, leading to bloodshed."

"How is that of any consequence to us?" asked Ludwig.

"With all due respect, sire, I was just getting to that. It has come to our attention that the individual leading these former sister knights fled here, to Hadenfeld, where you've given them safe haven."

"What if they have?"

"The Primus feels justice must be done. He's not suggesting all the former sister knights be turned over, only their leader, Charlaine deShandria."

"And if I turn over Temple General Charlaine?" Ludwig noticed the wince on the Temple Commander's face at the mention of her rank.

"Then the council shall be directed to reverse their position on Hadenfeld and yourself."

"And just like that, we'd no longer be considered heretics?"

"That is correct, sire. You and your queen will once more be embraced by the Church of the Saints."

"Is that all?" asked Charlotte.

"Naturally, we'd expect you to order the sister knights disbanded, but you'd be free to hire them on as knights of your own order if you so chose."

"An interesting offer," said Ludwig.

"Will you give it some consideration, Majesty?"

"I will, although I have some questions if you don't mind."

"Of course, sire. I shall be glad to be of any assistance."

"As the rulers of a Petty Kingdom, we see the Halvarian Empire as the greatest threat to our future prosperity. I wonder if you might tell us the Church's opinion on the matter?"

"I'm not certain I understand the question."

"Your own order is the sword of the Church, is it not? The premier fighting force of the entire Continent?"

"Most assuredly," replied Amarand.

"Then why did your order fail to help the Kingdom of Arnsfeld when the empire invaded it?"

"In our defence, the war was over before any of our knights could make it there."

"I have it on good authority that your Temple Knights withdrew all their companies from that realm prior to the invasion. As a man who understands strategy, can you explain the logic of that to me?"

"The idea was to enable our reserves to quickly mass and react to an invasion, regardless of where it might present itself."

"But you didn't," stated Ludwig.

"As I said, there wasn't enough time to muster our forces."

"Yet the Temple Knights of Saint Agnes and Mathew both intervened on behalf of the King of Arnsfeld, despite many having to travel from neighbouring realms. You are said to be a highly disciplined order, are you not?"

"I assure you we are, sire."

"Then I must admit to some confusion about this strategic decision of yours, not that I'm blaming you in person, you understand."

"We followed the orders of our superiors, as we have been trained to do," said Amarand. "I must also point out that during times of war, communication often breaks down, leading to uninformed decisions on occasion. Although we are Temple Knights of Saint Cunar, we are still Human. In hindsight, our strategy failed, but had we not attempted it, we would've been quickly overrun."

"Your sisters held the line."

"They were present, yes, but the Army of Arnsfeld did most of the fighting. I already admitted it was not the best strategy, but I fail to see what bearing that has on this current situation."

"The Temple Knights of Saint Agnes fought the empire and won. Why, then, would I wish to disband them when I know they'd fight to protect the people of this realm?"

"Their continued existence is no longer a viable option. As I said, you may hire them on as your own personal knights if you so desire, but they no longer represent the ideals of the Church and are not permitted to don the apparel of the Temple Knights of Saint Agnes. I must also remind you that they are of little interest to us. Hand over their leader, and all will be forgiven."

Ludwig thought back to his meeting with Charlaine. She'd be the first to sacrifice herself if it meant her fellow sister knights would be saved, but he knew that was the wrong choice. She was the future of the order, and he'd do everything in his power to keep them safe, even if it meant war.

"I'm afraid I shall have to refuse the offer," said Ludwig at last. "They came here seeking sanctuary, and I agreed. What kind of king would I be if I went back on my word?"

Temple Commander Amarand bowed respectfully. "You have made your choice, Majesty, and I shall not argue any further. You will pardon my manners if I do not wish you well, for in the not-too-distant future, we shall be facing each other across a battlefield. I only hope that when that time comes, you travel to the Afterlife with a clear conscience."

"I have not compromised my principles," said Ludwig. "Can you claim the same?" He nodded at the guards. "Captain Gustavo, please escort the

Temple Commander from our presence, and be so kind as to find an escort to ensure he reaches the border safely."

"Yes, Majesty."

They waited as their guest was escorted from the room.

"Should we have arrested him?" said Charlotte. "Saints know, we had enough cause."

"That would be contrary to our best interests," replied Ludwig.

"What is it you're not telling me?"

He nodded at the door. "He's going to tell us where the Holy Army is."

"Why do you say that?"

"He intends to face me on the battlefield; he said as much."

"How does that help us?"

"It tells me he expects to march with the Holy Army. All we need to do is follow him, and we'll discover where he's heading."

"But he could cross north into Deisenbach, then head east to Zowenbruch, and we'd be none the wiser."

"Ah, but you're assuming his escort will be the only ones watching him. I intend to have someone nearby who can blend in with the locals."

"Then perhaps his coming was fortuitous after all."

Ludwig waited as Captain Gustavo rode up to join him. Behind trailed a dozen of his men, his escort to Eisen. He planned to meet with Temple General Charlaine and then ride north to where Sig waited with his army. The autumn nights were already cooling off, and although winter was still a good two months away, he doubted any offensive would start until spring. When it did come, however, he needed to know what their strategy would be. He hoped Charlaine could answer that question, for she would've received training in how to conduct a crusade, or at least he assumed she had.

His assumption could easily prove false, for as far as he was aware, the Temple Knights of Saint Agnes had never participated in a crusade. She did, however, have battle experience, something which made her a valuable ally. And more importantly, she'd out-fought and outwitted the Cunars who'd been sent to stop her march to Hadenfeld.

Charlaine was no longer the young woman who'd captivated his heart long ago. The years had hardened her, turning her into a fierce warrior who'd bested the Halvarian Empire on multiple occasions. He chuckled at the thought of how different their lives would've been had his father not objected to their union.

"Something funny, sire?" asked Gustavo.

"I was just thinking how strange my path has been."

"This is the road to Verfeld. What other path might we take?"

"No, I mean my life. If you'd asked me in my youth where I thought I'd be today, I'd never have guessed here."

"When was it you left Hadenfeld?"

"I arrived in Erlingen in the spring of ninety-five."

"Thank the Saints you came back," said the captain, "else we'd be living under a tyrant."

21

EISEN

AUTUMN 1107 SR

Temple Captain Nicola stood in front of her superior's desk, waiting patiently until Charlaine paused her writing. "Yes?"

"A runner arrived from the city's gates, General. It appears we're about to have a visitor."

"Are you being deliberately vague as to who it might be, or do you simply not know?"

"It's the king."

"I imagine he's heading north, to check on his general."

"No. He told the sentries he's here to meet with you, General, which is why they dispatched a rider."

"I've received no correspondence from His Majesty recently informing me of a visit?"

"Nor have I seen any," replied Nicola, "but it must be important if he came in person."

"Indeed." Charlaine saw the hesitation in her aide's face. "What's wrong?"

"I'm not certain what the etiquette is for a Royal Visit."

"You were the aide to the grand mistress for years. Are you now telling me there are no protocols for a visit of this nature?"

"I am. No king ever set foot inside the Antonine, thus there are no guidelines within which to operate."

"If the Matriarch of Saint Agnes were to appear at our door, what would you do?"

"Likely spit in her face," replied Nicola, "but that's hardly a suitable greeting for a king."

Charlaine laughed. "Admittedly, we no longer serve under the matriarch, but surely there must've been customs in place that would dictate the correct behaviour?"

"For the matriarch, most certainly."

"Then think of King Ludwig as the patriarch of a trusted ally."

"Understood." Nicola turned to leave, then paused in the doorway. "Do you go down to meet him, or do I bring him up here?"

"For Saint's sake," replied Charlaine. "He's not just any king—he's OUR king. I shall greet him in the great hall."

"Yes, of course." Temple Captain Nicola disappeared into the hallway.

Charlaine sat back, her writing forgotten. Ludwig being here in Eisen was surprising, but his unannounced arrival suggested that something had happened, something important enough that he didn't have time to send advance warning.

Her thoughts immediately turned to Sigwulf's army camped some fifty miles north of Eisen, ready to repulse any invasion that might threaten. Had something happened there, or had Ludwig received news from the Antonine? Perhaps the Church had rescinded the order to disband the Temple Knights of Saint Agnes?

She shook off the notion. With a Cunar in command, especially one in the service of Halvaria, there was little chance a pardon would be granted by the Council of Peers. If anything, they would've sent out a demand for her arrest. Likely the reason for the visit was to warn her, but if that were the case, why come in person?

"Are you coming, General?"

Charlaine almost jumped out of her chair. "Nicola, I thought we were done."

"You said you wanted to meet the king down in the great hall?"

"Oh yes." She rose. "Come. Let's not keep His Majesty waiting."

Ludwig entered the great hall to find Charlaine standing at the head of the very table that he, as prince, had used to confer with the eastern barons. She'd donned a plain cassock, rather than her customary armour, but still wore the blue shoulder sash denoting her rank as Temple General.

She bowed her head as he approached. "Majesty, you honour us with your presence. To what do we owe the pleasure of your company?"

"I've come seeking guidance of a military nature." He looked around the room, noting the Temple Knights standing guard. "Can we dispense with all this formality? Let us sit and discuss the current state of affairs." He nodded towards his captain. "Captain Gustavo commands my Royal Guard. He'll be joining us, and I imagine you'll want your aide present as well. Temple Captain Nicola, wasn't it?"

"Yes," said Charlaine. She swept her hand to indicate they should all sit, then regarded the other Temple Knights. "You may leave us."

They dutifully filed out, leaving the four of them. Nicola grabbed a bottle from the table and poured wine into goblets, then passed them around.

"I assume you're here concerning the Holy Army," said Charlaine.

"Yes," replied Ludwig. "I hoped you might be able to provide some insight into its composition along with some suggestions as to what strategy they could potentially employ."

"I've never led a crusade."

"True, but I'm told senior Temple Knights are well-educated in such things. You've also fought the Cunars and bested them: not an easy thing to do by any means."

"Their arrogance is their undoing," said Charlaine. "They believe they are unbeatable despite evidence to the contrary. One thing is true, though: they never surrender. By all accounts from the Battle of the Wilderness, they fought to the last man, refusing offers of leniency."

"I've heard all about that battle. I understand they were supported by an army under the Duke of Erlingen's command."

"That's correct. The only accounts we have of the battle come from survivors of the duke's forces." She paused. Something had occurred to her, but she was hesitating.

"I sense there's more," said Ludwig.

"When I was in the Antonine, I discovered the Temple Knights of Saint Ansgar held a man by the name of Sir Raynald, a Knight of the Sceptre."

"That's Erlingen's order of chivalry. What in the name of the Saints was he doing in the Antonine?"

"He went there voluntarily, hoping to reveal treachery within the ranks of the Temple Knights of Saint Cunar. A regional commander of the order, Talivardas, conspired to launch a crusade without the Church's approval, which led directly to the debacle at the Battle of the Wilderness."

"Disturbing," said Ludwig.

"Even more so when you realize this very same man became the Primus, changing his name to Wilmar to cover his past misdeeds. And this same individual is a Sartellian, a family name I know you're familiar with."

"So the empire controls the Church?"

Charlaine forced a smile, though it was far from comforting. "Now you understand why the fighting orders were disbanded, save for the Cunars."

"Had this Raynald fellow any proof?"

"Yes, a letter purporting to be from the grand master of his order authorizing the crusade."

"And?"

"The letter was dated, and short of magic, it was impossible for a courier to make the trip from Corassus to Ebenstadt in that short a period."

"And the Church doesn't employ mages?"

"The Ragnarites do, on occasion, and my own order has one now that Teresa has returned to us, but certainly not the Cunars."

"Yet you claim this Talivardas fellow is a Sartellian. Doesn't that make him a Fire Mage?"

"Most assuredly, and knowing all this put me in a difficult position, particularly when they took steps to intercept orders meant to call me back to the Antonine."

"I don't understand," said Ludwig. "You left the Antonine to come here, didn't you?"

"Yes, but I received my orders to travel there in the spring of 1106. I arrived there in the summer of last year only to discover my grand mistress had summoned me much earlier. I managed to uncover the schemes of Talivardas while I was there, but by then, it was too late; he'd already seized power."

"I assume that's when he ordered the other fighting orders to disband?"

"There'd been rumours of that happening for a while, but the Council of Peers never supported it. Things didn't come to a head until the new Augustine patriarch was named." She fell silent.

"You mentioned you fled the Antonine. How did that come about?"

"The Grand Mistress suspected she was about to be dismissed. As I said before, only the Matriarch of Saint Agnes can name a new one, so she made me a Temple General and gave me the task of saving the order."

"That was a chaotic day," she continued, "but we were prepared. The Cunars surrounded our commandery, so we fought our way out."

"Isn't the Antonine walled?"

"It is, but the Ragnarites also refused to submit, and so they seized the gate that day, holding it long enough for us to leave, though we still had to fight our way out."

"I'll say!" added Nicola. "The Temple General broke both her legs jumping from the gatehouse. If it hadn't been for Sister Teresa, she'd have died."

"So began the trek of the Five Hundred," continued Charlaine. "We took losses along the way and were forced to fight a group of Cunars to get across a bridge. We lost more in a delaying action, including a couple of my best officers. We only made it into East Hadenfeld because a worshipper of Akosia helped us."

"Akosia? She's the Sea Goddess, isn't she?"

Charlaine nodded. "The ships of the Temple Fleet are blessed in her name."

"Yes. I recall a priestess of Akosia being present at my wedding. How did they know you needed help?"

"I was told the goddess embraced me as a champion of the old religion. I wasn't about to argue the point. In any case, we entered the eastern woodlands of Hadenfeld, which is when we ran across the Elves. The rest, you already know."

"You must scribe an account of your flight; it would inspire future generations."

"It may surprise you to know I already have. We Temple Knights like to document everything. It's how we pass on wisdom to future generations. Now, enough talk about me. Let's get to the real reason you're here, shall we? The composition of the Holy Army."

"Yes," said Ludwig. "I understand the Cunars will comprise the mounted contingent of the army, but I'm uncertain what to expect in terms of the extras."

"You mean the volunteers?"

"Yes."

"The Church prefers the term auxiliaries. They'll make up the numbers based on how recruitment proceeds. Generally, that means lots of foot, some bow, and, on rare occasions, cavalry."

"How many should we expect?"

"Few things can break the discipline of the Cunars' ranks, but our order defeating them on the field of battle will likely infuriate them. Do they know we're here?"

"They do," said Ludwig. "They offered to call off the crusade if I turned you over to them."

"You should've agreed. You could've saved the kingdom a lot of bloodshed."

"At the cost of forever being beholden to the Church. You know as well as I that was never an option."

"Since they're aware of us, we can make a few deductions."

"Those being?"

"We escaped the Antonine with just over five hundred Temple Knights. To ensure victory, they'll need to scrape together every knight they can muster. Fortunately for us, they took a terrible drumming at the Battle of the Wilderness, enough that their numbers in the east were drastically curtailed. Not so helpful is that there were a lot of Temple Knights in the Antonine. I suspect when they come, there'll be at least a thousand, possibly more."

"And the auxiliaries?"

"Once again," said Charlaine, "it's hard to give an exact estimate. The Army of Erlingen suffered a great many casualties in the last crusade, so they won't be too interested in another campaign. In all likelihood, the Church will recruit from areas hostile to Hadenfeld. In other words, those lands with which you don't currently have an alliance. You'd have a better idea than I of the number of men they could raise. How many have you under arms?"

"Thirteen hundred, although presently, that's split into two armies: one facing Deisenbach, the other, as you know, is north of Eisen."

"But you have the Elves, don't you?"

"They've pledged five hundred warriors."

"To which you can add my own five hundred. If you gathered everyone together, you might be able to match the enemy's numbers."

"It's not their number that has me worried, it's their quality. Few horsemen can stand up to the might of a Cunar Temple Knight, let alone all these auxiliaries."

"Auxiliaries vary greatly in quality and, with rare exceptions, are generally ill-led. It's what comes of being recruited from so many different kingdoms."

"The Duke of Erlingen led the ones in the east."

"True," replied Charlaine, "and by all accounts, his own men acquitted themselves admirably, but the rest of his army varied in both experience and equipment, not to mention training or a lack thereof. I might also remind you, that in the end, they lost the battle."

"Any idea what strategy they might employ?"

"This is no simple invasion; it's a crusade, which is a completely different beast. They'll cross the border in force and occupy any town or village within a day's march. Then, the Holy Fathers of Saint Cunar will move in, searching out those who oppose the Church. Once they find them, they'll attempt to convert them to their cause."

"And if they refuse?"

"I hate to admit it, but that would likely be a death sentence."

"I thought the Church preached acceptance of other religions?"

"It does. The words of the Saints were clear on the subject, but the Holy Army is not bound by scripture, only results. Cunars refer to themselves as the sword of the Saints, doing the work others are too timid to contemplate."

"That's barbaric."

"I agree, though in their minds, there is justification for this behaviour. Cunar Marthune, after whom their order is named, advocated the creation of a single church to rule over the entire Continent, something the Temple Knights of his order believe wholeheartedly. Up until now, they've followed the orders of the Council of Peers, allowing their more radical beliefs to be put aside, but that changed with the new Primus."

"Agreed," said Ludwig, "but that's only because the Halvarians made it so."

"Are you suggesting someone could convince them of the error of their ways? That would take a miracle."

"Yes, I suppose it would, but I believe we're past the point of diplomacy."

"What will you do now?" asked Charlaine.

"I'll ride north to check how Sig is doing, then head for Zowenbruch."

"Is that wise?"

"I have some experience dealing with King Konrad. I'm hoping to convince him to remain neutral in our conflict with the Church."

"And if he arrests you?"

"He won't," said Ludwig. "He's a man of his word."

"Still, he might not agree to remain neutral."

"True, but it's a bit late in the year to start a military campaign, particularly if this Holy Army intends to conquer all of Hadenfeld. If this attack is coming, it won't be till next spring, and I'll be well out of Zowenbruch by then. Of course, the crusade could still be coming from Deisenbach."

"It's not," said Charlaine. "I'm in contact with the Agnesite Temple Captain there. Had she heard anything, I would've known by now."

"I don't suppose you have anyone in Zowenbruch?"

"I'm afraid not. Our order was banned from assembling within their borders, so those there fled some time ago, some making their way here to Eisen."

"So you've increased your numbers?"

"Enough to make up our losses from our march here, but that's about it. I've also sent word out to other commanderies scattered throughout the Petty Kingdoms, but I expect it to be a while before I hear from any of them."

"And what about the Temple Fleet?"

Charlaine smiled. "Danica should be back in command of it by now. I've written, telling her of our whereabouts, but once again, it will take time for my letter to find its way to her."

"I assume you're using the Dwarven smiths guild?"

"Yes. It's the only option left to me. We certainly can't rely on couriers from the Church."

"I'm glad to hear the fleet is safe," said Ludwig, "but I'd feel more comfortable if I knew where that Holy Army was assembling."

"I shall write once more to Temple Captain Giselle in Deisenbach. Her command there is new to her, but she's quite capable. I'll have her send riders across the kingdom. I doubt they'll find the army, but there's a good chance they might hear something about the Church recruiting for this crusade, which would at least confirm they're massing in Zowenbruch."

"Thank you. That's greatly appreciated. There is one more thing I should tell you."

"Yes?"

"I told you the Church offered to put this matter behind us if I turned you over. What I didn't mention is that I have a man following the Temple Commander who presented that offer."

"And you trust this fellow of yours not to get caught?"

"Indeed. I recruited Rikal while I was still the Baron of Verfeld, and he's served me ever since."

"Long service doesn't guarantee he won't be seen."

"True, but he's an archer and an expert in tracking, not to mention one of the stealthiest people I've ever met. I won't hear anything from him till he's found what he's looking for, so that could still be some time yet."

"Meanwhile, you'll travel to the capital of Zowenbruch seeking answers?"

"Yes, I have people there at court already. My official reason for going there is to meet with King Konrad, but I see no reason why I can't do both." He nodded at his companion. "Captain Gustavo has also proven himself a valuable asset. When I find capable people like him, I like to keep them around."

"A sentiment we share," replied Charlaine.

22

KURSLINGEN

AUTUMN 1107 SR

Ludwig wandered through the camp, stopping to chat with the soldiers. The men were nervous, and rightly so, for no one knew how many enemy soldiers they'd be facing once the invasion began.

Sigwulf followed along, adding to the king's reassurances. He waited until they were finally free of the tents before diving into the real reason for this visit. "Have you heard anything from Zowenbruch?"

"No," replied Ludwig. "That is to say, I've heard from Lord Darrian, but nothing concerning the Holy Army. There is, however, plenty of activity from the Church in Kurslingen, their capital."

"What sort of activity?"

"Darrian thinks they're trying to whip up the crowd, badmouthing Hadenfeld to justify a crusade, even going so far as to portray us as a pack of filthy heathens."

"And is that working?"

"Apparently not, and that's largely Konrad's doing. He was thankful for the way we treated him after his failed invasion, and he's been vocal in defending us. Unfortunately, that isn't being received well by the Church."

"Interesting," said Sigwulf, "but I doubt that'll make much of a difference. That Holy Army will cross that border with or without the help of Zowenbruch, although I'd prefer the latter."

"As would I, which is why I'm travelling to Kurslingen. I may not be able to stop the Holy Army, but I'm hoping to convince Konrad to remain neutral in this affair."

"And you believe your presence there will make a difference?"

"Letters can be misleading, with words taken in a different context, while talking face to face prevents that sort of misunderstanding."

"I hope you know what you're doing," said Sigwulf.

"Konrad is a reasonable man and a follower of Saint Mathew. I intend to use the Saint's own words to try to convince him how wrong this crusade is."

"I think he already knows, but he's trapped. He dared not object, or his kingdom would suffer the same fate as ours, and he's not the military leader you are. The Holy Army would crush his army if it came to a fight."

"I shall bear that in mind," replied Ludwig. "My first order of business will be meeting with Lord Darrian and Lady Esmerelda. She's been at Konrad's court far longer than he, so I expect she'll have a much better idea about the political climate."

Sigwulf's gaze wandered over to where Gustavo and his men waited, along with Ludwig's horse. "Are you certain you shouldn't bring more guards?"

"I'm heading there on a diplomatic visit, not invading. The last thing I want to do is to give the impression I fear for my own safety."

"Good luck, then," said Sigwulf. "I've a feeling you're going to need it."

They reached Zwieken by the end of the week, and then crossed the river into the village of Seiburg in Zowenbruch. The terrain here was similar to that of northeastern Hadenfeld, consisting of open plains with occasional patches of forest.

The road was easy to follow, leading to a pleasant journey. They occasionally passed travellers heading north or south, intent on going about their business. Ludwig often engaged these individuals in conversation, but the threat of an impending war was the last thing on anyone's mind. They were more concerned with the price of bread than an army massing somewhere within their borders.

Over the next two days, the terrain turned hilly, and they learned from a roadside inn that the capital was within a hard day's ride.

Late in the evening, they topped a rise to see Kurslingen sitting off in the distance, a sprawling city devoid of any defensive structures. Quite a different sight than Harlingen, whose great walls had kept the capital of Hadenfeld safe on at least two occasions.

They entered Kurslingen unchallenged, with only the occasional city dweller remarking on their passing. Finding the king's palace was easy enough, for it sat atop a dominant hill to the west of the city, surrounded by fields full of livestock.

Gustavo nodded to the west. "Is that where we're headed?"

"Eventually," replied Ludwig, "but we must speak with Lord Darrian first."

"That'll be the north end of the city."

"How do you know that?"

"That's where the wealthy people live, or so said the barkeep at that last roadside inn. Do we have an address, or are we going to ride around and ask for their whereabouts?"

"It's a red-bricked house off Fountain Square, wherever that is."

Gustavo halted, looking around until he caught the gaze of a man selling apples from a stall. "You there," he said. "Where can I find Fountain Square?"

The merchant pointed. "Up that way, five streets, then turn right. You can't miss the fountain as it sits in the middle of the square."

"Thank you." The captain tossed him a coin, and they continued on their way.

Once they found the fountain, locating the house was easy. The captain knocked on the door, which was answered by a surprised servant who ushered them inside as others came to take their horses.

Lord Darrian and Lady Esmerelda, who were sitting in the parlour, stood as Ludwig entered.

"Sire!" said the baron. "I wasn't expecting you."

"It was a last-minute decision," replied Ludwig. "I trust you are well, my lord, Lady Esmerelda."

"Would you care for something to drink?" asked Darrian.

"By all means. You remember Captain Gustavo?"

"Yes, of course. Where are my manners? Please sit, both of you. Have you eaten?"

"Yes, earlier," said Ludwig.

"Are you here to meet with King Konrad?" asked Lord Darrian.

"I am, but first, have you heard anything new about this crusade?"

"I have. In fact, I dispatched a messenger only last night; it likely passed you on the road. Word is they're massing to the east, in a town called Esthafen."

"How did you come about this knowledge?"

"By being clever," chimed in Esmerelda. "Our cook was complaining about the scarcity of meat at the local market, so Darrian decided to investigate the situation. Turns out, the Church has been buying up as much meat as it can get its hands on, along with other supplies."

"Yes," added Darrian. "Once I discovered that, it only took a few coins in the right places to loosen some tongues. By my estimate, they're stocking up for winter, which has driven up the cost of linen, as they use it for making tents. I also learned the Church took control of many buildings in Esthafen for their winter billets."

"Could this be a ruse?"

"I seriously doubt it," replied Darrian. "From what I've been able to gather, they're still waiting on volunteers to trickle in from across the Petty Kingdoms."

"And Konrad?"

"He has yet to order his army to muster, but that makes sense if the campaign is due to start in the spring. I haven't had an opportunity to talk to him in person, but I've made some enquiries by letter. Unfortunately, he's not yet responded to my correspondence."

"Assuming he's seen any of it," said Ludwig. "Any news of Stormwinds or Sartellians at his court?"

"None whatsoever. It seems he ordered them to leave after his aborted attempt to capture Eisen."

"It seems?"

"As I said, I haven't been there myself to confirm it, and my good wife has heard no mention of their names, aside from the knowledge of their dismissal, that is."

"That's a relief," said Ludwig. "It gives us more time to prepare."

"Shall I send word to the palace that you're here and request an audience?"

"Yes. I'd prefer not to drop in unexpectedly."

Ludwig and Gustavo were met by an escort of Konrad's, who led them up the hill to the king's residence, its white stone walls seemingly going on forever. As he neared the ornate building, he noticed images of the Saints decorating the large columns out front.

A captain stood near the two guards outside the front door, and after a quick nod towards Ludwig, he ushered them into a large room whose white marble floor was polished to a mirror finish.

King Konrad sat at the far end of a long table, but stood as they entered, offering a nod of acknowledgement. "Good to see you, Ludwig," he said, "although I'm sorry it couldn't be under better circumstances."

"As am I," replied Ludwig.

"You are here, I assume, to discuss recent… developments?"

"I am, and to remind you that you swore an oath to never again cross our border in anger."

"And I meant every word, but I am under a great deal of pressure from the Church. Even as we speak, an army is forming, and if I don't submit to the will of the Church, I face utter ruination."

"How did it come to this?" asked Ludwig. "Did you invite them here?"

"They invited themselves, and before I knew it, hundreds of Temple Knights marched into Esthafen. They assured me they were no danger to my own realm, but there was an implied threat."

"Allow us to proceed or face the consequences?"

"Precisely. You see my dilemma. As you know, my army is neither numerous nor particularly experienced in the art of war. A contingent of Temple Knights would've made short work of my forces. If you recall, at the Battle of Eisen, my knights refused to engage the Mathewites. How, then, could I expect them to face off against the Cunars?"

"I sympathize with your plight," said Ludwig, "but the very existence of my own kingdom is being challenged by these same Temple Knights."

"I understand that," replied Konrad, "but I see no other way to proceed."

"Can you at least reveal how many Temple Knights I'll be facing?"

"Close to eight hundred, not including their initiates, who fight on foot."

"Are you suggesting they've had a sudden increase in the number of recruits joining the order?"

"I'm not suggesting at all; I'm telling you. I've seen them for myself. Each one is a trained knight, drawn from across the Petty Kingdoms."

"Do we know who's leading this army?"

"I believe it's a Temple General of Saint Cunar, but I'm afraid I don't know his name. Why? Were you expecting someone in particular?"

"That they've assigned a Temple General instead of a Temple Commander indicates how important they're taking this, and it also tells me that, in all likelihood, the person in charge is both capable and experienced, making my job far more difficult."

"I wish it were better news, but as I said, I have little choice in the matter."

"And if they ask you to march with them?"

"I shall do my best to avoid that particular entanglement, but should they force the matter, I have few alternatives. A refusal would likely lead my barons to rebel, perhaps even cost me my head."

Ludwig found himself at a loss for words. The very notion that Konrad would not keep his word destroyed his last hope of preventing a disaster. Although the Army of Zowenbruch wasn't large, its numbers gave the Holy Army a huge advantage by freeing the most experienced of their men, the Temple Knights, to continue the campaign while Konrad's forces garrisoned the captured towns and villages of Hadenfeld.

Without those additional men at their disposal, Ludwig could've worn down the attackers, sacrificing towns to reduce the enemy's strength. Now, he'd have no option but to confront the enemy before they could ravage his kingdom.

"If it's any consolation," said Konrad, "I don't like this any more than you do." He lowered his voice. "I shall do all I can to avoid this… entanglement, and I will provide you with what information I can regarding the composition of the Holy Army."

"I thank you for that at least." Ludwig shook his head. "I should've seen this coming. I know from experience how much pressure the Church can exert on a kingdom."

"It takes courage to stand against the might of the Church, and I applaud you for that, but I am not blessed with that particular characteristic. I'm a weak man and fell prey to the influence of the Stormwinds, and my kingdom has now become a vassal of the Antonine."

"A vassal?"

"Not officially, but we might as well be. The Church makes demands, and my nobles are far too eager to placate them. I sometimes wonder if I have any real power left."

Ludwig stood, silently contemplating his next move. Konrad waited, and the silence grew. Even the servants remained still, caught up in the seriousness of the moment.

"Your thoughts?" prompted the King of Zowenbruch.

Ludwig met his gaze, then spoke calmly. "I will return to Hadenfeld, but I make you this promise. My army will destroy the Holy Army, and in doing so, we will break the power of the Church once and for all. If your army stands in our way, then they shall suffer the same fate."

"I understand."

"We are done here. Come, Gustavo. It's time for us to be on our way." Ludwig strode from the room, his captain rushing to catch up.

They were soon mounted and on their way back to the border, bypassing the city of Kurslingen altogether.

Ludwig's mind whirled, his gut twisting with indecision. "Was I right to threaten him so?" he asked.

His words startled Gustavo, but the fellow recovered quickly. "What choice did you have?"

"None, but perhaps a more diplomatic statement might've been more appropriate."

"Nonsense, Majesty. You have a reputation as a great warrior. Better to put fear in the enemy's heart than show them weakness."

"Bravado will only get you so far."

"True," said Gustavo, "but that wasn't bluster—it was a promise. And if there's one thing I've learned over the years, it's that you keep your promises."

Ludwig laughed. "So now I must follow through with an empty threat because I gave my word?"

"Indeed. As Saint Mathew once said, 'A person's word should be taken as an oath.' To do otherwise would be considered a lie."

"I never took you for a religious man."

"Oh, I can be a devout worshipper when the occasion demands, and, I believe it's appropriate in this case, don't you?"

"What would you do, were you king?"

"Me? King? Now you're just being silly, sire. I'm but a humble captain of the guard."

"No," said Ludwig. "I'm being serious. You were there when Temple Commander Amarand first arrived in Harlingen. Were you in charge, would you have refused his demands?"

"That's difficult to say. If I'd known it would lead to war, perhaps not, but then again, we all hoped the queen's refusal would be the end of the matter. I don't think anyone expected it to reach the Council of Peers. And to declare us heretics? Why in the name of the Saints would they do that?"

"Because the Primus is an agent of Halvaria, which is why we have to fight. Unfortunately, even if we win, we lose."

"How's that?"

"The Halvarian Empire has wanted to conquer the Petty Kingdoms for centuries, but so far, they've limited their expansion to one realm at a time. This war, however, opens the door to a continent-wide invasion."

Ludwig noted the captain's look of confusion and asked, "What prevents the empire from expanding faster?"

"The threat of the Holy Army?"

"True, but along with that, we must consider the regional powers in the Petty Kingdoms. Hadenfeld once possessed one of the largest armies on the entire Continent. Any war between us and the Holy Army, win or lose, would result in a drastic reduction of our numbers."

"Making it easier for the empire to conquer us?"

"Yes," replied Ludwig. "In that sense, this entire war weakens us all."

"But what choice do we have?" said Gustavo. "We can't be expected to surrender, surely?"

"Of course not. Doing so would leave the Holy Army intact, and we know it's under the control of a Halvarian agent."

"That being the Primus?"

"Precisely."

"So what do we do?"

Ludwig grinned. "We fight, just not in the way they expect us to."

"And how do we do that?"

"I have a few thoughts, but I need a second opinion. To that end, we'll delay our return to Harlingen in favour of Eisen. I need to arrange a meeting with the Temple General and the High Lord of the Goldenwood."

"What of General Marhaven's army?"

"We'll order them back to Eisen as we ride by; there's no sense in leaving them out in the middle of nowhere with winter approaching."

"And our other army?"

"Cyn will return to the capital, but come the spring thaw, she'll bring them east, to Eisen, so we can carry out our campaign."

"I don't suppose you'd care to share your thoughts on this campaign?"

"Not quite yet, my friend. I'm still considering several possibilities, but you're welcome to sit in on the meeting. Who knows, perhaps one day you'll become a general yourself."

"Me, a general? I'm a captain, sire. I command but a single company."

"Well, maybe a commander, then. Would that be more acceptable? It comes with a pay increase."

Gustavo grinned. "An increase in pay, you say? No offence, sire, but you should've led with that."

They both laughed as they rode south, leaving the rest of the escort to wonder what had been said.

23

WAR CLOUDS

AUTUMN 1107 SR

"They're massing east of Zowenbruch's capital," said Ludwig. "I'm afraid there's no doubt. This man"—he pointed to Rikal—"followed Temple Commander Amarand all the way to Esthafen, confirming what we already suspected."

"That is good," replied Sindra. "We can now take decisive action." The High Lord regarded the people standing around the table. Sigwulf was there, as was the Temple General and Talon Elonin. Charlaine also invited Temple Commander Hamelyn, who'd travelled to Eisen and placed his own Temple Knights at her disposal.

"I've sent word to Cyn," said Sigwulf, "but her command is still at least a week away."

"We cannot wait," insisted the High Lord. "Doing so gives the initiative to the enemy."

"That means invading Zowenbruch," said Ludwig. "Our treaty is one of mutual defence; it says nothing of attacking another realm."

"All here understand what is at stake," replied Sindra. "If you march your army across the border, we will participate in the campaign."

"As will the Temple Knights," added Charlaine. "If you intend to go ahead with this, though, we need to do so quickly before the auxiliaries gather in larger numbers."

"I would be interested in hearing your thoughts on this Holy Army, General."

"The enemy will likely begin their campaign next spring."

"Why is that?" asked the High Lord.

"The Temple Knights of Saint Cunar lack the footmen and archers needed to successfully carry out their strategy. To solve that, they've sent a call out to the Petty Kingdoms asking for volunteers."

"And will they come?"

"Most definitely, but it takes time to reach the farthest kingdoms, and even more time for those interested to travel to Zowenbruch. If we strike now, before the onset of winter, we can hit the Crusaders while they're vulnerable."

"That makes sense," said Sindra. "What would be our strategy, Majesty?" The Elf turned to Ludwig.

He pointed to a specific location on the map. "The town of Esthafen lies here, approximately seventy miles east of their capital. The land there is mostly flat, ideal for an army mustering point, making it eminently suitable for the deployment of cavalry."

"And our attack route?" asked Sigwulf.

"I propose we divide our forces into three separate commands. Sig's army will cross here, at Zwieken, capturing the village of Seiburg, but instead of marching north to Kurslingen, you'll head northeast, cross-country, towards Esthafen."

"Wouldn't that make it easier for the Army of Zowenbruch to cut off our supply lines?"

"It's a risk, but I'm hoping the campaign will be over before that becomes a problem."

"You said three commands?" prompted Charlaine.

"Yes. I'd like your Temple Knights to proceed north through these hills here."

The Temple General looked at the map. "The Barrows? Not exactly the most welcoming of names."

"It's rumoured there are long-lost tombs up there, but it's likely superstitious nonsense."

"It is not," said Sindra. "A group of Humans inhabited the area in the distant past."

"How distant?" asked Sigwulf.

"Approximately fifteen hundred years ago, although I do not have my notes here to consult. I still remember their chieftain, a Human named Garulf. His grey eyes were most intense as if he could see into a person's soul."

"Grey eyes? Are you suggesting he was a Therengian?"

"That would've been centuries before the founding of the Old Kingdom," said Ludwig, "although I suppose even Therengians had ancestors." He turned to the High Lord. "Did all his people have grey eyes?"

"I do not recall. It was, after all, some time ago. Perhaps Elonin has a better idea?"

They all looked at the talon.

"There is nothing I can add to the High Lord's accounting. At that time, I spent most of my days in the east."

"Ah, yes," said Sindra. "You were still living in Thalune then."

"Is that another Elven city?" asked Sigwulf.

"It is."

"Just how many cities do you folks have hidden away in the Goldenwood?"

The High Lord merely smiled. "That is not something I wish to discuss at present. Now, can we get back to strategy, or will the conversation take another turn into a different topic? It appears to be something you Humans do quite often."

"Our deepest apologies," said Ludwig. "Now, where was I?"

"You'd suggested I take the Temple Knights through the Barrows," prompted Charlaine. "I assume there's a ford north of them?"

"There is. Sig can tell you more."

The huge northerner grinned. "I've been working with people from the area for the last few weeks, gathering as much information as I can to anticipate any alternate invasion routes. According to my sources, there's a ford where the Zowen River meets the Goldenwood. Hug the edge of that forest, and it should lead you right to it. There's also the chance the enemy knows about it and has it guarded, so you'd best take precautions."

"I don't anticipate any trouble on that account," said Charlaine. "If it's guarded, it won't be by Temple Knights."

"Why's that?"

"The Cunars will view it as being beneath them. If soldiers are there, they're likely King Konrad's, which brings me to the question of whether we attack, if that's the case?"

"I prefer you didn't," said Ludwig, "but getting across that river is a priority, or the entire strategy falls apart."

"Then we shall force the ford, if necessary, without bloodshed."

"And if they fight?" asked Sigwulf.

"They won't," replied Charlaine. "Not with hundreds of Temple Knights crossing in full plate armour."

"We can act as your advance scouts," offered Temple Captain Hamelyn. "The soldiers of Zowenbruch refused to engage us the last time they invaded. Hopefully, the same will prove true there."

"I shall leave that at the Temple General's discretion," said Ludwig, "but once you're across that river, you must head directly for Esthafen. Now, as for the Elves—"

"I know what you are about to say," interrupted Sindra. "We are to make our way north, using the Goldenwood to conceal our movements. Although we lay no claim to that portion of the forest, my glade wardens know the area well."

"How close can you get without being detected?"

"I cannot say with complete accuracy, but our estimates put the town of Esthafen some twenty-five miles from the woods, perhaps a little more. The road east of that town runs along the northern edge of the woods, so I suggest we use that route to approach."

"The key to all of this is staggering our attacks," said Ludwig. "To that end, you'll need people out front, watching for activity. I'd like Sig's group to attack first. Their aim will be to draw the enemy out of their camp. At that point, the Temple Knights come in from the south, hopefully catching them in the flank. The Elves will enter the camp while the enemy is busy and destroy as much as they can, then bid a hasty retreat before any retaliation."

"Coordinating all this will prove difficult," said Charlaine.

"Our Earth Mages can utilize magic to give us a bird's-eye view," said Sindra. "I shall ensure each group involved has one available before we march."

"That is most appreciated, but we must act quickly. The days have become significantly cooler, and we need to be in and out of there before the snow arrives."

"Your plan is bold and daring, which may tempt the enemy to retaliate in some manner prior to winter arriving. Are we prepared for that?"

"They won't enter the forest," noted Charlaine, "which leaves only two possible invasion routes: down through Zwieken or the Barrows. My suggestion is that we hold them off at the river."

"Would that stop the Temple Knights of Saint Cunar?"

"No, but they would only be able to cross a few at a time, incurring heavy losses in the process. This is a campaign of attrition, so we need to wear them down as much as possible before we make the last stand."

"Last stand?" said Sigwulf. "You make it sound like we're going to lose."

"A loss is always possible," replied Charlaine, "but I'm referring to the last battle, the one to end their dreams of a crusade. There's also the matter of the enemy's morale. Not that the Cunars will break, but inflicting a loss forces those auxiliaries to think twice about whether they want to be part of this campaign."

"An excellent point," said Ludwig. "As to the Army of Zowenbruch, we shall try to avoid any direct contact, but if they stand in the way, they're to be considered the enemy. Now, are there any other questions?"

"Are we correct in expecting them to pursue?" said Sigwulf. "If this works, they'll have no supplies or auxiliaries to help."

"If they do, they won't go after you," replied Charlaine. "The Temple Knights of Saint Agnes defeated them during our flight from the Antonine, and they'll be eager to take revenge."

"I have an idea," said Elonin. "If our archers were along the edge of the Goldenwood near that ford, we could pick off the Cunars as they tried to cross."

The Temple General nodded. "I saw how effective Elven bows were at the Battle of the Brinwald. I think it's an excellent idea, but won't you need them with you in the north?"

"Our part in this is to act as raiders, which our cavalry is particularly well-suited for. I doubt the absence of our archers amongst the enemy camp would make much of a difference."

"I shall leave it to you two to coordinate that," said Ludwig. "Out of curiosity, what's the likelihood of the enemy having crossbows?"

"Slim, I would think," replied Charlaine. "Crossbows are more expensive than bows and require a lot more maintenance. They're common enough amongst the armies of the Petty Kingdoms, but I doubt you'd find individuals who own them flocking to the Holy Army anytime soon."

"That's a relief. It means their archers have a much lower chance of penetrating our armour."

"There's a good chance we won't have to worry about archers at all. The Temple Knights of Saint Cunar look down on them, seeing them as an inferior but necessary part of any army."

"And if they do loose arrows at you?"

"Then we shall reply with a hail of bolts," replied Charlaine.

"Bolts?" said Sigwulf. "You have crossbows?"

"We came across them in an old storeroom in Eisen. I took it upon myself to commandeer them in the name of the order. I hope I didn't overstep my authority?"

"Not at all," said Ludwig. "I gave you the keep, including anything found inside, but I'm curious how you intend to use them."

"My knights are still training, but with almost five hundred to choose from, it wasn't too difficult to find enough capable to establish two companies. Now, having said that, they're not the heavier crossbows like the Dwarves use, but that makes them easier to handle while mounted."

"What tactics would you employ?"

"Their main task will be to discourage pursuit, although I suppose they could be used to soften up an enemy line before charging. Does Hadenfeld employ crossbows?"

"Not at present, but some of our allies do. The Duke of Erlingen had them at the Battle of Chermingen, although admittedly, they didn't contribute much. They say Dwarven armies use an all-metal crossbow that's extremely effective."

"Yes," replied Charlaine. "They call them arbalests. The Temple Fleet has them mounted on their decks, though those are naturally larger than the ones used by their archers."

"There is an area where we have the advantage," said Sigwulf. "Leadership."

"Agreed," said Sindra. "Both King Ludwig and the Temple General have experience in battle, although I suppose the Cunar leader will have some expertise in that area as well."

"We have one more advantage," offered Charlaine. "As a Temple Commander, I was required to study strategy and tactics from the same books as the Cunars, so I know what to expect from them."

"Which is?"

"Their books suggest a variety of tactics, but historically, they favour flanking manoeuvres while the auxiliaries pin down the enemy."

"Have your studies included the Battle of the Wilderness?"

"They have," replied Charlaine, "although in that battle, the Cunar commander defied all logic. The auxiliaries advanced on the right, but the Cunars sent their initiates forward on the left with very little support, save for a few crossbowmen on loan from the Duke of Erlingen."

"And the enemy?"

"They deployed on a hill, with woods reaching out on either side, rather like arms offering a place of concealment on the flanks of the Holy Army."

"I'm surprised the duke didn't send men into the woods to clear them."

"Oh, he did, but he didn't count on the tenacity of the Orcs, who put up a spirited defence, drawing the duke's forces farther into the forest, then they used Fire Mages to set it alight. The results were catastrophic."

"But the mounted Temple Knights were still intact, weren't they?"

"They were, but they had another surprise waiting for them. The accounts are sparse and oftentimes contradictory, but it appears a group of Orcs came from the east riding some sort of large creatures."

"How large?" asked Ludwig.

"Somewhere between two and five times the size of a warhorse, although I believe we can safely rule out the upper estimates. Regardless of their actual size, their hides proved tougher than the Temple Knights' armour, leaving the Cunars unable to wound them. They were also supported by mages wielding a variety of magic. Therengians and Orcs, it seems, are blessed with an abundance of spellcasters."

"It was, by all accounts, a terrible battle," continued Charlaine, "resulting in a great loss of life, including the Duke of Erlingen."

"And the leader of the Cunars?"

"He chose to make a stand with his men, fighting to the last and refusing surrender; at least that's the way it's portrayed. I should've liked to learn more from Sir Raynald, but matters were quickly spinning out of control."

"Who's Sir Raynald?" asked Sigwulf.

"A knight in service to the duke who was captured during the battle, then released after swearing an oath to never attack the Therengians again. Of course, I say Therengians, but at that time, they'd yet to declare their realm. I should mention the oath also applied to not attacking any of the Orc tribes."

"Orcs," said Sindra. "They are vile creatures."

"Why do you hate them so?" asked Charlaine.

"My people fought a great war with them two thousand years ago. The losses we sustained there led directly to the ascendancy of Humans."

"How did that happen?"

"The war itself lasted for more than one hundred years and saw death on a massive scale. By the end, we Elves had destroyed all the Orc cities, but in the process, we lost a tremendous number of our people. We withdrew to our own lands, leaving the wilderness to be claimed by you Humans."

"Two thousand years ago?" said Ludwig. "And you say there were Humans? I thought Herani was the birthplace of Humanity?"

"That is a myth," offered Elonin, "likely created to justify the existence of your Church of the Saints. Humans have existed in Eiddenwerthe for far longer than you might imagine, although when we fought the Orcs, your species had yet to discover civilization. By that, I mean they were largely limited to tribal villages; the concept of a realm or kingdom had not occurred to them."

Charlaine shook her head. "I always suspected Herani wasn't the first Human city, but to hear we were around a thousand years prior to that is a difficult thing to absorb."

"There is much your people do not know," said Sindra. "My own people encouraged the first Humans to settle down. When we initially met your kind, they were simple hunter-gatherers. We showed them how to farm, how to build proper shelter, even how to fight when needed."

"Did they help you during this war with the Orcs?"

The High Lord's face darkened. "No. We were betrayed. In our hubris, we believed Humans would look to us as pillars of wisdom and adopt our ways, but we did not count on the unique trait of your race."

"That being?"

"An unquenchable thirst for knowledge. The more we taught them, the more they wanted to know. Our own rulers balked at their demands, feeling that too much knowledge would prove dangerous. You were like children in those days, and when you expressed an interest in learning magic, we feared that, should you learn to wield such power, you would destroy the world of Eiddenwerthe. In frustration, you Humans turned to another species for help."

"The Orcs," said Ludwig. "Is that why you went to war with them?"

"The reasons for the conflict were many," replied Sindra. "I was not one of the ruling class in those long-ago days, so I cannot speak to the final spark that led to war, but certainly, the Orcs' growing influence amongst the Humans was a contributing factor. We fought that war to cleanse the land of their presence, and now you inform us that Orc tribes have risen in the east. This news is most disturbing."

"We Humans have gone to war with our neighbours in the past, but that doesn't mean we're still enemies."

"Ah, but you forget a key difference in our species. I marched in the Great War, fighting shoulder to shoulder with my fellow Elves as we destroyed the cities of the Orcs one by one. It is a distant memory, but I experienced it first-hand, and such brutality leaves a lasting mark on even the toughest of warriors."

24

THE ARMY ASSEMBLES
AUTUMN 1107 SR

Ludwig watched as Sigwulf's division lined up, getting ready to march. The lighter cavalry would lead, followed by the archers, and then the footmen, while the Knights of the Sacred Shield hung back to protect the baggage train. An enormous amount of food was required to feed an army, and the wagons seemed to stretch all the way to the keep. They carried meat and bread to feed the warriors, smiths to keep weapons sharp, armourers to maintain their mail, and a host of other specialists, everything from bootmakers to purveyors of ale and wine.

Adding to the confusion were the many helpers and family members accompanying the army, which further increased the burden of finding enough food. Ludwig had even heard that cows followed, herded along to provide fresh meat when required. Altogether, the camp followers outnumbered the army itself.

"Well?" said Sigwulf. "What do you think?"

"I wish we had more. When we helped Otto, I had four hundred men under my command, and I was only one baron."

"True, but many of those were little more than a local militia. This army consists of well-trained and well-equipped veterans who'll not let you down."

"I'm certain they won't," replied Ludwig. "If you could have more men, what would you wish for?"

The great northerner paused to gather his thoughts. "I'd like more of everything. Horsemen to scout and provide screening, another company of knights for that extra punch, three more companies of footmen to hold the line, and a hundred more archers."

"So, a division of one thousand souls?"

Sig smiled. "That sounds about right."

"If I allowed you that, I'd have to do the same for Cyn."

"Aye, you would, but would that be so bad? A standing army of two thousand warriors would show the Continent that we're not to be trifled with."

"Yes, and dividing it into two commands makes it easier to react to a variety of threats. I like your thinking, my friend. We'll look into raising those extra troops as soon as we take care of this Holy Army threatening us."

"About that," said Sigwulf. "A lot of the men have concerns."

"Concerns about what?"

"Misgivings about fighting the Church. They see it as a betrayal of their beliefs."

"The Church declared the crusade, not us."

"True, but the average soldier knows nothing about politics. What do I tell them?"

"That they're not fighting the Church, they're fighting for what the Church truly represents. Remind them that the Temple Knights of Saint Agnes are on our side, and those of Mathew as well. Tell them that if we fail to destroy this Holy Army, they risk losing everything. There comes a time in a person's life when they are forced to make a choice: do the easy thing or the right thing. I intend to be on the right side of history, as should they."

"Inspiring words," said Sigwulf. "I wish I had your knack for speeches."

"You're a plain-spoken man, Sig. They respect you for that. As for the men, simply remind them of why they need to fight. They'll soon come around."

The huge man shook his head. "If you'd asked me twelve years ago where I'd be today, I couldn't have imagined this in my wildest dreams."

"Don't tell me you have regrets?"

"Only the loss of comrades. We lost a lot of friends at Chermingen."

"That we did," agreed Ludwig, "and it's a heavy price to pay. You know, I recall my father once telling me that armies are the playthings of great men. I always found that statement disturbing."

"As you should. A man joins the army to fight for his kingdom, his comrades, or his family. The last thing they want is to be considered expendable."

"Do people no longer fight for their king?"

"They will for you," replied Sigwulf, "but you're no ordinary king. You hold the promise of a better future for everyone, regardless of their station in life. A person could ask for no one better to lead them in battle."

"These are your men."

"This is my division, yes, but it's your army. Look, don't misunderstand. I'm happy to take on the responsibility of looking after this lot, but you're the one who'll lead them into battle. You've got the experience, the know-how, and, most importantly, their unwavering loyalty."

"That's quite the statement."

"It's a fact. Most of the men here today helped you take the crown from Black Morgan."

Ludwig raised his eyebrows. "Black Morgan? Is that what we're calling him these days?"

"That's what the men call him on account of his heart turning putrid, along with his wits. At least, that's the popular opinion. It may not be entirely accurate, but you know how people are; no one seems to care whether it's the truth or not."

"If it helps inspire the men, I'm not one to stop such talk."

Sig gave a yell, and the horsemen at the front of the column advanced, beginning the march. Each group behind them waited for a count of thirty before they followed. "Look at them… grinning like fools."

"Yes," said Ludwig, "but they're your fools."

"I suppose they are." Sigwald turned to regard his king. "Do we have any chance of winning this, or are we the fools for even trying?"

"I wouldn't march men to battle if I didn't think we could win. Our strategy here is not to annihilate the enemy in one fell swoop but to wear them down, making their invasion as unpalatable as possible. Only time will tell if we can accomplish those aims, but we're better off going on the offensive rather than waiting until they cross the border in greater numbers than us. Now, you must excuse me. I need to see to other matters."

"Shall I see you when we camp tonight?"

"Definitely," replied Ludwig. "And I'll bring the wine." He turned his horse around and trotted off towards Eisen's keep.

Charlaine entered the room to see Ludwig standing by the window, seemingly peering outside, but she recognized that far-off look; he was lost in thought.

"Did you come here to see me, Majesty?" she asked.

He turned around. "I did, though, for the life of me, I can't remember why." He remained silent for a moment. "It's strange, isn't it? Seeing each other after so many years?"

"I'm not one to believe in fate, but it seems to me I always find myself in places where I'm needed most."

"The will of the Saints?"

"Perhaps, although I tend to ascribe it to a more mundane reason."

"Such as?"

"The grand mistress of my order was good at recognizing when trouble was brewing, and her orders dictated my assignments."

"But not here, surely?"

"Even here, in a manner of speaking," said Charlaine. "She ordered me to get the sisters to safety, although she didn't specifically mention Hadenfeld."

"Yet you knew you'd be safe here."

"I hoped we'd be safe. I didn't know for certain."

"For two people separated years ago, we do seem to be running into each other a lot."

"Only twice. Once in Reinwick, and now here."

"I might remind you that my own father forced you into the Church. Imagine how differently our lives may have turned out had that not happened."

"I don't need to imagine, I know. The Halvarians would control the Shimmering Sea, Reinwick would have gone to war with Andover, and Arnsfeld would be the latest conquest of their empire. Oh yes, and Hadenfeld would now be run by a mad king."

"Not necessarily," countered Ludwig. "Neuhafen might've conquered us instead."

"A valid point, but I choose to think everything happens for a reason, and I'm right where I need to be. Do you not believe the same?"

"I sometimes wonder if I'm doing more harm than good. My only desire was to return home and take care of my lands, but I seem to have made a mess of it."

"You did what you had to do to save the kingdom, sacrificing your way of life for the betterment of others, something worthy of a saint. We cannot change the past, Majesty, but that doesn't mean we should forget it. Our actions determine our path in life: mine to rise in rank in time to save my order, yours to rise through the ranks of nobility to save your kingdom. Do you regret your marriage to Charlotte or the birth of your son?"

Ludwig momentarily looked down at his feet. "No, of course not." He met her gaze. "They are my strength."

"As they should be. Now, enough of this introspection. Why don't you tell me why you're here?"

"I'm here seeking your opinion on military matters."

"Your plan is solid. What, in particular, is it you have doubts concerning?"

"Am I right to split the army into three?"

"Only time can determine if that was the best strategy, but I believe it will succeed. The enemy won't be expecting an attack while it gathers troops, and though the plan relies on coordinating three divisions, it has the advantage of never having been tried before. Thus, the Cunars should have no effective counter to it."

"Yes," said Ludwig, "but can we reproduce the loss they suffered at the Battle of the Wilderness? As far as I'm aware, it's the only time the Cunars have been defeated."

"That's a more difficult question to answer. The Therengians had Orcs screening their flanks, and a significant number of mages."

"The Elves have mages."

"So I've been informed," said Charlaine, "although I cannot comment as to the effectiveness of the magic they wield. As for the last advantage, we have no great beasts to counter their Temple Knights."

"True, but we have Temple Knights of our own, thanks to you."

"While we did outfight the Cunars at Silver Vale, our later encounter proved less successful, resulting in the loss of almost two entire companies. Given the numbers we've heard concerning this new army of theirs, I would expect a similar result."

"So you're predicting disaster?"

"Not at all. As you've already indicated, the strategy here is to wear them down, rather than destroy them straight away. We are, in essence, running up to them, slapping them in the face, then riding away."

"Do you think they'll take the bait and pursue?"

"Anything's possible, but I think it unlikely. For all their flaws, the Temple Knights of Saint Cunar are highly disciplined. An attack of this nature will, however, force them to maintain garrisons at the crossing points to avoid possible raids, thus reducing the number of men they can commit to a future campaign."

"While we try to keep our own casualties at a minimum."

"Agreed," said Charlaine. "What can you tell me about the Elves, from a military point of view?"

"At the Battle of Eisen, they fielded some three hundred warriors."

"Of what type?"

"They were split evenly between foot, horse, and bow. Speaking of bows, they proved quite deadly."

"Yes, I'm familiar with them. We had some at the Battle of the Brinwald, along with their foot, and they were most effective."

"How many men did you command?" asked Ludwig.

"Taking the Elves into consideration, close to sixteen hundred, of which three hundred and fifty were Temple Knights, which includes our brother knights of Saint Mathew, who held our northern flank when all seemed lost. Why? What are you thinking?"

"Cyn's division would boost our numbers by a significant margin. Perhaps we'd be better off waiting until she arrives?"

"We haven't the time," replied Charlaine. "The cold weather is fast approaching, and the last thing we want is to be marching in the snow. We need to hit the enemy hard, then let winter force them to wait. With a little luck, their auxiliaries will abandon the effort, thereby lessening their numbers."

"That only works if the Elves can destroy their stores."

"You're having doubts."

"I am."

"May I ask why? It's a good strategy, and the warriors under your command have faith in you. What gives you pause?"

"I've seen my share of battles, but none with the stakes so high. If I mess this up, the entire kingdom will be crushed."

"If we fail, Hadenfeld will endure, just not under your stewardship."

"True, but you and I both know the stakes here. A weakened Hadenfeld is an invitation for the Halvarian Empire to invade, and next time it won't be a border kingdom, not with the Holy Army under their control."

"It sounds so strange," said Charlaine, "hearing it out loud like that."

"But it's true."

"Yes, unfortunately, it is. To that end, we must preserve what forces we can to meet the inevitable reach of Halvaria."

"Any idea when that might be?"

"We know the empire learns from its mistakes. We defeated them in Arnsfeld, but I imagine it took some time for the details to reach the Halvarian capital. If they're anything like the fighting orders, they'd scrape together every report they could find and analyze them in great detail to prevent a recurrence."

"And to what do you ascribe your victory over them?" asked Ludwig.

"We were able to lure a portion of their forces away by manning a keep that ran alongside the road to the capital, forcing them to deploy an entire cohort to siege it. A good thing, too, for had they been at the Brinwald, we would surely have lost."

"We have no keep near the border."

"True," countered Charlaine, "but if this raid works, it will have the same effect on the Cunars, drawing numbers away from their offensive. We must acknowledge we are already fighting the empire; they've simply cloaked their true identity in the raiments of the Church."

"And how long do you suppose it'll be before their legions cross back into the Petty Kingdoms?"

"Two years, perhaps three?"

"That soon?"

"Soon?" she replied. "The Brinwald was four years ago; the legions of Halvaria will be eager to avenge their defeat. Have you any idea of how many warriors make up a legion?"

"I can't say that I do."

"At full strength, they number twenty-four hundred, divided into four cohorts of six hundred, each a balance of horse, foot, and bow. In the past, the empire typically unleashed a single legion to conquer an enemy, but I fear those days have come to an end."

"Why is that?" asked Ludwig.

"In a word, reputation. Although once considered unbeatable, their superiority has now been brought into question. They'll be eager to re-establish themselves as the legendary warriors who've conquered more realms than any other kingdom in the history of the Continent. If I were them, I'd throw everything I had at the Petty Kingdoms."

"Everything, being?"

"Multiple legions, two or three at least, perhaps even more."

"Let's hope your prophecy proves false," said Ludwig, "but you make a compelling argument. If they attack again, I think we're agreed they won't settle for a border kingdom; they'll come after all of us."

"The sheer scale of such an endeavour staggers the mind," said Charlaine. "You're well-versed in the politics of the Petty Kingdoms: how many men could they assemble against such an invasion?"

"Were it only a matter of numbers, more than enough, but uniting the kingdoms would prove an impossible task. Each ruler would insist on commanding their own troops, and then who'd oversee the battles? Tell me this, did any neighbouring realm send aid to Arnsfeld when the need arose?"

"No. None at all."

"I suspect the same will happen when that final invasion comes. The empire will pick off the Petty Kingdoms one by one, thanks to petty jealousies and indifference to the fates of our neighbours. The only realm with a sizable army these days is Erlingen, and they'd be hard-pressed to fight off a single legion, let alone two."

"There is hope," said Charlaine. "We must have faith that other kingdoms will unite under the banner of self-preservation."

"A fine dream," said Ludwig, "but it would take an extraordinary individual to bring together traditional enemies, even to save their lands."

"Then we must set an example. Hadenfeld used to field a powerful army. If I recall my training, before Otto's time, we were considered the strongest army in all the Petty Kingdoms."

"Sadly, that's no longer true. Oh, the men we have are fine soldiers, but we can't raise the numbers we used to. Two civil wars saw to that."

"Then we need to develop superior tactics."

"And how, precisely, do we do that?"

"By learning as we go. At the Brinwald, there was little finesse to their attack. They held their cavalry in reserve and sent a mass of men towards our line in an attempt to overwhelm us."

"Do you think the Cunars will use the same strategy now that they're under the empire's thumb?"

"I doubt it. For all their bravado, the Holy Army is at the mercy of their auxiliaries. Cavalry often proves the decisive edge in battle, but without foot and bow, they'll do a poor job of holding conquered lands. I assume your foot employs spears?"

"Most do," replied Ludwig. "Why?"

"I had a lot of time to read when I was at the Antonine. Amongst the books I digested was a recent translation of *The Campaigns of Aeldred*."

"He was the Therengian who defeated the Thalamites."

"He did, even though his men fought on foot. Do you know why?"

"No, but I've a feeling you're about to tell me."

"He taught them to use a formation known as the fist of spears. The warriors formed a rough circle with their spears pointed outward and the butts of their weapons planted firmly in the ground. It is written that horses feared the formation and refused to close the distance."

"An excellent idea," said Ludwig. "Please excuse me. I must ride to Sigwulf and instruct his men to practice that tactic!"

25

THE MARCH NORTH
AUTUMN 1107 SR

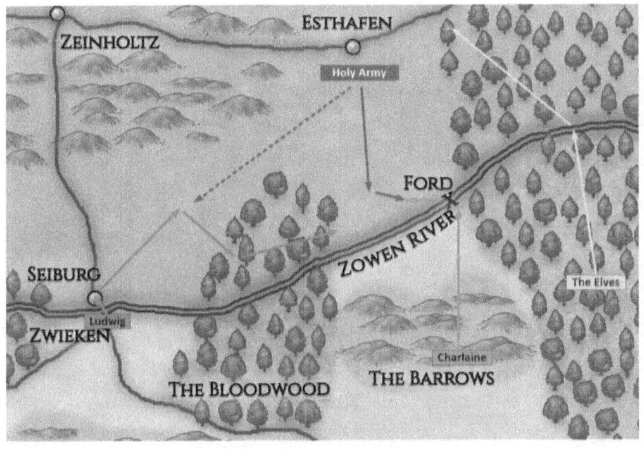

The column stretched on as far as the eye could see, with Ludwig and Sigwulf leading, both staring north towards Zwieken. Their cavalry had already scouted the area, reporting nothing of note across the river, yet they still sent men up and downstream to ensure it remained safe.

"I sense no sign of a trap," said Sigwulf. "At this rate, the entire division will be across before nightfall."

"You've talked to the men regarding Seiburg?"

"Yes. They're to treat the villagers with proper respect, or we'll risk Konrad's army breathing down our necks."

"And if they encounter soldiers from Zowenbruch?"

"Then they are to notify us immediately, although I must admit I don't know why."

"It falls on our shoulders to convince them to stand aside."

Sigwulf stared at him. "You really believe they'll stand down?"

"Given the likely disparity in numbers, I think they'll do just that. Unless you feel a small village garrison would be willing to fight hundreds of men?"

"I suppose that makes sense."

A rider approached from the north, and Ludwig recognized him as he drew closer.

"Sire," Captain Gustavo called out. "Our scouts are standing by at the bridge."

"Dare I ask why they've yet to cross?"

"There are men standing guard on the other side." The captain drew closer, then turned round to ride beside his king. "No more than a dozen, but they appear intent on preventing a crossing."

Sigwulf chuckled. "It appears the men of Zowenbruch have some guts after all."

Ludwig spurred on his horse. "Come along, Captain. You and I need to have a little chat with these folks."

Gustavo, briefly surprised by the sudden increase in speed, soon caught up. "Are you certain that's wise, Majesty? One arrow and you could be killed."

"Were there archers at the bridge?"

"No, not that I could see."

"Then it appears the danger isn't as great as you fear."

"Couldn't you send them a message instead?"

"I could," replied Ludwig, "but what kind of a king would I be if I placed every burden on the shoulders of someone else?"

"Even at the risk of personal injury?"

"Would I not be risking the same for someone I sent in my place?"

"I suppose so."

"Now, come along. I'm curious to learn who's leading this contingent."

They rode into Zwieken, passing by a tavern where people had gathered to watch the proceedings. The bridge was visible from their vantage point, as were the men on the other side. They'd cobbled together a makeshift barricade, consisting of barrels and crates, behind which they held their position. One individual amongst them stood out, as he wore mail, along with a kettle helm that did nothing to hide his thick, bushy moustache.

Ludwig dismounted, handing the reins to one of the scouts who secured his side of the border. Gustavo followed his example, and then both stepped onto the bridge.

"Stop right there!" came the command.

"I am Ludwig Altenburg, King of Hadenfeld," he announced. "I seek to parley. Who's in charge here?"

"I am," the moustached man replied. "The name's Eimar."

"We mean you no harm."

"Yet you come with armed men."

"My quarrel is not with the people of Zowenbruch," said Ludwig. "It is with those who would oppress my people."

"I have no quarrel with you, either, Majesty, but I will do my duty and protect this village from the ravages of war."

"If that's true, then you'd best stand aside. Behind me march hundreds of warriors, but I would prefer not to loose them on the poor people of Seiburg."

"So you expect me to stand aside and let you march past to attack the capital?"

"We are not marching to Kurslingen—we're marching to the Holy Army gathering at Esthafen."

"How do I know this isn't a ruse to get us to abandon our post?"

Ludwig stepped closer, keeping his hands well away from his sword. "If you think I'm a threat to the realm you hold so dear, then strike me down."

Eimar pushed aside a barrel and stepped out, drawing his sword. Ludwig remained calm as the man advanced, the tip of his weapon held out in front of him, finally coming to rest on Ludwig's breastplate.

"I could kill you in an instant," the soldier proclaimed.

"Then why don't you?"

Eimar lowered his sword. "I consider myself devout, but these days, the Church is preaching nothing but hatred. Were I in your shoes, I suppose I might do the same thing." He leaned to one side, peering behind Ludwig. "Hundreds of men, you say? You'll need a lot more than that if you aim to take on those Temple Knights."

"You're not the first one to tell me that, and I doubt you'll be the last, but I shall take my chances."

"Why?"

"Why?" replied Ludwig. "Because I have no choice. Were your kingdom threatened by the Church, would you sit back and wait for the invasion, or do all in your power to destroy their ability to wage war?"

Eimar nodded. "I'll let you pass, Majesty, but only if you promise me you'll spare Seiburg."

"I give you my word."

"Move aside, lads," the man bellowed. "His Royal Majesty has chosen not to fight today."

"Thank you, Sergeant."

"I'm no sergeant."

"Truly?" said Ludwig. "You had the courage to stand up to a king. Were you in my army, I'd insist you be promoted. I shall remember you, Master Eimar, and wish you well."

The warrior bowed his head. "You honour me, sire. Now, if you will excuse me, I must see to removing the barricade." He returned to his post, berating his men for not moving fast enough.

"That was neatly done," said Gustavo. "For a moment there, I feared he might actually kill you."

"He values the people of this village too much to risk a reprisal."

"You only spoke to him for but a moment."

"What can I say? I'm a good judge of character." Ludwig returned to Hadenfeld's side of the bridge. "I have a job for you. I'm going to give you some coins to spend at whatever passes for the local tavern. Buy some rounds, assure the folks here that we mean them no harm, but above all, ensure our people behave. The last thing we need is ill will behind us as we march towards the Cunars."

"Understood, sire."

The border crossing continued throughout the day. Under any other circumstances, it would've taken no time at all to cross six hundred fifty men, but the bridge was in disrepair, and Ludwig didn't want to risk damaging it further. Instead, he sent them across in small groups, no more than twenty at a time, interspersed with the supply wagons. Ludwig watched it all from the Seiburg side of the river.

Sigwulf crossed at midday, riding over to assume a position beside his king. "That bridge is a death trap."

"I agree," replied Ludwig. "Perhaps, when this war is over, we can convince King Konrad to allow us to make repairs?"

"Repairs? The wood is so rotten, you'd need a whole new bridge."

"Then I shall make that a priority once we've given the Holy Army a good thrashing." Ludwig went silent.

Sigwulf shifted in his saddle. "Something wrong?"

"How deep would you say the water is here?"

"Deep enough to require a bridge. Why? Surely you're not suggesting we use boats to cross?"

"No, but it occurs to me that the weight of heavily armoured Temple

Knights might prove a bit too much for that bridge, particularly if we took pains to weaken it further."

"We still need it to retreat," said Sigwulf.

"I wasn't suggesting we do it right now, merely that we have someone take a look and determine if it's even possible. The next time we pass through here, we'll be heading home, possibly with an army in pursuit. If that comes to pass, we'll have little time for such considerations."

"A clever idea, but who do we have with knowledge of such things?"

"Ask around," said Ludwig. "You might be surprised. These men must've done something before they became soldiers."

"Not necessarily; ever heard of a career soldier?"

"Of course, but I know that's not true of all of them. I suspect that the vast majority are from rural areas, many of whom were born to farmers. Gustavo was recruited in Roshlag, not to mention lots of our archers."

"I'll have someone check into it. I'd do it myself, but I need to escort these men out of the village."

"Thank you," replied Ludwig.

They camped in a field northeast of Seiburg and set guards to prevent any soldiers from trying to sneak into the village.

Captain Gustavo returned from the town after dark to find Ludwig finishing his meal.

"My apologies, sire. I didn't know you were eating."

"Nonsense. I'm almost finished." He turned to regard his servant. "Fetch some food for the good captain, will you?"

"That's not necessary, Majesty," said Gustavo. "I ate something in the village."

"How did things go?"

"The locals were hesitant to talk at first, but a few rounds soon loosened their tongues."

"Did you learn anything of interest?"

"That largely depends on how you define interesting. The folks around here all consider themselves good worshippers of the Saints, but I noticed quite a few still wear pagan symbols."

"The Saints wrote we should live in harmony with those of other religions."

"Yes." The captain quickly added, "I didn't mean it as a slight, merely an observation. As I was saying, they talk of their devotion, but few seemed ardent about it. I think they're as afraid of this Holy Army as we are."

"I can understand that," said Ludwig. "War has a way of disrupting or even ruining the lives of folks, even if they aren't part of the conflict."

"It's more than that. The Cunars have a reputation as being... well, I suppose strict would be the best word to describe them."

"Some might say disciplined."

"Perhaps, but the way they were speaking, I think unforgiving a more apt description. The rumour is they don't take prisoners, and anyone who opposes them, even in small ways, is considered an enemy."

"That surprises me," said Ludwig, "although I suppose it shouldn't. It's not uncommon for the empire to spread malicious tales ahead of a campaign to sow fear amongst their enemies."

"But these are people from Zowenbruch."

"Yes, which is troubling."

"Could it be that the rumours are merely that—a lie meant to unsettle us?"

"Anything's possible, but I did read an account somewhere concerning a battle after which the Halvarians massacred all survivors save for ten."

"Why ten?"

"They wanted someone still able to spread word of what happens to anyone who dares to oppose the empire. Oh, and to make it worse, each was maimed in some capacity."

"Maimed?"

"Yes. They blinded some in one eye, while others lost a hand, but nothing that would stop them from telling of the horror of war, just enough to remind anyone hearing the tale of how brutal the Halvarian Empire can be."

Gustavo took in a sharp breath. "You don't think the Holy Army would do that, do you?"

"I very much doubt it. They serve the Church, and it wouldn't do to have it spread amongst its followers that they massacred people. The scriptures of the Saints also decry torture of any sort, not that many rulers pay heed to such preaching."

"That's a relief. If you don't mind me asking, what can we expect from them? Are the Cunars as fearsome as they're made out to be?"

"That's an excellent question," replied Ludwig. "We've fought beside Temple Knights of Saint Mathew, but aside from the accounts of Temple General Charlaine, I have no knowledge of those of Saint Cunar. I suppose, though, we could make some suppositions."

"Go on," urged the captain.

"One must already be a knight to seek entrance to the Temple Knights of

Saint Cunar, which means much like those of other orders, their skills would vary considerably. Oh, they'd know how to fight, but most lack the discipline the order requires. To compensate for that, every new initiate is required to serve their first year of service on foot. Presumably, this is where they're introduced to the rigid discipline the Cunars are well known for."

"And are they as disciplined as they say?"

"The Mathewites certainly are, and the Temple General's accounts of her own order indicate they are as well, but I suspect in the case of the Cunars, their own training methods might work against them."

"How so?" asked Gustavo.

"In my experience, a knight of the Petty Kingdoms is an individualist, more concerned with taking captives than defeating an enemy."

"Why is that?"

"In a word, ransom. When a knight or any noble is captured in battle, it's customary to set them free in exchange for coins. The more important the individual, the higher the sum."

"The very idea is repugnant."

"I agree," said Ludwig. "There are, of course, other types of knights, men who claim to fight for honour and glory, but often cause the most trouble by disobeying orders and charging into a fray to achieve their objectives, regardless of the risks involved."

"There is an even rarer type, sire."

Ludwig raised his eyebrows. "You surprise me, Gustavo. I didn't take you as someone interested in such things."

"As you know, I've seen my share of battles. You've missed the most important type of knight."

"Which is?"

"Those who fight not through choice, but through necessity. Doing their duty to their sovereign lord because it's the right thing, rather than through any desire to enrich their own lives. That describes you to perfection, Majesty."

Ludwig barked out a laugh. "Now, you're just trying to flatter me."

"I am most earnest, sire. Your behaviour is an inspiration to us all."

"I thank you for the compliment. I'm the first to admit I never wanted to be king, or prince, for that matter, but if one intends to assume such a position, they must do their best to make the most of it. I took a vow to better the lives of my people, and I take that promise seriously."

"As you should," replied Gustavo.

"I've never asked you this before," said Ludwig, "and feel free to refuse to answer if you feel so inclined, but do you like to read?"

"I'm always eager to learn more, but I must admit my reading skills are somewhat lacking."

"But you can read?"

"Yes, just not well."

Ludwig stood, moving over to his travelling chest, where he began rooting through it. "Ah, here it is." He withdrew a book and placed it before the startled captain. "I found this to be most informative."

The well-worn tome's leather cover, a once brilliant green, had faded to a duller shade of its former self.

Gustavo picked it up. "*The Age of Chivalry*, an interesting title."

"Yes. An old friend, the Baron of Mulsingen, sent it to me. He thought it would amuse me."

"And did it, sire?"

"It did. It lays out the guiding principles of knighthood as seen by Lord Deiter Heinrich, the former Duke of Erlingen. A lot of it's sheer nonsense, but I think you'll understand the fundamentals."

"You want me to read it?"

"I do," said Ludwig. "But take your time; there's no hurry."

"Am I to practice what's written in here?"

"I think you misunderstand my intentions. I want you to read it so you understand the minds of our enemy."

"Does this book deal with Temple Knights?"

"Admittedly, no, but as I said earlier, all Cunars must be knights before joining their order; thus, they would take lessons like that to heart. I'm told that book was very much in demand amongst the wealthier members of the nobility, particularly those with more than one son."

"You'll pardon my ignorance," said Gustavo, "but why more than one?"

"The common practice is that the first-born male inherits, while the second and subsequent sons, should they be born, are spares. To prevent disagreements between siblings, it's often the case that these other sons join either the Church or a fighting order when they come of age."

"A strange custom, sire. Is this where all knights come from?"

"Not all," replied Ludwig. "Generations ago, knights were mounted warriors who could afford better armour than their contemporaries. Eventually, good armour became so expensive that only the wealthy could afford it, and thus the nobility became the most dominant example of such men."

"And now all knights are nobility?"

"There are still a few who gain knighthood through exceptional service to their sovereign, but by and large, yes. Most knights strive to accumulate wealth in the hopes of advancing within society, while others wish for fame for the same reason. Some even join for the thrill of battle, but few see enough of it to satisfy those sorts of cravings."

"And does a knight earn a lot from their lands?"

"That's where it gets more complicated," replied Ludwig. "A knighthood is not hereditary, but sometimes comes with an award of land, along with an estate. In such cases, this is considered a sort of payment for serving their lord."

"You mean their king?"

"Or duke. In some kingdoms, they even swear service to barons; it varies considerably. In Hadenfeld, they're all sworn to the Crown."

"And with all due respect, are all knights such pains in the arse?"

Ludwig chuckled. "I wish I could say no, but many cling to their place in society with an iron grip, delighting in rebuking those of a lower station. It's their way of proving themselves superior to others."

"And where, might I ask, do I rank in the hierarchy of court?"

"You are the Captain of the Royal Guard. I'm not entirely certain how other realms would rank you, but in my opinion, that makes you superior to them. If any knight tries to tell you otherwise, you can bring it directly to my attention."

"Yes, sire." Gustavo stood, clutching the book. "I shall begin reading this tonight." He bowed, then left.

Ludwig watched him go. His captain was a good man, and those were hard to find. Would he survive the coming campaign?

26

THE CROSSING

AUTUMN 1107 SR

Charlaine halted the march. Before them lay the Barrows, dark and foreboding hills that were unnaturally quiet.

Temple Captain Teresa rode up beside her. "I feel as if the hair on the back of my neck is standing on end."

"I don't suppose your magic has the power to ward off ghosts?"

"Not precisely, but if we run into any undead, I may be able to help."

"Undead?"

"Yes. You know, animated skeletons, creatures of rotting flesh—that sort of thing."

"Are you suggesting such things exist?" asked Charlaine.

"The Elves have a multitude of documentation to prove it."

"And if we did run into these undead, can your magic banish them?"

"No," replied Teresa, "but the same spell that heals wounds also inflicts damage to a creature of that nature."

"And here I was thinking all you could do was heal. Now tell me, and be serious, what do you make of those hills?"

"They look ominous."

"The Elven High Lord, Sindra, says there are tombs of an ancient race of Humans up there."

"Ah," said Teresa. "That explains the absence of wildlife." She pointed. "You'll notice there's no sign of birds, nor trees."

"Does that represent a threat?" asked Charlaine.

"I can't rightly say. I don't suppose we could ride around them?"

"That would put us behind schedule."

"Then into the hills we must go."

Temple Captain Nicola joined them.

"All set to go into some haunted hills?" asked Teresa.

"Haunted?" replied her comrade. "Surely you don't believe in such superstitious nonsense?"

"Hauntings are real!"

"Let's not have an argument," chided Charlaine, although her tone was light. "Teresa learned all about the undead while amongst the Elves, though I don't remember her mentioning hauntings."

"A haunting is simply a place where the undead dwell," said Teresa.

Nicola wasn't convinced. "And what, precisely, does the category of undead include?"

"Skeletons, animated corpses, wights, ghosts, and various other obscene mockeries of life."

"I've heard of some of those, but what is the difference between a wight and an animated corpse? Aren't they the same thing?"

"Not quite," explained Teresa. "A wight has intelligence, and, according to some accounts, can control other undead creatures. There's also some speculation they might be able to wield Necromantic magic."

"So they were Death Mages before they died?"

"No, that would be a liche."

"Just how many of these undead things are there?"

"Dozens. So many that the Elves break them down into categories. The most powerful are—"

"That's enough for now," said Charlaine. "The last thing we need is everyone imagining the worst. Nicola, close up the ranks. I want everyone within easy reach should we encounter anything untoward."

"Untoward?" said Nicola. "Are you telling me you expect to run into the living dead?"

"Something in those hills is keeping the birds at bay, and I don't intend to find out the hard way what that might be. And let's not talk anymore about the undead. I don't want it said the Temple Knights of Saint Agnes get spooked by shadows."

"Shadows," said Teresa. "That's another type of…" Her words trailed off as she noticed Charlaine's look of disapproval. "Never mind."

"Should I call in our scouts?" asked Nicola.

"No, but instruct them to remain within visual range of our column at all times. Once the sun sets, and it starts to get dark, they are to rejoin us. Speaking of the dark, when we make camp, instruct the sentries to operate in groups of three, and divide the night duty into four shifts. I shouldn't like anyone to be tired for tomorrow's march."

"Yes, General." Nicola rode off to begin issuing orders.

. . .

They entered the Barrows, with everyone on high alert, feeling as if every living thing save for them had been stripped from the area. There were no plants, no animals, not even any insects, as if some sort of supernatural power held them at bay.

Charlaine kept them moving despite a growing sense of unease. She was not usually the type to believe in superstition, but Teresa's words nagged at her. Where was the line between the superstitious and the actual existence of undead creatures? An image invaded her mind, one of skeletons rising from the ground at night and running amok, slaying them all in their sleep. She tried to shake it off, but the more she attempted to divert her thoughts, the quicker they returned to torment her.

That night, they set up camp atop a single hill. Nicola set sentries out with lanterns, dim beacons in an otherwise inky blackness, for clouds had rolled in, obscuring the moon.

A distant groan awoke Charlaine, and she was instantly alert, reaching for her sword as her fellow sister knights rose from their slumber.

The horses whinnied nearby, spooked by the strange sounds emanating from the darkness. Charlaine ordered knights to secure the mounts, then sought out Nicola. "Any idea what's making those sounds?"

"No," replied the Temple Captain.

"Where are they coming from?"

"Everywhere. Could it be the wind?"

"That's no wind." Teresa stepped forward, her white surcoat seeming to glow as it captured the light of the nearest fire. "Something's out there."

"That something, being?" asked Nicola.

"I thought you didn't believe in all this superstitious nonsense?"

"Yes… well… I may have to reconsider that opinion."

"Have you anything to help us?" asked Charlaine.

Teresa closed her eyes and began murmuring. The air seemed to come alive, as if thousands of insects swarmed the area. Then the Sister of Mercy held out both her hands, palms upward, and a small ball of light appeared, growing in intensity until everyone was forced to turn away. Another word of command, and the sphere floated upward, illuminating the camp.

Charlaine noticed shadowy figures hovering at the edge of the light. At first, she assumed they were her Temple Knights, but none wore tabards. Instead, they wore ancient armour, links of mail rotting in numerous locations. When they stepped into the light, their faces were no more than blackened skulls, but the brilliance of Teresa's spell drove them back, and they vanished into the darkness once more.

"How long can you keep that spell up?" she asked.

"Some time yet," replied Teresa.

"I thought you said you couldn't ward off ghosts?"

"I can't, but creatures such as that don't like bright lights. As for my spell, I can maintain it all night long if necessary."

"I think that would be for the best," replied Charlaine. "But won't that leave you tired?"

"It will, but I'm a Temple Knight. I can sleep in the saddle if need be."

"I'll have some people keep an eye on you tomorrow. I shouldn't like you to fall while we're on the march."

"Thank you. That's most appreciated."

"What were those things? Skeletons?"

"That would be my guess," replied Teresa. "The more worrying question is, why are they here?"

"High Lord Sindra spoke of tombs; might that explain their existence?"

"The existence of skeletons, most assuredly, but I'm curious to know why they're animated. The dead don't get up and wander around on their own; it takes an act of Necromancy."

"Are you suggesting there's a Death Mage in the area?" asked Charlaine.

"An area such as this would naturally draw the attention of such a person."

"That makes this even more disturbing. An Elf lord informed us of the tombs, which would indicate they're the only ones who know about the place's reputation."

"In other words, an Elven Necromancer?" said Teresa. "It's certainly not beyond the realm of possibility."

"If that were the case, why would they attack us?"

"Animated creatures, like skeletons, have no ability to reason. They carry out the last orders given to them by whoever brought them back from the dead. I would theorize that we're camped close to one of their tombs, one which the Death Mage didn't want discovered."

"Didn't or doesn't?" asked Charlaine.

"It's possible the caster in question may have been dead for years. Then again, if they're Elvish, they could be out there in the dark, watching us."

"If it comes down to it, can we defeat them with weapons?"

"Most assuredly," replied Teresa. "Skeletal warriors are a little harder to destroy than living ones, as they have no vital organs, but can still be broken into pieces. I suggest employing maces or hammers, but even a sword can prove effective. I think it's unlikely, though, for them to attack us; they're not particularly good at fighting."

"I'm surprised to hear you say that. I would've thought ancient warriors would retain their knowledge."

"That's a common misconception. They are not the spirits of the dead, merely animated corpses that no longer hold any flesh, imbued with dark magic, enabling them to carry out basic tasks, but they lack a true mind."

"Yet they can fight?" asked Charlaine.

"Yes, but the skill they fight with is based on the relative power of the mage who created them. My advice is to double the number of sentries and ensure everyone on duty is wearing their plate armour. And we might want to move the horses a little closer as a precaution."

"Will skeletons attack horses?"

"I doubt it. I'd be more concerned with our mounts panicking and running off. I don't like the thought of spending all morning chasing them down, do you?"

"No," replied Charlaine, "most definitely not. It seems your presence here has proven most fortuitous."

Teresa kept the camp lit using her magic, but by daybreak, she was exhausted. The Temple Knights were mounted and on the move before long, eager to escape the hilltop and the shrieks that had echoed through the darkness.

A full day's march brought them to the northern edge of the Barrows, where the land stretched out into a grassy plain. The presence of birds, along with the occasional hare, was proof that the desolation of the hills was well behind them, lifting everyone's spirits.

They rode northeast until the Goldenwood came into view, then paralleled its edge. By Charlaine's reckoning, they should reach the ford by mid-afternoon, but maps of the area were notoriously inaccurate, and she didn't want to raise her command's hopes until the river was within sight.

Teresa was riding beside her, her bare head basking in the radiance of the sun, when she suddenly turned eastward. "Did you hear that?"

Charlaine was instantly on the alert, raising her hand to signal the column to halt, then waited. "See anything?" she asked, her hand now resting on her sword.

"I can't be certain," replied the Sister of Mercy. "I thought I caught a glimpse of something moving, but I suppose it could be the wind."

Behind them rode the company commanded by Temple Commander Katinka. Usually, a captain led a company, but since the flight from the

Antonine, the order found itself with an overabundance of senior officers. Katinka also acted as the second-in-command of the expedition, in case something should happen to their Temple General.

"Outriders, if you please, Temple Commander," called out Charlaine, "and keep a close eye on that forest."

"Yes, General," came Katinka's reply. Twelve Temple Knights left the larger formation, taking up a position to the east. They marched two abreast, their column extended to protect the flanks of the expedition. The other companies sent out their own riders, the effect rippling down the length of Charlaine's entire command.

"Resume the advance," she ordered, urging her horse, Stormcloud, into a trot.

Having been on edge in the Barrows, the possibility that something was on their flank left their nerves worn thin. Charlaine wondered if she was being overly cautious, but it was better to be prepared than not, even if there ended up to be no real threat. "Where's our Elf?" she asked.

"Back chatting with the Mathewites," replied Teresa. "Shall I go and fetch him?"

"If you would be so kind."

Teresa veered off to the side, waiting for the company behind to pass, then headed south, towards the trailing end of their army.

A glint of light flickering in the distance caught Charlaine's attention. Was it sunlight reflecting off the surface of the river, or just her imagination playing tricks?

Theran Silverhand was of indeterminate age, yet his hair was white as the purest snow. Like the other Elves of the Goldenwood, he wore silver fish-scale armour, but no helmet, nor, it appeared, did he carry any weapons other than a short dagger hanging loosely from his belt. "You wished to see me, General?"

"Yes," replied Charlaine. "We've detected some movement in the woods to our right, and I wondered if you could use your magic to determine what's causing it."

"That will be completely unnecessary."

"Why is that?"

"I can plainly see what you are referring to."

Charlaine strained, but at this distance she could discern little more than trees. "Then perhaps you might explain what's moving around over there?"

Theran paused, his eyebrows raised as if something had just occurred to him. "I must apologize. I sometimes forget you Humans do not possess the keen eyesight of us woodland folk. Over yonder is a spear of Elves, likely led by a talon."

"A spear? How many warriors is that?"

"A close approximation would be one of your… what do you call them?"

"A company?"

"Yes, precisely."

"I'm surprised they haven't announced their presence," said Charlaine.

"But they have… Ah. I see the problem. They, too, overestimated your ability to see them. Would you like me to ride over and invite them out into the open?"

"That won't be necessary. I assume they're on their way to guard the ford?"

"I presume so, for I cannot conceive of any other reason why they would be this far from Nethendril." He paused. "Of course, they might be from Halieth; that's a little closer."

"How many Elven cities are there?"

"There are… My apologies. I received orders not to speak of such things. It seems I may have revealed a little too much."

"I shall not repeat it," replied Charlaine, "but is this city of Halieth in danger if the Holy Army marches this way?"

"I should think not," said Theran. "It lies some miles to the east." Again, a pause. "My goodness. Once again, I have let slip information meant to be kept secret."

"We are no threat to the Elves of the Goldenwood."

"This I understand, but even the best-intentioned people may be captured, or inadvertently reveal information they shouldn't."

"Like you just did?"

The Elf smiled. "Quite. Not to appear rude, but are there any other matters which require my attention?"

"Do you know how much farther it is to the ford?"

"It is right ahead of us. Can you not see the duck sitting on its bank?"

"I cannot," replied Charlaine.

"Then you must take my word for it that we are close, so close, that you shall likely be crossing within the hour."

"I wasn't aware Elves measured time in hours."

"Really?" said Theran. "Who do you think invented the sundial?"

"With all due respect, Magister, we Humans are long past using those. We have clock towers now, or at least we do in our larger cities."

"Then how do you tell time in smaller villages?"

"It's the Church's responsibility to ring the bell. In larger villages and towns, they use an hourglass, but in more rural communities, they only ring the bell to mark sunrise, noon, and sundown. I'm told the traditions vary a little across the Petty Kingdoms, but that's how it works in Hadenfeld."

"Remarkable. I have never seen a clock."

"So you've never been to Eisen?"

"No. If you recall, I joined the march once you were already on the road."

"I'm well aware," said Charlaine. "I'm not complaining, but I'm curious whether there was a reason for your late arrival?"

"The cities of men are filled with vermin."

"You dislike us that much?"

"Not at all," said Theran. "I refer to literal vermin—rats and such. I find such creatures most repugnant."

"Do you not have these creatures in Elven cities?"

"Not the ones I have been in."

"But you're an Earth Mage!" said Charlaine.

"I fail to understand what that has to do with anything?"

"I would think you could use your magic to get rid of them."

"Theoretically, I could, but from what I have observed, Eisen is a large city, and it would take weeks, if not months, to cleanse the place of them. Then, they reproduce so frequently the city would fill up again. An army of Earth Mages would be needed to make any sort of progress on an endeavour of that magnitude."

"And have you an army of mages?"

"Admittedly, we have more than our fair share," replied Theran, "but they are spread throughout the cities of the Goldenwood. Mind you, Nethendril has more than usual, including the High Lord, but Enchanters are more common."

"And will they accompany the Elven expedition to Esthafen?"

"Some may, although I cannot claim to know the High Lord's mind."

"Out of curiosity, how does one employ such magic in battle?"

"Enchanters typically use their spells to enable warriors to fight better. This can be achieved by temporarily enchanting their weapons to penetrate armour or by imbuing the warriors with a powerful enchantment that makes their armour more effective. There are more spells than that, but I focus on the magic of nature."

27

SKIRMISH

AUTUMN 1107 SR

Ludwig arose to a thick fog that obscured his view of the camp. He called out and soon heard Gustavo's voice approaching.

"I'm afraid we'll have to delay the march, sire. I don't think I've ever seen a fog as thick as this. I can barely make out our men."

"Hopefully the sun will soon burn it off," replied Ludwig. "For now, send some men to the supply wagons and find out if they need any help distributing the rations."

"Blasted fog," boomed out a distant voice, and then Sigwulf came into view. "Can't see a thing. It's unnatural, I tell you."

"You suspect that it's magical? Surely you're not suggesting the Holy Army has mages amongst its ranks?"

"Years ago, I would never have thought the Stormwinds or Sartellians were working for the empire. Times are changing, and so must we."

"And what would you have us do?"

"Let's find that Elven mage of ours. Perhaps she can do something."

"Like what?" asked Ludwig. "She's an Earth Mage, one whose primary focus is the living world. I doubt she could lift a fog."

"It couldn't hurt to ask?"

"True enough. Let's see if we can locate her, but stay close. I don't want to spend all morning trying to find you again."

"What should I do?" asked Gustavo.

"Make your way to the wagons, and I'll join you once we've located Karalindel."

The captain disappeared into the fog.

"Where do we begin?" asked Ludwig.

"I thought I heard her earlier," said Sigwulf. "She was over in that direction." He pointed but then turned to his right. "Or was it over there? I appear to have lost my bearings."

"Then pick a direction, and we'll call out as we go."

Sigwulf froze. "Did you hear that?"

"Hear what?"

"It sounded like horses."

"Hardly surprising, given the composition of our army."

"I suppose that's true." He shrugged. "I could've sworn the horses were behind us."

The clatter of steel drifted towards them.

"That sounds like fighting," said Ludwig.

"Agreed, but we're still miles from the Holy Army, aren't we?"

"We assumed they'd be camped near Esthafen, but perhaps that's not the case."

"We saw no sign of them when we set up camp."

"Then it's someone else," offered Ludwig. "Either way, we must investigate." He drew his sword, then began jogging towards the sound.

A rider briefly emerged from the fog, visible for only a moment, but his dark grey tabard left no doubt about his loyalties.

"Cunars!" yelled Sigwulf. "How in the name of the Saints did they find us?"

The sound of fighting grew more pronounced, and then a man stumbled into view, blood pouring from a gash on his temple. He took three steps before collapsing, face down, onto the ground. Ludwig rushed towards the fellow, only to witness his exposed spine, the result of a massive axe wound to the poor man's back.

"You must be careful," said Sigwulf. "Perhaps you should turn back and don your armour?"

"We haven't the time."

They advanced farther, the battle noises growing in intensity, the ground slick with blood, bodies lying left and right. The attackers finally came into view, a half-dozen mounted Cunar knights trampling bedrolls and attacking with wild abandon. This was no organized offensive; it was a slaughter!

Sigwulf let out a roar and rushed forward, striking out with his sword. It did little against the plate armour of his opponent, but it served to draw the fellow's attention away from his current target.

The knight turned, smashing out with a mace, but the huge northerner pulled back, avoiding a direct hit as the head of the mace grazed his chest, ripping some links from his mail shirt.

Ludwig stabbed out, trying to hit the Cunar's armpit while his arm was extended, but once again the knight's armour protected him.

The Cunar lifted his arm in preparation for an overhead strike against his foe, and Sigwulf used the opportunity to step closer, discarding his own sword to grab the knight's leg. A grunt of exertion escaped as he pulled the man from the saddle, but the huge northerner hadn't anticipated the knight would fall towards him, sending them both crashing to the ground.

Ludwig reached out, grabbing the Cunar's arm, trying to prevent the mace from being utilized. The Temple Knight had the presence of mind to swing his shield around, driving it into Ludwig's side, knocking the King of Hadenfeld off his feet.

Sigwulf, even with the breath knocked from his lungs, managed to push his opponent off him, then drew a dagger from his belt, and in the blink of an eye, was on the knight, thrusting the blade into the helmet's eye slits. The man went limp, the mace and shield falling from open hands.

A weight bumped against Ludwig's back as the bulk of a warhorse pushed against him. He turned, prepared to restrain the beast, only to find a second Temple Knight smashing down with a warhammer. A quick shift to one side avoided the blow, and then Ludwig stabbed out, the blade striking armour, but once again doing no damage. He backed up, hoping to avoid being hit by a further attack.

The warhorse pressed forward, knocking him to the ground, and he rolled to the side, narrowly avoiding the shod hooves. Hands grabbed him, dragging him to safety, and then Gustavo was there, leading a group of men armed with spears. They stabbed out, driving the horse back until the Temple Knight turned and fled, joining his surviving comrades, their rampage complete.

"By the Saints," said Sigwulf, walking amongst the wounded. "They carved their way through an entire company."

The fog had lifted, revealing the path of destruction where the Temple Knights had wreaked such terrible damage.

Ludwig stood, letting a limp hand drop from his own. "I knew this man," he said. "He served me in Verfeld, and now he's dead. How did they know we were here?"

"Perhaps I can answer that." The Elf's high-pitched voice interrupted them. She moved closer, staring down at the dead warrior. Tall, even for an Elf, her golden hair and pale face gave those around her the impression they were in the presence of something ethereal.

"You suspect magic?" asked Ludwig.

"That is but one possible reason."

"But not the one you suspect?"

She smiled, but it seemed unnatural, as if she was struggling to present a friendly face. "Before I answer that, let me ask you a few questions."

"Go ahead," said Ludwig.

"Is it possible a traitor could be in your midst?"

"Possible, but not likely."

"Would a rider from Seiburg have had enough time to reach the Holy Army and warn them?"

"No. The road through Kurslingen takes much longer, and our sentries would've spotted any rider coming our way."

"Then there remains but two possibilities."

"Which are?"

"The use of magic, or a military leader who anticipated possible threats and put out patrols of their own. Which do you think is more likely?"

"The latter."

"Then I would concur," said Karalindel. "I saw no indication the fog was magically induced. However, once those Temple Knights return to their camp, whoever commands the Holy Army will become aware of our presence here. I therefore suggest you alter your strategy."

"Excellent point," said Ludwig. "Can you send word to Temple General Charlaine?"

"Yes, but bear in mind it will take time to reach her. Birds may be fast, but they still must travel dozens of miles to locate her. What message would you like sent to her?"

"Ask her to withdraw south of the river. We'll send further instructions once we know more."

"You realize you may already be too late? If the enemy has scouts this far west, they're likely watching the river to their south as well. The Temple Knights of Saint Agnes may be marching into a trap."

"You think them that clever?"

"You tell me," said the Elf. "My experience with Humans was in the distant past, while your race was still struggling with the very notion of civilization. Would you consider Temple General Charlaine to be a great strategist?"

"Based on her history, yes."

"Then you should expect no less from the enemy. According to your own accounts, the Temple Knights of Saint Cunar are the finest warriors in the Petty Kingdoms. With such a reputation, would you expect them to be incompetent?"

"No," replied Ludwig. "I would not." His mind whirled. This entire campaign had been designed to surprise the enemy, and now it was becoming painfully apparent that whoever led them had anticipated his move.

His obvious choice was to retreat to Zwieken and destroy the bridge, but that would give the enemy the initiative. He must find another way to turn things back to his favour, but how?

"What's the terrain like between us and Charlaine's position?"

"I am not certain I understand your question," replied Karalindel.

"From the village of Seiburg, we marched northeast, which has the advantage of being mostly open terrain. What I want to know is what lies directly to our south, along the northern banks of the Zowen River?"

"A forest, although I am not familiar with its name."

"Are those the same woods that lie east of Zwieken?"

"Yes."

"Then that would be the Bloodwood."

"That is an unpleasant name for a forest," said the Elf.

"It's named for the vibrant colour of the leaves in the autumn," replied Ludwig. "Do you not see the same thing in the Goldenwood?"

"The trees of the Goldenwood certainly change colour, although the colours tend to be more yellow than red, a result, I suppose, of having a preponderance of other species of trees. In any case, the Bloodwood, as you call it, extends north of the river some twenty to thirty miles."

"Do you think it would be navigable?"

"I can send a hawk to investigate, but having never been there myself, I would rather not say."

"Then please do so."

"Hang on a moment," said Sigwulf. "What's the plan here? Even if there is a woodland trail, we can't take the wagons in there."

"We send the baggage train back to Zwieken, along with the injured and some people to keep them safe."

"And the rest of us?"

"We'll march south," replied Ludwig, "towards the woods, and then use the cover of the trees to continue east, assuming the forest permits. To a casual outside observer, it'll look as though we're retreating."

"I don't think it will fool the Cunars, do you?"

"No, but I doubt they'd expect us to traverse through the forest either."

"And how are we supposed to feed our men?"

"We'll issue rations for three or four days. My concern is that the Agnesites are heading into a trap, and our presence might be enough to save them."

"I'll get on it right away," said Sigwulf.

"And I shall send my messenger," added the Elf. "Though, once again, I must warn you it will take a while to reach its destination."

Charlaine halted the advance. They'd crossed the Zowen River, heading north, and were now in open countryside, with the Goldenwood still visible to the east. The city of Esthafen was off to the northwest, too distant to be seen, but something about the ease of their progress bothered her.

"Trouble?" asked Teresa.

"What makes you think that?"

"The fact that we've halted with plenty of daylight left. I may not be an expert in strategy or tactics, but I can tell when you're worried. What's on your mind?"

"Were I the one commanding the Holy Army, I'd have taken pains to watch the crossing points."

"Perhaps they don't expect us to attack?"

"I've lost a lot of respect for the Cunars over the years, but that doesn't mean they're not capable strategists. We crossed the Zowen with almost six hundred souls, more if you include the wagons. Doesn't it strike you as odd that we've seen nothing in the way of defences? At the very least, I'd expect the King of Zowenbruch to be guarding that ford."

"Perhaps he's unaware of its existence?"

"I suppose that's possible."

"But you don't think so," said Teresa. "I can tell by your manner. You've always done right by the order, Charlaine. We must trust your instincts. Let's assume it's a trap. What do we do about it?"

"I suppose it depends on where the enemy is located. Be so good as to fetch Theran, would you? I feel the time has come to utilize his magic."

"I shall be back directly."

Charlaine scanned the area. Somewhere, out there, an entire army waited, but where? If she advanced too far into enemy territory, she risked being cut off from her line of retreat.

It didn't take long for Teresa to return with the Elf accompanying her. "I found him," she announced.

"Master Theran, can your magic spy out the enemy?"

"It most certainly can. One moment, if you please." He closed his eyes, uttering words of power so quietly that it appeared as though he was only mouthing the words. The air seemed to buzz, and then a bird flew down from the east to settle on the mage's arm.

"I shall send this falcon aloft," he announced. "If the army is near, I will know soon enough." He touched his forehead to the bird's and then sat back in his saddle as it flew off, heading north.

"Can you see through its eyes?" asked Teresa.

"Were I an Air Mage, most certainly, but being a practitioner of the magic of the earth, no."

"Then how will you know if it worked?"

"Once it returns, I shall exchange information with it."

"So you speak bird?"

"No," replied Theran. "The communication involved is more akin to seeing memories."

"Can you call any kind of bird?"

"Any in the area, yes, but from a practical consideration, I try to call upon birds of prey."

"Might I ask why?" said Teresa.

"For the simple reason that any other species could fall prey to a predator."

They sat on their horses, watching the bird until it was no longer visible. Even then, Theran kept focused on the area where it was last seen.

"It is heading west," he announced.

"How can you tell?" asked Charlaine.

"I can still see it. Superior Elven vision, remember?"

"Yes, of course."

"Ah. Now, that is most interesting."

"What is?"

"It is circling. I think it has found something." He fell silent before finally nodding. "It is returning. See?" The Elf pointed.

The bird finally came into their view, swooping down to settle on the mage's arm. Once more, their foreheads touched, and then Theran turned to Charlaine. "A large force of Cunars is heading west."

"Is Ludwig in trouble?"

"If he is, the falcon saw no signs of it. Perhaps they discovered the army and are moving to intercept?"

"Did the bird see any indication of where they're camped?"

"Yes, far to the north. From what I could tell, it did not appear well-guarded. Do you wish to attack it?"

"No," said Charlaine. "We'll leave that to the Army of Nethendril. We shall march west instead."

The Elf swallowed. "But that brings us into direct conflict with the Temple Knights of Saint Cunar."

"Precisely."

"But we are dangerously outnumbered."

"Our aim is not to defeat them, merely draw them back towards us."

"A strategy of strike and run," noted Teresa. "That's a dangerous game."

"Find Nicola," said Charlaine, "and tell her to pull the wagons back across the river with two companies of Temple Knights to guard them."

"And the others?"

"Four companies will ride with me, while the rest remain here, at this location."

"Including the Mathewites?"

"I'd like Temple Captain Hamelyn to use his men to form a picket line to give us advanced warning of any enemy approach."

"Which companies will you take?" asked Teresa.

"The most experienced. We'll strike quickly, then withdraw. If all goes according to plan, they'll pursue. The idea is to lure them across the ford, so the knights here need to be ready to move at a moment's notice."

"Why not send them across now?"

"I may require their help. The Cunars are disciplined warriors and might pursue before we've had a chance to complete our retreat. Should that prove true, I'll need fresh Temple Knights to prevent them from outrunning us."

"I'll let Nicola know, but shouldn't you be telling this to Katinka? She is your second-in-command."

"I need her to organize the defence on the other side of that ford. Now, off you go, before I change my mind."

Teresa rode off.

"You Humans are a most fascinating species," said Theran. "We Elves will often ruminate on things for days before making decisions, but your people seem to thrive on short notice. One might even be so bold as to say you flourish when reacting to unexpected developments. I envy you."

"You do?" said Charlaine.

"Like most Elves, I have lived for thousands of years, and I find little in this world that excites me the way it does you Humans."

"Is that your way of saying you're bored?"

"I suppose that is one way of putting it. Having said that, I must admit to a slight thrill at the thought I may soon be embroiled in a battle."

"Then it appears we are not so different after all."

28

FLANKED

AUTUMN 1107 SR

Karalindel raised her head from that of the falcon. "The Temple Knights of Saint Agnes engaged the enemy and are now withdrawing back towards the ford."

"And the Cunars?" asked Ludwig.

"They are pursuing, albeit at a slower speed. I imagine they are wary of being lured into a trap."

"Then a trap we shall make it. Sigwulf, you take the cavalry and ride to the ford. Hopefully, you can catch them in the rear as they're crossing. The rest of us will follow, but I don't want to slow you down."

"How far is it to the ford?" the northerner asked.

"I can answer that," replied the Elf. "It varies depending on where you emerge from these woods, but thirty miles would be a good estimate."

"Can you cover that in a day?" asked Ludwig.

"We can certainly try," replied Sigwulf, "but we won't get very far if we don't get a move on." He hesitated. "Won't this leave the rest of the army dangerously exposed?"

"It will, though we'll use the cover of the woods for the first part of our trip."

"That won't help you once you reach open terrain."

"Agreed, but I'm confident in the discipline of our men."

"What does that mean?" asked Karalindel. "Surely you are not suggesting your footmen can attack and defeat cavalry?"

"Attack, no, but if they maintain their discipline, they'll be able to defend against them."

"How does a footman stand against a horse?"

"A horse won't charge into a wall of spears."

"And your archers?"

"Mixed in with the foot. If the Cunars get too close, they'll be met with a hail of arrows."

"I am led to understand that, like your own knights, the Temple Knights of Saint Cunar wear full plate armour. Your bows will have little effect against such warriors."

"They won't be targeting the knights."

"Then who, pray tell, will they loose their arrows against?"

"Their horses," replied Ludwig.

"The Cunars are still capable of fighting on foot, are they not?"

"They most definitely are, but it reduces their effectiveness. Without the mobility their horses offer, they'll be easier to flank."

"An interesting tactic," said the Elf. "I shall be watching closely to see whether it proves effective."

"How far until we clear these blasted woods?" grumbled Sigwulf.

"At the most a mile, then you can be on your way."

"Then I'd best get going,"

"One more thing," said Ludwig. "If the fighting proves too difficult, retreat and draw them back towards us. With a bit of luck, you'll force them to divert some of their men, which gives the Agnesites better odds."

"You Humans are strange," said Karalindel. "Always talking of luck. Do you truly think you can influence chance events simply by wishing it were so?"

"Do the Elves not believe in luck?"

"It was not luck that helped us defeat the Orcs; it was careful planning and a solid strategy."

"Perhaps, but surely chance made an appearance every now and then. Did your patrols never stumble across each other unexpectedly?"

"They did, but that was the result of each side's strategy clashing with the other. They were not chance encounters, merely the logical results of conflicting plans."

"And did your warriors ever take advantage of such unexpected clashes?"

"On occasion, yes. Why?"

"I can't speak for all Humans, but many of us believe good fortune often results when one plans for the unexpected."

"How can one plan for something if one cannot predict it?" asked the Elf.

"It's not prediction, it's expectation. I like to plan for every eventuality I can think of, which makes us more flexible as an army. That's one reason we crossed into Zowenbruch rather than wait in Eisen for the invasion."

"That still does not explain how you plan for the unexpected."

"No," replied Ludwig, "it doesn't, so let me put it another way. I cannot predict precisely what the enemy will do, but I know Human nature, so I use that to reason out what I would do in their place."

"Yet you were caught by a surprise raid."

"Admittedly, we were, but we survived that encounter and adapted. They'll not surprise us a second time."

"Fascinating. Perhaps it is due to our long lifespans, but Elves like to plan things down to the tiniest detail, yet you appear willing to march on little more than hope."

"Hope and guts," added Ludwig.

Karalindel laughed. "Now you are suggesting your intestines are responsible?"

"We use the term to describe courage or bravery."

"Then why not simply use those terms?"

"I have no answer for that. Perhaps, once this is all over, I'll present that notion to the scholars in my court."

"I would be most interested to hear their reply."

"You'd be most welcome to come and hear it in person," said Ludwig. "Actually, I'm surprised we haven't had more visits from your folk."

"Elves are reflective creatures, weighing all the advantages and disadvantages before settling on a final course of action."

"Meaning…"

"They are hesitant to visit a Human realm after centuries of solitude. I must say, you Humans of today are far different from your ancestors."

"In what way?"

"They were primitive folk, prone to aggression without provocation, as I recall."

"How long ago was this?"

"Two thousand years ago, give or take a century or two."

"Just how old are you?"

She smiled. "Three thousand, two hundred and fifty-two years, but I advise you not to ask that of every Elf you meet."

"Why? Is there shame in Elven society concerning one's age?"

"Not shame so much as sorrow."

"Is that because you cannot have children?"

"How did you know?"

"Something I overheard while I was a prisoner in Nethendril," said Ludwig. "Has it always been that way?"

"No. We once bore children as the other races do, but during the Great War, we lost that ability."

"How?"

"Those who ruled us realized we were losing the war. To stave off our own demise, our mages began exploring things previously forbidden. They unlocked magic that had long remained dormant, allowing us to win the war, but at a great cost."

"Your people became sterile?"

"Yes, though we did not come to that realization for many centuries."

"Centuries? Surely Elves must've tried having children in the meantime?"

The Air Mage's reply took on a hard edge. "We Elves are not driven by primitive urges to reproduce like you Humans!"

"I didn't mean it as an insult," replied Ludwig. "Though our respective peoples are similar in some ways, there are other differences that are still foreign to us. My apologies if I upset you."

"Your apology is accepted. Now, if you will excuse me, I require time to recover from the expenditure of my magical energy."

Charlaine risked a glance over her shoulder. The Temple Knights of Saint Cunar were gradually falling behind but kept their pace steady. She held no doubt that the grey-clad knights would pursue them for as long as possible; she only hoped the ford proved a defensible enough position.

Temple Captain Nicola fell back to her general's position, noting her gaze. "They're determined. I'll give them that."

"And so you should," replied Charlaine. "I only wish we could've done more damage. As it stands, we've done little more than slap them in the face."

"True, but our objective was to pull them away from the king, and we've managed to draw their full attention. It's odd, when you think about it."

"What is?"

"This entire situation. We quite literally came to blows with those Cunars, yet here they are, trailing along behind as if following us on a parade."

"What else would you expect them to do? It's not as if they can catch us; their horses are no better than ours."

"True," said Nicola, "but we must camp at some point."

"So must they, eventually."

"You intend to lose them in the dark, don't you?"

"What makes you think that's my strategy?"

"You have a devious mind, General, although I'm not certain it'll work to our advantage in this instance."

"Why?"

"Because the only way out of here is across the ford, a ford, I might add, that they are likely already familiar with."

"If what you say is true," said Charlaine, "then losing them in the dark wouldn't make any difference."

Nicola regarded her commanding officer. "I know that look; you're up to something. What is it?"

"We'll keep the column moving, just as you said."

"And once it's dark?"

"We'll deploy a light rearguard to watch the enemy while the rest get some sleep."

"You want them to continue following us, even though they outnumber us?"

"That's the point, isn't it? We want to draw them to the ford."

"So the Elves can slaughter them."

"I doubt it would be a slaughter, although it would likely slow them down a little."

"Then we could hit them from the south, while they're reforming on the other side of the river," said Nicola.

"Yes, though we must be careful to time the strike carefully. If we let too many across that river, their numbers may overwhelm us."

"We'd still need to fight them, eventually."

"Would we?" Charlaine whistled, causing the Elf, Theran Silverhand, to turn in his saddle towards them. "You called, General?"

"Inform the good Temple Captain here of what you told me earlier."

The mage slowed his horse until they caught up, then moved alongside the duo. "I received a message from Karalindel, the Earth Mage accompanying King Ludwig."

"And?"

"He has sent his general, Sigwulf, to attack the rear of the Cunars with all his cavalry."

"They'll be ill-matched."

"Which is why we must tempt them towards the ford."

"And when is this attack to commence?"

"That depends on what the enemy does," replied Charlaine. "It's another ten miles to the ford. Ideally, I'd like to arrive early tomorrow morning."

"Couldn't we push on through the night?"

"We could," said Charlaine, "but then we risk them turning around to deal with the king's cavalry. We need them to be preoccupied with chasing us, remember?"

Sigwulf sat in the dark. He'd ordered his reduced command to make camp without fires so as not to give the enemy any sign of their presence. So far, their strategy had worked, for a Cunar rearguard hadn't made themselves known. Off in the distance, the glow of campfires marked the enemy's position.

He'd considered a nighttime attack, but as much as the dark would help hide their approach, it made the attack itself more difficult. Without light to guide them, the uneven ground could cause a horse to stumble or his own men to lose their way when withdrawing from the enemy camp.

Far better, he'd thought, to continue with the plan of following along out of sight, until the Cunars broke ranks to cross the ford. And that was the moment they'd strike, when the enemy least expected it.

His thoughts turned to Ludwig. If the Cunars turned around to face Sig and his men, the knights would soon overwhelm them. He wondered how far behind him the rest of the army was, but he had no way of knowing. Instead, he must have faith the men of Hadenfeld would be there when needed.

"We must make camp, sire," said Gustavo. "Stumbling around in the dark does us no good."

"Yes, of course," replied the king. "Please convey my thanks to everyone and tell them we made excellent progress today."

The captain left, issuing orders to those within earshot, leaving Ludwig to his thoughts. They'd cleared the Bloodwood and were now north of the Zowen River, so close that if one listened carefully, they'd hear running water.

"I hope we do not run into more fog tomorrow," came the Elf's melodic tones. "That would greatly hamper my efforts to spy out the enemy."

"It would be helpful to know where they are at this moment," said Ludwig. "I don't suppose you could summon an owl?"

"I am a master of Earth Magic, not an Air Mage."

"You summoned a falcon."

"I can well understand your confusion," replied Karalindel. "I did not summon those creatures from thin air. They are friends of mine whom I have established a particular affinity with."

"Then where did they come from?"

"The Goldenwood. You failed to notice them following us. I find that Humans often lack the ability to absorb the majesty of their surroundings, particularly where the natural world is involved."

"As an Earth Mage, you must have many spells upon which you can draw."

"And you wish to know how they might help you in battle tomorrow?"

"Precisely."

"That depends on what you are looking for. My magic is not capable of inflicting significant damage on armies, although it is able to deal with individuals, but that is perhaps not the best use of it. By the same token, I could summon creatures to aid us, but I doubt they would be very effective against heavily armoured Temple Knights."

"I was thinking more along the lines of the terrain," said Ludwig.

"Broken ground comes to mind. The spell makes the ground uneven, very useful in preventing cavalry charges, but that would also affect your own horsemen, so perhaps not. How about a defensive mound?"

"I assume that creates some sort of hill?"

"It does," replied the Elf, "but I would need to cast it multiple times to provide enough benefit to your entire army. I could increase the effectiveness of some of your men's armour."

"How many could you affect?"

"One or two companies at most, and even then, the effect is relatively mild; it does not make your men impervious to weapons."

"I knew an Earth Mage some years ago," said Ludwig. "He was able to manipulate earth and stone."

"As can I, though there is little need for it these days. What is it you have in mind?"

"I'd like to be able to cross the river."

"We are some miles from the ford, with an army blocking our way."

"Could we not create a ford of our own?"

"I am not a Water Mage," replied Karalindel. "I am unable to reduce the water level."

"Ah, but could you not raise the riverbed to make the water shallower?"

The Elf stared back, her head tilted to one side. "I must congratulate you, Majesty. That thought never crossed my mind. All I would need to do is create a defensive mound in the middle of the river."

"And you can do that?"

"Most certainly, although I must warn you, the water has to go somewhere, and would presumably flood around the hill to whichever side of the river is lower."

"But you control the size of this mound, yes?"

"Of course."

"Then I propose you raise the ground just enough to make a shallow crossing."

"That would require a great deal of concentration."

"But you could do it?" asked Ludwig.

"I believe so," she replied.

"And how long does it take to cast a spell of that nature?"

"Not long at all, providing I have a clear view of the area in question."

"We're well clear of the Bloodwood. I should think it would be easy to see the river."

"It appears I did not explain the nature of the spell in a clear and concise manner. To raise the ground, I must be able to see the ground I am affecting, which means I need to see the riverbed. That should not pose a problem come morning, providing we do not suffer another fog."

"How long would this ford of yours last?"

"I am not sure I understand the question."

"My impression of magic," said Ludwig, "is that the effects only last for a brief time."

"Your impression is false," replied Karalindel. "Well, not entirely false. Many spells are limited in such a manner, but with the manipulation of earth or stone, the effects are permanent."

"So the enemy could also use the ford you created?"

"Yes, although I could always reverse the spell and be rid of the effects. That, however, requires recasting, which would drain me of more of my magical power. Have you a particular section of the river in mind?"

"Not at present, but I like to know what's at my disposal when going into battle."

"You are, I assume, familiar with the limitations of magic?"

"Only those you mentioned earlier. Why? Is there something else I should be made aware of?"

"Most definitely," replied the Elf. "Are you familiar with how magic works?"

"From what I've been told, it's in the blood. I've seen healing at work, and when I was in the north, I watched an Earth Mage manipulate stone, but for the life of me, I couldn't explain how it works."

"Mages draw their power from within, a reserve, if you like, of magical energy waiting to be utilized. The greater the reserves a caster has, the more spells they can cast in a given period."

"Are you suggesting this energy gets used up?"

"Only temporarily. It builds back up, but it places a limit on how much casting a particular mage is capable of."

"And have you a large reserve of this magical energy?"

"Relative to my colleagues, reasonably so, although I am by no means the most powerful caster in the Goldenwood."

"Then I count it good fortune you agreed to accompany us."

29

BATTLE

AUTUMN 1107 SR

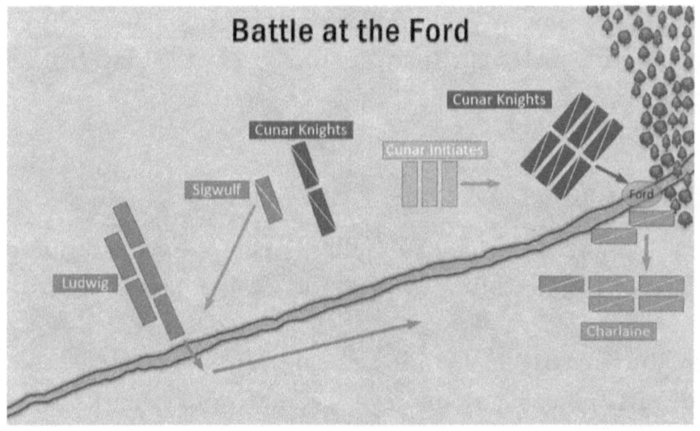

Ludwig ordered his men into a line and pressed forward, spears out, the archers following, ready to loose arrows over the heads of those in front should the opportunity present itself. They'd likely do minimal damage against the heavily armoured Cunars, but the action served to give his command hope. The grand melee drew closer, the Mathewites being pushed back towards him. Soon they'd break, and then the grey-clad Temple Knights would be upon the warriors of Hadenfeld.

Ludwig called a halt, ordering his foot to plant their spears in the ground so as to present a wall of steel. The brown-clad Mathewites, no longer able to hold their line, retreated south, and then the sea of grey rolled forward like a wall of death.

A horn sounded to the south, faint, but there was no mistaking it. He was about to risk a glance in that direction, but then the Cunars struck, charging forward, attempting to break the wall of spears. The knights were determined to penetrate the formation, but their horses veered away from the possibility of impalement.

Ludwig had anchored his left flank on the river, his men stretching out in a line heading due south. His spears would hold, of that he had no doubt, but the Cunars were pushing back Charlaine's knights, jeopardizing his right flank.

Another horn sounded, this time much higher in tone and coming from the north. He feared it might be the Army of Zowenbruch, but then spotted the Elves of Nethendril across the river, advancing towards the ford.

The Cunars must have noticed them as well, for their fighting reached a fevered pitch as they pushed south with renewed energy, desperate to break the Agnesites before the Elves arrived.

Ludwig ordered his men to advance three paces. They carried out the manoeuvre with great precision, then planted their spears again, ready to ward off the Temple Knights, but the enemy's attention remained riveted on defeating their nemesis—the scarlet-clad sister of Saint Agnes.

He repeated his order again and again, slowly pushing further towards the Cunars' rear.

Charlaine's knights started to falter. They were outmatched and outnumbered, with the initiates of Saint Cunar having joined the fight, seeking out those of her fellow sisters who'd been unhorsed.

A horn sounded from behind her, and hope rose in her heart as the green-clad warriors of Cyn's division surged through her knights, a wall of spear tips driving the enemy back. With their right flank protected by the forest and their left by Cyn's cavalry, the general's late arrival had given the Agnesites a fighting chance.

Ludwig watched as an arrow sank into the back of a Cunar. The fellow twisted in the saddle to locate his attacker, but then toppled to the ground.

More arrows flew from across the river as Elven archers lined the river-bank, and the enemy began to falter. The densely packed ranks of the Elven foot were crossing the ford, their silver scale armour glinting in the sun.

Ludwig held his breath. The Temple Knights of Saint Cunar were surrounded on all sides; would they fight to the death, as they'd done at the Battle of the Wilderness, or had that loss taught them a lesson in humility?

The Cunars disengaged, backing up to form a square, and an eerie quiet fell over the battlefield, broken only by the moans of the injured and dying. It was as if some great power had placed a gigantic hand between the two sides and swept them apart from each other, leaving a blood-soaked gap, littered with the bodies of men, women, and horses, a scene worthy of the Underworld.

A grey-clad knight stepped out from the enemy, his sword sheathed. He halted five paces short of Ludwig's men and removed his helmet. Temple Commander Amarand stood there, covered in sweat, his hair plastered to his face, dents and scratches marring his plate armour. His breath came in gasps, looking as though he might collapse, but then he straightened himself.

"I would parley," he called out.

Ludwig dismounted, pushing his way past his men to stand before the Cunar commander.

"Majesty," said Amarand. "Your men fought most valiantly. I yield the battlefield to you."

"It is not to me you must surrender," replied Ludwig.

"I am not proposing that I surrender, merely that we vacate the field of battle."

"You seem to be under the impression that you have a choice. You are surrounded, Temple Commander. The Elves block your only escape, and we have fresh troops to the south and west. Unless you intended to try to escape through the forest? If so, I should warn you, there are plenty more Elves there to block your way."

"You fail to take into account the might of my Temple Knights," replied Amarand. "They are the finest warriors on the entire Continent."

"No longer. Your defeat at the Battle of the Wilderness robbed you of your best men. Now you stand here, surrounded by enemies, a shadow of your former strength."

"We are not afraid to die."

"To die without reason is the height of folly. Your order has already been weakened by its crusade in the east; would you now make it even more so by needlessly sacrificing those under your command?"

Amarand cast his gaze about, quickly coming to the realization that they were severely outnumbered with no avenue of escape. He stared at the ground a moment, perhaps collecting his thoughts, then lifted his head to meet Ludwig's gaze. "To preserve what's left of the Temple Knights of Saint Cunar, we surrender."

"As I said, it is not to me you must surrender."

"Then to whom?"

Ludwig pointed to his right, where Charlaine was riding towards them, threading her way through the gap between the two armies.

Anger darkened the Temple Commander's face, and Ludwig feared that he'd pushed the man too far, but then Amarand drew his sword and offered it, hilt first, towards the Temple General.

"What is this?" asked Charlaine.

"He offered his surrender," replied Ludwig, "but I insisted he must do so to you, for your Temple Knights bore the brunt of the fighting."

"What are your terms?" asked Amarand.

Charlaine took the sword. "Your men must surrender their arms and mounts."

"And their lives?"

"That is up to His Majesty, the king, for we stand upon his lands, not mine."

"You fought an unjust war," stated Ludwig. "A war that should never have occurred in the first place, and why? Because we dared to refuse you a commandery?"

"My superiors wanted you broken, a demonstration of the Church's power. Instead, you've broken us."

"You did that yourself," said Charlaine, "when your Primus disbanded the orders."

"I shall not debate your words, Temple General. You bested us when you fled the Antonine, and have proven the strength of your convictions by defeating us yet again. The Saints look upon you with favour."

"I am a devoted follower of Mathew," said Ludwig, "but too many men and women died today because of your Church's twisted beliefs in its own supremacy. What would the Saints say if they witnessed such greed and arrogance amongst those who would use their teachings to their own advantage?"

"What else would you have of me?"

"Each and every Temple Knight of Saint Cunar must swear an oath to not take up arms against Hadenfeld ever again, nor any other Petty Kingdom."

"And if they refuse?" asked Amarand.

"Then they shall be given the opportunity to receive the same punishment meted out to those they conquered in the east."

"The history of the eastern crusades is a bloody one," said Charlaine, her attention on Ludwig. "They slaughtered those who refused to accept the Church of the Saints."

Ludwig kept his eyes on Amarand. "I said my piece. You command this Holy Army, do you not?"

"I do, under the authority of the Temple General of Saint Cunar."

"Then order your men to surrender their arms and mounts, or I shall let my reinforcements destroy what remains of your dignity."

The Cunar nodded before turning and marching back to his army. Moments later, his men dismounted and discarded their weapons.

Another rider trotted between the two armies, coming to rest a few paces short of where Ludwig and Charlaine stood.

"Sorry I was late, boss," said Cyn. "For a moment there, I was worried we wouldn't get a chance to fight."

"Fear not," replied Ludwig. "Your timing was perfect.

30

VICTORY

AUTUMN 1107 SR

Ludwig surveyed the field of battle. His men had come through relatively unscathed, but the Temple Knights, particularly those of Saint Agnes, had suffered tremendously.

Temple Captain Teresa moved amongst the wounded, helping those she could, and even the Elf healer, Galrandir, was using his magic to aid the survivors, but the stench of death was still overpowering.

Sigwulf's cavalry came through unscathed, but the Knights of the Sacred Shield had made a great sacrifice, dying almost to the last man in a heroic defence of the western ford that Karalindel had created.

"What now?" asked Cyn, drawing Ludwig from his thoughts.

"The Cunars are being rounded up as we speak," he replied. "The problem is what we should do with them. Were it up to me, I'd send them home, but this is no regular army; it's the Church."

"So send them back to the Antonine."

"How? Do I send them through the Goldenwood, or abandon them across the river in Zowenbruch?"

"Perhaps neither," came the voice of Talon Elonin. "Riders approach from the north, bearing the banner of King Konrad."

"Not to fight, I hope," said Cyn.

"Let's go meet them and find out," replied Ludwig. "Gustavo? Six men to escort us, if you please."

"Aye, sire."

Ludwig waited as they formed up on either side, then headed towards the old ford. Cyn rode alongside him, as did Elonin. Ludwig had thought to ask Temple General Charlaine to join him, but she was busy seeing to those under her command. They splashed across the Zowen River, then halted, waiting for the other party to approach.

King Konrad brought his horse to a halt before Ludwig. "I once promised you that I would never again cross your border in anger. I am here today to honour that pledge."

"I'm not certain I understand," said Ludwig.

"My army sits a few miles behind me. Had I chosen to, we could've marched to support the Holy Army, but I held true to my promise." He peered across the river, taking in the sight. "It appears you've been busy. My congratulations on your victory. Not only have you saved your kingdom, but mine as well."

"I have?"

"You may not yet realize the ramifications of what you've done here today, but I do," replied Konrad. "The Church of the Saints no longer has a sword with which to threaten the Petty Kingdoms. For that, I must thank you."

"Then perhaps there is something you can do for me," said Ludwig.

"What would that be?"

"I find myself in possession of a large number of prisoners. I'd escort them to my eastern border, but I'm afraid the terrain there makes such a journey most difficult."

"I assume they've been disarmed?"

"Yes, and their horses confiscated."

"Indeed? And what about their armour?"

"That we allowed them to keep," said Ludwig. "Were you to escort them to your eastern border and see them on their way, you might be justified in confiscating something of value as recompense."

Konrad smiled. "I like your way of thinking, Ludwig. I agree to do so once I've made some arrangements. You realize this won't sit well with the Antonine, and they might even send another army to attack my realm?"

"Do this for me, and I will assist you should any enemy threaten your lands."

"Indeed? I find that particularly encouraging, considering you have an alliance with Erlingen. As you know, we've been at odds with them for years."

"I've yet to visit Erlingen since becoming king, so any alliance arranged by my predecessor is no longer binding."

"So you offer me one instead?"

"Not an alliance, a mutual pact of defence. We only agree to help each other if invaded. I'll not support a war of conquest."

"What a refreshing idea," replied Konrad. "I don't believe I've seen its like before."

"I've used it in the south to secure my borders, and intend to offer it to all the neighbouring realms."

"A lot of people are talking about you lately."

"Are they? And what are they saying?"

"That you wish to restore the former glory of Hadenfeld. To be frank, it has many worried you'll start a war."

"I bear no desire to go to war," replied Ludwig, "but I shall defend my borders and those of our allies with all my might."

Konrad shook his head in disbelief.

"You find that amusing?" asked Ludwig.

"No," replied Konrad. "Quite the contrary, I find it an admirable quality. You have, in your short time as king, drawn support from the most unlikely of allies. First, it was Elves, then the Temple Knights."

"And now the Kingdom of Zowenbruch?"

"Agreed, although give me a few months to convince my nobles. I shouldn't like a rebellion on my hands."

"Then I invite you to visit Harlingen when you feel you're ready."

"I should be delighted." Konrad looked over his shoulder. "Now, with your permission, I shall fetch my men to take possession of those prisoners."

"That would be most appreciated."

Early the next morning, Ludwig met with his senior commanders. Sigwulf and Cyn were both there, as was Temple General Charlaine and her aide, Temple Captain Nicola. Not surprising was the added presence of High Lord Sindra, who'd accompanied Talon Elonin on the initial raid against the Holy Army's camp.

Ludwig didn't waste any time getting to important matters. "How much longer till all the Cunars are handed over to Konrad's men?"

"Likely another day or two," replied Nicola. "We're still treating some of their wounded."

"You took the brunt of the fighting. What were your casualties?"

"Half our fighting force," said Charlaine, "although many of those will recover thanks to the efforts of our healers. I must also thank the Elves of the Goldenwood for the loan of their Life Mage."

"You are most welcome," replied Sindra. "Having witnessed the damage dealt by your Temple Knights, I am pleased to know they will be on our side in any future conflict."

"We also lost many horses."

"That won't present a problem," said Ludwig. "Under the terms of their surrender, we have all the Cunars' mounts. You're welcome to take however many you need."

"Won't you need them for your knights?"

"A few, most certainly, but there are far more than we have a use for. As it stands presently, we'll have to recruit more knights to compensate for our losses, so it'll be a while before they're able to take to the field again."

"There's still a company amongst my division," offered Cyn, "but if the empire comes calling, we'll need more."

"You mean when," countered Charlaine. "Given recent events, there can be no doubt they're coming. Unfortunately, our victory here helps their cause."

"How so?" asked Cyn.

"We've effectively eliminated the threat of the Cunars. Not entirely, for they'll eventually rebuild, but it leaves the Petty Kingdoms vulnerable."

"But wouldn't their order help the Halvarians? After all, you're the one who revealed that they'd corrupted the Church."

"I'd hoped their aim was to neutralize the Holy Army, rather than control it. If that's true, then they'll likely attack as soon as they hear of its defeat."

"Can they, though?" asked Sig. "It takes a lot of preparation to invade a kingdom, let alone the entire Continent. I doubt they'd just wake up one day and decide to attack, even if events did play into their favour."

"You're forgetting one important detail," said Charlaine. "They've been dreaming of the final conquest of the Petty Kingdoms for generations. I imagine they'll have a multitude of contingency plans at their disposal."

"Then we should concentrate on the future," said Sindra. "If this invasion is to come, how do we best prepare for it?"

"By rebuilding the army and making it as strong as we can. Temple General Charlaine has fought them before, so she's the best person to advise us."

All eyes turned to the Temple General.

"The might of the empire," she began, "lies in the organization of its legions. At full strength, each has two thousand four hundred warriors, with each legion further divided into four cohorts. From our experience, half of those are comprised of Imperial troops, while the rest are provincials."

"Which are?" asked Cyn.

"People recruited from previously conquered regions. These provincial warriors are typically less well-equipped than the Imperials and are often sent in first to soften up their opponents. At least that was their strategy at the Brinwald, though they may have learned their lesson. I've read that the legions of Halvaria adapt quickly to changing tactics."

"But they can be defeated," said Cyn. "You proved that in Arnsfeld."

"The situation in Arnsfeld was unique in that we engaged an entire cohort by occupying a keep. I doubt they'd fall for that trick a second time. I believe that when the next invasion comes, it will consist of more than one legion."

"How do we fight that?"

"From what I've seen," replied the Temple General, "you've already taken the first step. Hadenfeld has brought its army under the king's direct control, and that centralized control makes it far more reliable in battle. You also have two capable generals, giving you flexibility in terms of strategy."

"It didn't help us here," said Ludwig. "In fact, if anything, it only made things worse."

"You could've done little to change the outcome. Your initial strategy was sound; it just didn't account for the enemy commander's abilities."

"A mistake I hope to avoid in future. What of you, High Lord? Have you an opinion on the matter?"

"I do. Several, in fact," Sindra replied. "But I am a politician rather than a warrior, so Elonin will speak on my behalf."

The Elf talon cleared her throat. "Though we won this battle, it exposed some weaknesses. Now, having learned what those are, we can take steps to rectify them."

"Those weaknesses being?" asked Sigwulf.

"The first relates to numbers. In simple terms, we all need more warriors under arms. At the same time, we must find the correct balance between foot, horse, and bow. I suggest we consider all our forces as one large army, dividing it up into two or possibly three divisions. We also need to increase our numbers to at least equal what a Halvarian legion would field, possibly even more."

"That would be expensive."

"Agreed," said Ludwig, "but we could reduce the burden by sharing it with our allies. At present, Sig and Cyn each command just shy of seven hundred men apiece, but we already plan to raise that to one thousand. If we press on with a diplomatic campaign, we might convince our neigh-bours to supply another thousand, all combined."

"Numbers aren't everything," said Elonin. "Each group, or division of your army, needs a balance of troops much like the enemy. Perhaps, Temple

General, you might share your knowledge regarding the makeup of these Halvarian legions?"

"Certainly," replied Charlaine. "At the Brinwald, roughly two-thirds of the provincials were foot, while the remainder were a balance of horse and bow. The Imperials, on the other hand, had a far larger contingent of horse, roughly one-third of each cohort, at the expense of their foot. The Imperial archers also utilized crossbows, giving them more stopping power than standard bowmen."

"And their tactics?"

"They were blunt, to say the least. They sent a swarm of provincials to pin our line in place, then tried to flank us, but we had a hidden surprise waiting for them."

"The Elves of Mythanos," said Sindra.

"That's correct. Even so, we very nearly lost the battle. The Temple Knights of Saint Mathew took a great number of casualties rushing in to prevent our other flank from collapsing. There is one more thing I should mention—an elite group of horsemen called the Emperor's Own."

"Were they part of the legion you defeated?"

"I'm not entirely certain. Even the prisoners we captured were unable to verify whether they were part of the legion or simply an extra assignment of warriors."

"How many elite horsemen were there?"

"Our best estimates suggest around two hundred, held in reserve till the very end, likely for the final push, but one of our Temple Captains rebuffed the threat with a counter-charge. These elite warriors wore plate armour, like us, although it soon became evident they lacked the discipline of Temple Knights."

"This is going to need a lot more thought," said Ludwig.

"Let's not overthink this," said Cyn. "We divide the army into divisions of one thousand to make things simple. Out of that, five hundred would be foot, with the rest divided equally between archers and cavalry."

"And what about the Temple Knights?"

"They become the reserve, to be utilized as the opportunity permits."

"And the Elves?" asked Sindra.

"We could distribute them amongst each division."

"That will not work," said Elonin. "Most do not understand the common tongue, making it very difficult to follow your orders. The Elves should form their own division, although it would naturally be smaller."

"Not necessarily," added Sindra. "The army we marched with is only that of Nethendril."

"Meaning?" said Cyn.

"There are other Elven cities, each with their own contingents. Were the entire Continent threatened, I am certain I could convince them to participate."

"And what warriors would they field?" asked Ludwig.

"Likely the same proportions as your own divisions, and our archers would be equipped with Elven bows. However, our cavalry is much lighter than yours, more useful for scouting and raiding than fighting against heavily armoured knights."

"Could you field one thousand?"

"I believe so, though it would likely take a year or two to organize."

"But you're the High Lord; couldn't you just order it?"

"We Elves do not rule in such a manner. We are, to use a Human term, more of a collection of independent cities. Though I am, in theory, their leader, I cannot compel them to march to war."

"These plans for expansion are important," noted Charlaine, "but we must be careful. We know the Stormwinds and Sartellians are agents of the empire, and though we have driven them from this realm, their reach is extensive."

"I agree," said Sigwulf. "But keeping a standing army of two thousand isn't something that we can easily conceal.

"Then we'll disperse them," replied Ludwig. "If they're not all gathered in one place, no one will likely notice. To the outside world, we'll look weak, a realm ravaged by internal conflict and two civil wars, while in reality, we'll be building a large, professional army that's ready to fight the Empire of Halvaria when the time comes."

"I like the idea, boss," said Cyn, "but if we're going to succeed in fooling the Halvarians, we need to be vigilant. By that, I mean we must limit who has knowledge of this plan. All it would take is one word in the wrong place, and the next thing you know, the empire would be knocking on our door."

"A good point. The queen will obviously need to know, as will Gita, since she'll be handling the treasury."

"Lord Merrick is in charge of the courts, so we'll need him to avoid any legal entanglements."

"Such as?"

"There are powerful people still working against you, boss. The attempted poisoning of the queen told us as much. If they get wind of any of this, they'll do everything in their power to stop us, which might include trying to use the law against you. I'm not suggesting they'd be in any way successful, but you need someone watching for signs of that."

Ludwig nodded. "Merrick and Gita are both to be informed. Any other suggestions?"

"Captain Gustavo," said Sigwulf, "so he can ensure no one overhears any of our discussions."

"Agreed. We'll begin by spreading our existing divisions across the kingdom. Cyn, you'll keep half your men in Harlingen, the rest will billet in Malburg. We'll work out something similar for Sigwulf's division, but with different towns. If anyone enquires, your entire command is in one and only one city. Just avoid revealing where."

"I get what you mean," said Cyn. "It'll look like we're trying to raise only five hundred men in Harlingen, while Malburg thinks the same, but isn't there a risk someone will discover the ruse?"

"I'll admit, it's not a perfect plan, but it's all we've got for the moment. Eventually, we could establish an army camp somewhere in the middle of nowhere. Still, even that creates problems, primarily how we supply them without anyone learning of their existence."

"And what about the cost?"

"Without the army to secure the kingdom, everything else becomes meaningless. We'll have to tighten our belts so we have what's needed to increase our numbers."

"You could do an Otto," said Sigwulf. "He was notoriously stingy."

"I never met King Otto," mused Charlaine. "What was he like?"

"I think you would've liked him," replied Ludwig. "He had a reputation for being stubborn, perhaps even bombastic, but once you got him away from court, he was quite pleasant. I know he cared a great deal about the people of Hadenfeld; it's a pity he didn't live long enough to rule over a reunited kingdom."

"He saw a little of it," said Cyn, "at least that's something. Then again, his death led to mad King Morgan, so perhaps it's just as well he didn't stick around."

"That makes no sense," said Sigwulf. "Regardless of how much longer he lived, we still would've eventually had Morgan as our king."

"Would we? Or would Otto have grown wiser and named Ludwig as his heir and thereby avoided the entire second civil war?"

"I doubt it would've come to that," said Ludwig. "There were too many other heirs in line before me."

"Regardless of Hadenfeld's history," added Charlaine, "or perhaps because of it, we are here today, planning for the future, rather than fighting over the past. Let us not forget who the real threat is—Halvaria."

31

WINTER

WINTER 1107 SR

"It's all so frustrating," said Ludwig. "Gustavo has questioned all the servants, yet we have no inkling of who tried to poison you. How can you remain so calm knowing they're still out there?"

"Getting upset serves no purpose," replied Charlotte. "And I have a theory that whoever placed that vial didn't do it out of malice. I think they were trying to help me."

"By poisoning you?"

"Travel across this Continent and you'll see all manner of folks buying good luck charms and supposed remedies that are little more than wishful thinking. Why, even the Church reportedly collects relics of long-dead Saints."

"The Saints were real people," said Ludwig.

"They were, but if I hear of another peddler claiming to have a finger bone of Saint Agnes for sale, I shall scream."

"You don't believe them?" he said, grinning.

She ignored his taunt. "I wonder how many finger bones the Church has?"

"Perhaps the Saints had ten fingers on each hand?"

She guffawed, almost spilling her drink in the process. "It amazes me how it's always a finger bone, never a toe or leg."

"A thigh bone would be too large for people to carry."

"But a toe wouldn't?"

"True, but didn't the Saints walk around in bare feet?"

Charlotte laughed a second time. "It would be a bone, not a dirty toe with toenails and calloused skin."

"It's good to see you in such fine spirits."

"I must admit it's nice to have you back. It feels like I hardly saw you this past year. First, you travelled south to stop a war, and then you returned only to fight a war. I think we deserve a little peace and quiet, wouldn't you agree?"

"I—" He started to answer, but then the door opened.

"Sorry for the interruption, Majesties," said Gustavo. "You have a visitor."

"Is it someone important?" asked Charlotte. "Not another representative from the Church, I hope?"

The captain hesitated.

"That doesn't bode well," she added.

"Who is it, then?" asked Ludwig.

"A man calling himself Brother Aiden," replied the captain.

"A Mathewite?"

"I couldn't say, sire. He wears no cassock."

"Surely you're not suggesting he's devoid of clothing?" said Charlotte with a wide grin. "How scandalous."

"He is dressed as a commoner, Majesty, but carries himself as a warrior."

"I assume he's been disarmed?" asked Ludwig.

"Yes, sire. Shall I escort him to the throne room?"

"Yes, but before you do that, see if you can find Father Vernan. If we are to speak with this 'Brother Aiden', it would be beneficial to identify which order he belongs to."

"Perhaps he's lying," added Charlotte, "and doesn't work for the Church at all."

"I hadn't considered that," said Ludwig. "Though calling himself brother would be an odd habit for someone of that nature."

"He could've left the Church?"

"You may be on to something there. Let's go find out, shall we?"

"My pardon, Majesties," said Gustavo, "but did you wish to see him right away, or wait for Father Vernan?"

"Hold him till we're in the throne room. I have faith that the good father will arrive in due course."

The man calling himself Brother Aiden stood in the centre of the throne room, surrounded by Royal Guardsmen.

The door behind him opened, and an out-of-breath Father Vernan rushed in. "My apologies, Majesties. I was at the Temple of Saint Mathew, conferring with the archprior." He came to a halt when he noticed the visitor. "Who's this?"

Aiden went down on one knee and bowed. "Majesties," he said, though he offered no further words.

"You bow like a Temple Knight," noted Charlotte.

The visitor raised his eyes, meeting her gaze. "That's because I am one."

"Of what order?" asked Ludwig.

"Saint Ragnar."

"A bold claim," said Father Vernan, "but how do we know you speak the truth?"

Aiden addressed his remarks to Ludwig. "You've given refuge to the Temple Knights of Saint Agnes, have you not?"

"I have," replied the king. "But that's common knowledge in these parts."

"And the person in charge of those knights is still Temple General Charlaine?"

"Indeed, but once again, that is known across the entire kingdom. How does that prove your claim?"

"I served with her in Ilea and Calabria. She will, I'm certain, confirm my identity."

"The Temple Knights are stationed in Eisen."

"And yet she is here," said Aiden, "in Harlingen. You are consulting with her regarding the reorganization of your army."

"How in the name of the Saints do you know that?"

"I make it a habit to learn as much as I can about the areas I operate in."

"In which you operate? Are you suggesting there's a Necromancer in Hadenfeld? That is what your order does, isn't it? Hunt down Death Mages?"

"That is but one of our duties, Majesty."

"With all due respect," said Father Vernan, "we've yet to prove the validity of his claims."

"True," replied Ludwig. "Could you, as a Holy Father, ask him questions to ascertain whether he tells the truth?"

"I wish I could, sire, but the Temple Knights of Saint Ragnar operate in secrecy, most often passing themselves off as commoners, the better to locate those practicing the dark arts. I did, however, pass the Temple General on the way here, as she was heading to visit the Archprioress of Saint Agnes. Shall I go and fetch her?"

"One does not fetch a Temple General," said Charlotte. "Extend to her a request for her to attend us here at her convenience. Brother Aiden will remain under the watchful eyes of the Royal Guard while we wait."

· · ·

Charlaine arrived at the Royal Keep as the bells tolled noon and was conducted into the throne room shortly thereafter.

"Majesties," she said, bowing in the custom of the Temple Knights. "I was informed you wished to see me?"

"We have a visitor who says he knows you," replied Charlotte. "A man claiming to be a Ragnarite. We were hoping you might be able to vouch for him."

"Where is he?"

"We're holding him nearby." Ludwig nodded to Gustavo, who left the room, then returned a short time later with the visitor, accompanied by six guardsmen.

"This is Brother Aiden," said Charlaine. "I met him in Ilea during my first assignment there." She approached the Ragnarite. "Is Brother Jarak travelling with you?"

"Not this time," the man replied. "His expertise was required elsewhere. I would offer you congratulations on your recent promotion, but I'm led to understand it came with some hardship."

"Have you returned to the Antonine?"

"No. We no longer serve the Church, although you may rest assured we still continue our work."

"Is that why you're here?" asked Ludwig. "Or are you seeking asylum?"

"Such things are of little concern to me, Majesty. I only wish to continue my work. As for my presence here in your kingdom, that, I fear, requires a longer explanation."

"You have our attention," said Charlotte, "and for once, we have no pressing issues demanding our presence." She looked at Gustavo. "You may dismiss the guard, Captain. I trust the Temple General's word that this man is who he claims to be."

"Yes, Majesty."

"Now," continued the queen, "where would you like to start?"

"My current investigation began some months ago, when I learned a mage in the court of Lubenstahl was delving into forbidden arts."

"Death Magic?"

"Not precisely," said Aiden. "He was trying to distill the elemental power that flows through the ley lines of Eiddenwerthe."

The queen leaned forward in her seat. "What would this distillation look like?"

"A bright green, glowing liquid that is poisonous in nature."

"We are a long way from Lubenstahl," noted Ludwig.

"Indeed, Majesty, but allow me to get to the heart of the matter. The originator of this process extracted three vials of this concentration before he succumbed to its effects himself. Three vials, I might add, that were nowhere to be found when I located him."

"How do you know all this if he was dead?"

"Through the journal he kept on his person at all times."

"And you're now attempting to track down these vials?"

"I am," said Aiden. "My investigation led me to the conclusion that one was sent here, to Hadenfeld, perhaps carried, unwittingly, by a member of the Church."

"And the others?"

"I have other avenues to explore in that regard, but for now, I'm concentrating on finding the first one."

"Then it seems we've done you a great favour, for we have it in our possession."

"It is most dangerous, Majesty."

"It was used in an attempt against the Crown," said Ludwig. "Temple Captain Teresa was the one who discovered its whereabouts."

"Teresa?" said Aiden. "I know that name." He turned to Charlaine. "Is that the same Teresa whom Jarak healed in Rizela?"

"It is," she replied. "After the Battle of Alantra, she spent time amongst the Sea Elves and learned Life Magic, then returned to us thereafter."

"How small Eiddenwerthe seems. Might I ask the current disposition of the liquid?"

"We placed it in a lead box," said Ludwig, "that is locked away in the dungeon. We've been advised that it's too dangerous to bury. Do you have a method of disposing of it?"

"Unfortunately, the late scholar's writings contain no information on that."

"Scholar?" said Charlotte. "You said earlier he was a mage."

"He was both, but spent his time researching the origins of magic. His research was funded by a fellow mage at the court of King Clemens, but there was no record of the individual's name in the journal."

"Likely a Stormwind," said Charlaine, "or possibly a Sartellian. We've had dealings with them in the past and discovered they're secretly in league with the Empire of Halvaria."

"They are both influential families," said Aiden, "with representatives in courts across the Petty Kingdoms. This news of yours is most disturbing."

"Can you relieve us of the burden of this elixir?"

"The Temple General's presence tells me you can be trusted, so I will leave it in your care, if that's acceptable to you?"

"It is," replied Ludwig, "though, while you're here, perhaps you could be of assistance to us?"

"What is it you need help with?"

"I am now of the belief this liquid was delivered to Harlingen by a Temple Commander of Saint Cunar by the name of Amarand. Now, as you mentioned earlier, this may have occurred unwittingly, but we know he visited several individuals before his departure. Perhaps one of those took possession of it prior to its use?"

"It certainly bears investigating. If you would give me the names, I could investigate the matter further."

"And if you discover they were complicit in the attempt to kill us?"

"Then I will take appropriate action."

"And what would that be?" asked Charlotte.

"We Ragnarites have always operated in the darkness, where evil dwells. With the fall of the Church, you must now trust us to take the necessary measures to keep your kingdom safe from such a scourge."

"When I first met Brother Aiden," said Charlaine, "he was chasing down a creature of the Underworld. Danica and I helped him kill it. I will not speak of the horror of that creature, nor what it was capable of, but I assure you that such things are the stuff of nightmares. Were I you, I would permit Brother Aiden to carry out his sworn duty in the manner he sees fit."

"That's good enough for me," said Charlotte.

"And me," added Ludwig, "though I would like a full accounting once you've done what's needed." He held up a hand to forestall any argument. "I will not condemn your actions, for you Ragnarites have kept watch over the Petty Kingdoms for generations. I merely wish an explanation of what happened in case such a conspiracy ever blights our kingdom again."

"Then I shall endeavour to do so, if I can," replied Aiden.

"Do you require any assistance with this?"

"Only the names and addresses you have, so I can examine the veracity of your suspicions."

"I'll make arrangements to give you what you need."

Brother Aiden bowed once more. "Thank you, Majesty. I shall do all I can to keep your kingdom safe from such threats."

"Temple General, would you be so kind as to keep our guest company while we retrieve the list of names?"

"I'd be delighted," replied Charlaine. She led Aiden out to one of the rooms where a guard stood.

"You can wait here," the fellow said. "I'll bring you the letter once I have it in hand." With that, the guard made his way down the hall, disappearing through a doorway.

"What happened to you after Alantra?" asked Charlaine.

"I stayed in the city for a few weeks before making my way south, along the coast, till I was free of Halvarian lands."

"But that's all wilderness, isn't it?"

"Not quite. There are small towns and villages all along the coast that serve no realm, and amongst one of them, I found a ship capable of taking me to Corassus."

"And Brother Jarak?"

"He elected to remain in Alantra, although I later learned he secured a berth on a visiting Kurathian merchant ship some months after I left."

"And what of Calabria?"

"I'm afraid one of the empire's legions moved in to crush all opposition. Many died, but the rebellion lives on, or at least it did, last I heard. It appears you've been busy these past ten years."

"After serving in Ilea, I was sent to Reinwick, along with Danica. There, we foiled a Halvarian plot to foment a war between Reinwick and Andover."

"And then you went to Arnsfeld," said Aiden. "I heard all about that. Is Danica back in Eisen?"

"No, in the north. She's a Temple Commander now, along with being the Admiral of the Temple Fleet."

"I admit I'm surprised the Council of Peers didn't demand the fleet be handed over to the Cunars."

"Oh, they did," replied Charlaine, "but Danica put in place a strategy to deal with that from the very beginning, thereby foiling their plans."

"What will you do now that you no longer serve the Church?"

"What our order has always done: keep the temples safe and protect women, at least in those kingdoms where we're still welcome."

"Will you remain in Hadenfeld?"

"Yes. The king granted us the city of Eisen to use as our base of operations. There's a keep there… Well, more of a castle, although the outer walls need some improvement."

"With the order officially disbanded, how will you fill its ranks?"

"We've received an influx of sisters who've fled to safety from those realms that sided with the Church. When needed, we'll train recruits in Eisen."

"Have you any recruits?" asked Aiden.

"Not as yet, although we've had plenty of enquiries. The current issue is the lack of facilities. It takes a great deal of skilled labourers to support so many knights, including armourers and weapon smiths, not to mention farriers, bakers... Well, you get the idea. Does your order experience similar problems?"

"Not really. There weren't very many of us to begin with, and we're scattered all over the Petty Kingdoms. Seldom would you find more than one of us in any given realm at the same time."

"My biggest problem is determining which companies of Agnesites still exist. I've sent messages off to various kingdoms, but only a few have responded thus far."

"The Continent is large," said Aiden. "It will be months before those in the east respond, and the same could be said of the north."

"I'm not worried about the north; Danica will see to them. How long ago were you in Lubenstahl?"

"I arrived there only three months ago. While there, I heard whispers of what had happened at the Antonine. Eleven days after my arrival, I learned our order had gone into hiding. We now work secretly, behind the scenes, making things more difficult for us, but our primary mission remains the same."

Charlaine chuckled. "If I recall, your order always worked in secret. They wouldn't even acknowledge your existence back in Rizela."

"True, but at least they provided a place of refuge when needed."

"Your order will always be welcome in Eisen, as I suspect it would be anywhere else in Hadenfeld, if you would but ask the king."

"How much do you trust King Ludwig?"

"I've known him for years."

"I've known many a soul for years," said Aiden. "That doesn't mean I trust them all."

"Then let me put this another way," said Charlaine. "When we discovered the machinations of the Stormwinds and Sartellians, I wrote to him, warning him about their treachery. Would I do that for someone I didn't trust?"

"No. I suppose not."

"He is a good man, and I trust him with my life. He's the reason I brought my people here when we fled the Antonine."

"And the queen?"

"She is his equal in every sense of the word."

"Is that admiration I hear in your voice?" asked Aiden.

"To some extent. Not every ruler puts the needs of the kingdom before their own, and both the king and the queen have acted in the best interest of their people despite the difficulties involved."

"High praise indeed."

The door at the end of the room opened, and the guard appeared, sealed letter in hand. "Your list," he announced as he approached. "His Majesty asks that you don't share the names on that with anyone, if at all possible."

Aiden took the missive, but left the seal intact. "I shall commit these names and addresses to memory, then destroy this letter. You may assure Their Majesties I will abide by their wishes." He turned to Charlaine. "I bid you good day, Temple General. May your Saint watch over you."

"I wish you the same."

32

SPRING

SPRING 1108 SR

Ludwig noted Lord Merrick's discomfort. He was normally very social, but today he sat quietly while the others talked around him. Gita appeared unaware of her husband's mood, spending most of her time relating stories of Kenley and Frederick's antics. Charlotte was similarly engrossed, as were Alexandra and Emmett.

He decided to broach the matter head-on. "Merrick, is something troubling you?"

"Indeed there is. A most perplexing situation has been brought to my attention, one which, quite frankly, has me baffled."

"And by situation, you mean?"

"A murder."

"I hate to admit it," said Ludwig, "but murder is not a stranger to Hadenfeld."

"It's not the murder itself that confuses me; it's the circumstances surrounding it."

"Why? What makes this death so unusual?"

"Late yesterday afternoon, the guards at the north gate were approached by an individual bearing a sealed letter for them."

"From whom?"

"That's just it. We don't know. No crest or sigil was on the seal, and the note within was left unsigned. The fellow delivering it claims he found it pinned to the door of a house by a dagger."

"I assume this was his way of alerting the authorities?"

"That is but the first mystery, for on the outside of the letter were instructions to take it to the north gate."

"The north gate specifically?" asked Charlotte.

"Admittedly, it was the closest," said Merrick, "but who pins a note to a door with a dagger in the first place?"

"And the contents of this letter?"

"Indicated the person at this address was served due justice. We assume it referred to the place the note was found."

"Have the guards looked into the matter?"

"They did, but that only deepened the mystery. They arrived to find the door unlocked, and upon entering, discovered the victim, stabbed clean through, likely with a sword, but no murder weapon was to be found. Someone also went to the trouble of searching the place."

"Are you suggesting it was ransacked?" asked Ludwig.

"Not at all. Whoever searched was methodical, moving papers around, but keeping them neatly stacked. Food was even removed from the pantry and placed on a table."

"Any indication of what they were looking for?"

"Not according to the guards. That's when they came to see me." Merrick took a sip of his wine. "I went there last night to examine the scene for myself, but to little avail. My suspicion is that the perpetrator found whatever they were looking for."

"That would make sense."

"Most certainly, but why go to the extent of keeping things neat and tidy? Whoever did this murdered the owner. For Saint's sake, what does it matter if his house is ransacked?"

A thought occurred to Ludwig. "What was the victim's name?"

"Hanford Schultz, a wealthy merchant. We asked around, but he seemed an ordinary enough man."

"Schultz, you say?" said Charlotte. "I recognize that name."

"As do I," added Ludwig. "He's from the list of people Temple Commander Amarand visited before he left."

"Does that justify his murder?" asked Merrick.

"I couldn't say. We still don't know his role in the poisoning of the queen."

"You could've arrested him."

"Without cause? That would make me no better than Morgan."

"Didn't we have people watching him?" asked Charlotte.

"Originally, we did, but interest waned after months of inactivity on his part."

"Yet now he's dead, and we have no idea who's responsible."

"That's not entirely true," said Ludwig. "To my mind, there are two possibilities. Either his death was at the hands of the Ragnarite or his confederates."

"What's this about a Ragnarite?" asked Merrick. "Are you suggesting they're operating here in Harlingen?"

"Only one, so far as I know. We met with him about two months ago and provided a list of names to help with his investigation, a list that included Hanford Schultz."

"So the Ragnarite must be responsible."

"Not necessarily. There is still the matter of the other individuals on that list. If they suspected Schultz of turning on them, it provided them a strong motive to silence the fellow."

"Then we should take matters into our own hands and arrest them."

"On what charge?" asked Ludwig. "It's not a crime to be on a list."

"Treason might work?"

"I'll not order someone's death on mere speculation."

"I agree," said Charlotte. "No doubt this is a most serious situation we find ourselves in, but we can't start arresting people on mere suspicion."

"Have we a way of contacting this Ragnarite?" asked Merrick.

"Not that I'm aware of, but I suspect if he were responsible, we shall soon hear of it."

"If he shows himself at court, he should be arrested."

"I can't do that," said Ludwig. "The Ragnarites perform an important role amongst the Petty Kingdoms. If we interfere with the performance of their duties, we risk a revival of the dark arts."

"I don't think so," said Merrick. "The days of Necromancers prowling the streets are a distant memory."

"Only because of the constant vigilance of the Temple Knights of Saint Ragnar," replied Charlotte.

"Are we then to believe Hanford Schultz was a Death Mage?"

"You tell me. You visited his house; did you find any evidence of Necromancy?"

"I did not," replied Merrick. "Then again, we weren't looking for anything like that. There was certainly nothing out in the open."

"Nor would there be," said Charlotte. "Practitioners of dark magic know their studies are illegal, so they'd go to great pains to hide anything incriminating."

"A good point. Should I have the guards conduct a more thorough search? Perhaps there's a hidden room that would answer our questions?"

"Seal the house for now," said Ludwig, "and keep a guard posted to ensure no one else enters. I'd like to give our Ragnarite time to come forward before we start making assumptions."

"Necromancers will often convince others to help them," offered Charlotte. "I remember reading about a cult back in Reinwick with close to twenty members. According to testimony presented during their trial, the vast majority believed they were following the old religion."

"Can people be that easily fooled?" asked Alexandra.

"Most certainly," replied the queen. "You must remember that the old religion isn't written down like that of the Saints' teachings—it's an oral history."

"You know a lot about this," noted Lord Emmett.

"I spent much of my youth going through my father's library, reading everything I could get my hands on."

"A habit she continues to this day," added Ludwig. "Our collection of books has grown by leaps and bounds these last few years, so much so that we'll soon need to find a larger room to house everything."

Alexandra smiled. "Perhaps you should use all those books to populate a library in the city. Scholars would visit from all over the Petty Kingdoms to see it."

"What a marvellous idea," said Charlotte. "What do you think, Ludwig? Shall we order the construction of a new library?"

"It's a grand idea, but we'll need to give it some thought. I shouldn't like to build it only to have to make it bigger ten years later. Why don't you sit down with some scholars and plan out what's needed, then we can set about looking for architects."

"While we're on the subject," said Alexandra, "you might consider making it a place of higher learning. There are academies devoted to training mages all over the Petty Kingdoms. Why not schools for scholars?"

"This is beginning to sound expensive."

"It likely will be, but it's an investment in the future of Hadenfeld."

"We'll add that to the list, along with tournaments," said Ludwig, "but presently, the priority is rebuilding the army, else the empire will put all our other plans out to pasture."

"Can we return to the topic at hand?" asked Lord Merrick. "Are we assuming this murdered man was coerced into some sort of cult, and his death was meant to conceal its presence?"

"Let's not panic quite yet, but we should add some of our soldiers to reinforce the Mathewites' street patrols. If Death Mages are prowling the city, I want everyone kept as safe as possible. I'll also alert the Temple Knights of Saint Mathew to what we know. They have connections amongst the commoners; perhaps they'll be able to help solve this mystery. Now, let's return to more pleasant conversation, shall we?"

. . .

When Brother Aiden arrived at court eight days later, he was conducted into the sunroom where Ludwig and Charlotte sat, sipping wine.

"My apologies for the interruption, Majesties," he began, "but I thought it best I share the results of my investigation so far with you, although I still have more work left to do."

"You've been busy," said Charlotte. "Are you the person responsible for the death of Hanford Schultz?"

"I am," replied the knight. "Though, that, in itself, requires a lengthy explanation."

"I'm all ears."

"Yes," added Ludwig, "as am I. I've no doubt his death was warranted, but I'm curious to discover what you were looking for at his home."

"I shall get to that in due course, sire, but let me start at the beginning. As you know, I arrived here seeking information about the green distillation we'd previously discussed. After you provided me with that list of names, I looked into each individual and uncovered some interesting details."

"When you say 'looked into', what precisely do you mean? Did you question the locals?"

"That is one of my techniques, yes. Another is to gain access to the addresses in question. I shan't go into individual cases, but typically such operations involve a ruse to gain entry. As you're aware, seven names were on that list, and while all were moderately wealthy, nothing suggested a connection between them all. They lived in different areas of the city, and so far as I was able to determine, no connection exists between their businesses."

"You must've eventually discovered something, or else you wouldn't be here."

"You are correct, sire. While they are not all connected to one another, they are each connected to another individual, aside from Temple Commander Amarand, of course."

"And this other individual is?"

"A woman by the name of Loralai Shozarin. Is that name known to you?"

"No," replied Ludwig. He looked at Charlotte. "You're more familiar with the wealthy and powerful of the Continent. Have you heard that name before?"

"The name Loralai is common enough in the north, but I can't say that I've ever heard of a family named Shozarin." She turned to regard the Ragnarite. "How is this woman involved in all of this?"

"The name first came to my attention when I overheard a discussion between two of the involved parties."

"I thought you said there was no connection?"

"My apologies. I should've explained myself better. What I meant to imply was that there was no commonality amongst all seven. There were, however, two sets of two, if you'll pardon the expression, who were on familiar terms with each other. I won't reveal which ones, for that might compromise my investigation."

"Understood," said Ludwig, "though I'm hoping you learned more than a name?"

"Indeed, sire. I suspect this Loralai Shozarin corresponded regularly with all seven suspects, but you'd find no evidence of that."

"Why is that?"

"They were in the habit of burning their correspondence after reading. Thankfully, I was able to retrieve some remnants from the fireplace of one while in the guise of a servant. Those fragments confirm there is an organized plot to ruin Hadenfeld."

"Ruin how, exactly?"

"I suspect the green extract was their first attempt, but far from their last. I have reason to believe they have agents amongst the Royal Staff, but I lack knowledge of their names."

"That's not surprising," said Charlotte. "We've suspected as much for some time and have taken precautions."

"That is most reassuring," replied Brother Aiden.

"And these other plots?" asked Ludwig.

"I overheard them discussing bribing some of your captains, but from what I gathered, that matter is still in the early stages of planning. I did discover they were attempting to turn your neighbours against you, although they have so far met with little progress."

"Should I arrest them?"

"I doubt it would do any good. This Loralai Shozarin is the one pulling the strings, but I've been unable to discover where she is."

"You say they exchange letters," said Charlotte. "The most logical next step would be to discover the destination of this correspondence."

"A task not easily accomplished, Majesty. The letters are taken by courier, typically a trusted member of the household."

"Ah, but if you notified us that one was on the way, we could have him intercepted, could we not?"

"The person behind this conspiracy has gone to great lengths to remain hidden. I suspect the letters pass through multiple hands before reaching their final destination. There is also another issue."

"That being?"

"They each use a phoenix ring to secure their letters." He removed a ring and handed it out for them to see. "I found this concealed in Hanford Schultz's house."

"I'm familiar with phoenix rings," said Ludwig. "They operate in pairs, and if anyone tries to open a letter sealed by one, they must have the other, else the message bursts into flames."

"I'm surprised you're familiar with such things, sire."

"The Temple General used the technique to warn me about the Stormwinds and Sartellians, though the courier held the ring, not me. That suggests whoever oversees these people doesn't trust their messengers."

"What I'd like to know," asked Charlotte, "is why you killed Hanford Schultz?"

"I didn't."

"You claimed responsibility earlier."

"I am, indirectly, the cause of his death, but my weapon wasn't what killed him."

"I'm afraid you'll need to explain that."

"I'd been watching him for days, enough to learn his schedule. I waited until he left, then followed him a few blocks to ensure I knew where he was going before I doubled back to his house, intending to search it. When I entered, however, I discovered that someone had already searched the place."

"Any idea what they were looking for?"

Brother Aiden held up the ring. "Likely this, but I suspect they'd hidden themselves within the house, waiting for Schultz to leave, and my return appeared to have interrupted their endeavours."

"Now," continued Brother Aiden, "we Ragnarites often find secret compartments under floorboards, and after a thorough search, I found a loose board in his bedroom, under which lay this ring, but then Schultz came home unexpectedly."

"Why?"

"I can only surmise he forgot something, possibly even this very ring. I then heard a slight commotion downstairs and rushed in to find Hanford lying in a pool of his own blood."

"And the attacker?"

"Fled out the back door."

"How could you possibly know that?" asked Ludwig.

"They left it open."

"I assume you wrote the letter pinned to the door?"

"I did. A man was dead, and although he likely deserved it, his murderer remained on the loose."

"You think someone in this cabal was aware of your investigation," said Charlotte. "That's why you blame yourself for his death."

"It is. In all fairness, I don't think they know my identity, merely that someone was onto them, but I believe that may have been enough to warrant the fellow's death."

"So what happens now?" asked Ludwig.

Brother Aiden withdrew some crumpled papers from his belt pouch. "I have these. They're not anything incriminating, merely correspondence regarding his business matters. It does, however, serve to give me an example of his handwriting."

"You intend to write to Loralai Shozarin," said Charlotte.

"I do. It's a gamble, but if even one letter comes back in response, it may provide some clue regarding their plans."

"Then you'll have to be quick about it. At least one of them is responsible for his death, and it won't take long for the others to learn of it."

"The only person who matters is the one responsible," said Ludwig. "Besides, the others have no connection to him, so his death would be meaningless. The risk is that the murderer will send word to Loralai Shozarin of what's happened."

"That's not much of a risk," replied the Ragnarite. "I can claim the attack was botched, and I somehow survived and went into hiding. Even if she does suspect something, the worst thing that can happen is she fails to reply to the forged letter."

"Are they doing anything else that would necessitate the interest of the Ragnarites?"

"The only reason I'm here is because of that vial of liquid."

"On that note, then, I'd like your opinion," said Ludwig. "I understand I might've been the intended victim, but what would be the objective? My queen is co-ruler, and we have a son to inherit the Crown? What would my death accomplish?"

"Under your rule, Hadenfeld represents a threat. You are an experienced leader of men, as you so amply illustrated in the recent defeat of the Holy Army."

"That was mostly the Temple General's doing, not mine."

"But as a result, you're increasing the size of your army."

"How did you know that? We've taken great pains to keep that secret."

"I'm trained to notice every detail, sire, and it's difficult to hide something on that scale without it coming to someone's attention."

"I suppose I was foolish to consider it a possibility. What do I do now?"

"I think your best option is to bring it out into the open. Move the army here, to Harlingen, and you'll make the job of these conspirators even more difficult."

33

REBUILDING

SUMMER 1108 SR

The hot summer day left those wearing armour suffering from the heat, and kings were no different. Ludwig watched as Cyn's division marched past, the sweat pouring off him in rivulets. He even felt it trickling down his back, but was determined not to show any signs of discomfort.

The men headed to the outskirts of the city for training, the sort that could only be done in the Hills of Harlingen. He remembered well the Second Battle of Harlingen, for in those very hills, he'd saved the life of King Otto and helped reunite the kingdom. It seemed so long ago, yet it had only been eight years. How much had changed in that time.

Ludwig wished Charlotte were with him this day, but she was bedridden due to an especially severe episode. This time, however, her visitors were restricted to a handful of long-serving handmaidens, ones they trusted not to do anything that might threaten her health.

Charlaine had billeted twelve Temple Knights of Saint Agnes at the Royal Keep, operating in groups of three to ensure the queen's safety at all times. Even now, they guarded her door, with one inside the room. Ludwig regretted that such protection was necessary, yet felt all the better for their presence.

"What do you think, boss?" Cyn's words broke him free of his maudlin thoughts.

"They're a fine body of men."

"We're still short some knights, but we've managed to meet all our other targets."

"And how are you doing? I know you miss Sig."

"He'll be back to visit once he's whipped his division into shape. Unfortunately, we don't have the housing to keep the entire army here in Harlingen."

"I hear you've decided to hold a mock battle."

"I have," she replied. "It's easy enough to march men around an open field, but battles are seldom that accommodating. There's also the notion of getting them comfortable with the terrain, as the kingdom has already had two battles in those hills. If the empire comes for us, we'll probably have to fight there again."

"And," she continued, "just to be clear, there won't be any actual fighting. I want to get them used to operating as part of a larger army since they're all under one unified command now, not following the orders of individual barons."

"I recognize the flag of Hadenfeld, but what are those others?"

Cyn beamed. "That was my idea: a system of signal flags to relay basic commands. I'm not certain how effective they'll end up being, which is one of the reasons we're doing this."

"Is Sig doing the same?"

"Not yet, but if it proves promising, I'll let him know. Speaking of promising news, any word on expanding our order of knights?"

"Oh, I see," said Ludwig, waving his hands at all the warriors. "All this was just an excuse to call me to task. Very clever, General."

"Does that mean you have news or not?"

"If you recall, when the kingdom was fractured, many of the knights continued their service in Neuhafen."

"Yes," replied Cyn, "and ever since reunification, their members have wanted back in, but that would cause no end of strife, particularly when it comes to seniority. Are you trying to tell me you've come up with a solution?"

"I have, though it may not be to everyone's liking."

"What is it you're thinking of doing?"

"I shall name myself Grand Master," said Ludwig, "then appoint someone else to see to the day-to-day operations."

"Won't there still be trouble?"

"They lost over half their numbers at the Battle of the Ford, and I intend to induct a host of new knights to get them up to where they should be."

"Clever," said Cyn. "You'll drown out their complaints with new members, but where will all these new knights come from?"

"Wherever I can find them. I've already written to Lord Darrian up in Zowenbruch. He's going to attend court and let them know we're looking for knights to take service with our order. From there, word will spread to other Petty Kingdoms, and hopefully, we'll see positive results. There are, after all, many knights who wander the Continent seeking sponsors."

"What gave you the idea?"

"Books, primarily, but also correspondence. Konrad, for example, limits membership in his own order of knights to only a hundred individuals to keep the cost down, but there are plenty clamouring to join. If we convince them to come here, it'll go a long way towards giving us the numbers we need. Until then, we'll rely on our footmen to do the brunt of the fighting."

"We have plenty of foot, so much so, we could easily raise another ten companies."

"That would complicate matters," said Ludwig. "Not only would we have to equip them, we'd also have to feed and house them on an ongoing basis. We'll stick to the plan for now, although perhaps we can revisit the situation in a couple of years."

He watched a group of bowmen march past, led by their captain, Rikal.

"How are we doing for archers?" asked Ludwig.

"We could always use more," replied Cyn, "but we've managed to fill our quota. If we take losses, though, we'd be hard-pressed to find replacements."

"Perhaps crossbows might be a good idea. I know Sig was looking into them to man the city walls."

"It's faster to train someone to use a crossbow, but the weapon itself is a lot more expensive. If you're willing to spend the coins, I'll be happy to train them for you."

"Let's not spend the entire treasury just yet," said Ludwig. "There are still so many other things requiring funding."

Ludwig sat on his throne, Charlotte beside him on hers. The realm's nobles had gathered for the midsummer feast, an occasion that monarchs across the Petty Kingdoms typically used to reward those of their subjects who'd somehow distinguished themselves, either through service to the Crown or acts of bravery. Today was of particular interest in Hadenfeld, for twenty-four knights were to be inducted into the Order of the Sacred Shield.

His thoughts turned to Brother Aiden. The Temple Knight had written to Loralai Shozarin in hopes of flushing her out, but so far as Ludwig was aware, the Ragnarite had yet to receive a reply. It was difficult to wait, knowing those behind the plot were still at large, but he calmed himself with the knowledge that they would eventually be brought to justice.

The crowd hushed as the far doors opened, and those seeking admittance to the Order of the Sacred Shield entered. Cyn led them, while her warriors marched on either side.

She halted them ten paces from the throne, calling for the first six to advance and kneel. Father Vernan blessed each before they took their oaths. With his task complete, the Holy Father turned to the twin thrones of Hadenfeld and offered a bow.

Ludwig remembered his own knighting, an impromptu affair in which he swore allegiance to Lord Wulfram in Erlingen. His service to the baron ended with the war, but the moment still lingered in his mind—a pleasant occasion set amidst a time of strife and struggle.

He stood, holding out his hand for Charlotte, and they both moved to the line of kneeling would-be knights, who now faced their monarchs.

Ludwig stopped before the first, and Brother Hamelyn, standing nearby, handed Charlotte the *Book of Saint Mathew*. She then held it before the initiate.

"Place your hand upon the Holy Book," she commanded.

He obeyed, then looked at his king.

"Do you solemnly swear to serve your monarchs in valour and faith, to protect the weak, and live by the realm's code of chivalry and honour?"

"As the Saints are my witness, I do so swear," the fellow replied.

She withdrew the book, and then Ludwig held out his hand, waiting for the ceremonial sword which Captain Gustavo was holding nearby.

Ludwig placed the tip of the sword on the initiate's right shoulder. "As Sovereign of Hadenfeld, and Grand Master of the Order of the Sacred Shield, I name thee worthy." He then shifted the blade to the left shoulder. "I command thee, as a knight, to protect the Crown and to serve the people of Hadenfeld to your last breath. Do you accept this duty?"

"I do, Lord King."

Once more, he moved the blade, lightly tapping the initiate on the top of his head. "Then I name thee, Sir Ingulf, Knight of the Sacred Shield."

Ludwig gave Charlotte a brief nod, and they moved to their left to stand in front of the next candidate. Father Vernan, meanwhile, stood before the first and placed his hand on the man's head. "I bless thee in the name of the Saints. May you, by your service, earn immortality in the Afterlife."

They repeated the process until all six inductees had taken the oath, then Cyn ordered them to their feet. They bowed in unison before stepping back to take up positions behind the other initiates.

The ceremony continued until all twenty-four were knighted. As the last group returned to join their comrades, Ludwig turned, ready to pass the ceremonial sword back to Captain Gustavo, but something made him stop.

The captain had served him loyally ever since he'd recruited the man back in Roshlag. Ludwig met his gaze, knowing without a doubt this fellow was deserving of recognition.

"Kneel," he commanded.

To say Gustavo was surprised was an understatement, but he did as he was ordered.

"You've served me faithfully, Captain. I shall not command you to protect the Crown, for you already do that. You've also proved yourself worthy, and I know you will serve the people of Hadenfeld to your last breath." He turned to Father Vernan. "Father, would you bless Captain Gustavo?"

"It would be my honour," replied the Holy Father. He placed his hand upon the captain's head, reciting the prayer. Once complete, he nodded, then stepped back.

Ludwig placed the blade lightly on the captain's head. "I name thee Sir Gustavo, Knight of the Sacred Shield. May the Saints bless you." As he withdrew the blade, the room broke into spontaneous applause.

"You may now rise," said Charlotte, "and congratulations."

Ludwig leaned in towards the captain and whispered, "I'm afraid it's not all good news. As a newly knighted member of the order, you're expected to buy a round of drinks for your brother knights." He nodded to Cyn, who came forward and gave him a small pouch, which, in turn, he handed off to Gustavo. "Here," said Ludwig. "These coins will soften the blow." He turned to the rest of his court. "Now let us celebrate!"

In Eisen, Charlaine sat at a table, eating a meal with Temple Captains Teresa and Nicola while they pored over a large amount of correspondence.

"Where do we stand?" asked the Temple General.

Nicola consulted her notes. "Ulrichen and Ardosa have no temple garrisons, but Lubenstahl and Abelard do, and they're both being evicted."

"Is evicted the right term?" asked Teresa. "I should think exiled more appropriate."

"The same is true of Zalista and Ostrova. Thankfully, Carlingen is still intact."

"That's where you sent Cordelia, isn't it?" asked Teresa.

"Yes," replied Charlaine. "She was promoted to Temple Captain and was due to travel there once her training was complete."

"True," said Nicola, "but her training was at the hands of her commanding officer, and there's no telling how long that would take."

"If she's not there by now, she should be soon enough."

"What about promotions?"

"I'm afraid that will have to wait. Although many here are deserving of a promotion, I have no positions for them to fill."

"Don't look at me," said Nicola. "I'm perfectly content being a Temple Captain."

"Or me," added Teresa. "I have no desire to be a Temple Commander."

"I was actually thinking of Temple Captain Giselle," said Charlaine.

"It's strange to think she's the same rank as when we first served together."

"She always had a cloud over her head for losing her first command. Unfortunately, with all that's happened, I haven't found time to promote her, but at least she's in command of a full company, rather than just a detachment. Do you remember Sister Rowan?"

"Of course."

"Giselle took her along as her aide."

"I know Temple Captain Nina ended up in the Antonine, but where are all the other sisters we served with in Ilea?"

"Aurelia died at Alantra."

"Yes, I remember now," said Teresa. "She drowned."

"Danica, as you know, is up north with Erika. Miranda perished at the Battle of the Brinwald, a victim of Fire Magic."

"And Florence?"

"She's up in Arnsfeld, in charge of her own commandery."

"We were a tight-knit group back then," said Teresa. "I miss them dearly."

"They were our sisters, and shall always be remembered as such." Charlaine pawed through the papers. "Did I see something in here regarding Arnsfeld?"

Nicola plucked out a letter, seemingly at random. "Yes, it's here. Temple Commander Isabeau writes that the border has been quiet of late. It appears the empire is not yet ready to avenge their defeat. She also indicates she's recalled all sister knights from Angvil after the ruler there decided he would rather side with the Church."

"How are our own numbers doing?"

"Due to the casualties we took, we're still well below five hundred, but our numbers are increasing as fellow Temple Knights trickle in from other kingdoms, albeit at a much slower pace than I would prefer."

"What about those kingdoms along the shores of the Shimmering Sea? Any luck there?"

"Other than Ilea, no, but that's to be expected. Between the fortress of Corassus and the Holy Fleet, there's a lot of pressure to obey the Church."

"Wait a moment," said Teresa. "I saw something about Thalemia." She dug through the letters, then brandished the one she was looking for. "Here it is. We still maintain a presence in Thalemia, although only one commandery." Her face fell as she skimmed through the words. "Perhaps it's not so good after all. It appears the Temple Captain there is under pressure to abandon their stronghold. Apparently, there's a Cunar commandery nearby that's giving them trouble."

"Not fighting, I hope?"

"Not that I can tell. It refers to them applying pressure at court."

"Any notes on Aldor?"

"That's firmly in the Antonine's hands," replied Nicola, "as is Amaria. It appears we are the largest concentration of sister knights in the central kingdoms. I suppose that only makes sense, considering the circumstances that brought us here."

Charlaine consulted her own notes. "Our order still maintains a significant number of Temple Knights, despite our recent losses. With few exceptions, we have commanderies spread across the northern coast, with little chance of being ousted, thanks to the Temple Fleet. We've also garnered a lot of goodwill amongst those kingdoms bordering the Halvarian Empire, due to our efforts in Arnsfeld. Once we get farther inland, however, that's no longer the case."

"So what's our next step?"

"We send out orders directing those knights in Church-friendly areas to find their way to safety."

"You want them to march across the Continent?" asked Teresa.

"If possible, or sail if it can be arranged. For those facing immediate danger, it may be advisable for them to split up and trickle across the border in small groups so as not to arouse suspicions. Fortunately, we now have a list of safe realms that we can pass on to the commanding officers."

"And if the Church gets hold of this list?"

"Ultimately," said Charlaine, "the rulers of those realms in question recognize our right to exist, so there's not much the Church can do about it." She glanced at her companions, both of whom looked forlorn. "I know it's not ideal, but consider how far we've come. Had the Church had its way, we'd no longer exist as an order. Not only do we have a home, but we've established communications with many of our commanderies."

"I suppose that is true," said Teresa without much enthusiasm.

Charlaine was determined to bring them around to her way of thinking. "Remember, with King Ludwig's help, we broke the power of the Church, and we no longer have to look over our shoulders waiting for the hammer to fall. We defeated the best the Holy Army had to offer, and as a result, we now have horses in abundance, along with a vast collection of weapons."

"Yes," said Nicola, trying to suppress a chuckle, "and Zowenbruch has a nice collection of plate armour."

"I never thought of it that way," replied Teresa. "I suppose we have come a long way, haven't we?"

"We have," said Charlaine, "but there's more to be done." She picked up her fork, ready to stab a piece of meat, then paused, staring at the plate. "It appears we've spent so much time talking, our food's grown cold."

"There's an easy remedy for that," noted Teresa. "Let's head down to the dining hall and get something fresh. It'll be just like old times."

"Well said, my friend. Well said."

34

WAITING

WINTER 1108 SR

Ludwig warmed his hands by the fire.

"It's freezing out there today," said Father Vernan. "I don't recall a winter this harsh for some years."

"Didn't you spend time in the north? Surely the weather was colder there?"

"Admittedly, it was. I suppose Hadenfeld has spoiled me; I've become accustomed to more moderate winters."

"At least the fire is warm," said Ludwig. "It's a shame I can't say the same for the rest of the Royal Keep."

"Ah, well. We shall endure." Father Vernan took a sip of his mulled wine. "They say no news is good news, and by that measure, things are going well."

"Well enough, but I'm beginning to wonder what happened to Brother Aiden. You don't suppose he's been discovered by this cabal, do you?"

"I wouldn't read too much into his absence, sire. Ragnarites are very thorough in their methods. For all we know, he may have left Hadenfeld to track down this Loralai Shozarin."

"Quite possibly," replied Ludwig, "but what about the conspirators back here in Harlingen? How do we know they're not still plotting?"

"You could always order the arrest of those individuals, Majesty."

"The affairs of these people are of great interest to the Crown, but as I've said on numerous occasions, I shall not arrest anyone without evidence of their guilt."

"I wish more of the rulers of Petty Kingdoms possessed your sense of morals. From what I've heard, it's common for people to simply disappear off the streets at the whim of a monarch, which raises an interesting philosophical question."

"How so?"

"Who is the servant, and who is the master? The prevailing attitude is that the people serve the monarch. This is borne out by the system of nobility, proof, if you like, that it's the destiny of the lowest layer of society to support those of the highest. You, however, see the monarchy as servants of the people, doing all in your power to better their lives, a most commendable attitude, but one which is far too rare these days."

"That's the influence of Saint Mathew," replied Ludwig.

"Were you religious in your youth?"

"Not especially. I attended all the required ceremonies at the temple, but never took the sermons to heart. That didn't come about until I went north to Erlingen and witnessed the horrors of war first-hand."

"War often changes a man. Some return from battle with horror in their eyes, living out a lifetime of nightmares and terror, while others become a shell of their former selves, disappearing into a life of solitude and isolation. The vast majority, thankfully, are able to get on with their lives."

"Do they? Or do they simply refuse to talk about such things and suffer in silence? It is no small feat to kill in battle, and not everyone is capable of doing so."

"I would agree," said Father Vernan, "although I daresay the common folk suffer the most in war. Their crops are stolen, their women violated, their animals slaughtered, all in the king's name." He stopped himself. "That's not to say I'm suggesting your men do that, sire, but the brutality of war cannot be denied."

"Thank you for that," said Ludwig, "but the alternative to war is to allow others to occupy our lands and slaughter those loyal to us. I wouldn't last long as king if I didn't take my duty to protect the land seriously."

"At least you were able to wrest control of the army away from the Barons of Hadenfeld. That alone goes a long way to reducing conflict. Back in Erlingen, the barons were constantly fighting with each other, and I think the duke encouraged it. After all, if they're busy fighting each other, they can't plot against him."

"Those are muddy waters. Such an attitude foments distrust, making it difficult for the barons to work together should an outside entity threaten the realm."

"Like during the invasion of Erlingen by Andover? What was that like?"

"Don't you remember?"

"I cannot remember what I did not witness," replied Father Vernan. "If you recall, I was sent off to Eidenburg to become a Holy Father."

"Of course, that completely slipped my mind. To answer your question, the barons were a fractious lot. I should also mention that two of them were openly fighting each other days before we received word of the invasion. It weakened them both so much that the duke ordered them to combine their forces so they could have a presence on the battlefield."

"That must've been awkward."

"Oh, it was, trust me."

"Still, it all worked out in the end."

"It did," agreed Ludwig, "although I do sometimes wonder if Andover would've invaded had the army been under the exclusive control of the duke."

"Wasn't it a legitimate grievance that led to the war in the first place?"

"It depends on what you consider legitimate. The King of Andover accused the duke of murdering the duchess in order to get himself a new bride. The duchess, in this case, was from Andover. Of course, it didn't help that the duke had already taken the woman on as his mistress before the duchess's death."

Father Vernan shook his head. "The things some people do defy all reason. Thank the Saints you were there to end it before too many lives were lost."

"Yes," said Ludwig. "I often wonder what would've happened if I hadn't travelled north all those years ago."

"Eiddenwerthe is all the better for your choice."

"Eiddenwerthe?"

"Well, some of the Petty Kingdoms at least. Erlingen may well have fallen, and had you not married Charlotte, then Reinwick might have been next."

"Whatever do you mean?"

"It's no secret that Andover and Reinwick dislike each other, or rather, it used to be that way. It's been a while since I was up there, so things may have changed considerably."

"Is there some imagined slight in their past, or is it two rulers arguing over who's more important?"

"Andover used to have more sea trade, but Reinwick has become the dominant trading entity in the last few decades, largely at the expense of their southern neighbour."

The door opened, admitting Charlotte, tears streaking her pale face as she clutched a letter.

"Whatever's the matter?" asked Ludwig.

She sat, taking a moment to compose herself. "I've received a letter from my father. Lord Wilfhelm Brondecker, the Duke of Reinwick, is dead, succeeded by his son, Lord Fernando."

"Does he mention how His Grace died?"

"In battle," replied Charlotte, "at a place called Ebenhof, in Andover."

"I didn't realize it had come to war," said Father Vernan. "Did you know His Grace very well?"

"Not as well as my father did. He will feel the duke's loss most keenly."

"How did this war come about with Andover?" asked Ludwig.

"It'd apparently been brewing for some time. My father didn't go into much detail about that, but he did mention sending emissaries to the court of King Dagmar in an attempt to prevent war."

"Clearly, it didn't work."

"No, it didn't," replied Charlotte, "but it resulted in some unusual circumstances."

"Unusual, how?"

"The timely arrival of a group of Orcs under the command of a Therengian, and not just any Therengian, the High Thane himself. I might also mention that a Water Mage by the name of Natalia Stormwind was present."

"That doesn't bode well," said Father Vernan.

"It's not what you think," replied Charlotte. "According to my father, this Natalia Stormwind broke away from the family and is now actively working against them."

"Therengia is a long way from Reinwick."

"Yes, it is, which begs the question of why they were in Reinwick in the first place. Unfortunately, this letter reveals nothing in the way of additional details."

"I don't remember Lord Fernando," said Ludwig. "Was he at our wedding?"

"No. I believe he was away on a diplomatic mission at the time."

"So you've met him?"

"Yes. I saw him more often than I saw his father. My father wished to arrange a marriage between us, but I convinced him that it was a bad idea."

"You would've become the duchess?"

She smiled. "Yes, but instead I am now a queen, and more importantly, married to a man who values my opinion."

"Are you implying Lord Fernando didn't take kindly to a woman's point of view?"

"Not only women, but anyone in general. Mind you, he was relatively young at the time, so perhaps age has mellowed him a little. It'll be interesting to see how he handles Reinwick now that he's the duke. He apparently acquitted himself reasonably well in battle, so perhaps there's hope for him."

"We should pay him a visit someday," said Ludwig. "Not yet, though. We're far too busy preparing for guests."

"Guests?"

"He means the Halvarians," replied Father Vernan. "We got tired of referring to them as the empire, so we now think of them more as unwanted guests."

"And does that help?"

"It does, actually. You wouldn't think a simple change of term would have that much of an effect, but it somehow makes them more palatable."

"It also reminds us," added Ludwig, "they are pests that need eradicating."

"When all this is over, we'll go and meet this new duke," said Charlotte. "Until then, we must continue being ever vigilant."

Ludwig stifled a yawn. It was late, but the business of running the kingdom waited for no one. Around the table sat all his advisors, save for Merrick, who was uncharacteristically late. Gita made her apologies on his behalf, but she had no idea what had delayed her husband.

"...and so the treasury is in good shape," she was saying. "Revenues are up, and now that you've sent cavalry patrols out to keep the roads safe, trade is increasing."

"That is most excellent news," replied Ludwig. "Have we any reports from Eisen?"

"We have. The Temple Knights of Saint Agnes submitted what will become their annual report outlining how they've spent the taxes collected. They detail several improvements, including the digging of three new wells within the city, repairs to the granary, and the creation of a fund designed to stimulate the economy."

"That comes as a surprise, although I suppose I should've expected no less."

An out-of-breath Merrick opened the door. "My apologies, everyone. I was unexpectedly detained by work. It's been a hectic few days."

"Anything we should be aware of?" asked Ludwig.

"Yes. In the last two days, we've had three mysterious deaths."

"Anyone we know?"

"Again, yes. All three were on the list of people Temple Commander Amarand contacted before his departure."

"Remarkable," said Father Vernan.

"Remarkable enough that I must ask if this was your doing, sire? Not that I would arrest you if it were, but you could save us a lot of bother if we knew this was by your command."

"It was not," replied Ludwig. "I wanted them to face justice in a public trial, not be silenced by having them killed."

"Could the Ragnarite be responsible? I know we assumed that last time and were proven wrong, but circumstances may have changed. Have we heard anything recently from Brother Aiden?"

"Admittedly, we have not."

"That's not unusual for a Ragnarite," offered Father Vernan. "Might I ask the manner of these deaths?"

"They vary," replied Merrick. "One was obviously murder, for we found a dagger protruding from the victim's back. The other two, however, simply collapsed."

"I assume that means we have witnesses?"

"One was found on the floor of his study after a servant, who went to wake him, discovered his bed hadn't been slept in. We found no visible signs of injury, so we assumed that he'd either died of poison or some illness, although his servants claim he was in good health last time they saw him."

"And the third victim?"

"He is the most perplexing of all. He showed up at a local tavern, The Green Fiddler, and ordered an ale. When it arrived, he took one sip, then fell to the floor, writhing in agony while foaming at the mouth. Witnesses report he thrashed around for a moment before going still. Needless to say, we checked the ale, but nothing appeared to be amiss."

"How did you check it?" asked Ludwig.

"The guards gave some to a stray cat, but the creature showed no signs of reaction, and the other patrons had ale pulled from the same keg and suffered no ill effects. Additionally, at least three of the staff swore the tankard itself had recently been washed, so the poison must've been administered prior to his arrival."

"This is most curious," said Father Vernan.

"Could it be Brother Aiden?"

"We've had this discussion before," said Ludwig.

"The problem," replied Merrick, "is that we don't know how the Ragnarites operate. Perhaps the Holy Father can provide more details about their practices?"

"Most certainly," said Father Vernan. "The Temple Knights of Saint Ragnar seek out those practicing the dark arts, but in the past, they've always been subservient to Church tribunals. In other words, they would collect the information concerning the accused and then present their evidence to a trio of Church officials."

"Which Church officials? Are they always the same ones?"

"No. Typically, they would pass on the information to the relevant Church authorities in the region in question, then request a tribunal. The Church would then select three senior individuals to judge the accused based on the evidence presented."

"Was this a public trial?"

"No. Only authorized members of the Church were permitted to participate, along with those who may be providing corroborating testimony."

"You mean witnesses."

"Yes, but they were sworn to secrecy regarding the trial and its outcome."

"Might I ask why?"

"To avoid panic," replied Father Vernan. "The mere mention of the presence of a Death Mage can send people into a frenzy. There was an incident some two hundred years ago when a witness leaked information about an arrest, and a riot ensued."

"Where was this?" asked Ludwig.

"A city called Caerhaven, in the Duchy of Krieghoff."

"I'm not familiar with it."

"Nor would I expect you to be. It lies far to the east."

"Near the new kingdom of Therengia?"

"South of it, I believe. If I recall, the Grey Spire Mountains separate the two realms."

"I don't much like the idea of a secret tribunal," said Lord Merrick.

"A complete record of all testimony would have been written down," replied Father Vernan, "and the entire volume then sent to be stored away in the archives of the Antonine."

"So only the Church has access to them?"

"Yes, I suppose it's not an ideal solution, but what other choice did we have to prevent panic in the streets? I might also remind you that the practice of Necromancy is an affront to the Church and, therefore, has always been considered a Church matter. Few Petty Kingdoms have laws regarding such things."

"We shall have to change that," said Ludwig.

"Agreed," said Merrick. "With your permission, I'll set about drafting a new law concerning Necromancy."

"You should also include Hex Magic," added Father Vernan. "It is often lumped in together with the magic of death."

"Hex Magic being?"

"We've all heard of Enchantments, spells that generally offer some sort of advancement to a recipient in the form of making them stronger, or able to wield a sword better. Hex Magic, however, has the opposite effect, making someone weaker, for example, or less capable of wielding a weapon. Of course, I'm speaking only in broad terms. I don't have a list of all the spells available to those who employ such magic."

"That's frightening," said Merrick. "I shall be certain to include that in the new law. Will you be available to assist? I may need to draw on your knowledge."

"I'd be glad to be of any assistance I can," replied the Holy Father.

"To get back to our original conversation," said Ludwig, "I think we should assume these individuals were killed by whomever is controlling them."

"That appears to be the case," said Merrick, "but what do we do about it? Do we arrest the remaining members of the group to protect them?"

"We can't," said Gita. "That would alert them that we're onto them."

"We can't just let them be murdered, can we?"

"It's a difficult choice," said Ludwig. "We had people watching them again after Schultz's death, but after months of nothing, we withdrew them, and now some are dead. Do you think they knew they were being observed?"

"It might explain why they weren't killed along with Hanford Schultz, and possibly why someone waited to murder these three."

"If that's the case," said Father Vernan, "then Brother Aiden may be in danger. Unfortunately, we have no way of contacting him."

"How do the Ragnarites contact their Temple Knights when needed?"

"Historically, they send word out to all the temples in the area and ask them to post a note on their message board."

"Then we shall do the same," said Ludwig, "and since the Antonine has abandoned us, we'll organize our own tribunals. To that end, I shall insist Lord Merrick preside over any that are called and that the Archprior of Saint Mathew and the Archprioress of Saint Agnes adjudicate."

"I shall coordinate your request with Their Graces," said Father Vernan.

"Thank you. And regarding the others on this list, I think it best we do nothing."

"Are you certain that's wise, sire?"

"Have any innocents been injured in any of these deaths?"

"No," replied Merrick.

"Then there is little more we can do for them. We cannot afford to pay people to keep a watch on them forever, and no one has acted since the death of Hanford Schultz in the spring. If you do find the guilty party, however, they are to be tried for murder, just as they would were these people not members of a cabal."

35

WARGAMES

SUMMER 1109 SR

"They're doing much better this year," Cyn said as the cavalry rode past.

The Army of Hadenfeld was marching to the fields north of Harlingen, ready to begin what was quickly becoming a yearly tradition of practicing war.

"How are the recent batch of new knights coming along?" asked Ludwig.

"Well enough, but a few more months of seasoning will see them improve."

"You and Sig did a remarkable job organizing all this."

"It wasn't just us, boss. The Temple General was a great help. That aide of hers is brilliant when it comes to making arrangements for things like this."

"That makes sense," said Ludwig. "They did march here all the way from the Antonine."

"Here they come now," said Cyn.

Temple Captain Hamelyn led the Temple Knights of Saint Mathew, his two companies having taken on the role of scouting for what was now known as the Temple Division. He saluted as they passed, and Ludwig nodded in reply. Behind them came Temple General Charlaine and the remainder of her contingent, including six individuals wearing white surcoats with three red waves.

"Who are they?" asked Ludwig.

"The Sisters of Mercy. Surely you remember Temple Captain Teresa?"

"Of course, but I had no idea they'd recruited other healers."

"Technically, they're considered novices even though most have been Temple Knights for years."

"Novices?"

"Yes. They're in training until they master the use of Life Magic."

"And how long does that take?"

"I have no idea," replied Cyn, "but you can bring up the subject this evening. You do remember there's a banquet planned?"

"Yes," said Ludwig. "I'm looking forward to it." He glanced skyward. "We couldn't have asked for better weather."

"Agreed, which is why we're hosting it outdoors."

"Are you pulling my leg?"

"No, I'm quite serious. Do you have any idea how many of our officers will be attending? There's no possible way we could fit them all into the keep."

"Just how many do we have now?"

"Between Sig's division and my own, we have forty captains, with almost as many Temple Officers, and that's not including Captain Gustavo or the Elven delegation."

"I can see now why you decided hosting it outside was a better option."

"We also have a little surprise for you, boss."

"You do?"

"We built a wooden tower to give you a better view of the battlefield."

"Does this mock battle of yours have a name?" asked Ludwig.

"It's not a battle so much as an experience. The Temple Knights will charge the foot to give them an idea of what to expect. They'll break off at the last moment, but it'll be frightening, all the same. I'm hoping it'll make our warriors less prone to panic should the enemy try a similar tactic. Of course, they've been drilled in the fist of spears, but it's one thing to do that in practice, quite another to hold the formation when tons of horseflesh is bearing down on you."

"We have veterans from the last campaign, don't we?"

"We do, but rather than group them all together, we've split them up, placing them alongside less-experienced men, allowing them to pass on their skills to others, thereby cutting down on training time."

"You're enjoying this far too much," said Ludwig.

"I can't help it if I'm enthusiastic. I never thought being a general would be this much fun!" She hesitated. "I'm not suggesting people getting killed is exciting—that would be horrible. On the other hand, training exercises like this are fascinating to watch, don't you think?"

"Some days I wish I were out there myself, but as king, I must take a step back and allow the professionals to do their jobs. Speaking of which, when are the manoeuvres to commence?"

Cyn looked skyward, judging the sun's position. "I was hoping to begin at noon, but we're a little behind schedule."

"Why is that? I thought everything was organized?"

"It was, I just hadn't counted on so much interest from the townsfolk." She nodded towards her left. "Those folks over there came out to watch the spectacle, which is fine by me, but their fancy carriages and long lines of servants have been clogging the roads all morning, which has slowed things down. I considered using men to deny them access, but that would strip my division of a good number of warriors, so I'll let them be for the meantime."

"Probably a wise move," said Ludwig.

The bells of Harlingen had rung noon some time ago, but the battle still wasn't underway. Ludwig climbed up into the tower Cyn had built to allow a better view of the spectacle and was about to sit when Gustavo pointed.

"It's begun, sire. General Sigwulf's division is advancing."

Sure enough, men in distinctive dark green and yellow surcoats were advancing, with a screen of archers in front, cavalry on either side. They kept their formation despite the relatively uneven ground, a testament to their training and discipline.

It was an inspiring sight, one that took his breath away. In the past, the warriors of Hadenfeld wore the colours of their baron, but that had changed now they were under the king's command. It had been suggested they wear the king's coat of arms, but to Ludwig's mind, that made little sense, for they'd be required to replace the surcoats whenever the monarch changed. He instead chose a deep green, offset by yellow trim, with their chest bearing the symbol of the crown of Hadenfeld.

Ludwig had to admit it had been a wise choice, for the uniform appearance of his warriors revealed to all that these were seasoned and disciplined soldiers.

Sigwulf's men advanced at a steady pace, closing the range until they were well within bow-shot of Cyn's division. They halted at this point, and then the archers ran back, milling in amongst the lines of footmen.

At the sound of a horn, Cyn's cavalry advanced from her left, threatening Sig's flank. The footmen under the northman's control calmly turned to their right, presenting a bristling wall of spears. The horsemen rode by, to the jeers of the foot, though it was good-natured.

Next came the Temple Knights of Saint Agnes, with only two companies advancing, but as they drew nearer, they broke into a charge. Ludwig noticed the footmen waver slightly, but the line held. The thunder of hooves must've been deafening down there, for Ludwig could hear it from atop the tower.

"I'd hate to be facing that," said Gustavo.

"That's rather the point," replied Ludwig. "Cavalry can't break a line of well-prepared foot, not unless they flank them or frighten them enough that their defence crumbles."

At the last moment, the Temple Knights broke off their charge, veering to the right. Their Temple Commander used her sword to salute the footmen, then the two companies made their way back to Cyn's line.

The marching and countermarching began anew with Sigwulf simulating a retreat while Cyn tried to get into a flanking position. Sigwulf's cavalry played a crucial role here, keeping the advancing enemy at bay. It was a constant battle of wits to see whose warriors could outmanoeuvre the others.

The battle halted while water was carried out to the men. From his vantage point atop the tower, Ludwig watched an exchange between Sig, Cyn, and Charlaine. He couldn't hear what was being said, but knowing the three of them, it was likely something unusual.

"This is about to get interesting," he mused aloud.

"How so?" asked Gustavo.

"That remains to be seen, but if you look down yonder, there's a discussion playing out. I suspect someone has decided to change today's plan. Were you given an itinerary?"

"No, sire. You?"

"Not so much as a hint. Well, I can't say I blame them. Besides, it's more interesting not knowing in advance, don't you think? It makes it more like a real battle."

"There's no fighting?"

"This isn't about fighting," said Ludwig. "It's about practicing the movements they learned in training."

"What makes a good army?"

"Did you read that book I gave you?"

"I did."

"What did you think of it?"

"To be honest, sire, most of it was self-serving, a deliberate attempt by a noble to enforce the idea that knights are everything."

Ludwig chuckled. "Did you learn nothing valuable?"

"The author did write about using the knights only when one could guarantee success."

"Think about that for a moment," said Ludwig. "Why do you think that is?"

"The fist of spears formation is cavalry proof."

"Only if the men wielding those spears stand solid. If even one or two broke, the entire formation would quickly fall apart."

"Is that the main lesson for those men out there?"

"Not the only one, but one of the more important ones. Having thousands of pounds of horseflesh bearing down on you is the stuff of nightmares. By experiencing it here today, the men will be more prepared for it in a real battle."

"Am I interrupting?" came Charlotte's voice.

Ludwig turned to see her struggling up the ladder. He took her hand and helped her reach the top. "Come to see the battle?" he asked.

"I couldn't let you two have all the fun now, could I?" She moved up beside her husband. "What's happening?"

"I couldn't say. The two sides just had a parley and are now returning to their respective commands."

"Has it been enlightening?"

"It has," replied Ludwig. "I must admit having a vantage point like this allows for an unfettered view of the entire engagement."

"You should take a tower with you when you march to fight Halvaria. You could build one that came apart easily enough, and then use a wagon or two to carry the pieces. It certainly wouldn't take you long to put it back together again."

"That's an excellent idea."

"With all due respect, sire," said Gustavo, "how would you issue commands?"

"Horns," said Charlotte. "They're used a lot in the north. They say the Dwarves were the first to employ them. Of course, you'd need larger ones to be heard over the din of battle."

"We already use flags," said Ludwig. "That was Cyn's idea. Each colour signifies a different command."

"A most interesting concept," said Gustavo, "but how do they know who's meant to be the recipient of the command? Wouldn't it be more convenient to send a messenger?"

"Convenient, most certainly, but slow. In battle, every moment counts. To take advantage of an enemy's weakness, you must be able to recognize the opportunity and then act quickly. A signal flag makes that easier to achieve."

"Something's happening," said Charlotte.

Cyn's men had formed into one massive formation, a great circle that bristled with spears. Her archers were safely ensconced within that circle, as were some of the Temple Knights, but as they watched, two full companies of Temple Knights rode straight through the lines of foot.

Ludwig stared in surprise, for it appeared they'd ridden over their allies, but then he saw the men shift their position, closing up the gaps as if it were a normal, everyday achievement. "Remarkable," he said. "I was not expecting that."

"Impressive," remarked Charlotte, "but if you look closely, some of Cyn's footmen are slightly out of place. Nothing a little more practice couldn't take care of, but it makes their formation less effective."

"I'm confident Cyn's already adding it to her list for practice."

"And did you notice that some of those Temple Knights carry crossbows?"

"I did," replied Ludwig. "Charlaine found them in the stores at Eisen when they arrived there, but this is the first time I've seen them in the field."

"A volley from those at close range might be enough to break open an enemy line," offered Gustavo. "That, in turn, would make it vulnerable to a cavalry charge."

"Another new tactic," said Charlotte. "It seems this is the day for military innovation."

It was almost dark by the time everything was said and done. All that remained was the meal, for which tables had been hauled out of the city and laid end to end, forming one massive line. Those farthest from Ludwig's end wouldn't be able to hear him, but he didn't mind in the least. The important thing was what he saw on everyone's face—the sense of accomplishment and pride that came with being part of something important.

Those assembled here were the future of Hadenfeld, maybe even the future of warfare itself. Baronial armies had been common for centuries, but other than the Halvarian Empire, no one had sought to unify command of all their warriors under an organization such as the one he saw before him today.

He spotted Talon Elonin amongst his captains, and it made him think about the Elves. Surely they must have fielded large armies against the Orcs during their Great War, yet they had no rank higher than talon. Then again, Elonin had led the Elves when they battled the Holy Army, so perhaps he misunderstood how they defined rank.

The Temple Knights had a rigid hierarchy of ranks from knight to captain, then commander, and finally general. Should he adopt a similar system? There were arguments both for and against it. On the one hand, a general had complete control over a division under a single command, whereas having commanders beneath them left room for incorrect interpretation of orders. Whereas, a commander could make decisions on changing circumstances far more easily than a general, who was usually farther away from the fighting.

Looking at all the captains seated at the table, he was struck by how many reported directly to each general. Could Cyn and Sig even keep track of twenty different captains each? Perhaps he should create commanders to make their divisions easier to manage, but then the question was, how to split them. Does he assign one commander each for foot, horse, and bow, or break down command by numbers, with each commander in charge of a quarter of the division? That was the most logical choice, but the empire could be crossing the border at any time, and he wasn't willing to reorganize everything now, especially when it looked to be running so smoothly.

Charlaine's words interrupted his theorizing. "I thought it went extremely well today," she said. "Is this something you do often, Majesty?"

"This is only the second time we've done it, and the first time the entire army was present. I do think, however, that it might become a regular thing. Would your Temple Knights be interested in further participation?"

"Most certainly. I know from first-hand experience how terrifying a real battle can be, and this exercise is just the thing to help steady one's nerves."

"Did your knights have trouble with nerves at the Brinwald?"

"Many of our Temple Knights were relatively new to the order, and few of those who'd served for years had any battle experience. If it hadn't been for our constant drills, many would've fled, but training can only go so far. What we did today gave them a sense of what a real battle feels like, minus the casualties."

"It wasn't completely safe," replied Ludwig. "I hear a few sustained minor wounds, mostly twisted ankles, although we did have one of our newer knights manage to unhorse himself, resulting in a damaged hip. Without Temple Captain Teresa, the poor fellow would've been crippled for life."

"That's a risk in any type of training. Even practice swords can do damage, and I've seen plenty of Temple Knights receive kicks from their horses. You learned to use a sword at a young age. Did you never get hurt by your trainer?"

He chuckled. "Kurt hit me more times than I care to admit, though thankfully, never seriously. You?"

"From training, no, though during my time in Arnsfeld, Danica and I were set upon by agents of the empire. I ended up taking a crossbow bolt to my left bicep that very nearly killed me."

"It must have nicked an artery," said Ludwig, "but you appear to have fully recovered."

"I was lucky Danica was there. She got me to a mage named Orlina Day, who healed me."

"Let me guess, a Life Mage?"

"No," replied Charlaine, "an Earth Mage, but thankfully, she knew a lot about the healing nature of herbs and such. It used to ache on occasion, but I got accustomed to it."

"I'm surprised Temple Captain Teresa hasn't healed you."

"She did. After I jumped from the Antonine's gate tower. Surprisingly, I miss it. It had a way of reminding me that I'm not indestructible."

"Wise words," said Ludwig, "though I think I'll refrain from injuring myself to remain humble."

She grinned. "Then how will you prevent your ego from growing too large?"

"I have two generals and a wife to remind me of my proper place. Mind you, I'm not complaining. A king should never forget that he's only a man and, as such, set a good example for his nobles. Far too many rulers come to believe they're infallible, or they surround themselves with sycophants, both actions that only result in failure."

"And if someone were to look back on your life, decades from now, how would you like to be remembered?"

"That's an interesting question, one I don't think I've been asked before." Ludwig contemplated her words. "I suppose I'd be happiest knowing I left Hadenfeld better off than before I began my rule."

36

ILL WINDS

WINTER 1109 SR

The snow crunched under Charlotte's feet as she walked through the park. The guards maintained a respectful distance, a Temple Knight on either side and four Royal Guardsmen behind, ready to rush in and assist should their presence be required.

"It's a brisk day today," said Gita. "Though a tad milder than I would've thought for this time of year."

"You should be thankful you don't live in Reinwick," replied the queen. "The winters up there are frigid."

"Is it that far north?"

"A substantial distance, but it juts out into the Great Northern Sea, a place that's said to get too cold to freeze."

Gita chuckled. "Is that even possible?"

"The rivers and streams freeze, but the sea doesn't. Scholars purport it's because of the salt in the water, but I prefer to think of it as a living thing."

"A living sea?"

"It is, in a sense," said Charlotte. "You might say it flows in the veins of northerners, or at least their trade routes. For that reason alone, we should all be thankful it doesn't freeze."

"Has this always been the case?"

"So far as I know. There are sporadic accounts of large chunks of ice floating in the far north, but few people venture there, for obvious reasons."

"Do you think you'll ever return for a visit?"

"We hope to, once the threat of Halvaria has passed. I'd like to give Frederick a sense of how I grew up. Speaking of my son, we should be moving along. I don't want to miss his lesson." Charlotte turned to a Temple Knight. "What time is it, Sister?"

"Almost noon, judging by the sun, Majesty."

"Then I think we should make our way to the stables. Frederick will be worried sick that I'm not there to watch him."

"He's become an accomplished rider," replied Gita, "and at only ten years of age. You must be proud."

"I'm ecstatic, but he's still a few months shy of his tenth birthday. Today, I told him that if he receives the approval from the riding master, he can begin instruction in the art of fighting from horseback."

"Trust me," said Gita, "I understand completely. Kenley's been going on for ages about how he and Frederick will put the other students to shame. I told him he should be humbler, but you know how children can be."

"It's difficult, watching them grow up," said Charlotte. "The years seem to fly by at the blink of an eye. The next thing we know, they'll be young men."

"Not quite yet. We still have a few years left to enjoy them."

A yell came from behind. Charlotte and Gita both turned to see a man running towards them, waving his hands around, screaming something. Sergeant Reiner ordered his men to subdue the stranger.

"They're coming!" the man yelled just before he disappeared from sight as a guard tackled him. Moments later, he was lying on the ground with a knee pressed firmly into his back, his arms pinned behind him. The other guards held drawn swords, while the Temple Knights placed themselves between the queen and her would-be attacker.

Charlotte stared at the fellow, who was dressed in the clothes of a commoner, though clearly one with means. "Who are you?" she asked.

"M-m-my name is Luther Berhaus."

"I know who you are," she replied. The fellow's mouth hung open in disbelief.

"You do?" he said.

"Yes. You and your companions plotted against the Throne. Were it up to me, the lot of you would've been thrown into the dungeons, but luckily for you, the king has a sense of justice."

"I never intended to hurt the Crown, Majesty. I had no choice; you must believe me."

"Shall I have him taken away?" asked Sergeant Reiner.

Charlotte stepped closer, then knelt to see the man's face. "You said they were coming; to whom do you refer?"

"The Halvarian Empire."

"And you know this how, precisely?"

"Please, I beg of you; save me and I will reveal all I know."

"Take him to the keep," ordered the queen, "and let the king know what has transpired here. He'll want to hear this man's tale, as will I, but I shan't miss my son's lesson for a traitorous villain like this."

"Yes, Majesty." Reiner gave the order, and two of his men lifted Berhaus from the ground and marched him off.

"That was interesting," said Gita. "What do you suppose he means when he said the empire is coming. Surely they're not here in Hadenfeld already?"

"I hardly think a Halvarian Legion is at our border, if that's what you're thinking, although we can't dismiss the possibility that there is some plot afoot to weaken our rule."

"You mean assassins?"

"That would be my guess, but then again, I'm not an expert in such matters."

"Should we cancel Prince Frederick's lesson?"

"Doing so demonstrates we're at the mercy of these traitors. We'll increase the number of Royal Guards, to be safe, but I'm not going to give them the satisfaction of scaring us into seclusion."

"Well said," replied Gita, "but we really should be on our way, not because of this interruption, but because if we don't get there soon, you'll miss everything."

Ludwig stared at the prisoner who'd been forced to his knees before the crown. The man's hands were manacled, as were his legs, and guards stood on either side, weapons drawn. Charlotte and Gita came through a side door into the great hall.

"Ah, ladies," said the king. "So glad you could make it. How was the lesson?"

"Frederick flew through it with full honours," replied the queen. "I see our new visitor has put in an appearance." She crossed the room, ignoring Berhaus and taking her seat on her throne. Gita stood on one side, watching with great interest.

"Has he said anything yet?" asked Charlotte.

"Nothing save for the occasional whimper. I thought it best to await your arrival before asking any questions." His gaze met that of Gita's. "I sent Gustavo to find Merrick as well, although he's likely to be a while yet."

"I think he'd insist you not wait for him, Majesty."

Ludwig's gaze swivelled back to Berhaus. "On his feet, if you please. I would look him in the eye when we speak."

The guards hauled the prisoner up to his feet but held on to his arms with a firm grip.

"You have a lot of explaining to do," said Ludwig.

To his credit, the man did not flinch, meeting the king's gaze with a remarkable calmness.

"I regret my actions, Majesty, as I'm certain the others do, though I know them not."

"Then how do you know there were others?"

"My correspondence with the woman in charge indicated as much, although she never named them."

"Let's start at the beginning of all this, shall we? You are a successful merchant, one who has built a business that has been both rewarding and profitable. How did you become embroiled in a plot against the Crown?"

"Some years ago, I had a… Well, let's call it a dalliance with a young lady. Mistress Shozarin somehow got wind of it and used it to blackmail me. My wife's family invested heavily in my business, and any controversy could've resulted in them demanding repayment."

"But you have plenty of coins," said Ludwig. "Why not simply pay off your blackmailer?"

"I did, and for several months, I thought that was the end of it, but then she threatened again to expose me unless I did her one last favour. It wasn't much. All I needed to do was deliver a charm to a member of the Royal Household. A charm, I might add, meant to remedy the queen's… condition."

"Can you describe this charm?"

"Yes, indeed," said Berhaus. "A glass vial containing a glowing green liquid that came with a note indicating it was a magic charm to calm the mind."

"Do you still have this note?"

"I do not. I burned it, along with all the letters I received from Loralai Shozarin, as per her orders."

"And how did this vial come into your possession?"

"Delivered by a Temple Knight, of all people. I didn't get his name, but he wore the grey tunic of the Cunars."

"Did you ever meet this Loralai Shozarin?" asked the queen.

"No, Majesty. Not in person, although she wrote to me often."

"How often?"

"I received letters at least once a month. The tone of her correspondence started off friendly, but as time wore on, she became more… What's the word?"

"Demanding?"

"More insistent than demanding. She was careful with her words, crafting them with great precision; I was utterly under her spell."

"But she was blackmailing you."

"That came later."

"I asked you to start at the beginning," said Ludwig, "yet now you're telling me the blackmail came later. How do I know you're not making this up as you go?"

"My apologies, sire. I first heard from her when she wrote to me about purchasing a shadowbark desk. Now, I don't make things like that myself. However, I have connections that allow me to acquire exotic items of that nature, so I began making enquiries on her behalf. As time went by, we continued to correspond, and while I'm ashamed to admit it now, I found myself enthralled at the thought of meeting her."

"Let me guess," said Charlotte. "This search for a desk led you to the woman with whom you had your dalliance?"

"I'm ashamed to admit it did."

"You were lured into a trap of your own making."

"I realize I made a mistake in bedding the woman, but what trap are you referring to?"

"I would've thought it obvious. The woman was sent to seduce you so Loralai Shozarin could use it against you. It was apparently quite effective, considering the result, and the stupid smirk on your face when you mention her. What was this woman's name? The one you slept with?"

"Marget, Marget Harford, but she disappeared shortly after our moment of passion."

"And you didn't think that suspicious?" said Ludwig. "You mentioned receiving the vial. Have you had any interaction with anyone else since?"

Berhaus dropped his head and stared at the floor, mumbling something.

"Speak up, man, or I'll have you beheaded where you stand!"

"Nothing more than simple tasks to watch and report on certain people. Then I received a letter this morning, sire, commanding me to go and kill the queen."

"Which you promptly set off to do, from the sounds of it."

"I did, but when I got there, I knew I couldn't go through with it."

"How did you know where I was?" asked Charlotte.

"Loralai told me in her letter where to find you."

"I find that most interesting, considering I only decided on that course of action this morning."

"Loralai must be here, in Harlingen," said Gita, "and someone within the queen's confidence is in her employ."

The door opened, and Gustavo returned, along with Lord Merrick.

"Ah, just in time," said Ludwig. "Captain, I need you to gather all the queen's maids and detain them immediately."

"Yes, sire." Gustavo immediately left to do the king's bidding.

"Sorry I'm late," said Merrick, "but there's been a string of murders, more people from that list."

"How many more?"

"All but one." Merrick stopped, noting the presence of the prisoner. "Luther Berhaus, I presume?"

"The very same," replied Ludwig. "He informs us that he was sent to kill the queen, and we've reached the opinion that one of Charlotte's servants has been passing information to Loralai Shozarin."

"How do we identify the guilty party?"

"We can narrow it down considerably," said Charlotte. "My trip to the park today was a last-moment decision. Gita and I were intending to go riding, but I changed my mind, so we went walking instead."

"That's right," said Gita. "There were, if I recall, three maids present. The guards were there as usual, but you sent Melinda to fetch a warm cloak while Selenia helped you with your boots. I can't remember who the third one was, but she was stowing your riding cloak, as you were concerned it was too long for walking and would drag on the ground."

"It was Elsie," said Charlotte.

He closed his eyes, willing himself into a calmer state. The betrayal felt fresh and deeply personal, a wound exposed and painful.

"You indicated they were coming," said Charlotte, directing her words to the prisoner. "Are you referring to your attempt on me, or is the kingdom in danger? And while you're at it, can you explain to us why you think the empire is coming?"

"Once I heard about the queen's illness, I took a greater interest in discovering just who, exactly, Loralai was. Over the years, there've been subtle hints that led me to believe she was not from the Petty Kingdoms. I tried to find out more about where she lived, but she was very guarded in her correspondence."

"It wasn't until I saw the queen in the park that all the pieces fell into place. She is beloved by all; who could possibly wish her harm but the Halvarians? The chaos resulting from her death would only play into their hands, and I couldn't be part of that."

"Have you anything further to add?" asked Ludwig.

"No, Majesty."

"Then we shall wait while the good captain gathers our suspects."

"Actually," said Charlotte, "if you don't mind, I have one more question."

"By all means," replied Ludwig.

She moved up to stand before the prisoner and stared at him. "How long ago was the original enquiry from Loralai Shozarin?"

"It was, if I recall correctly, the summer of oh-six."

Gustavo returned, his men escorting ten women.

"Just those three," said the queen, pointing. "The rest may be excused."

The captain lined up the maids, watching them closely. Charlotte moved to stand in front of them, looking each in the eyes. Melinda and Selenia both looked down, but Elsie stared back.

"It was you, wasn't it?" said the queen.

A sly smirk creased the corners of the woman's mouth. "Congratulations, you made the right choice. How did you know?"

"You undertook your service here roughly the same time as our friend here began corresponding with Mistress Loralai."

"Clever."

"Where is Loralai Shozarin?" demanded Ludwig.

Charlotte backed up a couple of steps. "This is Loralai Shozarin."

"You're too clever for your own good," replied Elsie, then strange words issued from her mouth as she raised her hands up, light playing over her fingers.

Gustavo thrust with his sword, a swift attack that sank deep into the woman's chest, causing her to collapse to the floor in an expanding pool of blood.

"My apologies," he said. "I only wanted to wound her."

"Don't apologize for doing your job," said Ludwig. "The queen is safe, which is all that matters. Someone fetch Kandam. Perhaps he can help."

Guards rushed to find the healer, but by the time he arrived, it was too late. Loralai Shozarin had taken her last breath. Then, her features began to change, including her height, but her face underwent the most remarkable alteration, for the woman who stared back in death was a stranger.

"Saints alive," said Ludwig. "What magic is this?"

"I believe it to be some sort of Enchantment," replied Kandam, "although I can't say what it might be called. This appears to be her true form, however." He reached down, confirming the lack of a pulse. "I'm sorry, sire," said Kandam. "She's gone to the Afterlife."

"That one's more likely to be in the Underworld than the Afterlife."

"I shall take men and search her quarters," said Gustavo. "Perhaps we might find something that explains who she's working for?"

"I doubt that would prove fruitful. She went to great lengths to conceal her trail of letters and never met any of her agents in person. If it hadn't been for Temple Commander Amarand, we would never have even discovered the existence of her agents."

"More could be out there," stated Charlotte. "We shall have to be extra vigilant."

"I agree," said Ludwig, "but I believe without this woman to direct them, they'd be aimless and unable to organize themselves. From what Brother Aiden discovered, not one knew the identities of all the others."

"She was a master manipulator. I suspect she would've used the same techniques on them all, but now that she's dead, I doubt we'll ever learn the full story."

37

NEWS

SPRING/SUMMER 1110 SR

The day had started well, with a clear sky and an unusually warm morning perfect for riding, but Ludwig couldn't shake the feeling that things were about to take a turn for the worse. Charlotte would've called it intuition, but he'd never believed in that. Now, as he returned to the keep, he faced a growing sense of unease. Something had happened, yet for the life of him, he couldn't explain how he knew.

He dismounted and passed off his reins to a stable boy, then noticed Lord Merrick standing by the door.

"Trouble?" asked Ludwig.

"We've received news from the north. The Halvarian Army crossed into Gotfeld, and as we speak, they're on the border of Erlingen."

"So quickly?"

"With all due respect, sire, it took time for the news to reach us. They attacked in winter, surprising everyone. They completely destroyed the Army of Gotfeld, then marched into Rudor and Angvil."

"Have any come our way?"

"Not that we're aware of," replied Merrick, "although details are scarce."

"Call everyone together. Have we heard anything from Zowenbruch?"

"Not as yet. I've sent word to Lord Darrian, but it'll be weeks before we receive a response."

"These sorts of things never happen at a convenient time."

"Will we march to Erlingen's aid?"

"Not until we learn more about the enemy's movements. Where's the messenger?"

"At the keep."

"Then come," said Ludwig. "Let us talk with him."

The messenger looked tired and hungry, the result of a gruelling ride over hundreds of miles. Ludwig felt sorry for the fellow, but the needs of the kingdom must take precedence, and the rider could rest later. At the arrival of the king and his advisors, the man stood straighter.

"What details can you provide?" asked Ludwig.

"The duke intends to make a stand against the enemy, but fears he's badly outnumbered."

"Outnumbered? Last I recall, Erlingen's army was substantial."

"It is, sire, but what hope has he against two full legions?"

"Yet you say he still intends to fight?"

"Yes, that's right. He's placed command of his army in the hands of a foreigner."

"What nonsense is this?" asked Merrick. "Has he lost his mind?"

"Tell me about this foreigner," said Ludwig.

"She claims to be a Mercerian General, whatever that is. She travels in the company of a Life Mage, an Orc, and a couple of men, one of whom is a knight."

"And the other?"

"Her husband, apparently, although what role he plays in all of this is a mystery to me."

"You said Mercerian," said Charlotte. "Is that a new Petty Kingdom?"

"No, Majesty. They claim it's a realm lying far to the west, beyond the Halvarian Empire."

"How odd."

"It gets odder still; a Temple Knight of Saint Mathew vouched for them."

Father Vernan perked up. "A Temple Knight, you say? Has this individual a name?"

"Brother Cyric."

Ludwig looked at his spiritual advisor. "Do you know him?"

"Only by name," replied Father Vernan. "His reputation is impeccable."

"What makes him so noteworthy?"

"He investigates matters on behalf of the Church."

"What sort of matters?"

"Everything from murder to corrupt officials. If he vouches for someone's credentials, then I'd be inclined to accept them, and I have no doubt the duke would as well."

Ludwig nodded at the messenger. "We'll accept this Mercerian General's qualifications and assume she's a capable leader. The question facing us today, however, is how we react to this news."

"They would have fought by now," said the messenger.

"Agreed, but we don't know if they've defeated the enemy or been destroyed themselves, which doesn't help us in the least. We must also determine whether there are other legions out there."

"You think there may be more than those two?" asked Merrick.

"If they only intended to capture one Petty Kingdom, as they have in the past, I'd say no, but to strike deep enough to threaten Erlingen indicates this is the war to end all wars."

"It occurs to me," said Cyn, "that if they're threatening Erlingen, their most likely path of attack would've been through Rudor and Angvil, placing them north of Zowenbruch, which could indicate their next target."

"Konrad's forces are not numerous," noted Ludwig.

"He had enough to threaten us," offered Father Vernan.

"Yes, but we were already a divided realm, thanks to Morgan. Hadenfeld now has a substantial army. Add to that the fact that we shamed the Holy Army and harboured a large number of Temple Knights, and it makes us a major threat to the empire. A threat, I might add, they'll be keen to rid themselves of."

"So what's the plan, boss?" asked Cyn.

"Once again, we're faced with two possible avenues of attack, through Zowenbruch or through Deisenbach, although this time, I think they'll choose the latter."

"What makes you say that?"

"Konrad's men escorted the remnants of the Holy Army to his eastern border, which tells the Church, and by association, the empire, that he's on our side. He'll also be on guard in case another Holy Army shows up. Deisenbach, however, has a smaller army, or at least it did, last I heard."

"That's true," said Merrick. "Though I recall the Temple General saying they were accepting of Temple Knights of her order, which at least gives them some decent cavalry."

"There are Mathewites there as well," added Charlotte. "If you recall, their regional commander is based in Agran."

"We'll send messengers to both realms in the hopes of gaining more information. Once we receive word back, we'll have to act quickly. To that end, I want Sig's division to march north through Eisen, but this time, they'll camp south of Zwieken. That way, they can march north into Zowenbruch if needed, or west through Valksburg and into Deisenbach. Cyn, you'll take your division north of Drakenfeld and camp in the hills near the border until further notice."

"We should also inform Temple General Charlaine," said Charlotte, "as well as High Lord Sindra, for she'll need time to gather her forces from all the different Elven cities."

"I'm well aware," said Ludwig, "but even if she can't gather them all in time, we'll still have the five hundred Elves from Nethendril."

"Where do you want them to assemble?"

"Have them rendezvous with Sig's division."

"How would you suggest the Temple Knights be utilized?"

"I'd like half of them placed under Cyn's command, with the rest joining Sig's division in the north, assuming the Temple General has no objection."

"I shall draft the letters as soon as we're done here," said Charlotte.

"Thanks to the efforts of our generals, our army is well-trained, a match for whatever the empire has to offer, but we must still be wary. If they've deployed two entire legions against Erlingen, we may find ourselves facing similar numbers. That reminds me, we need to alert Hollenbeck and Mirantha of what's happened."

"Yes, I'll see to it," said Merrick. "Our alliance with them requires them to send troops."

"It does, but I doubt they'll get here in time. We will need them, however, if the empire makes it to our own border." He looked around the room. "I intend to take the fight to the enemy instead of waiting here for them. Gaining the initiative here is crucial to victory, but we can't do that till we know where they are."

The hour was late, and Ludwig was struggling to stay awake. Before him lay a map that purported to show the Petty Kingdoms, although it was woefully out of date. For the last few days, he'd been trying to work out the enemy's strategy, but the more he stared, the more indecisive he became.

A knock came at the door, then Gustavo entered, bearing a letter. "This just came for you, sire."

Ludwig took it, then examined the seal. "This is the Duke of Erlingen's seal."

"Indeed."

He broke it open and read through the contents.

"Good news, sire?"

"Definitely. It appears the Halvarians are not so infallible as everyone believes. The Army of Erlingen has bested them in battle."

"A cause for celebration, then."

"Yes. Grab a bottle and pour us both something to drink, will you?"

Gustavo made his way over to a side table, selecting a wine and popping the cork. "Any details?"

"This new general of theirs caught the enemy with a feint."

"Does it say how?"

"One legion withdrew west, in an attempt to lure them into following, while another tried to outflank them, but the duke's army turned it to their advantage. They inflicted heavy losses on the enemy, yet were forced to retreat back to Erlingen due to the presence of the second legion."

"Wasn't the battle in Erlingen?"

"No, in Angvil. In any event, they sustained casualties and need time to recover. His Grace expects it will be a month or more before anything further comes of it."

"Why is that?"

"The empire suffered a defeat. They won't continue the campaign till they've reasoned out how they lost and devise a strategy to avoid the tactic being used against them again. Say what you like about the Halvarians, but they learn from their mistakes."

Gustavo placed a goblet of wine before his king. "Is that a good thing or bad?"

"That's hard to say. It does mean that two legions are tied up fighting Erlingen. However, that in no way implies more aren't out there marching straight for us."

"If I recall, Zowenbruch is south of both Erlingen and Angvil, isn't it?"

"Yes. That's correct."

"Then I doubt they'll be coming through Konrad's lands."

"A very astute observation," said Ludwig, "and one I would agree with, although I'm curious to hear how you came to that conclusion."

"If two legions are west of Erlingen, the roads will be clogged with their supply wagons. It would be difficult to send a third marching down through those very same roads into Zowenbruch, let alone potentially a fourth, which suggests if they're coming, it'll be through Deisenbach."

"Interesting," said Ludwig. "Deisenbach also gives them a shorter supply line back into the empire, which means we now know what route they'll be taking."

"Assuming they're coming at all."

"Even if they're not coming for us, we need to join Cyn's division, but I can't cross into Deisenbach without their king's permission."

"We'll need maps," said Gustavo. "I'll see what I can dig up."

"Before you go, aren't you forgetting something?" Ludwig stood, amused at the captain's confusion. He raised his goblet. "Here's to the Battle of the Pines."

"The Battle of the Pines?"

"That's what the duke is calling this victory."

"It's as good a name as any."

They tapped their goblets together before downing the wine.

"Right," said Ludwig. "You'd best be off. I have work to do."

The distance from Harlingen to Eisen was close to two hundred fifty miles, requiring significant time for a messenger to reach Temple General Charlaine.

By the time the Temple Knights of Saint Agnes reached Cyn's division, the general's command was firmly ensconced in the hills northeast of Drakenfeld. They met in a tent, where Charlaine produced a map of Deisenbach.

Ludwig looked it over. "This is one of the better maps I've seen. Where did you get it?"

"Temple Captain Giselle sent it. She commands our detachment in Agran, Deisenbach's capital."

"She must have been quick to send it to you."

"Not in the least," replied Charlaine. "She sent it almost two years ago, when I contacted her after coming to Hadenfeld."

"Thank the Saints she had the foresight to do so, else we'd be stumbling around in the middle of nowhere."

"Surely you've been there before? You must have travelled through Deisenbach when you went north to Reinwick to marry the queen."

"That's true, we did, but we had no maps to guide us." He pointed. "This is the route we took, up through Volbruck and Agran, then on to Bessin, crossing into Zowenbruch at Santrem. It looks so different seeing it marked on a map."

"Where do you think the most likely place for the empire to attack?"

"From what I see here," said Ludwig, "there are three routes that look possible, though the northernmost one, through Herst, would involve a much longer march to reach the capital. By that reasoning, we can assume it's unlikely to be their choice, which leaves us with two others: Rotmar and Freizel."

"Rotmar is a more direct route to the capital."

"It is, but if they brought more than one legion, as they did in the north, they might cross the border at both locations."

"That puts us in a difficult position," said Charlaine, "or at least it might, but our first task is getting to Agran. Have we had any requests for help from King Justinian?"

"Not as yet, but every day we sit here waiting consumes more of our supplies."

Cyn entered the tent, wearing a grin, and brandishing a scroll. "Guess what I have here?"

"An invitation to a midsummer feast?" said Ludwig.

"There's a feast?"

"No. What is it you've got there?"

"A letter from King Justinian of Deisenbach." She handed it over, and Ludwig broke the seal.

"It's official," he said. "The king has asked us for help. He has word that a legion is marching south through Gotfeld and fears they'll soon be at his border. He's asking us to march to Agran and join with his forces to repel a Halvarian invasion."

"Any idea where the enemy is expected to cross the border?" asked Charlaine.

"No, but that's to our advantage. It means they're not close enough to be seen, which gives us time to march. Cyn, dispatch riders to Sig. They can take the road through Deisenbach to save time. Tell him to cross the border at Valksburg and march down through Trivoli."

"Will we wait for him at Volbruck?"

"No. He can join us in Agran. We haven't the time to wait."

"I shall dispatch a pair of Temple Knights to carry word of our march to Agran," said Charlaine. "Any word on where Justinian's army is?"

"He doesn't mention it specifically, but I imagine they'd be in the capital. He did say he wanted us to join him there."

"So we march at first light?" asked Cyn.

"Yes, and I want your cavalry leading the way, at least till we get to Volbruck."

"And the Temple Knights?" asked Charlaine.

"I'd like them to bring up the rear. If any enemy scouts are out there, I'd prefer they not know you're marching with us. A little secret, if you will, for us to spring on them when the time is right."

They set out at dawn, reaching the river mid-afternoon. A small bridge was the only means to cross, but no sign welcomed them to Deisenbach, nor were there guards to challenge their crossing: merely the flowing waters of the Rasfeld River.

Ludwig rode at the head of his footmen, the road already secured by the cavalry. The clear sky promised a pleasant march, and he drank it in. If they weren't marching to war, it would've been most enjoyable.

Gustavo soon caught up to him.

"Any problems?" asked Ludwig.

"Not at all, sire. The foot are keeping a steady pace, and the wagons are managing well enough. I shouldn't be surprised, though, if they fall behind a little later this afternoon."

"You think the oxen will tire?"

"It's not the oxen I'm worried about, it's the camp followers. We've also got a herd of cattle and a flock of sheep to provide fresh meat, which requires a lot of work to control."

"I hadn't considered that," replied Ludwig. "It's amazing when you think about it. All those animals just to feed the army, but then we have to add more men to look after the animals, and they, in turn, require food as well. It's like an ancient puzzle that can never quite be solved."

"There must be a perfect balance somewhere, sire. A point after which we'd get diminishing returns."

"Diminishing returns? You've been taking more lessons from that book I lent you."

"I have," admitted Gustavo, "and I think I've finally gotten to the point where I begin to understand your message."

"That message being?"

"The true measure of an army is its blend of foot, horse, and bow. Knights are a tremendous advantage when the enemy is broken, or against an undisciplined enemy, but you need footmen to capture and hold territory, and bowmen to help protect the foot."

"And what about the lighter horsemen?"

"The author barely mentioned them; it is, after all, a book about the age of chivalry."

"But you must have some thoughts," said Ludwig.

"The obvious use would be for them to scout ahead of the army or act as messengers, although I suppose they could also be useful in melee, provided the enemy isn't too well-armoured."

"Light cavalry, as we like to call it, is lightly armoured men mounted on smaller horses. We tend not to use them against a well-formed enemy, but they're capable of fighting when the occasion demands it. When we fought Zowenbruch six years ago, the Elven cavalry was an immense help. Without their intervention, we might've lost the battle."

"But we don't have light cavalry of our own," said Gustavo. "We have knights, and then we have mounted warriors in mail, neither of which is particularly well-suited to scouting."

"Which means?"

The captain stared back a moment. "We… need to raise some?"

"Are you asking me, or making a statement?"

"We definitely need light cavalry."

"Agreed," said Ludwig. "Unfortunately, that requires time we don't have, so we'll have to make do."

"I do have one question."

"What would you like to know?"

"What was your impression of *The Age of Chivalry*?"

"As I mentioned when I loaned it to you, much of it is complete nonsense, but it makes a few good points."

"Yes, but are we truly living in the age of chivalry, or have we gone beyond it?"

"Now, that," said Ludwig, "is a question for the scholars."

38

OLD FRIENDS

SUMMER 1110 SR

The men were tired and with good reason. The Army of Hadenfeld had set a gruelling pace, and now, ninety miles later, the end was finally in sight. Despite the ordeal, they straightened their shoulders and fell into step: once more, the professional army Ludwig had raised.

He rode at the forefront, along with Cyn and Captain Gustavo. Although he wasn't expecting a ceremony to celebrate their arrival, he was disappointed to see naught but a pair of Temple Knights of Saint Agnes waiting outside the city. Ludwig couldn't help but wonder where the Royal Army of Deisenbach was camped.

"Where are they?" he mused, talking to himself.

"Perhaps they're north of the city?" said Gustavo.

"I got a bad feeling about this," added Cyn. "You don't suppose we're too late, do you?"

"The city's not burning," replied Ludwig, "and I see no sign of foreign flags. That, at least, is a good sign. Gustavo, you'd best go fetch the Temple General."

"Yes, sire." The captain turned his horse around, galloping off towards the rear of the column.

"At least it's not a trap," said Cyn. "The terrain around here is far too flat to hide any Halvarians."

"Unless, as Gustavo suggested, the city is blocking our view of them."

Cyn nodded towards a distant field. "Farmers wouldn't be out in the fields if an enemy army were in the vicinity."

"Good point," said Ludwig. "Let's go and see who's there to greet us, shall we?"

The two Temple Knights waited off the road, allowing the army to pass without hindrance. As Ludwig and Cyn approached, their new hosts trotted towards them.

"Greetings, Majesty," one of them called out. "I am Temple Captain Giselle, and this is my aide, Sister Rowan."

"Good day to you," replied Ludwig. "My companion is General Cynthia Hoffman of the First Division." He slowed, pulling off the road to intercept his greeters. "Are you here at the behest of King Justinian?"

"Not precisely," replied the Temple Captain. She looked past Ludwig to where a small group of riders were now heading directly towards the group.

Charlaine slowed her horse as they drew closer, a big smile lighting up her face. "Temple Captain Giselle, it's so good to see you. You remember Teresa?"

"Of course. And this must be Temple Captain Nicola?"

Charlaine turned to Ludwig. "Teresa and I both served under Giselle in Ilea. At that time, she was one of the few Agnesites with any battle experience."

"Yet she is still only a captain? How can that be?"

Giselle straightened in the saddle. "I lost my command as a result of the battle, and the Antonine felt that having Temple Knights fight in a regional war set a bad example. As punishment, I was sent to command a remote outpost on the coast of the Shimmering Sea."

"Thank the Saints you did," he replied, "else you wouldn't have inspired the Temple General, and then where would we be?"

"She set us a fine example," said Charlaine, "and in many ways she was my mentor." She looked at Nicola, who nodded, then reached into her satchel and handed over a bundle of scarlet cloth. The Temple General took it, holding it out in front of her. "This is for you, Giselle. You've earned it."

"What is it?"

"Why don't you take a look and see?" Charlaine tossed it to her. Giselle unrolled the bundle, revealing a standard surcoat of the order, save for the three waves of Saint Agnes, stitched in gold.

"Congratulations, Temple Commander. It's about time you had a rank commensurate with your abilities."

"I... don't know what to say. I never expected to receive this. Thank you."

"The thanks are all mine. Had it not been for your influence, Arnsfeld would have fallen, not to mention there'd be no Temple Fleet. I'm certain Danica would offer you congratulations were she here, but I'm afraid she's far too busy taking care of things in the north." Charlaine nodded at Giselle's companion. "Good to see you, too, Rowan. How have you been?"

"Well, but I'm happy to remain a knight."

Charlaine turned to Nicola. "I told you, didn't I?"

Her aide shrugged her shoulders. "I can't be responsible for keeping track of the wishes of every single member of the order."

"Nor would I expect you to."

"I hate to interrupt," said Ludwig, "but where is King Justinian?"

"My pardon, Majesty," replied Giselle. "He's taken his army north. I urged him to reconsider his strategy, fearing the capital would be left defenceless, but he insisted. I elected to remain here with my company to do what we could, should the enemy appear." She peered around Ludwig, taking in the warriors of Hadenfeld. "Is this your entire army?"

"No, only one division. Our other one had a longer march and is likely a day or two behind. Tell us more about the king. How did he hear about the trouble in the north?"

"I think it best if you allow me to escort you to Queen Helisant. She's better equipped to answer any questions you may have."

Ludwig nodded. "Cyn, you're in charge until my return. Temple General, I wonder if you would accompany us to speak with the queen. Your experience fighting the Halvarians might help us put things into perspective."

"It would be my pleasure," replied Charlaine.

"Gustavo, you're with me."

"Yes, sire."

"This way, everyone," said Giselle. "I'll take you directly to the queen."

"Anything in particular we should know?" asked Ludwig.

"There has already been one plot to kill the king, and she fears another."

"Not from a fellow king, surely?"

"I'm not suggesting she'd suspect you, sire, merely that she may be suspicious, perhaps even demanding."

"I promise I shall be on my best behaviour."

They entered the palace after having traversed the city of Agran to reach it. The massive building was the largest structure in the area, making it easily identifiable. Two guards waited at the main doors, ready to challenge any interlopers, but at the sight of Temple Commander Giselle, they relaxed.

"The queen is in the great hall," said the shorter of the pair. "I shall escort you to see her."

"Thank you, Rillian," replied Giselle.

The guard took a few steps before stopping unexpectedly and turning to the visitors. "I should mention, Her Majesty is not alone. She has a visitor."

"That being?"

"Bloodrig."

"Strange name," said Ludwig.

"They're an Orc," said Giselle. "A shaman of the Sky Singers."

"Does that make him a mage of some sort?"

"The closest approximation would be a Life Mage, and they're not a he, they're a she."

"What are Orcs doing in the court of Deisenbach?" asked Charlaine.

"Did I not mention the king's illness in my reports?"

"Only briefly. Then again, such topics are not what's expected to be passed on to a superior officer."

"What sort of illness are we talking about?" asked Ludwig.

"Rather a strange one," replied Giselle. "Without the help of the Mercerians, I doubt he would've survived."

"Mercerians?" said Ludwig. "That's the second time I've heard mention of that realm. Was one a general, by chance?"

"Yes. Lady Beverly Fitzwilliam, the Baroness of Bodden. She travelled in the company of her cousin, a gifted healer by the name of Lady Aubrey Brandon, along with some other individuals whom I believe were part of her retinue. They claimed their land lies to the west of the Halvarian Empire."

"And how did they come to be here?"

"They were stranded by magical means. Sister Rowan spent more time in their company than I did; they arrived as the tournament was preparing to start, but I digress. Lady Aubrey sought the aid of the Orcs to help cure His Majesty."

"Might I ask why?"

"Apparently, there are many Orcs in Merceria, and she'd worked with their healers before. She informed us it was not a sickness but a strange sort of magical poison held within a glass vial."

"Let me guess: it was green and glowing?"

The Temple Commander stared back. "How did you know?"

"We ran across the same thing back in Hadenfeld. Does the Crown still have it?"

"My order was originally tasked with burying it, but then Brother Aiden, a Ragnarite, showed up and insisted it be sealed in a lead box."

"Brother Aiden was here?" said Ludwig. "How long ago was this?

"Just after the spring thaw."

"It seems our Ragnarite friend was busy after all."

Their escort stopped at a door, then knocked. "You have guests, Majesty. King Ludwig of Hadenfeld and a small entourage."

"Send them in," came the reply.

Rillian opened the door, then stood aside, allowing them entry. The room was much like any other great hall, although it was presently devoid of any furniture. The queen was in conversation with an Orc, but turned, giving the new arrivals her full attention.

"King Ludwig," she said. "I'm so glad to see you. I was just saying to Bloodrig we expected you any day now, and here you are."

"Greetings. I hope we're not interrupting anything important?"

"Nothing that can't wait. I assume you brought your army with you?"

"I did, although, admittedly, only half are here with me; the rest will be here in a day or two."

"Good," said Helisant. "Once they arrive, you can march north to assist my husband."

"Might I ask why he marched?"

"We received reports that an army was sighted north of Herst, one of our northern towns."

"I've seen a map of the kingdom," replied Ludwig, "but I'm afraid I don't recall its exact location."

"It is only about twenty miles from our border with Rudor."

"Have you not heard about Erlingen's great victory over the empire?"

"We have," said the queen, "which is why we suspect they're choosing to march on our realm. They lost a frontal assault on the duke's lands, and now they're coming south in the hopes of flanking them."

"Using that logic, would it not be better for them to march through Zowenbruch?" asked Ludwig.

"I do not claim to be a strategist," replied Helisant, "but it seems to me the conquest of Deisenbach would shorten their supply lines, making a campaign against Zowenbruch easier as a result."

"Do you not find that suspicious?"

"In what way?"

"How far away is Herst?"

"Close to a hundred and sixty miles by road."

"And how long ago did your husband march?"

"As soon as we heard."

"Which was?"

"Four days ago."

"With all due respect," said Ludwig, "if the enemy were spotted close to Herst, a message would take at least a week to reach here, by which time the empire would be within striking distance of Agran."

"Which is why you must march to his aid. For all we know, he's facing them on the field of battle even as we speak."

"I suspect he's chasing ghosts," said Charlaine.

"Yes," added Ludwig. "A clever ruse to draw his army north, away from the capital, while the real attack comes from Gotfeld, to the west."

"This is mere speculation on your part," said Helisant. "What if you're wrong, and the legions that fought Erlingen are coming south for us? Surely you can see the best course of action is to march to my husband's aid?"

"Let me take my knights north," offered Giselle. "We'll locate the king and discover whether or not there's a Halvarian Legion in the area."

"Very well," replied Charlaine, "but on the off chance there is, you'll need more Temple Knights. Take one of my companies as well. Do not leave, however, until the rest of the Army of Hadenfeld arrives."

Helisant's anger was evident to all. "You must do more than send a token force! You have the chance to destroy the enemy once and for all; do not waste the opportunity by being timid!"

"Timid?" said Ludwig. "I assure you we have only the best interests of your realm topmost in our hearts, but I will not leave Agran defenceless without proof of the enemy's intentions."

"And while you wait, my husband stands to lose his army. This is completely unacceptable."

"You mentioned earlier you'd received reports of an enemy army to the north," said Charlaine. "Might I ask the source of these accounts?"

"From people fleeing the north," replied the queen. "The first was, I believe, a merchant and his wife. Then, less than half a day after that, a pair of farmers."

"And where are these people now?"

"How would I know?"

"Did you not think to question the veracity of their stories?"

"No. Why would I? What possible motive would they have to lie?"

"They were likely paid to give you false information. It's a common tactic for the Halvarian Empire to seed confusion and chaos amongst an intended opponent. They've even been known to insert agents at court. You don't perchance have a court mage by the name of Stormwind or Sartellian, do you?"

Helisant's jaw dropped, but she quickly recovered. "There was one, a woman by the name of Ludmilla Stormwind. We suspected she was responsible for poisoning my husband, but she escaped custody."

"Escaped?"

"Yes. We locked her in one of our cells, but when we opened the door to interrogate her, she was gone. All that was left were chunks of ice."

"She must've used her magic to escape," said Charlaine. "Was she your only court mage?"

"Yes, until Bloodrig and her tribe came to our assistance."

The Temple General regarded the Orc. "Do you speak the common tongue of Humans?"

"I do," she replied.

"I understand there is some enmity between your people and the Elves."

"The woodland folk tried to wipe us from Eiddenwerthe many centuries ago."

"That was generations ago. Do your people still bear a grudge?"

"I do not understand what you mean."

"Do you hate the Elves?"

"I cannot say. I have never met one, nor have any of my tribe."

"What has this got to do with anything?" said Helisant. "You are here to discuss fighting the empire."

"We've allied ourselves with the Elves of the Goldenwood. An Elven army accompanies our second division."

"And how many of these Elves are coming?"

"At least five hundred."

"I thought you called it an army."

"They're few in number," replied Ludwig, "but their quality makes up for that shortcoming."

"Can they fight?"

"Most definitely. They've helped us twice now, the first time in battle against the Army of Zowenbruch, the second as raiders against the Holy Army. Their horses are fast, albeit lightly armoured, and their bows can penetrate the heaviest armour."

"This is not good news," said Bloodrig.

"I'm certain they can put up with the presence of a single Orc."

"But it's not," replied Helisant. "Not a single Orc, I mean. Bloodrig has sent for others of her tribe to help in the war."

"You should have told us," said Giselle.

"Word was only just sent."

"Then recall the messenger."

"There was no messenger, or rather, Bloodrig was the messenger."

"I'm afraid I don't understand."

"Nor do I," added Ludwig. "This is all very confusing."

"I can explain," said the Orc. "I used my magic to talk to Garok back in Ag-Dular. He, like myself, is a shaman of the Sky Singers."

"I assume you've dispatched an animal to carry word, like the Elves?"

"Not at all. I speak with him using the spirit realm."

"Spirit realm?" said Charlaine. "Are you suggesting Garok is dead?"

"We Orc shamans have a connection with the spirit realm, which allows us to communicate over great distances."

"How great a distance?"

"There is no limit, but we can only reach those we know."

"And when did you contact your people?"

"First thing this morning. By now, they will be well on their way."

"Fascinating," said Ludwig, "but I must admit to not being familiar with the land hereabouts. Where is your village located?"

"In the Grey Hills," replied Bloodrig. "They lie to the northeast, some eighty miles."

"So we have some time before they arrive."

"They will be here in less than four days."

"Eighty miles in four days? We're lucky if our footmen cover fifteen miles a day, and you're suggesting your people can do twenty?"

"Twenty-five if the weather remains clear."

"It makes sense," said Charlaine. "They're likely wearing much less armour than our foot troops, and if Bloodrig is any indication, they have a longer gait."

"You are correct," said the Orc. "The pace of an Orc is lengthier than that of a Human. This became evident when we accompanied the Mercerians here to Agran."

"I'm not complaining," said Ludwig, "but I'm curious why you decided to help King Justinian. Is there a history of Orcs working with the Crown?"

"No," interjected Giselle. "Quite the opposite; they were bitter… Well, I'd say enemies, but from what I've learned, the reality of the situation was very one-sided. There used to be a bounty on capturing Orcs until the Mercerians intervened."

"They intervened?"

"Yes. They were adamant that they needed the Orcs' assistance to cure the king. They claimed that back in Merceria, Orcs work side by side with Humans, even going so far as to integrate them into their army."

"Remarkable," said Ludwig.

"That's not the only place where Orcs and Humans work together," said Charlaine. "Accounts of the Battle of the Wilderness indicate they worked with the Therengians to defeat the Holy Army."

"Do your people have mages, Bloodrig?" asked Ludwig.

"Yes," replied the Orc. "We are called the Sky Singers because we have masters of air."

"I'm no expert in magic," said Ludwig, "but I imagine that would be of great benefit during a battle. The Elven mages we've worked with have primarily been Earth Mages and used birds to relay messages."

"That is most unusual," said Bloodrig. "That sort of thing is typically limited to masters of air. Then again, they call themselves the Chosen of Tauril, so perhaps their goddess has granted them that ability."

"Their goddess? Are you suggesting the gods are real?"

"Is there reason to believe otherwise?"

"We must respect their beliefs," said Charlaine. "It is not our place to call into question the existence of gods."

"No, of course," said Ludwig. "You're quite right. Thank you, Bloodrig. You've been most informative."

39

REINFORCEMENTS
SUMMER 1110 SR

They'd adopted a local tavern in Agran as their command centre, much to the owner's delight. Ludwig sat with Cyn, Gustavo, Charlaine, Giselle, and Temple Captain Hamelyn.

Ludwig looked around the table. "Thoughts?"

Charlaine was the first to answer. "King Justinian was convinced a threat came from the north, but the circumstances surrounding this discovery are troublesome, to say the least. I believe it to be a ruse."

"As do I. The rest of you?"

"I think we all agree," said Hamelyn. "No doubt the Army of Deisenbach will march all the way to their northern border only to find open fields and a lack of enemy soldiers."

"To my mind," said Ludwig, "that confirms my initial suspicion that the attack is coming through Rotmar."

"They could still attack farther north, crossing at Freizel."

"Then why lure Justinian's army north? They'd be better off keeping them in the south. No, they're coming through Rotmar."

"What do we do about it?" asked Cyn.

"Let's see that map again."

She pulled it from the oversized scroll case and unrolled it onto the table.

"We need eyes and ears on Rotmar," he said. "What's this here?" He stabbed down halfway between Rotmar and Agran.

"Tormaline," said Giselle. "It's a relatively small village, but a popular spot to rest on longer journeys. There's an inn there called the Spotted Dog that sees a lot of traffic."

"And the rest of the village?"

"A few farms, a blacksmith, and a shrine to Saint Mathew, that's about it."

"What's the terrain like in the area?"

"Mostly flat plains. A few trees, but nothing major, and certainly not anything that might be construed as a forest. Why? What are you thinking?"

"If we have to fight the Halvarians, that might be the place to do it. What of this forest to the north?"

"It's hard to tell from this map, but that's close to twenty miles away."

"You appear to know the area well."

"My company patrols the king's roads on behalf of the Crown."

"It's a common enough practice," added Charlaine. "Some realms have their own road wardens, or rangers, but most haven't the resources, so they allow the fighting orders to ride the countryside on their behalf."

Ludwig looked down at the map. "Tormaline appears to be halfway to the border with Gotfeld, is that accurate?"

"Yes," said Giselle. "When we first heard that Halvaria crossed into Gotfeld, we feared they were heading straight for us, but then they turned north, into Rudor instead, and... well, I suppose you could say the rest is history."

"Wait," said Charlaine. "Why am I only hearing of this now?"

"I sent Sister Consuela with a report months ago."

"She never arrived in Eisen."

"She must have been waylaid," said Ludwig. "That's just the sort of thing the empire would do."

Giselle shook her head. "Had I realized you knew nothing of this, I would have mentioned it earlier."

"We can't do anything about that now; we need to deal with the present. Have you any information about what's happening in Gotfeld?"

"Only scattered reports from refugees. The Halvarians defeated Gotfeld's army at a place called Rasgalen. They say very few survived."

"Any idea how many legions were present?"

"Only one," said Giselle. "The Ninth. They reportedly executed almost all their prisoners, allowing only a few to survive to spread word of their invasion. Make no mistake, sire, the Halvarians are a brutal enemy."

"And you say there was only the one legion?"

"That's what we heard, but you must bear in mind that was last winter. Since then, they've sent men to secure the border, and it's been quiet ever since."

"They're most likely busy subjugating Gotfeld," offered Gustavo. "Isn't that what they usually do?"

"Yes," said Charlaine. "Then again, they used to be content with conquering a single kingdom. This time, they've marched deep into the Petty Kingdoms, so we can't rely on them following their usual practices."

Ludwig mulled over all they'd learned. "Have we any information on how large Gotfeld's army was?"

"Justinian believed it to be somewhere between five and six hundred men. Hardly sufficient to stand up to a full-strength legion."

"Yet they somehow did exactly that. Why wouldn't they have retreated towards Deisenbach?"

"I can answer that," said Giselle. "Deisenbach and Gotfeld have never been on friendly terms."

"Why is that?" asked Ludwig.

"It boils down to the complex web of alliances that exist across the Petty Kingdoms. Justinian never liked to play that game, but Gotfeld and Erlingen reportedly have some sort of agreement."

"I doubt that's true," offered Ludwig. "It certainly wasn't true under Otto, though admittedly, Morgan didn't take me into his full confidence, so that may have changed. Still, if Erlingen had an alliance, why didn't they march to help Gotfeld?"

"Because they couldn't," said Cyn. "At least not without marching through someone else's lands."

"A Halvarian invasion would be convincing enough to get around that limitation."

"Not necessarily. As was mentioned earlier, the empire typically invades only a single Petty Kingdom. If the Halvarians started their campaign in Gotfeld, people may have figured this was going to be like all their other invasions and only concerned the one kingdom."

"Which is precisely why we have alliances in the first place."

"I would suggest otherwise," said Charlaine. "The alliances that dot the Continent are more about preventing other Petty Kingdoms from going to war with each other than they are about fighting the empire. If that wasn't true, they'd all be in one great alliance against Halvaria."

"You make an interesting point. Not that the past matters right now, as there can be no doubt about their true intentions this time. What we need to do now is locate this legion of theirs."

Temple Captain Hamelyn cleared his throat. "I have a suggestion, sire. If you'd permit it, my Temple Knights would undertake the journey to Rotmar to ascertain the strength of the enemy. We wouldn't engage them, merely observe, sending back riders to report on our findings."

"I like the idea," said Cyn, "but you should take some of my cavalry with you to act as messengers. That allows you to maintain your companies at full-strength while still reporting back to us here in Agran."

"Agreed," said Ludwig. "You can set out first thing tomorrow. It's getting late, everyone. Let's get some rest."

Charlaine and Teresa stood watching as the rest of her Temple Knights arrived, along with Sigwulf's division and the Elves.

Upon sighting the woodland folk, Teresa shook her head. "I'm surprised so many showed up, considering their alliance is a defensive one."

"The Halvarians give no thought to alliances. Were they to defeat the Army of Hadenfeld, the Goldenwood would be next. High Lord Sindra understands that and has been working diligently to encourage the other Elven cities to assist us."

Sigwulf spotted them and rode over, the rest of his division proceeding towards the camp. "Greetings," he called out. "I trust I'm not too late?"

"You've arrived just in time," replied Charlaine. "General Hoffman is waiting to direct your men to the area marked out for them. I expect you'll want to see His Majesty?"

"Eventually, yes, though if truth be known, I could use something to drink first. It's been a long, dry march."

Teresa tossed him her waterskin. "Here. That should quench your thirst."

He drank deeply, then stopped suddenly. "That's water!"

"What else would you expect from a waterskin?"

"Wine? Or ale, perhaps?" Despite his protestations, he took another gulp, then passed it back. "My thanks, Sister."

"How were the Elves?" asked Charlaine.

"You know them, always keeping to themselves." He glanced at the line of marching soldiers. "The bulk of their cavalry is bringing up the rear, so you should see them any moment now." Sigwulf waited a little longer, but there was no sign of the mounted woodland folk. "It seems my timing is terrible today. Ah, here comes Talon Elonin. I expect she'll want to know where to camp."

The Elven commander rode up to them, but as she drew closer, something behind Charlaine caught the talon's eye, and she stopped, a scowl forming on her face. They looked behind them to see the Orc shaman, Bloodrig, approaching.

"What is this?" said Elonin. "What is that… creature doing here?"

"That is Bloodrig," replied Charlaine. "A Shaman of the Sky Singers."

"This is no place for an Orc."

"They've offered help."

"The only help we need from them is for them to leave."

"With all due respect, Talon, that's not your decision to make."

"High Lord Sindra will not be pleased they are here."

"Then it's a good thing she's back in Nethendril," said Sigwulf. "Besides, it's only one Orc. It's not as if they'd be a danger to the Elves of the Goldenwood."

"You were not there when they slaughtered our people," said Elonin, "so I will excuse your ignorance."

"Perhaps," offered Charlaine, "this is a subject better discussed with the king?"

"Yes, of course." Elonin ignored the Orc and turned to the Temple General. "What is the strategy?"

"We believe the enemy will be coming from the west, but we're waiting on confirmation."

"And the Army of Deisenbach?"

"They've gone north, following rumours of an invasion, but we've heard nothing since."

"That sounds like ill tidings."

"Admittedly, it's not the best of news, but once King Justinian discovers it's all a ruse, I'm certain he'll march back here, to Agran."

Bloodrig reached them but halted as she took in the Elf. To her credit, she offered no insult, merely a blank stare, but was quick to recover. "Greetings, one and all. King Ludwig asked me to come and speak with you."

"You have news?" said Charlaine.

"I do. The Orcs of Ag-Dular will be here before nightfall."

"That quickly? I thought they could only manage twenty miles a day?"

"Closer to thirty, and I might remind you that this... What did you call it? Division?"

"Yes."

"It was due to arrive yesterday."

"That wasn't my fault," said Sigwulf. "We were caught in a storm two nights ago, which slowed us considerably."

"Well, you're here now," replied Charlaine. "That's the important part."

Elonin regarded the Orc. "How many of your people should we expect?"

"We will not know until they arrive."

"Is this how you run your army? With unknown numbers? Tell me, do they possess armour, or cavalry?"

"We are hunters, not warriors."

"Then they are useless to us."

"Now, now," said Charlaine. "Let's not judge them too harshly."

"They are an uncivilized group of savages," insisted Elonin.

"Those savages, as you called them, helped defeat a Holy Army. I wouldn't be too quick to dismiss them if I were you."

"We're all on the same side here," said Teresa. "The empire doesn't discriminate when it comes to killing its enemies."

"I will try to remember that," replied Elonin, "though I cannot promise there will be no incidents involving my people and these... Orcs."

"I understand your hatred runs deep, but no Orcs alive today had anything to do with the war you fought centuries ago."

"Yet many of us remember it, having experienced the horrors of that conflict first-hand. It is what comes of being immortal."

"You must let go of your hatred," said Charlaine, "for it will only lead to further pain and suffering."

"What would you know of such things? Were your people pushed to the point of extinction?"

"I might've been born in Hadenfeld, but my heart is Calabrian, a realm where the empire has subjugated and murdered dissenters for years. So, yes, I understand your pain, but I also know those who survive can either thrive or allow their memories to lead to despair and ruin."

The Elf stared back. "I had no idea."

"Nor would I expect you to. We Humans don't generally talk of such things, as it's considered too painful to address."

"You refer to those who survive. I assume you speak of your parents?"

"Yes. My father embraced life in Hadenfeld, while my mother grew more bitter with each passing year, yearning for what she was forced to give up because of the Halvarians."

Elonin nodded. "I see the wisdom in your words. I shall strive to keep them in mind in the days to come."

It was almost dark when the Orcs finally arrived. Wary of possible friction with the Elves, Charlaine went to meet them, bringing along Giselle as well as their shaman, Bloodrig.

The Sky Singers were a fearsome-looking bunch of hunters armed with bows and large axes. Their wide shoulders and broad chests made them appear enormous despite being similar in height to humans.

As they approached, Bloodrig grinned, showing off her ivory teeth. "Welcome, Garok!"

The lead Orc grinned back. "It is good to see you again, Bloodrig. Long has it been since you graced us with your presence."

"You're both speaking our language," said Charlaine. "I must admit to some surprise at that."

"Garok and I are the only ones who speak it so well thus far," explained Bloodrig, "but we are encouraging others to learn." She swept her hand to indicate the two Humans. "This is Temple General Charlaine, head of the Temple Knights of Saint Agnes. Sister Giselle, you know already, but you might notice her surcoat now bears the gold thread of a Temple Commander."

Charlaine looked at Giselle. "You've met before?"

"Indeed. Garok and Bloodrig take turns as court healers here in Agran. It's an arrangement they came to after the king's illness."

"Greetings, Garok," said Charlaine.

"And to you, Temple General," replied the Orc. "We are honoured by your presence."

"Why have you joined us here? I would've thought you'd march to aid the king?"

"That was Giselle's idea," replied Bloodrig. "She felt it best to keep some hunters here, in the capital. Of course, at that time, she was unaware that Elves would accompany the Army of Hadenfeld."

"Elves?" said Garok. "Why was I not informed of this?"

"I only recently found out myself."

"We thought it best to keep your respective people at opposite ends of the encampment," said Charlaine. "The better to avoid any trouble."

"The Sky Singers will not cause trouble, but they will defend themselves if threatened."

"I shall do what I can to maintain the peace, but ultimately it will be Talon Elonin and you, Bloodrig, who are responsible for the behaviour of your respective people."

Bloodrig bowed. "This I understand, and I will do all within my power to prevent any unnecessary contact with the Elves of the Goldenwood. Now, with your permission, I shall show my tribe mates where they may set up their camp." She called out in the tongue of the Orcs, then began making her way past the Army of Hadenfeld, heading east, the hunters of the Sky Singers following.

"I sense trouble," said Charlaine. "Are we certain we can trust them to behave?"

"What choice do we have?" replied Giselle. "They're hunters, used to moving around in the dark."

"What makes you say that?"

"They have what they refer to as moon sight."

"So they can see in the dark?"

"Not in complete darkness. According to Bloodrig, they see by the light of the moon almost as well as we Humans do in the daytime, but it's not absolute."

"Meaning?"

"The moon must be visible for it to work. If any clouds block it, their moon sight won't work."

Charlaine looked at the sky. "Just our luck, a cloudless night."

"Should I post sentries to keep them away from the Elves?"

"I fear that would be a waste of resources. Unlike the Orcs, our sentries would be blinded by their own lanterns, unless you're suggesting our Temple Knights stumble around in the dark?"

"No, of course not, but we must do something?"

"I should bring this to the king's attention."

"What can he do?"

"Not much," said Charlaine, "but at least he'll be forewarned about the potential for trouble."

"Pass the bottle, Sig. We'll do this the old-fashioned way." Ludwig held out his hand, and the great northerner laughed. "You're the king; you can't drink from the bottle!"

"Why not? I'm still a person, aren't I?"

"Go on," urged Cyn. "Give him the bottle, before he orders you to."

Sig shrugged, then handed over the wine.

Ludwig was lifting it to his lips when Gustavo opened the tent flap. "Temple General Charlaine is here to see you, sire."

Ludwig raised his eyebrows, then looked at Sig. "I suppose this means we'd best break out the cups." He waved at Gustavo. "Let her in, Captain." He waited until she was inside before speaking. "This must be important to bring you here so late."

"It is, Majesty, or at least it might be."

"This sounds like it's going to quickly become complicated. Have a seat, Temple General, and let's not waste time on formalities. What's this all about?"

"The Orcs have arrived to help."

"Let me guess; you believe there'll be trouble between them and the Elves?"

"Precisely."

"You've spent time marching with the Elves, Sig. What's your take on this? Will it be a problem?"

"That's difficult to say," replied the northerner. "Elonin said more about the Orcs earlier today than she did on the entire march. We know they fought the Orcs way back when, but it's not the sort of thing one brings up in casual conversation."

"Way back when?" said Cyn. "How about we be more precise? The war ended something like two thousand years ago."

"And you feel that 'something like' is more precise?"

"Let's not worry about that right now," said Ludwig. "We must bear in mind the Elves don't die by natural causes, which means every Elf here with Talon Elonin may have fought in the Great War."

"Yes," added Cyn, "a war that ultimately resulted in them withdrawing into secluded areas of the Continent."

"Not just that," said Sigwulf, "but they can't have children."

Cyn looked away, but Charlaine noticed it. "Is something wrong, Cynthia?"

"She needs a moment," replied Sigwulf, his voice softening.

"I'm fine," said Cyn, wiping a tear from her eye. "I know what it's like being unable to have a child; I can't imagine an entire race being cursed in such a manner."

40

OLD ENEMIES

SUMMER 1110 SR

Ludwig awoke to someone shaking him and opened his eyes to see Gustavo bending over him, a worried look on his face.

"Sorry, sire. You wouldn't waken."

Ludwig looked around. "It's still dark. Is something amiss?"

"You might say that."

"We're not under attack, are we?"

"No, but fighting may break out if we don't do something."

"I suppose that's what I get for staying up so late." He sat up, dropping his feet over the side of the bed. "What's going on?"

"The Orcs and Elves are threatening violence, sire, or at least I believe they are. It's difficult to tell when they're speaking different languages. I have men keeping them apart at present, but they're not making things any better."

"Let me get some clothes on, and I'll come and see what I can do."

"Shall I fetch the generals?"

"No. Let them get some sleep."

"The Temple General, perhaps? She brought this possibility to your attention in the first place."

"Yes. Do that, then come straight back here. I should be dressed by then."

"Yes, sire." Gustavo left to find Charlaine.

Ludwig rose, making his way to a nearby bowl to splash water over his face in an attempt to wake up. He should've known better than to stay up late drinking with Cyn and Sig, especially with the possibility of trouble between the Elves and Orcs.

Gustavo soon returned.

"Did you find the Temple General?" asked Ludwig.

"Yes, sire. She'll meet us there. She's just donning her armour."

"It's that bad?"

"I couldn't say. Do you want help donning your own armour?"

"No. I'm not going to war with them, but I will take an escort."

"I have six men standing by, sire."

"You think of everything, Gustavo. Thank you." He went to leave, then, almost as an afterthought, strapped on his sword and scabbard. "Come along, then. Let's see what we can do."

They threaded their way through the darkened camp. Off in the distance, Ludwig could make out an area lit by a bevy of lanterns. "I assume that's where we're headed?"

"Yes, sire."

Voices grew louder as they approached, and then they rounded a tent to see a large mass of people. To one side stood the Elves, weapons drawn, while across from them, the Orcs brandished axes. Between the two stood twelve men of the Army of Hadenfeld, looking like they'd been caught in the jaws of some fearsome beast.

"What's going on here?" called out Ludwig.

Shouts came back at him in the language of both Orc and Elf, drowning out any attempt at a civilized conversation.

He leaned close to Gustavo, raising his voice to be heard over the din. "Go and find Talon Elonin, and the Orc Shaman, Bloodrig." His captain nodded, then disappeared back into the camp.

Ludwig placed himself between the two groups, holding out his hands on either side, palms outward, signalling for silence. He had no idea if it would work, for the mind of an Elf was still difficult for him to discern, while the Orcs were a complete unknown, but he could think of nothing better to calm the situation.

The area quieted, and he breathed a sigh of relief. Temple General Charlaine appeared, along with Temple Captain Teresa.

"I don't suppose," said Ludwig, "that the good Temple Captain has a spell to speak Orc?"

"I'm afraid not," replied Teresa, "but I spent years amongst the Sea Elves, and I'm fluent in their language."

"Then I hope you can get to the bottom of this argument. I can't figure out if they bumped into each other accidentally or came looking for trouble."

Teresa turned to the Elves and began speaking their language. It made for an odd sight, at least from Ludwig's point of view, for the Temple Captain looked nothing like an Elf, yet the words that tumbled from her lips seemed to calm the woodland folk. She continued for a time, and then one of the Elves replied. The language might be foreign, but there was no mistaking the fellow's intent, so harsh were his words.

"What's he saying?" asked Ludwig.

"This Elf claims Orcs were responsible for the death of his wife."

"When did this happen?"

"He used the Elven calendar, so I'm not entirely certain, but it sounds like he's referring to the Great War."

"Tell him that war is ancient history and that he should live in the present."

"I tried that, Majesty, but he indicated he's taken an oath to avenge her death."

"This is ridiculous."

"I would concur," said Teresa.

Gustavo's voice cut through the night. "I have them, sire!" It was followed shortly thereafter by another call. "Make way, give us some room!"

The entire camp was now awake, crowding the area to watch what was transpiring. Elonin and Bloodrig moved to either side to stand before their people. Words were flung back and forth, but Ludwig understood none of it. "This is getting us nowhere," he said.

Charlaine stepped forward. "If you would allow, Majesty, I would volunteer my services as arbitrator."

"With all due respect, your captain tried that already, and it has gotten us nowhere."

"Have we an alternative? We cannot fight the enemy effectively if we are busy arguing amongst ourselves."

"I completely agree, but their hatred runs deep. How will you convince them not to kill each other?"

"I shall appeal to their survival instinct."

"You're welcome to give it a try."

"Thank you," said Charlaine. "Talon Elonin, if you would be so kind, I would have words with you. You, too, Shaman Bloodrig."

The two leaders hesitated.

"That was not a request," she added, a little venom in her voice. "It was an order."

They both nodded, then approached her, each staring at their counterpart with a look of disdain.

"Teresa, come with us," said Charlaine. "We shall discuss the matter in private."

. . .

She led them through the camp, finally stopping before the command tent of the Temple Knights of Saint Agnes. "Guards, ensure we are not interrupted. Teresa, you're with me. You two"—she nodded at the Elf and the Orc—"come inside."

Charlaine waited for them to enter before speaking. "I understand the Orcs and Elves have hated each other for generations, but I know few of the details."

They both started to speak at once, but she raised her hand to interrupt. "You shall each get a chance, but first I must have my say. Now, where was I? Oh, yes. I was talking about not knowing your history. Elonin, since you're the oldest, I shall let you begin."

"What would you like to know?" asked the Elf.

"How did this Great War of yours come about?"

"That is lost to the annals of history."

"Do you take me for a fool?" said Charlaine. "You claimed to remember the details of the war from first-hand knowledge, but now claim otherwise? Which is it? Did you experience the war in person, or is that story a mere fabrication?"

"It is no lie," replied the talon. "I fought the Orcs, even participated in the destruction of Ard-Uzgul, but that pales in comparison to what the Orcs did in the Forest of Shadows."

"Which was?"

"A massacre where they killed more than five thousand Elves, including children."

"It is easy to make accusations," said Bloodrig. "Particularly when there are no living Orcs who can counter them. I would summon my Ancestors to recount their fates at the hands of the woodland folk, but only I would be able to hear them."

"Convenient," said Elonin. "How typical that the green-skinned savages would deny the slaughter of Elves."

"You shall each get your turn," said Charlaine. "Please continue, Elonin, but refrain from resorting to insults."

"I shall do my best. Yes, we destroyed the cities of the Orcs and drove them into the wilderness, but they deserved that fate after what they did to our people. I admit we were not paragons of purity, and that we, too, committed acts of war that should never have been considered in the first place. The Orcs ended up a wandering race, but we Elves are now doomed to extinction."

"What has that got to do with the war?" asked Charlaine.

"The Great War raged for centuries, a conflict so all-encompassing in scale that you Humans could barely comprehend its scope. So fierce was the struggle that the Elves were forced to turn to new magic to have a chance of winning."

"New magic? Surely you don't mean Necromancy?"

"Some did, but I speak of a power even greater, the ability to harness the ley lines that form the very lifeblood of Eiddenwerthe. We learned how to use that power to transport our warriors over great distances. It altered the course of the war in our favour, yet the price of employing this magic was the eventual sterilization of all who travelled in this manner."

"Surely you had healers?"

"We did," said Elonin, "but they understood little of the power of the ley lines and even less about the longer-lasting effects it left on our people. Only after the war was over did we realize the full implications of what we had done, and by then, it was too late."

"It is never too late," said Charlaine. "Surely there is a way to repair the damage? Temple Captain Teresa can regenerate lost limbs, would that not restore your people to full health?"

"Do you take us for fools? Do you not think we have tried precisely that? The greatest minds of the Elven realm have spent centuries trying to cure our people, to no avail."

"And yet," said Bloodrig, "there is hope."

"What makes you say that?" asked Charlaine.

"The Human healer, Lady Aubrey, with my assistance, was able to cure an infection of the mind brought on by the green liquid extracted from those very same ley lines."

"Yes, that's right," said Charlaine. "Giselle told me all about it."

"What nonsense is this?" said Elonin. "Is this some sort of ruse to gain my trust?"

"It is no ruse," said Charlaine. "Bloodrig speaks the truth."

"I do not believe you."

"It is easy enough to prove," said the Orc. "Lady Aubrey taught me how to use the spell, and I, in turn, taught it to Garok."

"Are you implying you could cure my people's infertility?"

"It would be easy enough to arrange a demonstration. You say all your people are sterile, yes?"

"Without exception."

"Then select two Elves, one male and one female, and we shall see if this spell can cleanse them of the curse."

"Why would you agree to help us?" said Elonin.

"I can tell you why," said Charlaine, "because, unlike you, they have no direct connection to the Great War. The conflict you see as a personal memory is nothing more than ancient history to them."

"I want to trust that you speak the truth, but I find it difficult to believe an Orc could solve a problem that has plagued my people for nearly two thousand years."

"I understand your reluctance," said Bloodrig, "but Lady Aubrey developed the spell, and she is a Human Life Mage, perhaps the most gifted healer I have ever encountered."

"I… shall consider your offer."

"I've given Elonin time to speak," said Charlaine, "and it's only fair we allow Bloodrig a chance to air the grievances of her people."

The Elf folded her arms across her chest. "I shall try to keep an open mind."

The Orc shaman straightened her back. "I have no doubt that both sides committed atrocities during the Great War. I was not there, but the Ancestors tell us that all the great cities of the Orcs were destroyed, their survivors slaughtered save for the few who managed to escape. We became a wandering race, ever on the move to avoid discovery by the Elves. Only in the last few centuries have we finally found the courage to settle down and build villages as in days of old."

"All the more reason to get past this anger," said Charlaine. "Both your peoples have suffered because of this hatred, to the extent that you were reduced to isolated pockets, cut off from the rest of the Continent. This, ultimately, allowed us Humans to thrive, but think how different Eiddenwerthe would be had you learned to live alongside each other in peace?"

Both Elonin and Bloodrig stayed silent as Charlaine continued. "Let me remind you about the empire, for it affects us all. They want to rule over all of Eiddenwerthe, and history shows us they'll do everything in their power to accomplish their objective."

"We Elves have done our part," said Elonin. "Did those of Mythanos not fight at the Battle of the Brinwald?"

"They did, most assuredly. In fact, they played a vital role in that battle."

"And what did the Orcs do to help?"

"The Sky Singers did not participate in that battle," replied Bloodrig, "but neither did the Elves of the Goldenwood. One of our masters of air, however, is now travelling in the company of the Mercerian General, Redblade."

"Redblade?" said Charlaine.

"The name our people have given to Lady Beverly. I can also tell you that other tribes are not sitting idly by. Those to the west march with the Mercerians as we speak, while those to the east form an integral part of the Army of Therengia."

"This war threatens us all," said Charlaine, "whether we be Elf, Orc, or

Human. Think of all that could be accomplished if you put aside your differences, focusing your hatred on those who deserve it."

"You make a great deal of sense," said Bloodrig.

"I agree," said Elonin. She moved to stand before the Orc. "Let me offer my hand in friendship and let us bury the past, where it belongs."

"Gladly." They shook hands, but Bloodrig held Elonin's in a firm grip. "My offer still stands. Give me two of your people and let us see if we cannot rid them of this curse."

"I cannot raise false hope only to have it crushed when it does not work."

"If that is your concern," said Charlaine, "ask for volunteers. Warn them that the chance of it being successful is slim and that it's unlikely to work. That way, they won't be disappointed if it fails. If, on the other hand, it succeeds, it will give your people new hope."

"I wish Sindra were here to hear this for herself. I shall do as you ask. When do you wish to do this?"

"Whenever your people are ready, even this night, if you so wish."

"Won't they all be asleep?" said Charlaine.

"Elves don't sleep," replied Elonin. "We rest in a meditative state. Please excuse me. I shall find two volunteers and return forthwith."

News of the Orcs' spell spread quickly, and the idea that a cure existed for the Elves garnered considerable interest. So much so, that some of the Human warriors had to be deployed to prevent them from crowding the Orc shamans as they conducted their ritual. Ludwig even came himself, along with Temple Captain Teresa, who was eager to learn what spell might be employed.

An Elven archer named Telieth lay on the ground, her head resting on a rolled-up cloak. Bloodrig closed her eyes and began chanting, her voice lower than Garok's when he joined her. The two voices, initially at odds with each other, created a discordant sound, then Garok's voice changed, and they blended together in miraculous harmony.

The air crackled with energy, and the hair on Ludwig's arms stood straight up. The chanting quickened until the two Orcs placed their hands on the patient, and as they went silent, their eyes became blank and unfocused. Everyone who bore witness to this strange phenomenon held their breath in anticipation.

Bloodrig spoke, first in her native tongue, then in the common tongue of Humans. "Strange. Like the king, this patient's body is riddled with peculiar green vines, but where his were fresh, these are sharp and brittle, likely due to their presence for many centuries." She hesitated. "They are not vines in the true sense of the word, but it is how our minds interpret this ailment." She lifted her hands up a finger's width above the patient, then Garok placed his hands atop hers. They moved them over the patient, from head to toe, as if they were feeling the growth within Telieth.

"I see now wherein the problem lies. It will take time to remove the vines, then further healing will be required."

Bloodrig started chanting once more, Garok joining in, but this time, their hands glowed with a faint light that slowly soaked into their patient, revealing a strange, vine-like pattern deep within the body, as if all the blood vessels there were emanating light.

The sweat built on the brows of both shamans, and Ludwig found himself once more holding his breath. The scene was mesmerizing, and he realized he was witnessing something that would have far-reaching consequences.

At last, the chanting stopped, and the two Orc shamans visibly relaxed.

"Our spell is complete," stated Bloodrig, "but there is more to be done."

"I do not understand," said Elonin. "You claimed you could cure her."

"And I can," replied the Orc, "but first I must rest and recover my strength. The malady that sterilized your race is gone, but centuries of its presence have done terrible damage to those internal organs that allow a child to be conceived. A spell of regeneration is all that is needed to counter that."

"And our males?"

"I suspect it will be much the same. Once we have recovered our strength, we will perform the same ritual on your male volunteer."

"And where do these vines come from?"

"From the energy of the ley lines. Your people used it to carry your warriors over great distances, did you not?"

"We did."

"The effect on you was very different from that of the king. I suspect each species reacts differently to its power. Lady Aubrey told me Orcs are immune to such effects, so perhaps it has something to do with our blood?"

"I don't understand," said Ludwig. "Do you not bleed like the other races?"

"We do, but our blood is black."

41

DANGER

SUMMER 1110 SR

Once more, Ludwig splashed water on his face, but it did little to freshen him. It had been a long night, for the Elves had seen fit to celebrate what they were now referring to as the second coming of their race.

In the end, Bloodrig's prediction had proven true, and the male Elf, Escarial, was now free of whatever the strange condition was. The Orc shaman described it as green vines, but she'd also said that was the way her mind interpreted it. Whatever it was, it was invisible to the naked eye, making Ludwig wonder what kind of magic had been used to see it. Was it a spell that the Elf mage, Galrandir, simply lacked? Or was it something only the Orcs could do? He shook his head. No. Bloodrig claimed a Human had taught her the ritual.

"Sire?"

Ludwig towelled off his face. "Yes, Gustavo?"

"A messenger arrived from Temple Captain Hamelyn. He confirms the enemy is crossing the border north of Rotmar."

"North? I thought the town sat on the river?"

"It appears there's low ground on either bank, sire, which leads to frequent flooding. As a result, the town was built some five miles from its banks."

"That's disappointing."

"On the contrary," said Gustavo. "According to the messenger, the bell tower in town gives one a commanding view of the crossing."

"It must be tall indeed to see that far."

"I can only repeat what I've been told, sire."

"And the message?"

"Carried verbally on the instructions of the Temple Captain. He feared the messenger faced the possibility of being intercepted."

"A wise move, considering who we're up against. Any more details?"

"He claims that somewhere between three and four thousand men are gathered on the other side of the border. As predicted, they consist of foot, horse, and bow."

"That's a large contingent for a legion. You'd best summon our generals; we'll need to make some decisions. Any word from King Justinian?"

"Not as yet, sire. Do you think he could've run afoul of another legion?"

"If that had happened," said Ludwig, "there'd be stragglers coming here, or at the very least refugees fleeing the invasion."

"We've seen neither."

"Precisely. Oh, while you're collecting people, ask Elonin and Bloodrig to join us. I would value their opinions."

"Yes, sire. Do you want them to meet here?"

"No, we'll meet outside, over by the horses. That'll give the men time to pack all this up."

"We mean to march?"

"We must eventually. Better to do so on our own terms than those of the enemy."

The faces around him looked glum.

"How many?" asked Sigwulf.

"Three to four thousand," replied Ludwig. "Enough to give us trouble."

"That's not so bad," countered Cyn. "We beat the Holy Army; this lot is a bunch of amateurs in comparison."

"I might remind you that the Temple Knights of Saint Agnes bore the brunt of that fight, not us, and the enemy didn't have a balanced mix of foot, horse, and bow, merely knights, some on horse, and some on foot."

"So what's the plan? We talked about marching on Tormaline; is that still what we're going to do?"

"That's what we're here to discuss," replied Ludwig. "Unfortunately, we have yet to hear from King Justinian. We could end up marching to Tormaline only for a second legion to capture Agran from the north."

"A difficult choice," offered Charlaine, "but we have reliable information that an enemy is crossing the border near Rotmar. We can't ignore that, nor can we afford to split our forces if the enemy has that many warriors."

"I agree," said Ludwig. "The problem lies in terrain, or rather, the lack thereof. By all accounts, the area between here and the border is a flat plain, hardly something that could conceal a surprise attack or allow us to flank them without being seen."

"With the terrain being so open, they'll try to use their cavalry to flank us."

"Then we'll have to count on your Temple Knights to prevent such a tactic."

"Perhaps we can surprise them another way?" said Bloodrig. "As I mentioned previously, Garok and I are able to use our magic to communicate over a great distance. If he went north to find King Justinian, we could pass on your strategy to His Majesty."

"I like the idea, but we need to decide precisely what that strategy is."

"The sooner he leaves, the sooner he will find the king. Remember, Garok does not need to know the strategy until I pass it on to him."

"He'll need an escort," said Ludwig.

"Then I shall provide one," said Elonin. "Our horses are fast and capable of making more miles a day than a single Orc on foot."

"Then it's agreed. Garok will travel north, seeking out King Justinian."

"Or Temple Commander Giselle," said Charlaine. "If you recall, I sent her to find the king."

"That's right, you did. Do we know how many men are in Justinian's army?"

"I believe it numbers eight hundred or so," replied Bloodrig, "but that does not include the two companies of Temple Knights."

"The problem," said Cyn, "is we don't know precisely how far north the king is. He could be two days away, or more than a week."

"We can easily find out," said Bloodrig. "Amongst our tribe, we have masters of air who could use their magic to seek out the Army of Deisenbach. They are also farther north than we are, allowing them to search areas that would take us days to reach. I can contact them through our other shaman who remained with the tribe."

"Excellent," said Ludwig. "Elonin, I'll leave it to you to arrange Garok's escort while Bloodrig contacts her tribe. In the meantime, I'd like a rider sent to Temple Captain Hamelyn. Have him retreat to Tormaline but avoid any contact if he can."

"We should reinforce that position," said Sigwulf. "At the very least, we could send some additional cavalry."

"Actually, I'd like your entire division to advance, along with the Elves."

"Does that mean we're definitely going to make a stand there?"

"Let's call it a working strategy for the time being, but I'm hoping we can do something else."

"Care to let us in on it?"

"My hope is that our presence in Tormaline will slow the empire's advance. You'll have to be careful of their cavalry patrols, but I'd like them to think you're going to make a stand. You might consider putting up some defensive works to give that impression."

"Impression?" said Sig. "As in, we're not going to fight? This is getting very confusing."

"I think it's safe to assume the enemy knows we're here. I'm hoping what they don't know is how many warriors we have under arms. If they believe they outnumber us, they'll be eager to engage."

"But don't we want to slow them down?"

"A legion is a large formation, particularly when it's oversized like the one we're likely to face. If we draw them towards us, it leaves their supply lines dangerously exposed."

"Where my cavalry can exploit it," offered Elonin.

"Your warriors did a fine job of tearing into the Holy Army's camp; I'm hoping you can do the same here. It won't stop them, but it will force them to divert men to safeguard their supplies."

"I like it," said Cyn. "But what does my division do in the meantime?"

"Your men and the Orcs will camp halfway to Tormaline. From there, you can either reinforce Sig or fall back to the capital, depending on what happens in the north. If Justinian has been crushed, we'll need to pull everyone back here, to Agran, but I'm starting to suspect that it won't be necessary. My gut tells me the sighting of troops in the north was a ruse, in which case, King Justinian will be returning, hopefully sooner rather than later, but we must plan for both eventualities."

"Including our allies," he continued, "the Army of Hadenfeld numbers over three thousand, but add in Justinian's men and we might be able to match the numbers of the empire."

"Will that be enough?" asked Elonin. "If the enemy numbers four thousand, they still hold a slight advantage, and they are experienced soldiers."

"As are we," replied Ludwig. "Two civil wars gave us lots of veteran warriors, not to mention an invasion from Zowenbruch and a Holy Army bent on a crusade."

"Bent?" said Elonin. "I do not understand the expression."

"He means determined," offered Bloodrig. "I have found that Humans often use strange terms when they become emotional. It is likely because they are such a young race."

"A very astute observation. It appears we have more things in common than I thought."

Ludwig couldn't help but smile. "Who rules in Ag-Dular?"

"Our chieftain, Lurzak," replied the shaman, "but he remains there to watch over the tribe."

"Then perhaps you can tell me a little more about your hunters. I know the Elves have bows superior to ours. Are yours of a similar construction?"

"The Elven bows are superior to our own, although I learned recently that our people to the far east have created a new bow with similar qualities. Our current bows, however, would appear to outdistance those of your archers. From what I have observed, you utilize your archers in formed blocks. Is this true?"

"Yes. We call them companies, and by grouping them in ranks, we increase their effectiveness."

"Our hunters rely on skill rather than numbers, and we tend to spread our archers out, the better to protect them when the enemy looses their own arrows."

"So they've fought in battle?"

"On rare occasions, we have found ourselves forced to protect our lands. More often than not, these were brigands intent on claiming a bounty the Crown put on our heads, but many years ago, it is said we fought the forces of the king."

"King Justinian?"

"No, one of his predecessors. During this conflict, we learned to spread our archers out to avoid excessive casualties."

"Skirmishers," said Sigwulf. "If you recall, Konrad had men leading his columns when we fought them."

"I do," replied Ludwig, "though in that case, they had axes and throwing spears, rather than bows. They proved ineffective, yet I suspect Orc hunters would be much more useful."

"Might I remind you," said Elonin, "we also have our two Earth Mages, Karalindel and Theran. They can use their magic to help create a fortified position."

"Yes," said Charlaine. "At the Brinwald, an Earth Mage created hills for us to make our stand on. We found it extremely effective."

"And I can use Enchantments," added the talon.

"We seem to be blessed with mages," said Ludwig. "I know we have healers as well, thanks to Temple Captain Teresa and our friends, the Orc shamans, so we can help keep our losses to a minimum."

"We can do more than heal," said Bloodrig.

"What are you suggesting?"

"We shamans have a connection with the spiritual world that allows us to call on the Ancestors to provide hunters of the past to assist us in our endeavours."

"Are you saying you can conjure ghosts?"

"We prefer the term spirits. They are not as effective as living hunters but can still fight."

"How does that work?" said Sigwulf. "Wouldn't they simply pass through everyone?"

"That is a misconception. When conjured, they take a physical form capable of fighting. Their weakness is that they can also be injured by the enemy, although they do not bleed, merely returning to the spirit realm once their temporary physical form is destroyed. It does, however, require a significant expenditure of magical strength to conjure enough of these hunters to make a difference on the battlefield."

"Perhaps not," said Elonin. "Humans are superstitious, are they not?"

"Many are," replied Ludwig. "Why?"

"The mere presence of ghostly figures may help wear down their morale."

"She's got a point," said Charlaine. "Typically, half a legion is made up of provincial troops, people forced into service from areas conquered by the empire, and they are less competent, thus possess a lower morale to begin with. That's not to say they're not effective troops, but they lack the discipline of the imperials."

"Imperials?" said Elonin. "I assume those are recruited and trained from territories that have been in the hands of the empire for a greater length of time?"

"Precisely."

"Another advantage for our side," said Ludwig. "Anything else I should know about?"

"Yes," replied the Elf. "As an Enchanter, there are several spells which might benefit our warriors. I can, for example, extend the range of our bows, or make our armour more effective, though admittedly, I can only do this for a small number of individuals."

"How many would that be?"

"A company, perhaps two at the most, and it would drain a good portion of my reserves."

"Would that spell work on Bloodrig's spirit hunters?"

"I do not know, but it would be easy enough to find out."

"Then please do so. I'm not saying I want you to use that particular tactic once we get into battle, but it would help to know what you're capable of. Any other spells you'd like to share?"

"My most powerful spell is that of far scrye, for it allows me to remotely view an area of my choosing, although I must have seen the location at some point in the past to target it. We used it to great effect when we raided the encampment of the Holy Army."

"I thought you had to be familiar with the area you were trying to target?"

"I do, but once I create the viewing point, I can move it at a regular walking speed. When we raided the encampment, I began the spell half a mile away, then moved my point of view until I was in their camp."

"This is getting better and better," said Cyn. "We could use that to locate their general."

"A legion is led by a commander-general," said Charlaine, "and each cohort by a captain-general."

"But we think this is an oversized legion, so wouldn't that make each cohort larger?"

"I suspect not. The organization of a legion is rigid. I think it's more likely they added additional cohorts rather than enlarging the existing ones, allowing them to keep the same chain of command."

"You've given me much to consider," said Ludwig. "I think I'll amend my previous orders. Sig, I still want you to march to Tormaline, but I'd like the Elven Earth Mages to travel with Cyn's division."

"To what end," asked Cyn.

"The land hereabouts is more plains than anything else, so instead of relying on hills that don't exist, we'll make our own." Those gathered around him were all intent on his words, but rather than making him nervous, he drew strength from them.

At that precise moment, everything fell into place. "Elonin," he said, "I'd like you to proceed directly to Tormaline with Sig's men. Familiarize yourself with its layout. Once the Halvarians take it, you can use your magic to spy on the enemy."

"I would be honoured to do as you wish, Majesty, but you already asked me to take the Elves there."

"Sorry," replied Ludwig. "I only need you there now. The rest of your Elves will be going with Cyn."

"Tormaline is small," said Cyn. "Not much more than a roadside inn and a few businesses."

"That will make my task even easier," offered the Elf.

"I don't claim to be an expert in magic," said Ludwig, "so I'll have plenty of questions over the next few days. Getting a more accurate accounting of our enemy's numbers is our most important task. Once I know that, I can finalize my plans."

"You said you wanted defences," said Cyn. "What did you have in mind?"

"You'll need to discuss that with our Earth Mages, although I suspect the Temple General has some ideas in that regard."

"I do," said Charlaine. "It's all about hills and ditches, but we can discuss that once we're done here."

Ludwig tried to get some sleep, but the thought of going into battle caused him no end of trouble. He wasn't afraid to fight; in fact, he was eager to engage the empire, but he was trying to juggle so many different elements that he found it difficult to keep track of everything.

He finally rose, deciding to seek out Gustavo. His captain was sitting outside his tent, finishing off a piece of barn bread. "Now that brings back memories," he said.

"Did you need something, sire?"

"I want to double-check I'm not forgetting anything."

"You need me to fill in some blanks?"

"Not precisely. I recall what the Elves were doing, and I know what Cyn and Sig's divisions were up to, but what did I end up doing with the Orcs?"

"Bloodrig was going to contact her tribe and convince their masters of air to use their magic to locate King Justinian."

"I remember that, but there was something else."

"Yes, the other shaman, Garok, was going to ride north in search of the army as well. The idea was to enable us to be able to talk to Justinian without the delay of sending messengers."

"Ah, yes, that's it. I must be getting old."

"You're not old, sire, merely tired. You should get some sleep."

"I've been trying to do that all night."

"What about some seaflower?"

"We left Kandam back in Harlingen, along with his remedies."

"We have a shaman," replied Gustavo. "Perhaps she has some? Or maybe she can put you to sleep using her magic?"

"You know, that's not such a bad idea."

42

MARCH TO BATTLE

SUMMER 1110 SR

"There it is," said Sigwulf. "Tormaline, although I must say it's much smaller than I expected. There can't be more than a dozen buildings along the main road."

"There are eleven," said Elonin, "but that is not important at this time. The Spotted Dog seems to be the largest, so I suggest you put people on its roof to watch for the enemy."

"I thought you intended to use your magic to do that?"

"My spell allows me to see things at great distances, but even then, I can only view one direction at a time. What will you do now that we are here?"

"My first task is to evacuate the town. The locals won't like it, but I'd prefer them safe and alive than suffer the ravages of the empire."

"The blacksmithy is a robust building," said the Elf. "Perhaps you might consider fortifying it."

"We're not here to fight a battle, merely delay their advance."

"And what better way to do so than to give the appearance you are constructing defences."

"You make a good point," said Sigwulf. "I'll take a look and see what can be done."

"While you are doing that, I shall see if I can locate the enemy, although I doubt I will have success this day."

"Why would you say that?"

"For the simple reason that none of the Temple Knights of Saint Mathew are within sight."

"Ah, but maybe they are, but they're just far enough away that you need your magic to see them?"

"I had not considered that. I shall cast my spell."

Sigwulf rode over to the smithy and was about to order his men to take the villagers to safety when Rikal interrupted him.

"Sorry, General. Talon Elonin needs to speak to you."

"I was quite literally just talking to her."

The archer shrugged. "She was staring off into nowhere and then snapped that she saw something and that I was to fetch you."

"Fetch me? What am I, a dog?"

"Those weren't her exact words, but you know how prickly Elves can be."

Sigwulf shook his head. "I've told you before, my lad, if you're going to carry a message, you need to be accurate. That means repeating a message word for word, not making things up."

"With all due respect, I'm an archer, not a messenger."

"Yes, and a good thing too. Now come along. Let's see what the good talon wants."

Elonin was staring off into the distance as they approached.

"You have news?" asked Sigwulf.

"I do. The Temple Knights are riding this way."

"Are they in a hurry?"

"No, which seems to indicate they are not currently under attack."

"Any signs of the enemy?"

"Not yet, but I have not extended my point of view past the Temple Knights."

"Rikal, take some men and escort the villagers from their homes."

"Where am I taking them?" asked the archer.

"Down the road to the east, away from the enemy. Tell them to bring whatever goods they can carry, but impress upon them that they should gather them quickly. I suspect that we'll be fighting before long."

"Why would you say that? The talon said she hasn't seen the enemy yet."

"I shall answer that question with one of my own. Why would the Temple Knights be riding towards us if the enemy weren't behind them somewhere?"

"Perhaps the Halvarians gave up and decided to go home?"

"That's what I like about you, Rikal; you're always so optimistic. I'm afraid this time, however, you're wrong. They're coming; I can feel it. Now off you go. I don't want those villagers becoming casualties of war."

Fifteen or so miles east, Cyn sat in the saddle, trying to imagine a battle.

"They're going to come down this road," she said. "The question is how we best use your magic to our advantage?"

Karalindel surveyed the area before answering. "I would suggest a defensive mound on either side of the road, at least for a start, with possibly some ditches in front."

"I don't suppose you can conjure trees out of nowhere?"

"Perambulating trees is not a spell I have ever felt a need to learn."

"Perhaps Theran has it?"

"Not that I am aware," replied the Earth Mage. "You must remember, we live in the Goldenwood, where trees are plentiful. Why in the name of Tauril would we have any interest in moving one?"

"To make room for a road?"

"We build our roads around trees, not through them."

"It was just a thought," replied Cyn. She spotted the Orc shaman, Bloodrig, in conversation with Ludwig. "You'll have to excuse me. I must talk with the king."

The Elf mage offered a bow. "Certainly, General."

Cyn rode over in time to witness a grin spread across Ludwig's face. "News, boss?" she called out.

"Yes, and it's good, for once. We've located King Justinian."

"And?"

"They're marching towards us with all speed."

"And Temple Commander Giselle?"

"She and her companies are with them. His Majesty was in Bessin when they finally caught up to him, but by then, he'd concluded it was all a ruse, meant to draw him away from the capital and was already returning. Thanks to the mages of Ag-Dular, Garok was able to meet them after they cleared the Wildwood. Bloodrig convinced them to ignore the road and march directly west from their present position. Barring the unexpected, they should arrive in two or three days."

"So this will definitely be the battleground," said Cyn.

"Most certainly," replied Ludwig, "but I'd feel better if there were some way of obstructing the enemy's view."

"Perhaps there is," offered Bloodrig. "Our masters of air can create a fog bank to block their view."

"But they're back in Ag-Dular, aren't they?"

"No. They, along with the tribe's remaining hunters, are now travelling with King Justinian."

"Still, wouldn't a wall of fog raise suspicions?"

"Not if the attack came in the early morning."

"That means delaying the enemy," said Ludwig. "If we do it properly, we can lure them on to our defences late in the day, then they'd have no choice but to wait until morning to begin their attack."

"Could they not attack at night?"

"Humans don't see particularly well in the dark, and controlling an army under such circumstances would be most difficult indeed. It does, however, require that Sig hold off the enemy to give Justinian time to get into position."

A call of alarm sang out from behind them. Moments later, one of Cyn's riders galloped into the camp, his horse lathered. "An army is coming, sire."

"From what direction?"

"From the southeast. They would've had to march right through Agran."

"It's too soon to be Justinian!" said Cyn.

"Get your footmen across the road," ordered Ludwig, "and place the wagons behind them to stop them from being ransacked."

Ludwig fretted as Cyn rode off, yelling orders as she went. He tried to figure out how the enemy had outmanoeuvred him, but for the life of him, he couldn't imagine how.

Gustavo appeared, leading Clay, the king's horse. As Ludwig climbed into the saddle, he was reminded of how the horse's previous owner, an Earth Mage, had died attacking a baron's stronghold. The creature had served him well for many years, but was beginning to show its age, which got him to wondering whether he himself was doing the same.

The Knights of the Sacred Shield rode past, and Ludwig spurred on his horse to join them. Captain Rostrik offered him a nod, which he promptly returned, falling in beside the captain.

"Any idea what we're up against, sire?"

"None whatsoever, but you're not to engage. Your task is to ascertain who this army belongs to and how many there are."

"You think it may be the empire?"

"That would be the most likely explanation."

"How in the name of the Saints did they get behind us?"

"That's a good question," replied Ludwig. "If I had to guess, I'd say they came by way of Talstadt, but at this point, it's mere speculation."

The other army appeared in the distance, stretched out in a long line on the road. The knights halted, their captain ordering his men to draw weapons.

"Hold on," said Ludwig, breaking into a grin. "That's no enemy." He urged Clay onward, towards the distant warriors. The knights, fearing for their king's safety, followed, although they kept their weapons sheathed.

A trio of riders broke off from those on the road, one of whom carried a familiar flag.

"Greetings," called out Ludwig. "You're possibly the last person I expected to see here in Deisenbach."

King Konrad smiled. "I thought I'd surprise you, although I must admit I might have broken my vow to you when I crossed through your territory to take a shorter route through Zwieken and Valksburg."

"But we have no alliance?"

"True, but the empire threatens us all. If we don't stand united, we shall fall one by one. I have only one request in return."

"Which is?"

"Well," said Konrad. "How shall I put this? Having demonstrated on several occasions that I'm not the best strategist, I ask that my men be placed under your overall command."

"It would be an honour. How many did you bring?"

"Seven hundred. I trust that will be enough. I would've brought more, but I had to leave a portion of the army to protect Zowenbruch."

"They shall be of great use to us. I am curious, however, why you didn't send word ahead of time?"

"It's easier to beg forgiveness than to ask permission. I was worried the King of Deisenbach would object, as our two kingdoms have never been close, politically."

"Because they were allied with your enemies?"

"Precisely. Thanks to the labyrinthine politics of the Petty Kingdoms, my realm is ringed with potential enemies."

"Those days are at an end," said Ludwig. "And coming here, in our time of need, proves how important your kingdom truly is to all of us."

"Is this where we are to make our stand?" asked Konrad.

"In a manner of speaking, yes."

"I'm afraid I don't follow?"

"My intention is to meet the enemy, most certainly, but I will do more than simply wait and defend."

"Are you suggesting you'll take the offensive?"

"I don't intend to march towards them, if that's what you're asking, but neither will we hide behind our defences. We'll let the enemy come to us, then destroy their legion."

"I like your confidence," said Konrad, "although it might be a tad misplaced. No Petty Kingdom has ever defeated the legions of the empire."

"I'm afraid you're misinformed," said Ludwig. "They were beaten in Arnsfeld and recently lost a battle against the Army of Erlingen."

"Erlingen? I had no idea! I'd heard about Arnsfeld, but that was at the hands of a Temple Commander, was it not?"

"That's Temple General Charlaine, and she's here, with our army. Surely you remember seeing their scarlet-clad surcoats when we defeated the Holy Army?"

"I most certainly did, but I was unaware their leader was the same one who defeated the empire. Saints alive, you've got Temple Knights and Elves on your side, along with an army that has, what, three victories under its belt? What more could you ask for?"

"Your arrival is of great benefit," replied Ludwig, "but there's more."

"More? Please, don't let me stop you."

"The Army of Deisenbach is marching to our aid even as we speak, along with the Orcs of Ag-Dular."

"What's this, now? Orcs? What's next, Dwarves?"

"I'm afraid there's none in the area," said Ludwig, "at least as far as I know."

"Where would you like my men?"

Ludwig looked over his shoulder, where Cyn had lined up her footmen across the road. "Have your captains report to General Hoffman; she's over there, by that flag bearer."

"I shall be pleased to have them do so."

"Once your men are settled in, come and find me; we have much to discuss."

"It will be my pleasure." King Konrad trotted back to his army.

"He seems in a fine mood," offered the knight captain.

"He's timed his arrival to perfection. You can dismiss your men, Captain. I won't be needing their services today after all."

Temple Captain Hamelyn removed his helmet, revealing his sweat-covered face. "It is as we feared, General. The enemy is marching in force. You received my earlier report?"

"Yes," said Sigwulf. "You estimated between three and four thousand men. Is that still your best guess?"

"It is."

"These extra men, any idea how they're organized?"

"If their regalia is any indication, it looks like they've raised two extra cohorts."

"Regalia? I'm sorry, I don't know much about the empire's organization."

"Don't worry," replied Hamelyn. "During my time with the Temple General, she told me all about how the empire operates. To put it in simple terms, a legion typically numbers twenty-four hundred men, divided into four cohorts of six hundred."

"Yes, I seem to recall something of that nature."

"Each cohort has its own standard emblazoned with its number, along with the legion's identifying mark."

"That being?"

"A legion has what I can only describe as a simplified coat of arms: a wreath of some sort, a representation of an animal, such as a lion or what have you, and the number of the legion."

"How many legions does the empire have?"

"I'm afraid I don't know. The one defeated at the Battle of the Wilderness was reported to bear the number five. I'd assume they're numbered sequentially, but the empire is reputed to be immense, so there must be quite a few more."

"But it was working with another, wasn't it?"

"That is my understanding, although I cannot claim to know which one. You must remember this invasion is unlike anything the Petty Kingdoms have experienced. Before, the empire only invaded a region with one legion. If two were at the campaign leading to the Pines, who knows how many more are marching through the Petty Kingdoms as we speak?"

"But the army you observed appears to be only one legion?"

"Yes, but one with six cohorts instead of four. Think of it as a legion and a half, if that makes it easier to digest."

"And you're certain these extra cohorts aren't from another legion?"

"As I said," replied Hamelyn, "their standards indicate they're attached to this one."

"Could you make out their number?"

"Unfortunately not. They were a fair distance away, and there was little in the way of wind, so the flags were only partially unfurled. They all bore the image of what looked like a stag's head, but I'm afraid I couldn't make out any numbers at such an extreme range."

"You did what you could," said Sigwulf. "The information you've provided has proven most valuable."

"Where is the king?"

"A few miles down the road, back towards Agran."

"And our orders?"

"General Hoffman is preparing defences, so we need to delay the enemy to allow her time to complete them. To that end, I'd like it to appear we're preparing to defend this village, small as it is."

"Appear?"

"Yes. We won't actually make a stand here; we'll withdraw back to her position."

"How do we delay the enemy if we're not going to defend the village?"

"We make it look like that's our intention," said Sigwulf. "If they think we've fortified our position, they'll take time to form up into a line of battle to attack. Once they do that, we'll retreat down the road, forcing them to chase after us."

"And if they don't take the bait?"

"They will. They didn't come all this way to sit back and do nothing."

"This is a dangerous game, General," said Hamelyn. "How can we Temple Knights assist? Should we send out men to form a screen so we have warning when the enemy begins forming up for battle?"

"I doubt that will prove necessary. Talon Elonin will be using her magic to keep an eye on them."

"There must be some way for us to contribute?"

"There is. Tell your men to rest. When we do eventually retreat, the enemy will be nearby, and we'll need someone to stop them from overwhelming us. I have two hundred and fifty horsemen under my command, a hundred of whom are Knights of the Sacred Shield. I would very much appreciate it if you would oversee their deployment."

"I'd be honoured, General."

"Good. See to your command, Temple Captain. It's going to be a busy day tomorrow."

As Charlaine prayed, she sensed something in the air, as if the Saints themselves were watching over them. Tomorrow, or possibly the day after, there'd be a titanic battle that would decide the fate of not only Deisenbach, but that of Hadenfeld and all its immediate neighbours.

She'd defeated the empire at the Brinwald, but that battle had cost the victors heavily, with many of her sisters lost, but they'd at least thwarted the territorial ambitions of Halvaria for a few years. Now, however, the empire had returned in even greater numbers, and she worried that, in some small way, her victory spurred them on to bring such a large force.

A calmness washed over her, a comforting embrace she attributed to Saint Agnes herself, assuring her that the invasion of the Petty Kingdoms wasn't the result of her defiance, merely the logical conclusion to years of conquest by the empire, and she was exactly where she was needed most.

43

EVE OF BATTLE

SUMMER 1110 SR

Sigwulf had hoped to hold the Halvarians at the small village for half a day, but as soon as the legion broke the horizon, he realized they'd quickly be overrun. With no other options, he'd ordered his men to retreat to the east, back towards the safety of the rest of the army.

He glanced over his shoulder. The enemy horsemen were closing too fast, threatening his withdrawal from Tormaline. He halted the column, then ordered the men to form up. In quick succession, each company of foot spread out on either side before they turned to face the threat.

The Halvarian cavalry, likely sensing victory, rode forward en masse, but before they closed within striking distance, a wall of spears appeared, forcing the riders to veer off to the side.

Sigwulf gave the order, and the ranks opened enough for archers to move up and loose a volley of arrows. Though the armoured riders were largely unaffected, their mounts were not so fortunate. The archers quickly withdrew, and the spearmen once more closed the gaps.

The enemy, having their dreams of a quick victory crushed, pulled back towards the mass of Halvarian footmen forming up to the west.

"This waiting has me on edge," said Cyn.

"I know what you mean," replied Ludwig. "Part of me wants the enemy here now, so we can finish this, but we must be patient. The longer they take, the more time Justinian has to get into position."

"Any word from Siggy?"

"Not as yet, but even if he sent a rider first thing this morning, we wouldn't hear anything till this afternoon."

"Perhaps we should've sent one of those Orc shamans to help pass on any news?"

"No," said Ludwig. "They're of more use to us to communicate with King Justinian."

"What do we know about his army?"

"Not much, I'm afraid. He has somewhere close to eight hundred, but no idea how that's broken down. I suspect the bulk of it will be foot."

"Does Deisenbach have any knights?"

"They do, though, to my knowledge, not many of them. Temple Commander Giselle is with them, and she has two companies of Temple Knights, so that helps."

"Don't forget the Orcs," said Cyn, "although I'm curious how they'll fight. They don't look the type to form up into companies."

"That'd be my assessment as well, but I expect they'll be excellent at skirmishing. Imagine how effective our archers would be if they were all skilled hunters?"

"Some of them are."

"Agreed," said Ludwig, "but not nearly enough. What we really need are better bows."

"You mean like crossbows?"

"No, Therengian bows. They're said to be as tall as a man, but take years to master. I'd warrant they'd be almost as effective as the Elven bows."

"That would be something to see," said Cyn. "The only problem with Elven archers is we don't have nearly enough of them."

The Elven Earth Mages created four great mounds to anchor the Hadenfeld line. Two sat north of the road, the others south, forming roughly a north-south line. Farther to the north stood King Konrad's army, a line of Elven archers in front; the rest of the Goldenwood's Elves held to the rear to be used as needed.

To the south of the Army of Hadenfeld, the Temple Knights of Saint Agnes waited, ready to engage should the enemy try to flank them. This formation made the north end of Ludwig's line appear weak in comparison, but that was his intention. If the Halvarian cavalry was going to attack, the north end was the likeliest point. Konrad understood this risk when Ludwig had presented his strategy, but the King of Zowenbruch was eager to prove his army worthy of victory.

The Orcs were spread out in a skirmish line in front of Cyn's men, ready to withdraw as the enemy came within melee range.

The day wore on, and Ludwig began to wonder if the enemy had decided to withdraw. His doubts vanished as a lone rider appeared to the west. With her white horse and silver hair, there could be no doubt as to Elonin's identity. She rode swiftly and was soon passing by the Orcs towards the flag of Hadenfeld that identified Ludwig's position.

"The enemy is coming," she said, wasting no time with introductions. "General Sigwulf is retreating slowly, but is in danger of being flanked."

"How far away is he?" asked Ludwig.

"He should be here by nightfall, but he's taking casualties. The numbers are not in his favour. Do we advance to assist him?"

Ludwig glanced over to the next hill where Cyn waited amongst the troops. No doubt she would insist on helping Sigwulf, but if they advanced now, they surrendered the advantageous terrain. This was the most difficult decision of his life, yet Ludwig knew he had no choice. "We hold here," he said. "We'll stick to the plan."

"Even at the risk of losing Sigwulf's division?"

"It's not a decision I make lightly, Talon, but we must do more than simply beat the Halvarians; we must utterly destroy them. If we march out of our prepared positions, we risk trading lives in equal numbers. Though that would still grant us victory, it would come with a heavy loss on our side."

"And so we wait?"

"What other choice have we?"

Elonin closed her eyes and began uttering words of power. The air buzzed, and then she snapped her eyes open. "I am viewing the battlefield from above, as if I were in the air."

"Through the eyes of a bird?"

She smiled. "In a sense. There is no bird present, but I am using my spell of far scrye to view Tormaline remotely."

"And what do you see?"

"The village is burning. Sigwulf was wise to evacuate the inhabitants."

"And the legion?"

"Marching through what is left of the village on their way here. Wait while I shift my point of view." Sweat broke out on her brow as she swivelled her head. "I see it now, a distant mass of horsemen harassing the general's division."

"And Sigwulf's men?"

"They appear to have made little progress since I left them. The Halvarians have them surrounded, cutting off any chance of retreat."

Ludwig held his breath, cursing himself for not ordering Sigwulf to withdraw sooner. His insistence on delaying the enemy would now cost the huge northerner his life. His throat tightened as the great loss threatened to overwhelm him. He fought down the sadness; the emotion would do nothing to help him now.

"A battle is raging," added Elonin. "The general's division is tiring, I can see it in the way they fight." Her silence stretched on, and then she suddenly took in a sharp breath. "Their lines have collapsed, and the enemy is in amongst them. I fear it is only a matter of time until they are all dead."

One thousand men had been under Sigwulf's command, and now they were gone, wiped out by a merciless enemy. Ludwig steeled himself, silently swearing he would make the Halvarians pay dearly for the death of the great northerner and his men.

"A significant loss," said Elonin. "Almost one quarter of our entire army."

Ludwig found his temper rising. "What would you have me do? Retreat? Throw away our best chance at defeating the Halvarians? I will not consider that!"

"I am not your enemy," said the Elf.

He forced himself to take a deep breath. "No, you're not. I'm sorry. I didn't mean to take it out on you."

"Your anger is understandable, given the circumstances. We Elves are not immune to such emotions. During the Great War, the fighting was savage, and though it shames me to admit it, atrocities were carried out by both sides. This is what happens when wars become prolonged and people lose hope."

"This war has only just begun."

"If you succeed in destroying this legion, it will put an end to their advance. Their claim of being an undefeatable enemy has already been tarnished; another defeat puts that to rest once and for all."

"We have lost our numerical superiority."

"Perhaps," said Elonin, "but not our spirit, and that is our greatest strength."

It was late in the day when Elonin scryed yet again. "They are almost here," she said. "You should get everyone into place. I doubt they would attack so late in the day, but I am led to believe that when Humans are flush with victory, they oftentimes feel invulnerable for a while. I fear their destruction of General Sigwulf's division will have them eager to continue the fight."

Ludwig turned to Gustavo. "Send word," he said. "Everyone is to take up their assigned positions. Skirmishers to the front."

"Were you the enemy," asked Elonin, "would you fight?"

Ludwig shook his head. "Not until daylight. The sun will be low on the horizon by the time they get here, and no one wants to fight in the dark; it's too easy to mistake friend for foe."

"Then perhaps we have an advantage."

"I'm listening."

She nodded upward. "The sky is cloudless."

"What are you implying?"

"Orcs have moon sight, provided the moon's rays are not blocked. They can see as well under such circumstances as Humans do during the day."

"Do Elves have the same?"

"No. We are able to see things in dim light, but only at relatively short distances, nor as well as when the sun is up."

"Do you think the Orcs would be willing to do a little raiding tonight? Not to cause casualties, but to keep the enemy from getting a good night's rest."

"I am afraid I am not in a position to ask them, considering the shared background of our people. Were you to ask, however, I think they would be amenable to your request. It will be some time yet before your eyes can behold the enemy."

"Then you must excuse me," said Ludwig. "I need to find myself an Orc shaman."

The sun was fading fast as Charlaine observed the Halvarian Legion's arrival. It was immense, easily dwarfing the army she'd fought in Arnsfeld, and for a brief moment, she wondered if they hadn't made a grave error in choosing to fight here in the middle of nowhere. She turned to speak to Teresa, who stood to her right, but before she put her thoughts into words, a calmness overcame her.

"I know what you're going to say," said the Temple Captain.

"Can you read minds now?" asked Charlaine.

"I don't need to—I know that look."

"And what look is that?"

"The one you get when you know Saint Agnes is watching over us. This is the second time I've felt it."

"When was the first?"

"At the Battle of Alantra, when they tied me to the mast of one of their warships. I remember the agony coursing through me before a calmness engulfed me, as if the Saint herself held me in her arms. I thought then that she had come to take me to the Afterlife."

"And now?"

"Now it feels as though she's telling me I'm right where I need to be."

"I feel the same," replied Charlaine. "It's as if all the worry has been lifted from my shoulders. I've felt it several times over the years."

"You are the blessed of Saint Agnes."

"Nonsense."

"As I've told you before," said Teresa, "your aura is white, which is very unusual, perhaps even unique. It marks you as gifted in some manner, and I think it's your spirituality. I've never seen anyone as devout as you when it comes to their beliefs. You truly live by the words of Saint Agnes."

Charlaine pointed towards the enemy army that was now spreading out to set up their camps for the night. "Those Halvarians care naught for spirituality, or beliefs other than their own. You and I have witnessed the horrors they inflict on their prisoners; we shall not allow them to be given the opportunity to act in such a manner ever again."

Teresa gave her a curt nod. "May the Saints watch over you, Charlaine."

The Temple General smiled. "I doubt we'll see fighting until tomorrow, so save your blessings for then."

Ludwig lay there, trying desperately to calm his nerves. Tomorrow, there would be a massive battle, the largest he'd ever witnessed. He was afraid, but he couldn't stop fussing over the tiniest little details. His plan was solid enough, even with the loss of Sigwulf's division, yet he'd never directly fought the Empire of Halvaria. They held a near-mythical status amongst the Petty Kingdoms: the unstoppable legions that had conquered dozens, if not scores, of realms over the centuries. Charlaine put an end to that at the Brinwald, then the Mercerian General gained a victory at the Battle of the Pines. Could he now add to those victories with one of his own?

There was also the matter of Erlingen. Last they'd heard, the Army of Erlingen had retreated back across their border. Yes, they'd defeated a legion but had taken tremendous losses and been threatened by a second. Would his fate be the same? He'd been confident in his strategy, but recent developments left him second-guessing himself.

He rose, then exited his tent to see Gustavo sipping a drink by the fire. "Don't you ever sleep?"

The captain looked up at his king. "Who can sleep with battle so close. What about you, sire? Not sleepy?"

"Too many things on my mind," replied Ludwig. "I hate to say it, but I may have bitten off more than I can chew."

"I know you'll lead us to victory."

"How can you be so certain?"

"Think about it. Your whole life has led you to this point in time."

"Couldn't you say that about everyone here?"

"Aye, I reckon you could, but look at everything that brought you here. Had you not become king, the army would be a shell of its former self. Not only that, but the kingdom might well have been at war with itself yet again. You were instrumental in reuniting Hadenfeld, then you defeated the invasion from Zowenbruch, and became king just when the entire realm needed your strength and guidance."

"You make it sound like it was my destiny."

"It's not only you, sire, and everyone knows it. This isn't just a battle of armies, it's a test of wills. The Saints versus... well, whatever it is the Halvarians believe in. And can you honestly say it wasn't fate that brought the Temple General to us?"

"She brought her Temple Knights to Hadenfeld because she knew I'd give them sanctuary."

"Yes, because you had a shared past, don't you see? The touch of the Saints has been with you your entire life."

"Are you suggesting it was fate?"

"What else could have sent you to Eisen and led to the discovery of the Elves? A lesser man would've died at the hands of the woodland folk, yet you convinced them to become our allies."

"You were there with me in Nethendril."

"Yes, and I witnessed how you turn enemies to allies."

"I wasn't alone."

"True, but your forethought allowed Konrad to keep his honour, despite defeating his army, and now he stands beside us, ready to fight to protect our way of life. Who else could've accomplished that?" Gustavo paused for a moment. "I say this not to inflate your ego, sire, but to remind you that you are here because you're the one best suited to defeat the empire."

"What if I'm not?"

Gustavo shrugged. "Then we'll all die tomorrow knowing we're doing our duty. There is no certainty in war; that book of yours taught me that, but you've done all you can to bring victory within reach. No one could ask for more."

"I'm flattered," said Ludwig, "but I doubt the author of *The Age of Chivalry* had much experience of actual battle."

"Then once this war is over, you should write your own thoughts on the matter."

"Me? Write a book? I possess no gift for the written word."

"Then ask the queen to help you," said Gustavo. "We all know her gift for prose."

"Who'd read such a book?"

"Anyone who wants to master the art of war." Gustavo lifted his finger in the air. "That's it!"

"What is?"

"The name of your book. You can call it *The Art of War*."

Ludwig shook his head. "I'm certain someone's already used that."

"The truth is, it doesn't matter what you call it; people will read it for years to come. Every ruler of the Petty Kingdoms will want it in their library, every general in their house. I know I'd read it, and I'm only a captain."

"You're much more than that, my friend; don't underestimate yourself. You may have been raised on a farm, but you're now Sir Gustavo of Roshlag, Captain of the Royal Guard. That's quite the accomplishment. You fought beside me at the Second Battle of Harlingen, were there with me in Nethendril, and you've been with me ever since. It's people like you who will make the difference tomorrow. Thank you."

"For what?"

"For reminding me what's worth fighting for."

44

THE BATTLE OF TORMALINE
SUMMER 1110 SR

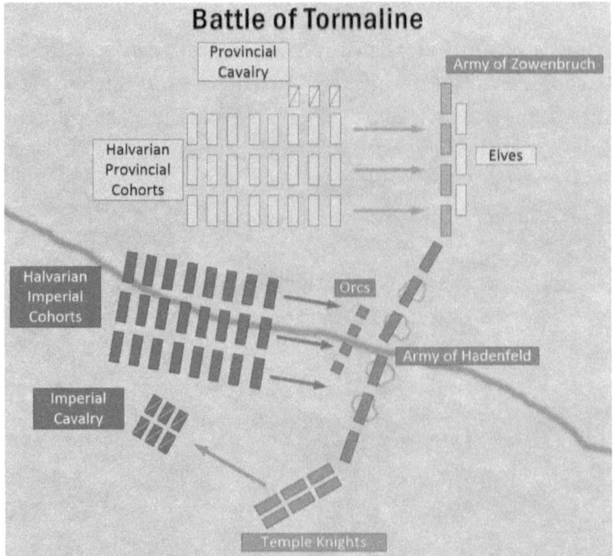

T he sun peeked over the horizon, revealing a field of ankle-deep mist that gave the impression the army stood on clouds.

Ludwig stared out at the formed-up enemy, ready to begin the assault that would seal the fate of the Petty Kingdoms. He'd expected the attack to commence at dawn, but to his surprise, the Halvarians stood there, waiting for something. A stirring amongst their lines drew his attention, and then he noticed a group of horsemen riding towards the front of their massive formation. Was this a display of might meant to intimidate his forces, or were they offering to parley?

All thoughts of negotiation disappeared as he took in what followed. Behind the riders came a wagon, which, in itself, was not unusual, for it looked like that of a farmer. However, the timbers attached to the back that formed a giant X held a man bound to them, his arms stretched out to the sides with his legs splayed wide apart, blood dripping down his face and the sides of his head.

The grotesque exhibit of their savagery advanced, turning to parade the sight before the Army of Halvaria. As it passed, the Halvarians let out a great cheer, the sound carrying across to Ludwig's own command. It wasn't until it reached the northern end of the enemy line and turned around that he realized who'd been made to suffer in such a horrific manner. There was no mistaking the huge northerner, now that Ludwig had a clear view.

Sigwulf's eyes had been gouged out, his ears cut off, and his body was covered in lacerations. A blind anger rose within Ludwig, and he instinctively looked north, to the next defensive mound, where Cyn waited.

"Saints alive," said Gustavo. "These Halvarians are nothing but barbarians!"

"They're trying to bait us into attacking," replied Ludwig.

"And it's working. Look!" The captain pointed at a Hadenfeld company where the men jeered at the enemy, their solid line becoming sloppy due to their rage. Ludwig spurred on his horse, passing through his own line to ride out in front of his men.

Gustavo trailed along behind, calling on six Royal Guards to accompany him. He snatched the Royal Standard, carrying it aloft to draw the attention of the warriors of Hadenfeld.

The king halted, then turned his back to the enemy. "Stand firm," he shouted at the top of his lungs. "Witness the barbarity of the empire. Today, we stand on the threshold of a new Eiddenwerthe, one where the Petty Kingdoms stand shoulder to shoulder, united in their desire to end the oppression of those who seek to end our way of life."

He turned slightly, pointing at the mass of Halvarian soldiers. "That is the enemy. They come seeking your death, but it is you who shall be filling the Underworld with their spirits this day."

Ludwig drew his sword, raising it into the air. "For Hadenfeld! For the people of Eiddenwerthe! For freedom!"

They began chanting his words, and it soon spread to other units. Ludwig urged his horse into a canter, riding along the line much as the enemy had done, his sword still raised high. Gustavo and his men followed behind him, the flag flying in the wind.

Ludwig rode all the way to the north end of their line, then turned around and headed back. He risked a glance at the Halvarians, but the wagon was no longer visible. Instead, their lines were straightening as the empire's sergeants pushed people into position. Flags were unfurled, and then horns sounded. The battle was about to commence.

———

At the sight of the atrocities done to Sigwulf, Charlaine tasted bile in the back of her throat. It brought her back to the Battle of Alantra, where the Halvarians had tied three of her sisters to the masts of their ships, a warning to all that resistance meant death. She couldn't help but look at Teresa, who'd endured the torturous practice. The Temple Captain stared at the enemy lines with a look of determination: the only sign of her distress, a clenched jaw.

"And so it begins," said Teresa.

"You should get to the rear," said Charlaine. "It's time for the rest of us to get to work."

"May Saint Agnes watch over you," replied the Temple Captain, then turned her horse around, heading behind the line. As soon as she'd left, Nicola filled her place.

"You know what to do?"

"Of course," replied her aide, "but we'll have to wait for just the right moment if the tactic is to prove successful."

"Then we must bide our time. Our chance will come, but we cannot be too hasty."

———

Ludwig had returned to his position atop the defensive mound by the time the enemy legion commenced its advance. Judging from their relatively light armour, the enemy had gathered their provincial troops to the north to assault King Konrad's army, while their cavalry attempted to turn the flank. That meant the bulk of their imperial troops would be assaulting Cyn's division, although he did note a large mass of cavalry to the south, ready to circle around his other flank.

"Bold," said Gustavo. "It appears they intend to assault the entire line at once."

"Not surprising, considering the disparity of numbers. Their strategy is to pin us in place with their foot while their cavalry attempts to come around either flank, which is exactly what I expected."

"What are their chances of success?"

"Those in the north will encounter the Elves of the Goldenwood with their Elven bows, while the south faces the Temple Knights of Saint Agnes, who are more than sufficient to maintain the hold on our position."

"Any orders, sire?"

"Yes, be so kind as to find Bloodrig for me, will you? I shall need her help if we are to time this right."

"Yes, sire." Gustavo rode off.

The enemy advanced at a ridiculously slow pace, perhaps as a show of force to shake the confidence of Ludwig's men, but as they drew closer, he noted how poorly some of the Halvarian warriors were at keeping their columns intact. There was only one explanation he could think of: the extra men who'd been added to the legion had been hastily trained, a sign of how desperate the empire was to fill its ranks.

A swarm of archers marched in front, eager to close the range and pepper his men with arrows, but they hadn't counted on the Orcs. The Sky Singers moved their archers up, their bows outdistancing those of the enemy. Instead of volleys, they took their time, making each arrow count. Scores of Halvarian bowmen fell, enough to halt their advance, but the real threat was behind them, imperial footmen who'd quickly outnumber the Orcs.

"You wanted to see me?"

Ludwig turned at Bloodrig's voice. "Yes. Please contact your fellow shaman, Garok, and ask where they are."

"I already know. They are on their way, but it will be a while before they arrive. Perhaps it would have been wiser for them to take a more direct route?"

"No, our strategy is sound; it just means we must hold on a little longer than expected."

"Their arrival will do no good if we are no longer here to be helped."

"A fact of which I'm well aware."

"Is there anything else I can do to help?"

"You can pray to whomever you worship for us to last the day."

"We Orcs do not pray."

"But you worship your Ancestors, do you not?"

"We venerate them, and are guided by their wisdom, but we do not worship them as gods the way Elves do Tauril, or as you do the Saints."

"I suppose that puts us Humans somewhere in the middle. We say we worship the Saints, but in truth, it's their teachings we follow, not them personally. They were mortal men and women, not gods."

"Belief in the Gods, Saints, or Ancestors does not guarantee success in battle. They do not intervene in the affairs of the peoples of Eiddenwerthe; they merely observe or judge."

"Yet they guide the actions of people."

"To whom do the Halvarians pray?"

"To their emperor," said Ludwig, "or so I'm led to believe."

"Then let us hope their belief is not stronger than ours, for in the end, that may well determine who wins this conflict."

The Halvarians kept marching until their archers were in range, then they stepped in front of the footmen once more and let loose with volley after volley, but the Orcs, dispersed as they were in such a loose formation, took little in the way of casualties.

South of Ludwig's position, a group of Halvarian crossbowmen advanced, not yet within range, but it wouldn't be long before they would begin loosing bolts at his men.

His archers moved forward, the ranks of footmen opening up to allow them to pass through. They'd only get a few volleys off, but every enemy warrior taken down now served to even the odds.

Ludwig's cavalry moved closer, resting just behind his footmen, prepared to charge forward should the opportunity present itself.

Arrows flew forth once more, and then a large group of Orc hunters rushed forward, past their archers and straight into the massed bowmen of Halvaria.

One moment, the empire's archers were calmly loosing arrows, the next, they were being hacked down with axes, the survivors fleeing to the rear of their own lines. The imperial footmen advanced to catch the hunters, while they were disorganized, but the Orcs of Ag-Dular were too cunning, withdrawing at a pace that easily outstripped the armoured footmen of Halvaria.

The empire's cavalry in the south continued their advance, the lighter horses leading the way, not even moving at a trot, and still they struggled to maintain their ranks.

Charlaine, seeing her chance, swept her sword down, and five hundred Temple Knights began their own advance. Nicola split off with three companies, attacking the crossbowmen who threatened Ludwig's position. The remaining Temple Knights headed straight for the Halvarian cavalry, their heavy warhorses sounding like thunder as they barreled towards their enemy.

As was their practice, the Agnesites started at a trot, increasing their speed as they drew closer, until the final moments of the charge, when they broke into a full gallop, their lances down as they crashed into the lighter Halvarian horsemen.

Charlaine was in amongst the enemy, no longer able to monitor the progress of her fellow sisters as she concentrated on dealing with the Halvarians in her immediate vicinity. The enemy fought as best they could, but their swords were next to useless against the Temple Knights' plate armour.

Having completed their charge, the Agnesites discarded their lances in favour of maces, axes, and hammers, weapons that would wreak far more damage to armoured opponents. They cleaved their way through the lighter horsemen, then found themselves up against the empire's finest.

Ludwig watched Charlaine's charge. She'd timed the attack to perfection, taking the enemy by surprise and was now deep into their ranks. A smaller group of sister knights had struck the crossbowmen, quickly carving through them as they cut their way north with Ludwig's own cavalry advancing to join them. The enemy's entire southern flank lay exposed.

The imperial foot was still massed in one gigantic column in the middle, crawling towards Cyn's position. The Orcs pulled back to the base of the hills, drawing their axes once they'd exhausted their remaining arrows.

On Ludwig's left, the Agnesites made short work of the majority of the crossbowmen and advanced into the flank of the column. The Knights of the Sacred Shield moved up to assist the Temple Knights fighting the imperial cavalry. He wondered, briefly, how the north was faring, but the other defensive mounds blocked his view of Konrad's line.

"They are here," said Bloodrig. She pointed to the northwest, where a distant fog was rolling towards them. "They will soon fall upon the rear of the enemy, and then the legion will be hopelessly trapped."

"My only fear," said Ludwig, "is that the Army of Zowenbruch may not hold their position. I'm glad that they're here, but they're not exactly renowned for their bravery, and the Halvarians' numbers may overwhelm them."

"The Elves are there to bolster them," the shaman replied. "Our people may not always see eye to eye, but there is no doubting how fiercely the woodland folk can fight."

"Let's hope you have the right of it."

Charlaine struck down with her battle axe, cleaving through the armour to penetrate the arm beneath. As her victim fell back out of the saddle, she looked around only to realize no enemy cavalry were left to fight. "Sound the order to reform on me."

Horns sounded, and the Temple Knights nearby responded, forming into a column as they took up their new positions. The enemy foot, realizing the danger the Temple Knights posed, ordered the rear ranks to turn around, forming a wall of spears.

"Nicola," she called out. "Crossbows forward. You know what to do."

The sisters fell into position, then each Temple Knight turned to the right, changing the formation from a column into two separate lines, three horse lengths between them.

Nicola held her sword out before her, then dipped it, signalling the advance. They trotted towards the wall of spears, but the enemy footmen jeered, feeling safe from attack, and why wouldn't they? What horse would willingly charge into spears?

The Temple Knights halted no more than ten paces from the enemy line, and then the crossbows sang out, concentrating on one section of the Halvarian formation. Dozens of the empire's finest fell, and then the knights using the crossbows halted as those behind them rode past into the middle of the Halvarian formation. As the Temple Knights of Saint Agnes surged in amongst the enemy, panic ensued.

Swords cut down, axes dug in, maces bludgeoned, and hammers crushed skulls. The entire area became a bloodbath. A few Halvarians tried to fight back, but for the most part, the plate armour of the knights proved impervious to their spears.

Ludwig stared in fascination. The imperials were being massacred, the Temple Knights in amongst them, dealing terrible damage to the tight formation. The legion's footmen were so densely packed that they couldn't get out of the way of the armoured horsemen.

Some tried to flee to the northwest, the only direction that looked safe, but then, the Army of Deisenbach emerged from the distant mist, their archers in front in a single line, bolts loaded and ready to let fly. Behind them came two great lines of footmen, their armour gleaming in the sun.

To their south rode King Justinian's knights, their plumed helmets a colourful display amongst the muted tones of the rest of his army. Onward they advanced, moving inexorably towards the rear of the provincial Halvarians fighting King Konrad.

Ludwig rode down the hill, heading towards Cyn's position, eager to get a better view of what was happening in the north. Her men were defending against a spirited attack by the imperials. Suddenly, ghostly figures appeared amongst the men of Hadenfeld, and the enemy broke, streaming down the side of the hill in disarray.

Cyn looked grim, her face sprayed with blood, the head of her mace covered in gore. Even as he watched, she ran forward, finishing off a Halvarian who'd somehow gained the top of the hill. There was a wild look in her eyes, as if the old Gods had taken possession of her wits. She rushed down the hill, her men screaming defiance as they streamed into the enemy.

Ludwig paused, taking a moment to orient himself. Bloodrig's spell had broken the empire's final push. The spirits continued the fight as he turned north to see the thin line of Zowenbruch holding. It appeared as though they'd taken tremendous casualties, but the glint of Elven silver mail told him all he needed to know. The Goldenwood's foot soldiers had intervened on their behalf, filling in gaps where losses would've proved disastrous.

The Halvarian attack was beginning to wane, with those on the front lines no longer advancing. Off to the northwest, the Army of Deisenbach was finally within range, its crossbows starting to make their mark, loosing volley after volley.

Gustavo was right there beside him, pointing to the distant north. "There, sire, do you see it? The Elven cavalry has flanked them. We have the Halvarians completely surrounded!"

Suddenly, Konrad's entire army pushed forward, one final heave to drive deep into the enemy ranks. Behind them lay a trail of blood and bodies, discarded weapons, and trampled flags. The Elven archers pulled back to the rear, having used up all their arrows, but their remaining forces continued the fight.

Ludwig spotted Konrad's banner with his knights, cutting a swath through the provincial cavalry alongside the Elven riders.

Elonin's pennant flew strong above the Elvish foot as they pushed into a mass of Halvarian axemen, and it made him wonder if she'd ended up using her magic to help her warriors fight.

The entire legion would soon be destroyed, and an enlarged one at that, but at what cost?

45

TRIUMPH

SUMMER 1110 SR

It was late in the day, the shadows growing longer as Ludwig walked across the battlefield, the stench of death lingering in the air. No threat remained from the Halvarian Legion, but the task of collecting the wounded had only just begun.

His warriors carried those who couldn't walk, while captured Halvarians saw to the gathering of the dead. The final toll wouldn't be known for days, but from what he could see, far greater losses had occurred on the empire's side.

The Sisters of Mercy had set up an area to the south of the battlefield, and he began moving in that direction, trying to ignore the cries of the wounded. He noted a trio of riders heading straight for him, so he halted.

Temple Commander Giselle led them, and the second person was evidently someone important, for his armour was of the finest quality. The third rider held a flag that hung limply, the earlier breeze having been replaced by the stillness of death.

"King Justinian, I presume?" called out Ludwig.

The King of Deisenbach dismounted, then stepped forward to offer his hand. "My congratulations, Majesty. Your strategy has given us a great victory and a fitting end to this invasion."

"End? We've defeated a legion, sire. There are likely still more out there."

"Then you haven't heard?"

"Heard what?" asked Ludwig.

"My apologies. I only received the news last night. I would've passed it on sooner, but with all the preparations needed for today's battle, it completely slipped my mind."

"News of what?"

Justinian beamed. "A great battle has been fought at Torburg, in Erlingen. Three entire legions were destroyed, along with a traitorous group of Temple Knights. That battle, and our victory here, has destroyed the threat to the Petty Kingdoms once and for all."

"There could still be other legions out there, somewhere."

"Perhaps, but after such a great loss, they'll be retreating across their border. The great war is over, Ludwig. We've demonstrated to the empire that when we stand together, we can defeat anything they send at us."

Ludwig looked at the Temple Commander. "You saw this message?"

"I did, sire," replied Giselle.

"Could it have been a forgery? Sent to distract us while they recover their strength?"

"The Duke of Erlingen's seal looked genuine."

"You should be celebrating," insisted Justinian. "A great alliance from Erlingen, Andover, and Reinwick came together with the Army of Therengia to deal the Halvarians a savage blow. Even Orcs were present, just as they were here. This is a momentous occasion!"

"True, but many men died today," replied Ludwig, "and families will be grieving once word reaches home. I hardly think that warrants a celebration."

The King of Deisenbach sobered. "Yes. You're correct. Their sacrifice shall be honoured. Perhaps instead of a celebration, we should give thanks to the Saints for guiding us to victory this day?"

"That would be acceptable."

"I shall have my people make arrangements. Sorry we interrupted you. Were you on your way somewhere?"

"To visit the wounded. Would you care to accompany me?"

"I'm afraid my attention is required elsewhere. I must see to making arrangements for all these prisoners, not to mention the proper burial of the dead. I can't say I entirely trust these captured Halvarians to observe our death rites, not when they worship their emperor as a god. Who knows what strange things they do with their own dead?"

"Then I shall leave you to your business," said Ludwig. "Now, if you will excuse me, I'll be on my way."

"Of course," replied Justinian.

Charlaine inspected her Temple Knights. They'd fared well in terms of casualties, with only seven of their number dead. More than one hundred had received wounds of varying degrees, but Teresa assured her that they would all recover in time, thanks to the application of healing magic.

After seeing the utter exhaustion on their faces, she made only a cursory inspection before dismissing them, then headed towards the awnings erected to keep the sun off the wounded.

Teresa and the other Sisters of Mercy were doing all they could, aided by the Orc shamans, Bloodrig and Garok, but the wounded outnumbered those who could help, leaving many still out in the field, their wails of pain and suffering drifting to her ears.

An anguished cry drew her attention, and she saw General Hoffman rushing over to one of the wounded.

"He'll be fine," came Teresa's voice. "I've used my magic to heal the more serious of his wounds, but I'm afraid regenerating his eyes and ears will have to wait until I've dealt with those nearer to death."

Charlaine moved closer, looking down at where General Marhaven lay, his head wrapped in blood-soaked bandages that covered both his eyes and ears. His clothes were likewise soaked, while his torn shirt revealed newly healed skin beneath.

A hand reached out, seeking Cyn's. "I've had worse," he said, his voice harsh and parched. "At least it wasn't a stinking badger!"

"You're going to be fine," replied Cyn, her voice cracking ever so slightly. "I'll stay here and make sure of it."

"No. You must see my division. There might still be some left alive."

"I'll look after them," said Charlaine. "You two need to rest." She met Cyn's gaze. "Stay with him. He needs your strength right now."

"The king," someone called out.

"Stay where you are," replied Ludwig. "This is a place of healing, not a Royal Court. Continue with your work." He moved to join Charlaine. "Sig, I'm so sorry. I never should have sent you to Tormaline."

"You had no choice. Besides, it was my own fault. I should've withdrawn sooner. Those cursed Halvarian horsemen were to blame; they were much faster than I thought they'd be."

"I'm just glad you're still alive. It wouldn't be the same without you."

"What happens now?"

"For someone so badly wounded, you're awfully inquisitive."

"I can't help it. I'm worried about another legion showing up."

"As am I," added Charlaine.

"You can put your minds at ease," said Ludwig. "I received word that a great battle played out in Erlingen, where three more legions were destroyed."

"That is good news, indeed," said Charlaine. "But are we certain that's all they had remaining?"

"There's only one way to find out. Perhaps you'd care to join me, Temple General."

"To what end?"

"We have the commander-general of the legion as a prisoner. Shall we go and have a chat with him?"

Ludwig gazed down at the prisoner. The Halvarian was sitting on the ground, his hands tied behind his back, while guards with drawn weapons stood nearby. The man's armour had been stripped from him, along with his weapons, which were now safely out of reach.

"Get him standing," commanded Ludwig.

The guards moved in to seize the prisoner by the arms and hauled him to his feet.

"What's your name?"

"Korvin Bandros," the prisoner replied. "Commander-General of the Eleventh Legion."

"No longer. That legion is gone, destroyed by the combined armies of Hadenfeld, Zowenbruch, and Deisenbach, with help from their allies."

"Allies?"

"Yes, the Orcs of Ag-Dular, and the Elves of the Goldenwood."

"Heathens."

"From our point of view," said Charlaine, "you're the heathens. We worshippers of the Saints are happy to coexist with other religions, but even those who worship the Old Gods would consider it blasphemous that a ruler would have the audacity to claim themselves to be a god."

"He rules through the power of his bloodline," insisted Bandros.

"Of that I have no doubt; it's common enough amongst the rulers of the Petty Kingdoms, but to claim to be a deity is the height of hubris."

"Do you not worship the Saints?"

"The Saints were mortals; it's their teachings we venerate."

"As we do the word of our emperor."

"Your emperor's teachings have led you to ruin," said Ludwig.

"I cannot argue the point," replied Bandros. "Your army proved superior to ours. I must therefore concede that you are the better strategist. May I ask a question?"

"You may ask, but I can't guarantee an answer."

The commander-general cleared his throat. "What is to be my fate? Am I to be executed?"

"No. Why would you be?"

"It is the accepted practice in the empire."

"This is not the empire," replied Ludwig, "and it is not our practice to kill those we capture, at least not if I have any say in the matter. As to your ultimate fate, that is for me to discuss with King Konrad and King Justinian."

"Please," begged the Halvarian. "Spare me the torment of imprisonment."

"What else am I to do with you?"

"Release me, and I shall tell you all I know of the empire's plans."

"Tempting," said Ludwig, "but how would I know whether or not you're telling the truth?"

"Teresa," offered Charlaine.

"You think she has a spell that might help?"

"I know she does. I shall send word and ask her to join us."

"And if she's too busy?"

"Then we'll ask Bloodrig."

"I'm not lying," insisted Bandros. "I have no reason to. I have lost my legion. My career is over, possibly even my life."

"Your superiors would execute you for failure?" said Ludwig. "I find that difficult to believe."

"I don't," said Charlaine. "The empire is ruthless. They execute prisoners after a victory."

"Ah, yes. I remember," replied Ludwig. "All except for ten, so they can spread word of the might of the empire. Perhaps that's what we should do here?" He glared at the prisoner. "They also maim those they release."

Beads of sweat dripped from Bandros's pale face.

Charlaine stepped forward, looking the prisoner in the eyes. "This is your lucky day, Commander-General. The Saints don't condone such behaviour from us Temple Knights. It's a pity the same can't be said of kings." She looked at Ludwig. "He's all yours." With that, she turned and left.

Charlaine heard footsteps and looked over her shoulder to see Temple Captain Nicola racing towards her. She halted, allowing her aide to catch up.

"I couldn't help but overhear," said Nicola. "Surely you're not going to allow the king to torture the prisoner?"

"Why would you think that was my intent?"

"You told him we don't commit such acts of barbarity, then left him at the mercy of the king."

"And do you honestly believe I'd do that if I thought His Majesty capable of doing such a thing?"

There was a long pause before the Temple Captain replied. "It was a bluff?"

Charlaine smiled. "I didn't lie, if that's what you're implying. I merely reminded the prisoner that the rulers of the Petty Kingdoms are not subject to the same strict rules that we Temple Knights follow."

"You continue to surprise me. I can see the Grand Mistress was wise in granting you the rank of Temple General."

"I never sought promotion, but I'm not one to shirk my duty. I took a sacred oath to preserve the order, and that's precisely what I aim to do."

"By fighting for Hadenfeld?"

"We didn't fight here simply to preserve one kingdom, but to ensure the people of the Petty Kingdoms could live their lives without fear of the oppressive rule of the Halvarian Empire."

"And once they're defeated, what comes next?"

"That is a matter for another day. Right now, we have need of Teresa."

"I shall go and fetch her."

Ludwig stared down at Korvin Bandros. His wealth was evident, for although they'd removed his plate armour, he still wore his gambeson, one decorated with exquisite embroidery and cuffs bearing gold thread. "How long have you been a commander-general?"

"Ten years."

"And before that?"

"I started my career as a captain of an imperial company of foot in the Second Legion. I gained distinction during the pacification of the south and was promoted to captain-general."

"The south?" said Ludwig.

"South of the empire, there is another continent, an area teeming with Orcs and other wild folk."

"And a captain-general commands a cohort?"

"Yes. A warrior of Halvaria usually serves in one legion for the entirety of their career, but in my case, no captain-general openings were available in the Second Legion, so I was sent north to fill a vacancy in the Eleventh, the same legion you destroyed today."

"So you've spent your entire adult life as a warrior?"

"Those of us who serve prefer the term legionnaire, or soldier, if you wish, but yes. What of yourself? You clearly have battlefield experience."

"Not through choice," replied Ludwig.

"Enough to allow you to claim the Throne of Hadenfeld."

"I never sought to rule over others, yet somehow my path in life led me to where I am today."

"So what happens now?"

"I have no desire to see more bloodshed, and by your own admission, your career is over. In all likelihood, I shall release you, although not until the war is over."

"And in the meantime?"

"That's an excellent question," said Ludwig. He sought out Gustavo, who stood nearby. "Housing and feeding all these prisoners will prove difficult. How do you suggest we proceed?"

The captain stared back a moment before answering. "You're the king, sire. That's your choice."

"I value your opinion."

"I'd suggest putting them to work. At least then we'd see some benefit to bearing the expense."

"What sort of work would we have them do?"

"Building roads? Perhaps a new commandery for the Temple Knights in Eisen? There's an awful lot of prisoners, maybe even enough to do both?"

"We shall do precisely that," said Ludwig. "I should like to confer with Lord Merrick once we return home, but I think we'd need to put a limit on how long they'd serve in such a capacity. That would be the humane thing to do."

"To my knowledge, the Halvarians have never demonstrated the slightest shred of humanity."

"That's true, which is what makes us different from them."

Charlaine returned, accompanied by Temple Captain Teresa.

"I hope we're not overtaxing you," said Ludwig. "I understand how treating the wounded drains your magical strength."

"I still have some reserves," replied Teresa. "Temple General Charlaine informs me you have the enemy general in custody. Is this him?"

"It is. Can your magic determine whether or not he's lying?"

"I know a spell that allows me to see his aura, which typically changes colour when someone is lying, but the changes can be subtle and difficult to detect."

"So does that mean you can or not?"

"I shall certainly try."

Bandros licked his lips nervously. "I thought only the empire had sentinels?"

"Sentinels?" said Charlaine.

"Yes, Life Mages who serve the emperor. We call them truthseekers. They judge guilt or innocence when needed."

"I am no judge," said Teresa, "merely an observer who has the power to inform others if you're being deceitful."

"You may begin your spell whenever you're ready," said Ludwig.

The Temple Captain began casting, setting the air abuzz with the feeling of magic. Her words of power ceased, and then her eyes glowed with a soft inner light. "You may begin your interrogation," she said.

Ludwig turned to the commander-general. "How many legions invaded the Petty Kingdoms?"

"To my knowledge, four," the fellow replied. "The Fifth, Eighth, Ninth, and my own, the Eleventh."

Teresa nodded, indicating he told the truth.

"And how many does the empire have in total?"

"Twelve, but last I heard, three were tied up in the Mercerian campaign with another three in the jungles of the empire's southern border."

"That leaves two unaccounted for."

"As far as I know, they were being held in reserve."

"He lies," said Teresa.

Bandros hung his head. "They've been sent to re-pacify Calabria and Herani."

"Calabria?" said Charlaine.

"There's been an increase in hostile activity since the fleet was lost at Alantra, and it has since spread to Herani."

"How do you know all this?"

"There are only twelve commander-generals, and although we tend to despise each other, we see the value of keeping in touch on occasion."

"Do you understand what this means?" said Charlaine. "It's over. We've won."

"Not so," said Bandros. "You still have to deal with the other legions facing Erlingen."

"He's telling the truth," noted Teresa.

Ludwig smiled. "He is, as far as he knows. However, we have information that he doesn't. A great battle was fought at Torburg in Erlingen, where three legions were annihilated."

"It's my fault," said Bandros.

"Why would you say that?"

"My legion was given the responsibility of subjugating the conquered kingdoms of Rudor and Gotfeld, but when reinforcements were sent from Halvaria, I used them to enlarge my own command and marched them here, seeking glory. Had I not done so, the empire's forces at Torburg would've been significantly larger."

"That's a decision that will likely haunt you for the rest of your remaining days," said Charlaine. "Your empire's invasion of the Petty King-doms has done what years of diplomacy failed to do: allowed us to put aside our petty grievances and stand together for the betterment of all."

"A new age is coming," she continued, "an age in which we will no longer live in fear of invasion by the empire."

"The empire will rebuild," warned Bandros.

"Perhaps, but we now possess the knowledge and the leadership to defeat them."

"This was always your destiny," said Teresa, her eyes flicking between Charlaine and Ludwig. "Years ago, your lives diverged, allowing you each to learn what was needed. You have come together just in time to save us from the threat of subjugation. If that's not the will of the Saints, I don't know what is."

EPILOGUE
SUMMER 1110 SR

Charlotte looked across the table to where Sigwulf and Cyn sat beside each other. "It's good to see you back to your old self. It appears Temple Captain Teresa's magic was put to good use."

"Indeed," replied the huge northerner. "Though I must admit it's a strange sensation. My eyesight was never the best, yet now, with my eyes regenerated, I can see so clearly." He smiled, though something else was obviously on his mind.

"What are you smirking at?" asked Ludwig.

Sig turned to his left. "Go ahead. You tell them."

Cyn looked as if she were about to burst. "We're going to have a baby!" She realized everyone's excitement and sobered. "Not right now, of course, but eventually." She stared at Sig with adoring eyes. "It seems Teresa's magic can heal a great many things."

"What of the Elves?" asked Charlotte.

"That's a story in itself," replied Ludwig. "The Orc shamans, Bloodrig and Garok, agreed to teach the Elves how to heal the rest of their people. They're meeting with Galrandir even as we speak. I wouldn't say they're the best of friends, but it's a sure sign that their relations are improving."

"Then it appears we are finally at peace."

"Hadenfeld is," said Charlaine. "But the war in the north continues. I received word this morning that Danica is taking the Temple Fleet west, to the land of Merceria, to assist them in staving off the remnants of the empire."

The door opened, revealing Gustavo. "Brother Aiden has returned, sire."

"Please show him in," replied Ludwig.

The Ragnarite entered, offering a bow. "Majesties. I believe I promised to inform you of my progress."

"Ah, yes, the green vials. I know you found the second in Deisenbach. Does this mean you found the third?"

"I'm afraid not, sire. The trail has gone cold."

"Are you saying you have no idea at all of where it is?"

"I have a suspicion, but no way to follow it up."

"Then let's hear it."

"I re-examined my findings and came to the conclusion it's most likely in the possession of Temple Captain Amarand."

"And where is he?"

"I came across second-hand information that revealed he and several of his fellow Temple Knights abandoned the order and left for parts unknown. I shall continue to keep an eye out for any signs of them, but I doubt he'll show his face in these parts again."

"I thank you for your efforts," said Ludwig. "Your order is free to use our kingdom as a place of safety should they need it."

"That is most gracious, Majesty."

"What will you do now?" asked Charlotte.

"I shall continue to reach out to other members of my order. We are few, and scattered, but still dedicated to carrying out our vows. Might I be so bold as to ask you the same?"

"After years of conflict, we are finally at peace," she replied. "It's time to build a better, brighter future for Hadenfeld."

<<<<>>>>

ENJOY THE STORY? LEAVE A REVIEW FOR WARRIOR KING TODAY!

If you liked *Warrior King* then *Ashes*, the first book in *The Frozen Flame* series awaits.

START READING ASHES

CHARACTERS, PLACES, AND ITEMS OF NOTE

CAST OF CHARACTERS

MAIN CHARACTERS
Charlaine deShandria - Temple General, Saint Agnes
Charlotte Altenburg - Queen of Hadenfeld
Cynthia 'Cyn' Hoffman - Baroness of Verfeld, General
Gita Sternhassen - Baroness of Drakenfeld, Treasurer of Hadenfeld
Ludwig Altenburg - King of Hadenfeld
Merrick Sternhassen - Baron of Drakenfeld, Chancellor of Hadenfeld
Sigwulf 'Siggy' Marhaven - Baron of Verfeld, General
Vernan - Holy Father, Saint Mathew, Spiritual Adviser to King Ludwig

THE LORDS AND LADIES OF HADENFELD
Alexandra Kuhn – Baroness of Dornbruck, wife of Emmett
Darrian Forst - Baron of Glosnecke
Emmett Kuhn - Baron of Dornbruck, husband of Alexandra
Esmerelda Boesch - Daughter of Merten
Evangeline Kuhn - Daughter of Emmett and Alexandra
Frederick Altenburg - Son of Ludwig and Charlotte
Gowan Forst - Son of Harvald, younger brother of Darrian
Harvald Forst (Deceased) - Previous Baron of Glosnecke
Jurgen Voltz - Baron of Bruggendorf
Kenley Sternhassen - Son of Merrick and Gita
Merten - Baron of Langeven
Meinhard Schafenburg (Deceased) - Baron of Luwen
Morgan II (Deceased) - Previous King of Hadenfeld
Nikolaus Wendt - Baron of Udenacht
Otto (Deceased) - Previous King of Hadenfeld

THE CHURCH
Aiden - Temple Knight, Saint Ragnar
Amarand - Temple Commander, Saint Cunar, the Antonine
Bernadine - Archprioress, Saint Agnes, Hadenfeld
Cyric - Temple Knight of Saint Mathew, Special Investigator
Erasmus - Holy Brother, Saint Augustine
Jarak - Life Mage, Kurathian, Servant of Saint Ragnar

Hamelyn - Temple Captain, Saint Mathew, Hadenfeld
Hieronymus - Archprior of Eisen, Saint Mathew, Hadenfeld
Hywell - Archprior, Saint Mathew, Hadenfeld
Ignacious - Holy Father, Saint Mathew
Malakai - Archprior, Saint Cunar, Hadenfeld
Ramone - Archprior, Saint Mathew, Hadenfeld
Wilmar - Primus, Church of the Saints, the Antonine

TEMPLE KNIGHTS OF SAINT AGNES
Aurelia (Deceased) - Temple Knight
Consuela - Temple Knight, Deisenbach
Cordelia - Temple Captain, Carlingen
Danica - Temple Commander, Admiral of the Temple Fleet
Erika - Temple Knight, Temple Fleet
Florence - Temple Captain, Arnsfeld
Genevieve - Temple Knight, Hadenfeld
Giselle - Temple Captain, Deisenbach
Helena (Deceased) - Temple Knight
Isabeau - Temple Commander, Arnsfeld
Katinka - Temple Commander, Hadenfeld
Miranda (Deceased) - Temple Captain
Nicola - Temple Captain, Hadenfeld
Nina (Deceased) - Temple Commander
Rhea - Temple Knight, Hadenfeld
Rowan - Temple Knight, Deisenbach
Teresa - Temple Captain, Sister of Mercy, Hadenfeld
Verushka (Deceased) - Temple Commander

PEOPLE OF HADENFELD
Clay - Ludwig's horse
Edwig - Captain, Therengian descent, Army of Hadenfeld
Elsie – Servant, Royal Keep in Harlingen
Gustavo – Captain, King's Guard, Calabrian descent
Hanford Schultz - Wealthy merchant
Ingulf - Knight of the Sacred Shield
Kalen Hasrich – Archer, recruited from Roshlag, Army of Hadenfeld
Kandam – Life Mage, Kurathian descent
Kerrigan - Vintner
Liesel - Wife of Emmet Kuhn's cousin in Eisen
Logrin - Knight Commander, Knights of the Sacred Shield
Luther Bernhaus - Wealthy merchant

Magret Hanford - Woman of Harlingen
Melinda – Servant, Royal Keep in Harlingen
Paran - Captain, Army of Hadenfeld
Reiner - Sergeant, Royal Guard
Rikal - Captain, Archer from Roshlag, Army of Hadenfeld
Rostrik - Captain, Knights of the Sacred Shield
Ruger (Deceased) - Former king of Neuhafen
Selenia – Servant, Royal Keep in Harlingen

Elves

Elonin - Talon (Captain), Enchanter, Nethendril
Escarial - Warrior, Nethendril
Fariel - Talon, Nethendril
Galrandir - Life Mage, Nethendril
Gwalinor - Sea Elf, Life Mage
Karalindel - Earth Mage, Nethendril
Nindaril – Talon, Silver Eagle Glade Warriors, Elandril
Sindra - High Lord of Nethendril, Earth Mage
Telieth - Archer, The Goldenwood
Theran Silverhand - Earth Mage, Nethendril

Orcs

Bloodrig - Shaman, Sky Singers, Deisenbach
Garok - Shaman, Sky Singers, Deisenbach
Lurzak - Chieftain, Sky Singers, Deisenbach

Others

Aeldred (Deceased) - Ancient king, Old Kingdom
Aubrey Brandon - Baroness of Hawksburg, Life Mage, Merceria
Augustinian II - King, Mirantha
Beverly Fitzwilliam - General, Baroness of Bodden, Merceria
Clemens - King of Lubenstahl
Dagmar – King, Andover
Deiter Heinrich (Deceased) - Duke of Erlingen
Diedrich (Deceased) – King, Neuhafen
Eduardo Stormwind - Water Mage, Court Adviser, Mirantha
Eimar - Warrior, Zowenbruch
Fernando Brondecker - Duke of Reinwick
Garulf (Deceased) - Ancient human chieftain, the Barrows
Gebhard Stein - Baron of Mulsingen, Erlingen
Giles - Farmer, Bedmar, Hollenbeck

Helisant – Queen, Deisenbach
Jaramel (Deceased) - High Lord of Herani
Justinian – King, Deisenbach
Konrad - King, Zowenbruch
Korvin Bandros - Commander-General, 11th Halvarian Legion
Loralai Shozarin - Unknown individual referenced only by name
Ludmilla Stormwind - Water Mage, formerly at the court of Deisenbach
Natalia Stormwind - Water Mage, Warmaster of Therengia
Orlina Day - Sacred mother of Tauril, Arnfeld
Raynald - Knight of the Sceptre, imprisoned in the Antonine
Rillian - Guard, court of King Justinian, Deisenbach
Roderick of Tollingsbruck - Knight, Hollenbeck
Rosalyn Haas - Daughter of the Baron of Regnitz, Erlingen
Rurlan - Dwarf courier for the smith's guild
Sirellia Stormwind - Water Mage, Mirantha
Stigurd Grossman - Elector of Malburg, Master of Taxation
Stormcloud - Charlaine's horse, a Calabrian
Talivardas - The primus, now using the name Wilmar
Ulfric Sternhassen - Duke of Hollenbeck
Wilfhelm Brondecker (Deceased) - Duke of Reinwick
Wulfram Haas - Baron of Regnitz, Erlingen

PLACES

PETTY KINGDOMS
Abelard - Kingdom, northern coast
Aldor - Kingdom, south of Hadenfeld
Amaria - Kingdom, southeast of Hadenfeld
Andover - Kingdom, south of Reinwick
Angvil - Kingdom, east of Arnsfeld
Ardosa - Kingdom, east of Hadenfeld
Arnsfeld - Kingdom, Halvarian border
Carlingen - Kingdom, northern coast
Corassus - City State, southern coast
Deisenbach - Kingdom, northwest of Hadenfeld
Erlingen - Duchy, north central Petty Kingdom
Gotfeld - Kingdom, west of Deisenbach
Grislagen – Kingdom, west of Hadenfeld
Hadenfeld - Kingdom, ruled by Ludwig
Hollenbeck - Duchy, south of Hadenfeld
Ilea - Kingdom, southern coast

Krieghoff - Eastern Duchy, south of the Grey Spire Mountains
Lubenstahl - Kingdom, northeast of Hadenfeld
Mirantha - Kingdom, south of Hadenfeld
Neuhafen - Former kingdom, now reunited with Hadenfeld
Ostrova – Kingdom, eastern Petty Kingdom
Regensbach - Kingdom, east of Hadenfeld
Reinwick – Duchy, north coast of the Petty Kingdoms
Rudor – Kingdom, Halvaria border
Talstadt - Kingdom west of Hadenfeld, past Grislagen
Thalemia - Kingdom, southern coast
Ulrichen - Kingdom east of Zowenbruch
Zalista – Kingdom, eastern Petty Kingdom
Zowenbruch - Kingdom north of Hadenfeld

OTHER REALMS OF EIDDENWERTHE
Calabria – Kingdom, western shore of the Shimmering Sea
Eloria - Island of the Sea Elves
Halvaria - Large empire, west of the Petty Kingdoms
Kurathia - Collection of principalities, south of the southern continent
Merceria – Kingdom, west of Halvaria
Mythanos - Elven realm, Arnsfeld
Old Kingdom - Ancient Kingdom of Therengia
The Goldenwood - Elven realm, east of Hadenfeld
Therengia - Realm, east of the Petty Kingdoms

HADENFELD
Arnsbach - Barony, Eastern Hadenfeld
Bruggendorf - Barony, Southern Hadenfeld
Dornbruck - Barony, Eastern Hadenfeld
Drakenfeld - Barony, Northern Hadenfeld
Eisen - City, Eastern Hadenfeld
Erhard's Folly - Hill north of Verfeld
Glosnecke - Barony, Northern Hadenfeld
Grienwald - Barony, Central Hadenfeld
Harlingen - Capital of Hadenfeld
Langeven - Barony, Eastern Hadenfeld
Luwen - Barony, Western Hadenfeld
Malburg - Free city
Ramfelden - Barony, Eastern Hadenfeld
Roshlag - Village, Barony of Verfeld
Tongrin - Barony, Eastern Hadenfeld

Udenacht - Barony, Eastern Hadenfeld
Valksburg - Barony, Eastern Hadenfeld
Verfeld - Village and Barony, North Hadenfeld
Zwieken - Barony, North Eastern Hadenfeld

Erlen River - River near Eisen
Forest of Shadows - Unknown location where Elves were slaughtered
Great Northern Sea - Sea forming north coast of Eiddenwerthe
Grey Hills - Range of hills in Deisenbach
Grey Spire Mountains - Mountain range in the eastern Petty Kingdoms
Hills of Harlingen - Hills east and north of the capital of Hadenfeld
Hollen River - river separating Hollenbeck from Hadenfeld
Rasford River - River separating Zowenbruch and Deisenbach
Shimmering Sea - Sea on the south coast of the Petty Kingdoms
The Barrows - Range of hills, north of Eisen
The Bloodwood - Forest straddling the Hadenfeld-Zowenbruch border
The Wildwood - Large forest, Deisenbach
Zowen River - River, border between Zowenbruch and Hadenfeld

CITIES/VILLAGES/OTHER PLACES

Ag-Dular - Orc village, Deisenbach
Agran - Capital, Deisenbach
Alantra - Capital, Calabria, under Halvarian occupation
Antonine - Centre of power of the Church of the Saints
Ard-Uzgul - Orc Village, Deisenbach
Bedmar - Village, Hollenbeck
Bessin - Town, Deisenbach
Bodden - Barony/village, Merceria
Caerhaven - City, Duchy of Kreighoff
Cathedral of the Saints - Hollenbeck
Chermingen - City, Erlingen
Ebenhof - Town, Andover
Ebenstadt - City, Therengia
Eidenburg - City, Agnesite training academy,
Elandril - Elven city, The Goldenwood
Esthafen - Town, Zowenbruch
Freimar - Capital, Mirantha
Freizel - Town, Deisenbach
Gryphon's Rest - Inn, Bedmar, Duchy of Hollenbeck
Halieth - Elven city, The Goldenwood

Herani - Holy city, under Halvarian occupation
Herst - Town, Deisenbach
Klermacht - Capital, Hollenbeck
Kurslingen - Capital, Zowenbruch
Nethendril - Elven city, The Goldenwood
Rasgalen - Village, Gotfeld
Rizela - Capital, Kingdom of Ilea
Rotmar - Town, Deisenbach
Santrem - Village, Zowenbruch
Seiburg - Village, Zowenbruch
Silver Vale - Village, Regensbach
Thalune - Elven city, The Goldenwood
The Spotted Dog - Inn, Tormaline, Deisenbach
Torburg - Capital, Erlingen
Tormaline - Village, Deisenbach
Trivoli - Town, Deisenbach
Verslacht - Village, Mirantha
Volbruck - Town, Deisenbach
Zarnau - Town, Hollenbeck

ITEMS OF NOTE

BATTLES

Battle of Chermingen (1095 SR) - Duchy of Erlingen defeats Andover
Battle of Eisen (1104 SR) Hadenfeld defeats Zowenbruch
Battle of the Brinwald (1103 SR) - Arnsfeld defeats Halvarian invasion
Battle of the Wilderness (1104 SR) - Therengia defeats Holy Army
Second Battle of Harlingen (1100 SR) - Hadenfeld defeats Neuhafen
The Great War (Date unknown) - Centuries long conflict between Orcs and Elves

SAINTS & GODS

Agnes - Saint, Protector of women
Akosia - Goddess of Water
Ansgar - Saint, The peacemaker
Augustine - Saint, Collector of relics
Cunar - Saint, The warrior
Mathew - Saint, Servant of the ill and poor
Ragnar - Saint, Hunter of Necromancers
Tauril - Goddess of the Forest

THINGS

Afterlife - The place where it is believed good people go after death

Council of Peers - Ruling council of the Antonine

Glade Wardens - Elven warriors, the Goldenwood

Holy Fleet - Northern fleet, Temple Knights of Saint Agnes

Ithilium - Metal that falls from the sky, godstone or sky metal

Knights of the Sacred Shield - Order of Knighthood, Hadenfeld

Magerite - Rare gem that can indicate some types of magical potential

Moon Sight - The ability of Orcs to see by moonlight

Phoenix Ring - Paired rings used to make letters tamper-proof

Primus - Head of the Church of the Saints

Sea Elves - Elves that left the Continent two thousand years ago

Seaflower - Herb, ground to a powder to induce sleep

Sister of Mercy - Temple Knight of Saint Agnes trained in Life Magic

Sky Metal - See Ithilium

Sky Singers - Orc tribe, Deisenbach

Temple Knight - Member of a religious fighting order

Temple Knights of Saint Ansgar - Polices the other fighting orders

The Age of Chivalry - Book of military strategy and tactics

Underworld - The place where it is believed bad people go after death

A FEW WORDS FROM PAUL

Warrior King marks the end of Ludwig's journey. He began as the spoiled son of a wealthy noble in Warrior Knight, and through trials and tribulations, ended up as a wise and benevolent king. From the very beginning, it was always my intention to reunite Ludwig and Charlaine as equals just in time to deal the Empire of Halvaria its fatal blow.

The Church of the Saints is now broken, having been destroyed by agents of the empire and reduced to a shadow of its former influence. The result of this will be felt across the Petty Kingdom and will have a bearing on future events. Though this series is now concluded, the survivors of the Temple Knights of Saint Cunar will rear their heads again in a future series.

Ludwig and Charlaine, however, will ride one more time, in Victory of the Crown, Book fifteen in the Heir to the Crown series.

It's not easy to finish a series, and I particularly owe a debt to my wife, Carol, whose encouragement helped me develop and write this tale. Additionally, her work of editing and promoting all my books allowed me to devote more time to writing.

I should also like to express my gratitude to Stephanie Sandrock, Christie Bennett, and Amanda Bennett for their continued support.

Thanks are also due to my BETA team for providing such valuable feedback, so a big shoutout to Rachel Deibler, Michael Rhew, Phyllis Simpson, Don Hinckley, Debbie Reeves, Joanna Smith, Barbara Raue, Diana Elliott Braddi, Kari Fredlund, Anna Ostberg, Steve Filson, Keven Hutchison, John Henniger, Lisa Hanika, Brad Williams, Lisa Hunt, and Charles Mohapel.

Finally, I thank you, my readers, without whom this series would never have been written in the first place. I hope you've enjoyed the Power Ascending Series, and I invite you to read some of my other series.

ABOUT THE AUTHOR

Paul J Bennett (b. 1961) emigrated from England to Canada in 1967. His father served in the British Royal Navy, and his mother worked for the BBC in London. As a young man, Paul followed in his father's footsteps, joining the Canadian Armed Forces in 1983. He is married to Carol Bennett and has three daughters who are all creative in their own right.

Paul's interest in writing started in his teen years when he discovered the roleplaying game, Dungeons & Dragons (D & D). What attracted him to this new hobby was the creativity it required; the need to create realms, worlds and adventures that pulled the gamers into his stories.

In his 30's, Paul started to dabble in designing his own roleplaying system, using the Peninsular War in Portugal as his backdrop. His regular gaming group were willing victims, er, participants in helping to playtest this new system. A few years later, he added additional settings to his game, including Science Fiction, Post-Apocalyptic, World War II, and the all-important Fantasy Realm where his stories take place.

The beginnings of his first book 'Servant to the Crown' originated over five years ago when he began running a new fantasy campaign. For the world that the Kingdom of Merceria is in, he ran his adventures like a TV show, with seasons that each had twelve episodes, and an overarching plot. When the campaign ended, he knew all the characters, what they had to accomplish, what needed to happen to move the plot along, and it was this that inspired to sit down to write his first novel.

Paul now has four series based in his fantasy world of Eiddenwerthe, and is looking forward to sharing many more books with his readers over the coming years.